# THOSE WHO TRESPASS

_A NOVEL_

**SYDNEY F. GREY**

*For my Lord, my husband, and my family*

# CHAPTER I
# CAPTAIN'S LOG

Journal of His Majesty's Ship *Relentless*
Frigate, 5th Rate, Lively Class, 38 Gunner
Johnathan Gresham, Captain

*LOG ENTRY DATE: AUGUST 8, 1818*

*LOCATION: 24°N 77°W, NORTHEAST OF THE NORTHERNMOST ISLE OF THE BAHAMAS, WEST INDIES*

Storm broke last night. Foreyard snapped in two. Eight men injured, no deaths. Decision made to anchor in the lee of a small uncharted island, to harvest timber necessary for repairs, instead of returning to Jamaica, in order to make for England as ordered, to begin new assignment posthaste.

Beads of sweat prickled his furrowed brow as Captain Johnathan Gresham surveyed the tiny island by which he had anchored the HMS *Relentless* just after dawn. The uncharted, kidney-shaped spit of land, not more than four frigates long, boasted groves of palms and mangroves on the two sides of the low land in the middle. Gresham noted with annoyance the lack of birds calling above the sounds of the surf, a sure sign the island lacked a source of fresh water to replenish his ship's store.

He hoped to find a tree suitable for repairing the foreyard, damaged in the wild squall that had bested his abilities the night before. A sudden bursting change in the wind's direction had taken hold of his fore course sail and snapped the yard like a twig. He had never seen anything like it in all his twenty-one years at sea. And at five and thirty, he had been at sea most of his life.

Gresham rubbed the back of his damp neck, rankled at this unanticipated delay, but more disappointed with himself for not having seen the storm coming the evening before. He was usually able to predict such things and hated being caught off his guard.

Pacing the deck and working his jaw, he licked the salt from his lips as sweat dripped onto his black cravat. He could feel the moisture seeping through his white linen shirt into his pale-yellow waistcoat. To top it off, his navy, gold-embellished captain's coat was suffocating.

He calculated they should be able to make repairs and set sail for England in a matter of a day or two. The quicker the better, if only to get out of this devilish heat. He was due for a furlough and still hoped to visit his sister and brother-in-law between commissions. It had been far too long since he'd seen them.

He was also anxious to get back to his own investigation

into London's rash of missing girls, which had consumed him the last time he was there. The kidnappings had continued, or so he had heard, and he could not get the plight of those poor little souls out of his mind. As much as he relished chasing pirates and capturing prizes around the West Indies, something pulled his heart back to England.

Donning his dark-blue bicorn hat, he prepared to go ashore. He could have let his ship's carpenter and mates supervise the choosing of the tree without him, but he liked to see that things were done properly. Besides, it was a good excuse to stretch his land legs a bit before the fortnight of sailing ahead.

"Boats all ready, Mr. Bowling?" Gresham shouted to his coxswain over the rail.

The weathered, red-faced sailor looked up and saluted. "All ready, Capt'n!" Bowling called as he settled his oarsmen in the launch and held the rope by the hull's outer steps for the captain to descend.

Two small wooden dinghies were already occupied by Mr. Jameson, the ship's carpenter, and his mates, along with a few other strong sailors who would help fell the chosen tree and hoist it aboard. Sweat dripped down their sun-leathered faces as they swatted at the swarm of insects hovering over them like a black cloud.

Gresham nodded to Bowling. "Let us make haste. No sense staying in this heat any longer than necessary."

Bowling grunted in agreement as Gresham lowered his frame to his seat in the stern sheets of the launch. The count was given, and they rowed the short distance to the beach and dragged the boats onto the shore.

Just as Gresham's boot sank into the white sand, his gut clenched with an eerie sense that something was amiss. The hairs under his queue stood up, and he heard the quickened

SYDNEY F. GREY

surge of his pulse in his ears. His eyes flitted to the stand of
trees past the beach, but there was nothing. All was strangely
quiet.

He shook off the unwelcome feeling. What could possibly
be a danger here on this pathetic little rock in the middle of
nowhere?

He waved his hand in front of his face to clear away the
buzzing swarm and the silly thoughts of buried treasure and
other bits of nonsense that flashed through his mind.

It must be the lack of sleep and his rattled nerves.

As the men marched behind Jameson up the slight incline
toward the large stand of trees to the northeast, Gresham
gazed around, still feeling in his bones that something was off.

He fell behind the men, and Mr. Bowling kept his pace as
they picked their way through the thick tropical flora. The
breeze whisked through the palm branches above, echoing the
sound of the waves on the shore. They stopped in their tracks
at a shout from Jameson up ahead.

"Capt'n Gresham! There's somethin' 'ere you should see,
sir!" Jameson beckoned to the little clearing under the trees,
where his crew circled.

Gresham and Bowling increased their pace and arrived to
find Gresham's curiously somber men looking down at the
ground. Some had even removed their caps.

There in the ground was a roughly made wooden cross
stuck into the sandy soil at the head of a long mound.

Gresham stopped short. "Dear God, what a place to be
buried!" His voice was rough with pity. Kneeling on one knee,
he removed his hat and examined the cross. There was no
name of the soul occupying the grave. It wasn't freshly made,
but certainly not older than half a year.

He looked up at his men. "Curious indeed. Be careful not to
disturb it and get on with the business at hand." With a wave

of his hat, he motioned them to continue, though he remained.

His feeling of alarm grew. "Hold up, Mr. Jameson."

The men waited as Gresham spoke to Bowling. "Mr. Bowling, take a few men and have a good look around."

"Aye, Capt'n." Bowling snapped into action. Borrowing three men from Mr. Jameson, they split up to search the island, while Jameson took the others deeper into the trees.

Gresham stood by the grave, the back of his fingers stroking the stubble on his chin. Now he felt the queer sensation that he was being watched. He searched as he paced beside the grave, fanning himself with his hat. Finally he stood still by the cross and lowered his head.

"Our Father, who art in heaven, hallowed be thy name. Thy kingdom come, thy will be done, on earth as it is in heaven. Give us this day, our daily bread and forgive us our trespasses, as we forgive—"

He was stopped short in his prayer by a call behind him from the southern end of the island. Replacing his hat, he moved in the direction of the voice.

A panting Mr. Bowling met him on his way. "Capt'n, we found somethin' else you should take a look at, sir!"

DEAR GOD! *They've come back.* Panic shot through her like a lightning bolt after spotting the British naval ship approaching. Her thin hands trembled as she strapped her Bible to her waist and ran from her shelter along the back side of the island to the tree she had selected long ago for just such an emergency.

Every beat of her heart slammed against her ribs as she struggled to climb to the security of the nest she had created.

Settling under the branches above the large clutch of coconuts, she caught her breath while slowing her racing heart and thoughts.

*Dear God, please protect me. Please don't let them find me.*

Her stomach rolled with fear and hunger. She had not had time to find much to eat before the ship neared the island in the pale light of dawn. Thinking it best to open a few coconuts before anyone came ashore, she'd used the butt of her knife to crack them open, partaking of one and setting the others aside.

Her mind raced with questions. How long would it take them to lower a boat and land on the beach? Were they coming to make sure she was dead?

Peering out from the leaves that surrounded her, she saw not just one boat but a launch and two dinghies lowered with a dozen men aboard them. Then her heart stopped dead when she saw the man in the captain's coat and bicorn hat come down the steps on the hull and take his place among them.

*My God! It is him.*

Her panic crescendoed to a fever pitch while her head swam, and tears of dread filled her eyes.

He'd come back to find her bones under the trees beside her husband.

Her gut lurched with the revelation.

But he would not find her bones, thanks only to God's mercy. And when they did not find her corpse, they would know that she still lived, and they would hunt her down.

Holding her breath, she watched in strained silence as the men made their way from the beach and up the small slope straight toward the stand of trees where she hid.

*Dear God! What shall I do? Have you saved me thus far only to have this monster come back and finish me off? Only you have helped me to survive. Only you can save me now.*

She bit her lips hard, trying to keep the sheer panic from

making her collapse in a faint and fall out of the tree. Closer, closer they came, looking up at the trees. Then she noted how the captain lagged behind the main group.

Wasn't that just like him? Sending others to do his dirty work for him.

Every muscle in her thin frame tensed in her effort to remain still while the men drew up directly under her, pausing to look at her husband's grave. Jarred by the shout of the man with the axe over his shoulder, she heard him calling for the captain.

*No!* she screamed silently as she gripped the branches. *Leave him alone! Haven't you done enough to him already?!*

She wanted to shriek down at them as the captain came near, removed his hat, and knelt by the little cross she had fashioned at the head of the grave.

Straining to hear what he said over the breeze hissing in the leaves of the trees, she could not quite make it out. Then she caught sight of a tall black sailor among them. Her heart gave a small leap of hope, but from her vantage point above them, she could not be sure if he was the same man who had helped her before she was left here to rot and die.

The captain pointed toward the trees and the men left, including the black sailor, leaving only the captain pacing beneath her.

Should she attack him while he was alone? She shuddered.

But how could she ever overcome a tall, strong man in good health? And what would the others do to her if she did?

Then something extraordinary happened. The captain stood by the cross and bowed his head, and this time she could just make out what he was saying. To her astonishment, he was praying.

GRESHAM SHIVERED as a tickling bead of sweat rolled down his back while Bowling led him toward the trees at the island's highest point. As Gresham approached, the murmuring men fell silent. Expecting to continue walking uphill, he was surprised when the terrain dipped downward just underneath the circle of trees, and his face cooled slightly from their shade.

"It's there, sir." Bowling pointed to a clump of bushes at the base of the tree trunks.

At first it wasn't plain what he should be looking at, but as he drew closer, something took shape.

They weren't bushes at all. Instead, a hut was fashioned out of layers of palm fronds, supported by the tree trunks and a few sturdy mangrove branches.

Naturally camouflaged, the dwelling was something more than a primitive lean-to and appeared to have been thoughtfully made. The joints were tied together with handmade braids of stems and vines, with layers of palm fronds thick enough to keep out the rain.

Gresham marveled at its engineering. Then his attention was drawn upward by a delicate, musical sound coming from the branches above. Hanging in little groups were strands of seashells, woven into braided lengths, gently clicking in the breeze.

The sound gave Gresham a haunted feeling. "Have you looked inside, Mr. Bowling?"

"No, Capt'n. I thought it better to wait for you, sir." Bowling's wrinkled face was flush with excitement. He rubbed his hands together like an eager schoolboy.

"Very well then." Gresham abruptly handed Bowling his hat and dropped down onto all fours to crawl through the low opening.

The space smelled earthy, and the first thing he saw was a shaft of light pouring in from the back side, where a break in the branches made a sort of small window, giving the occupant a view of the sea and beach below and, presumably, to let in the breeze.

"Hmm, not as dark and cramped as I expected," he said.

"What's that, sir?" Bowling called from the entrance. "Shall I join you inside?"

"No, Mr. Bowling," he barked. "Please stand guard. Especially since we don't know who owns the place."

"Aye, Capt'n."

The ceiling allowed just enough room for Gresham to rise to his knees. He found himself facing a Royal Navy–issue hammock exactly like the ones his men slept in side by side belowdecks. The hammock was secured to the tree trunks supporting the shelter, from one side to the other.

His mind swirled with the possibility of another survivor of the shipwreck he presumed the occupant of the grave might have experienced. Someone had to have buried whoever was in it. The hut wasn't new and showed signs of having been lived in, but it didn't show the wear of more than a season or two.

But how could someone be alive here that long with no evidence of a water source? His gut twisted with pity at the thought of someone so alone and with little hope of rescue in such a place.

Something in the shadows under the little window caught his eye, and he pushed the hammock up and over his head so he could reach the back of the dwelling. Crawling along fresh palm fronds covering the floor, he sat down next to a large box against the back leafy wall.

It was, in fact, a traveling trunk, not like a locker used by seaman but something that had cost its owner more than a shilling or two. Gresham shuffled the trunk around to better catch the light. The wood was grayed from water damage, the latch from the hinged lid was broken, and some nails from the corners were missing.

"Hmm, unexpected indeed," he muttered.

On instinct he reached to lift the lid, but halted, feeling he was about to invade someone's privacy. He reconsidered and even shot up a quick prayer for wisdom.

Leaving the box to itself for a moment, he sat back against the wall and looked up at the ceiling. How long would it take someone to construct such a sturdy little shelter? With its positioning and the way it huddled down so the wind would roll off its curves, it might very well protect someone from the terrible storms that would certainly have beaten down upon the island.

Shifting to retreat, he was strangely reluctant to leave this quiet, cool, yet lonely little place. Deciding to respect the owner's privacy and not examine the contents of the trunk for now, Gresham took one last wondering glance around and stooped under the hammock. His hand landed on something sharp.

"What the devil?"

Taking the offending object up and angling it toward the light, he found a beautifully carved tortoiseshell comb, the kind a woman used to secure her hair up off her shoulders.

Gresham sat back down and stared at the delicate thing in his hands. His perspective altered. His thoughts raced. A woman? Here? How could it possibly be?

Crawling back to the trunk, he threw open the lid. A lady's trunk, filled with the scraps and ragged remains of a lady's belongings. Pieces of muslin clothing, a petite sewing kit, hairpins, a small broken mirror, even a lady's reticule containing buttons, and an embroidered well-used handkerchief.

The revelation stunned him.

Gresham scrambled out of the shelter and ran into the startled Mr. Bowling.

"Where are the others?" Gresham growled.

"I sent 'em to look round, sir. I thought we might need to be looking for whoever lives 'ere, sir. I 'ope it was the right thing to do, Capt'n," Bowling reported.

Gresham nodded. "Gather the men, all of them, on the beach, even Jameson and his crew." He barely looked at Bowling before pushing past.

Bowling led the others back to the beach soon after. Jameson and the rest of the men now carried a straight tree trunk on their shoulders.

Gresham gathered them around. "Now, men, we have found more evidence besides the grave that someone is living here. Perhaps a castaway from a shipwreck."

Gresham glanced from face to face and knew he had piqued their curiosity. "And I believe that this person may possibly be a woman."

Their eyes widened, but they held their tongues.

He turned to the ship's carpenter. "Mr. Jameson, I want you and your men to load your timber onto the launch immediately. Mr. Bowling will convey you to the ship. Have some men also take one of the dinghies. Tell Master Mackenzie to take charge. And fetch Lieutenant Compton, Mr. Latch, Dr. Braxton, and Mr. Green here." He pointed to three sailors. "And leave me these men."

The men sprang into action. Gresham put those remaining to work. "Now, gentlemen, we're going to search the island more carefully."

He turned to Thomas Smith. Although Gresham was a tall man, Mr. Smith was at least half a foot taller and a good deal broader in the shoulders. He was a freed slave from Jamaica and an experienced topman. Most importantly, Gresham knew him to be a capable and trustworthy fellow. "Mr. Smith, I want you to walk down to the beach and then circle the island to the north."

Smith nodded to Gresham with a salute and departed.

"Mr. Hodgkins, I want you to do the same, only travel to the south. You understand?"

"Aye, Capt'n!" Hodgkins saluted and did as ordered.

"Mr. Patterson, you will walk straight across the island from here to the opposite side and meet up with the others. Then the three of you cross through the middle of the island again, spread out to cover as much ground as possible, and report back here to me."

Patterson stood up straight and saluted like the others. "Aye, Capt'n!"

As the men strode away, Gresham found shade and awaited the arrival of his two lieutenants, the ship's surgeon, and his steward, Mr. Green. He wondered what the others would think about him summoning his steward, but he felt prompted to include him.

He had known Mr. Green for several years as a good Christian man with a keen intuition. Gresham trusted him implicitly and did not want to intimidate this poor soul, whoever she was. Gresham knew from experience that he could be intimidating, even when he tried not to be. His impatience and a tendency to rush ahead had given him a reputation for being impetuous in his youth and overbearing in his adulthood.

Furthermore, Mr. Green was small in stature and had cared for his sick Irish mother until the day she died. Gresham was sure that Mr. Green's presence would be an asset.

Gazing out at the *Relentless*, Gresham rolled over a multitude of questions and possibilities. Looking up to the sky, he prayed, "Dear Lord, have you led us here by your providence to make this discovery? Is it really a woman? How did she get here? Give me wisdom, Lord. Help us find this poor soul if it is your will. I am your servant."

# CHAPTER
# TWO

Gresham paced the beach, the constant weight of his orders to timely return to England lurking in the back of his mind despite the current intrigue. The trip for the dinghy would not take long. However, the difficult task of hoisting the tree trunk aboard, using the ship's main yard and capstan as a crane, was no small task. And the sticky heat was taking its toll.

He took a metallic-tasting draught from his canteen, but not much water remained. Looking around for a source, he saw nothing and shook his head, still wondering where one would get fresh water to survive on. His heart sank again for the plight of the castaway, but impatience quickly took its place.

In good time the new landing party came ashore. It was clear the men had already heard the fantastic news about a castaway and the possibility that castaway was a woman. Their eagerness to be of service did not seem dampened by the rivulets of sweat running down their cheeks.

First Lieutenant Timothy Compton, a tall, rather dashing young man except for his sadly crooked nose, which looked as though it had been broken more than once in battle, stood to attention and saluted Gresham.

"You sent for us, Captain?"

"Indeed, Mr. Compton." Gresham was relieved to see the melancholy Dr. Braxton, his closest friend, who gave him a fresh canteen of water. With a look of gratitude, Gresham took a long drink and gave the vessel back to Braxton.

"Thank you for thinking of me, Doctor."

"Of course, Captain," Braxton replied with a slight smile and friendly nod. His cropped hair glistened with perspiration.

More refreshed, Gresham led the men into a shady spot on the beach, where he apprised them of the situation. "Well, gentlemen"—he looked down at Mr. Green first with a slight nod—"it seems the hand of providence has guided us, by way of our little skirmish with the storm last night, to an unusual discovery. As I am sure you have heard, there seems to be someone living on this godforsaken island, and there is also evidence this person could possibly be a woman."

Gresham paced in front of their line, conveying an unruffled countenance. "I know that you are thinking the same as I. How in God's name would a woman get to such a place, let alone survive? We also discovered a grave today but have yet to find out who lies in it. So perhaps, at least for a while, the person or persons living here have not been by themselves the entire time." He paused, wiping the sweat from his brow with his handkerchief.

"Now, if someone is living on this island, where are they? Why don't they simply come out and gladly be found? Perhaps they are ashamed of their current condition, or maybe they are afraid. They may consider British sailors to be enemies." This last thought made him uneasy, but he ceased his pacing.

"Whatever the case, we have a delicate situation on our hands and will need to take care with how we proceed. I have already sent three men to circle the island and then traverse back to here. They shouldn't be long in—"

His speech was interrupted by a commotion some twenty-five yards away toward the waist of the island. Gresham and his men sprinted toward the incident. When they arrived at the lowest point, they spotted Hodgkins and Patterson rushing from the other direction toward the sound of someone thrashing under the dense foliage. Pushing back the enormous leaves of the plants, they discovered Mr. Smith, his leg sunk knee deep in the ground at the plant's base, struggling to free himself. Patterson and Hodgkins laid hold of Smith's armpits and pulled. A strange sucking sound filled their ears as they dislodged him, and when his leg popped free, they all fell backward in a pile.

Gresham offered Smith a hand up. "Are you all right, Mr. Smith?"

"Aye, Capt'n," he replied, obviously embarrassed.

"Good! Now then, what in the world took hold of you here?"

The others joined Gresham in lifting the leaves to examine the soft ground underneath.

"It is damp here, Captain." Lieutenant Compton squatted, showing the spot where the sandy soil was soggy. And there, where Mr. Smith's leg had made a deep impression, lay a pool of water.

"That's groundwater, sir." Hodgkins crouched beside the puddle, dipping in his finger and licking it. "There's a good deal of limestone down there by the taste of it, but it's drinkable. Would you like to try it, Capt'n?" He dipped in his hand and offered it up to Gresham.

Gresham laughed. "No indeed, Mr. Hodgkins, for I have no interest in drinking anything that has lately had Mr. Smith's foot in it!"

The others had a good laugh with him, roughly slapping Smith good naturedly on the back.

Gresham looked at the group. "What's to be made of this, lads? A water table perhaps?"

Mr. Latch nodded. "Perhaps, sir." Although Latch was Gresham' second lieutenant and barely seventeen, his discipline in his studies and aptitude for all things scientific had garnered him the reputation of being a know-it-all amongst the officers. "Indeed, if this island were a bit larger and this spot a bit lower, there might even be a bit of a spring or pool here, sir."

Gresham pondered for a minute. "So that solves the question of water then, but we seem to be no closer to discovering our castaway. Come this way and I will show you the shelter we discovered."

The others were as impressed as Gresham with the construction of the dwelling. And he made one new and significant discovery as well. On the back side of a tree near the hut were hash marks, made by something sharp. They were in groups of seven. A way to mark time, and if one slash represented one day, the sum was figured to be around four and a half months. Not far from his earlier estimate.

While the men took to searching for more clues around the exterior, Gresham motioned for Dr. Braxton to join him off to the side. With the others not near enough to overhear his lack of formality, he crossed his arms over his chest and asked, "What do you think, Paul?"

Braxton pushed his spectacles higher on his narrow nose and looked Gresham in the eye. "To be quite honest, I am in a bit of shock and awe. It is disturbing, alarming even. To discover a castaway is unlikely, the stuff of novels, but for a castaway to be a woman, now that is something that has never crossed my mind."

The doctor rubbed his high forehead and drew a heavy breath. "But there is one thing I know for sure—that she has survived this long is a testimony to the remarkable human will to live, but no one would be able to survive in a place like this forever, nor would one want to, unless there is something desperately wrong with their way of thinking."

Gresham's heart sickened as he asked the lurking question. "And what if there is something wrong with their way of thinking, as you say? Perhaps she has gone mad and that is why she does not show herself?"

Braxton's brows lifted. "It is a distinct possibility, being in a place like this, her companion dead, isolated, perhaps even suffering from an injury or illness. We will have to deal with her as we find her. And we must find her, John. We really have no other choice. To leave someone here, man or woman, would be cruel beyond words." Braxton folded his arms, as if settling the point.

"Of course we cannot leave her, but she is making things awfully difficult." Gresham slapped his thigh with his hat. "How could anyone keep themselves this well hidden in such a small place?" He pressed his lips and flared his nostrils as he kicked at the rock by his foot. Then he stood still, his eyes narrowing. Looking at Braxton with a tilt to his chin, he turned his eyes to the trees above the hut until they rested at the tops, where the leaves swayed gracefully in the breeze.

The doctor followed his gaze. "How on earth would she get up there? One thing is sure—if somehow she is up there, she won't survive there long in this heat."

Gresham met his eyes again and shook his head incredulously, not sure of the idea himself.

They were interrupted by Mr. Green. "Pardon, Capt'n, but Mr. Compton has made a discovery, sir." The Irish lilt to Mr. Green's tone sounded too cheerful for the circumstances.

Compton reported finding the remains of a firepit on the back side of the hill from the dwelling. "There is evidence of someone cooking over a fire there, sir. Empty coconut shells, bits and pieces of shellfish remains. And there is this, sir." Compton held out his hand, a small stone in his palm.

Gresham took it and inspected it closely. "A flint! Now that is handy." He showed it to Braxton, then shoved it safely into his pocket.

"And we found a few footprints, Captain. Very small to be a man's, sir." Mr. Latch lifted his foot. "They only came to here on my foot." He outlined to a spot just at the ball of his boot.

Gresham took a long, pondering moment. He clasped his hands behind his back, looking up at the treetops, then took note of the position of the sun in the summer sky. "Right then." He pursed his lips as he collected his thoughts. "First, I will show you the grave, and then I want every inch of this island searched. Not one bush or rock is to be unturned. If there is someone here, I want them found. However"—he raised a hand and glanced at Braxton—"it is possible that this person needs to be handled with the greatest of care. Doctor, what advice would you have for us in that concern?"

Braxton breathed deeply in through his long nose and clasped his hands behind him. "Well, assuming that this person is indeed a woman, there is a good possibility that she may, shall we say, not be dressed as modestly as she might wish to be."

Gresham noticed that though Braxton didn't stumble in what he said, he was, nevertheless struggling to sound discreet, considering the subject. Anyone could imagine what a group of sailors were conjuring up in their heads at the thought of finding a half-naked woman under the bushes.

"We must be extremely considerate of her modesty if this is the case," Braxton continued. "There is also the possibility that she might be confused in her mind and, therefore, may be frightened and intimidated by a group such as ourselves, so we must not appear to be aggressive in any way. With that in mind, if you do find her, it would be best to keep your distance while keeping her in sight until we can assess the situation and make her feel as comfortable as possible."

"And that, gentlemen, is where Mr. Green comes in." Gresham motioned for Mr. Green to step forward.

Gresham put a friendly hand on Mr. Green's shoulder. "Since Mr. Green is smaller in stature than most of the men on the ship . . . uh, no offense, Mr. Green"—Gresham smiled down on the shorter man—"and because he cared for his own mother until she passed, may God rest her soul, he is perhaps the man amongst us with the most experience in knowing how to make a lady feel at ease. Therefore I requested that Mr. Green be on hand, and even if this lady does not speak English, I thought him the best man to be the first to communicate with our castaway and be our noble ambassador of goodwill."

Poor Mr. Green's face flushed bright red, but Gresham clapped Green on the back with a chuckle and a smile of brotherly affection. "So if you do find this poor soul, give her the dignity that any lady deserves and do all you can not to frighten her. You shall search in pairs, so if she is found, one of you can keep her in sight whilst the other fetches Dr. Braxton and Mr. Green to do all the talking. And now I feel I must turn my attention back to the ship and the repairs in progress. If she is found, send for me immediately."

He donned his hat and waved them on. "All right. Be about your business now. Mr. Latch, would you be so kind as to convey me back to the ship?"

"Of course, Captain." Latch snapped to attention.

With a meaningful glance back at Braxton, Gresham left him in charge and strolled with Mr. Latch toward the boats.

THE SHIP'S bell chimed three in the afternoon when Gresham stepped back on board. After examining the progress of the repairs and finding all in good order, he sent a topman aloft supplied with a spyglass and orders to look at the top of each tree and report immediately if anything unusual was found.

To his great disappointment, nothing was sighted, either in the treetops or on the ground. Incredible. His frustration mounted. He had been through battles, chased pirates, found out men's secrets, and sailed this ship to the other side of the world and back, but he could not find one little woman on a tiny little rock like this? Ridiculous.

A few hours later, Gresham called for Mr. Bowling to collect the search party. "Tell them we will resume in the morning. They need their dinner by now." And so would she. Better to give her some time to herself.

Gresham asked Braxton to join him in his cabin for dinner. The stern cabin was the private domain of the ship's captain, and Gresham's was divided into a small night cabin, where he slept in a hanging berth, and a day cabin, furnished with a large table and chairs, desk, and cabinets, with a full view out the gallery windows of the sea as it drifted past the rear of the ship.

"I'll be jiggered." Gresham growled. "Either there is no one here, or she has a hidden cave we cannot find the entrance to." He raked his hands through his hair, which had, as usual, fallen out of its queue. Sighing wearily, he propped his long legs up onto the empty chair next to him. "Well, Paul, what do we do now?"

"I am as baffled as you, John." Braxton rubbed his long auburn sideburns with the back of one hand, his wine in the other. His hazel eyes stared intently at the table, as if searching for ideas. "Perhaps there is a way to entice her to come out from hiding of her own accord. Food maybe, or clothes?"

"Hmmm. Now, my friend, you are onto something." Gresham lowered his feet to the floor and leaned forward, taking a long sip of wine. "We must give her a good reason to show herself." He bent his head, staring down at the green damask tablecloth. He worked the muscles in his jaws as hard as his mind, and a cloud darkened his thoughts. When he finally looked up at Braxton, he added a heavy gravity in his voice. "Perhaps the reason will not be a pleasant one."

# THREE

T hey would have to exhume the body from the grave.

But dear God, how could they do something so cruel? Gresham hated cruelty toward anyone, especially a woman. Several times during the night, he'd knelt, fighting to quiet his racing thoughts and still his soul, begging God to speak to him, only to be left with a feeling of dread and self-recrimination. At last he'd resigned himself to being the worst of jackanapes.

Just after dawn he heard a knock at the door, and Mr. Green entered with a breakfast tray without waiting for an answer, as was his custom. "Top o' the mornin' to ya, Capt'n!" He placed the tray on the table and was out the door before he could hear Gresham's grunted reply.

He leaned his head back, stretched his neck up, and slid his shaving blade along his tanned skin. Might as well look presentable if he was going to be a devil. He glowered at his reflection in the mirror.

He gulped down his coffee, crammed his biscuit into his mouth, buttoned up his blue double-breasted day coat, and took his bicorn from its hook. Marching out the door, he tossed a quick "Morning, Quist" over his shoulder as he swept past the red-clad marine sentry standing guard outside the captain's cabin. He took the steps up the companionway two at a time.

The boatswain piped his tune, announcing the captain's presence on deck, and the starboard side was cleared for his pleasure. The first item on his agenda was to send Mr. Smith up to the mizzen top with a glass to have a look around. Next, he checked the progress Mr. Jameson was making on the repairs of the yard and other damages. "Things look like they're coming along nicely, Mr. Jameson."

"Aye, Capt'n! Should be able to finish sometime late today or tomorrow at the latest, sir."

"Excellent. I am anxious to get us out of this heat. Now, Mr. Jameson, I do not wish to cause you any delay in your work, but I need something made as quickly as possible, if you please."

"Of course, Capt'n. What is it you need, sir?"

"I am in need of a box. It needs to be so long, so high, and so wide." Gresham demonstrated the required dimensions with his arms. "And it will need a lid, but do not attach it, as it needs to remain loose until its contents have been placed inside. And I will need to borrow a hammer and a pouch of nails."

"Right away, Capt'n. 'Ave it done in 'alf an hour, sir." Jameson sent two men to take on the project. "'ere, Capt'n. You can use my 'ammer." He handed it over with a leather pouch of nails.

"Thank you. That should do the job." Gresham turned to go, but paused. "And have that box dropped down to the launch when it is finished, if you please, Jameson," he called over his shoulder as he strode away. *Blasted awful business this.* The knot from the night before still lingered in his stomach.

Since he had a bit of time on his hands before the box was ready, he strode to the quarterdeck to check in with Lieutenant Compton and his helmsman. Then he proceeded back to the foremast and called up to Mr. Smith, his hand cupping the side of his mouth. "Anything to report, Mr. Smith?"

"No, Capt'n, nothin' to report, sir" came the low, bellowing reply.

*Blast.*

Mr. Green appeared with a second cup of coffee for Gresham. It was a bit bothersome how this little man could anticipate him and show up with just the right thing at just the right time. "Thank you, Green. Now would you please go and gather the men from yesterday's search party. I will need their services again this morning. And bring another seaman besides Smith today. He is a good fellow but a bit daunting, I'm afraid."

"Aye, Capt'n," Green chirped.

Just before he was out of earshot, Gresham called after him, "And find me some shovels, will you? Three or four should be enough."

Green lifted his hand in assent and disappeared down the companionway.

The box appeared at last and was lifted over the railing. He sickened at the sight of it. Of course it looked like a coffin. Everyone could see that it was a coffin. It was, after all, a coffin, wasn't it? Gresham gripped the rail and tried not to vomit. He had always hated coffins, ever since the death of his little sister and he'd been obliged to see her ghostly white body in one, and the familiar guilt of being responsible for her lying there came crashing in on his conscience like a giant wave on the shore. With no small effort, he stuffed the guilt back down.

*Better to bury people at sea,* he quipped to himself. *No nasty coffins to deal with.*

The search party assembled. Every man was furnished with a canteen, and Green handed out the shovels and tools. Gresham was a bit irritated by the slight tardiness of Braxton, but he shortly emerged. Gresham fought with success the urge to chuckle out loud at the sight of the doctor. Braxton had a canteen slung over one shoulder, a small medical box hung on a strap from the other, and a wide-brimmed straw hat on his balding head. He looked at once like a man going on an expedition or to a picnic, but when he met Gresham's eyes, his gaze was gray and somber.

"All right, gentlemen, off we go."

GRESHAM SAID nothing as they rowed the short distance to the shore. His sullen mood made the others subdued as well. He kept quiet as he led them up the little incline to stand with his hat in his hands, looking down at the cross at the head of the grave, pursing his lips and hating what he was about to do.

He motioned for the men to gather closer and spoke in a low tone. "I am sure you have all guessed what it is we are about here. The reason for this exercise is an attempt to give our castaway the impetus to come out of hiding. It is a dreadful deed, I know, but the only leverage we seem to have." Gresham caught a glimpse of Braxton's grim face. "Now, I want you all to stand around the grave, and when I give you the order, I do not want you to actually start digging but to pretend to—just shuffle some sand around as if you are digging. Then we shall see what happens. If that is not enough, we will have to get more serious." Gresham caught Braxton's dubious nod of approval and motioned the men to their places.

Raising his voice so that anyone on the island could hear, he began. "Gentlemen, we have before us a somber task today. Since we have not been able to find anyone alive on this island to help us identify the poor soul who lies here, we have no other choice but to remove the body and take it with us back to England. It is not what I would have wished, but . . . well . . ."— his speech faltered, and he added weakly—"as I have said, it seems we have no other recourse."

With one last glance at Braxton, he continued, nearly shouting. "Now, gentlemen, I would ask you to kindly remove your hats in a gesture of respect for this poor soul and join me in reciting the Lord's Prayer." Gresham took a deep breath and slowly released it. He bowed his head and closed his eyes. "Our Father who art in heaven, hallowed be thy name. Thy kingdom come, thy will be done, on earth as it is in heaven. Give us this day our daily bread, and forgive us our trespasses, as we forgive those—"

Gresham stopped short at the sound of a great rustling in the treetops overhead. Looking up, he was blinded by the sun's rays shooting through the dancing gaps in the leaves, and just as he shielded his eyes with his hand, the end of a rope dropped down and the flurry of bare feet, bare legs, ragged skirts, and flowing hair of a woman slid down the rope and landed with a whirl on top of the grave.

Gresham's mouth gaped, and he stood back, taking her in. There she was, clothed in rags, her long, sun-bleached hair flying around her slim body. One hand clung to a worn leather Bible strapped by a cord to her waist, and the other gripped the handle of a long-bladed fighting knife. He was only aware of this knife being held directly at his face by his peripheral vision, as his gaze was locked with her gray-blue eyes, full of fury as they blazed at him under her angry brows. Gresham couldn't breathe. She was the most beautiful thing he had ever seen.

His mind wouldn't cooperate. "Oh! Well then," he stammered. "I mean, good day to you, madam. Uh, yes, well, you see, we were just, uh, I mean, my name is Captain—"

At the mention *captain*, the lady took a menacing step toward him, her eyes narrowed and her jaw set harder still. Gresham stepped back with his hands up. "Oh! Yes! I see! All right then, uh, my name is John Gresham, and my men and I are from the ship, as you see, over there, called the *Relentless*. If you would, please allow me to introduce these kind gentlemen to you." He gestured to the men behind her.

She kept her ground and did not turn around, the knife steadily pointed inches from his face. He could see the men behind her were ready to spring upon her, but he gave them a slight shake of his head. "Yes, well, let's see now. There is Mr. Compton over there, and that's Mr. Latch next to him, and next is Mr. Hodgkins, Mr. Patterson, and Mr. Brice, yes, and now here to my right is Mr. Green. He is a very fine chap, you see, and here to my left is Dr.—"

This time it was *Dr.* that jarred her, and she swung to face Braxton, pointing the blade at his nose, the fury on her wildly beautiful face turning to horror. She spun her leg to the left, kicking Gresham in the stomach, and took off like a shot in the direction of the boats on the beach.

"No! Don't chase her!" Braxton cried as he held out his hand to help Gresham to his feet.

Gresham stood doubled over, trying to breathe the air back into his lungs.

"Are you all right, sir?" Braxton asked.

Gresham nodded and followed the lady down to the shore, with his men in tow, still gasping for air. By the time they reached the beach, she had already tossed her Bible into one of the dinghies, put her knife between her teeth, and pushed the boat out into the water. She swung herself in, grabbed the oars, and rowed madly away from them.

"It's all right—she cannot get far," Gresham sputtered. "The surf is too strong."

His command of his thoughts was returning. "Mr. Bowling, I want you to take Compton and Latch in the launch and get around behind her. Not too close, mind you. Take your time and slowly herd her close to the ship. Mr. Hodgkins, take Dr. Braxton and Mr. Green with you in the other dinghy. Get them as close to her starboard side as possible without posing a threat, just near enough so that Dr. Braxton and Mr. Green can try to speak to her. We want to get her on board the ship of her own accord."

"Captain," Braxton warned, "what about the heat? She will not last forever out on the water in the full sun. What if we cannot reason with her?"

The urgency in Braxton's tone alarmed Gresham even further. "You are right, Doctor. In that case, if all else fails, then signal me by waving your hat and we will have to go back to digging."

SHE ROWED AWAY from the shore in violent desperation, her heart pounding in terror and her mind wild with fear. *Dear God*, she prayed frantically, *help me! Give me strength or give me death. I cannot face such monsters again!*

But her prayer for strength went unanswered as the ache in her arms forced her to stop rowing while the other boats moved closer and closer, trapping her against the looming hull of the ship. She slapped at the water with her oars, splashing at them as they drew nearer, and was ready to fight them off if they tried to attack her, but exhaustion and the scorching sun were sapping her of any fight she had left.

Drowning in irrational thoughts and seeing the boat with the doctor edging ever nearer, she succumbed miserably to her helplessness and buried her face in her hands, silently weeping. *I cannot go through this again, God,* she prayed. *Please, please do not ask it of me.*

Even now, in her troubled soul, there remained a small remnant of quiet faith. Even before, when there had been nothing but torture and death to endure, and then never-ending days of the effort to survive one hour at a time, this one tiny thread had held her together like a lifeline of sanity. And now, once again a still, small voice made its way through the rest of the cacophony of silent screams in her mind.

*I am here, daughter. Surrender to me.*

Utterly defeated but never abandoned, there was nothing left for her but to obey. She stood to her feet in the little boat, and raising her arms to the heavens, she surrendered to God and to the inevitable doom that surrounded her.

Braxton's chest twisted at the sight. Seeing someone so powerless, so completely at the mercy of people she feared so intensely was a torture to behold. That he was part of the gang entrapping her made him want to retch. The look of horror on her face when she had learned he was a doctor had felt like a sword in his belly. He had never experienced such fear and hatred from anyone.

He watched as, exhausted, she let go of the oars and bent her head over her lap, her face in her hands hidden by her tumbling hair. Her thin back shook with silent sobs. A sickening helplessness gripped him as he motioned for Mr. Green to start talking.

Mr. Green leaned over the edge of the dinghy. "Please, dear lady, ya have nothin' to fear. We are friends, ya see, and God has sent us ta find ya and take ya home ta yer fam'ly. Now, if ya would just row o'r ta those steps on the ship, we'll help ya on board and have a nice cup o' tea and a bit o' supper. Wouldn't that be nice?"

No response.

Braxton could see her strength waning. Moments later she stood in the jostling boat, her face tilted skyward, covered in tears. She lifted her arms, reaching high overhead, as her lips moved soundlessly, and he realized she was praying.

Braxton had never seen anything so heart wrenching. He could hear Mr. Green whispering prayers behind him. Besides heartbreaking pity, something else rose to the surface of his soul. He was terribly frightened. *But,* he argued with himself, *haven't I been through battles and plagues, seen men cut in two by cannon balls shattering the walls around me while never once losing focus on the task at hand? I have never given way to panic—why now?*

Watching the hopeless woman in the dinghy, his mind flashed with memories. The last time he'd felt like this was as a child. Oh yes, he had prayed then, begging God to rescue him when he'd heard his father calling him to come downstairs and be taught a lesson in God's judgment. He had prayed in vain then. He would not pray now. He would rely on himself and his own mind, as he had vowed to long ago.

Again she sat down, rowing desperately. The fight was draining from her. Braxton knew he didn't have much more time. Gripping the side of the dinghy, he tried to be heard over the waves. "I am sorry. I am so very sorry."

The merciless heat waged war on all of them, the sun's rays

scorching their backs and its reflection off the water blinding their eyes. Braxton pulled the strap of his canteen over his head, and with a swing of his arm, lobbed it in her direction. To his great relief, it landed in her boat at her feet. "Please, dear lady. Please drink it all," he called.

She darted him a fierce look, then picked up the canteen and removed the lid, letting it hang on its little chain. She sniffed at the opening, glared at Braxton with defiance, then slowly poured the water from the canteen over the side of her boat into the sea. Then she threw it back at him as hard as she could, and Braxton caught it just before it slammed into his face.

"No, oh no! Now why would she go an' do a thing like that, sir?" Mr. Green said behind him.

Braxton replaced the lid on the canteen. "Because she thinks it is poisoned." With a heavy sigh, he pushed to his feet and removed his straw hat. With a fling and a spin, he sent it flying in her direction, again relieved that it landed in her boat, this time behind her. "Please, madam, please put it on."

She twisted to pick up the hat, and once again her smoldering gaze locked with his. Holding the hat by the brim, she plunged her fist through the straw crown and flung it back in his direction. This time it didn't quite reach them, and Mr. Hodgkins fished it out of the water with an oar.

Defeated, Braxton looked down at the dripping hat in his hands, raised it over his head, and waved. She must have known it was a signal. She stood as she watched Gresham on the beach wave his bicorn in reply. He motioned for the men with him to take up the box on the beach and carry it up the little berm and into the brush.

Standing only a moment longer, she swayed and collapsed.

CHAPTER

# FOUR

Gresham watched the whole drama unfold from his helpless position on the shore. He chastised himself for not joining the men in the boats, but since she had kicked him and fled, he'd thought it better for him to stay away and not cause her more of a threat than she already felt. His heart nearly burst out of his aching chest when she stood, arms lifted toward the glaring August sky in a desperate petition to God. He hung his head in his own pleading prayer, begging God to forgive him for his impatience and forcing her hand. If only he had put more faith in God's timing and stopped worrying about the plans of men, even if they were made and ordered by his superiors in the King's Royal Navy.

He had to admit he'd had no peace in his spirit, no confirming release from the dread he had felt in his gut when he'd forged his plans.

*Blast it all, Gresham,* he berated himself. Why couldn't he have waited at least until the repairs were finished? Why couldn't he have tarried one more day before he bullied her?

He watched in horror as she rejected Braxton's overtures

and knew the clock was ticking. Who knew the last time she'd had some water. When Braxton stood waving his pathetic hat over his head, Gresham could hardly breathe for the solid lump in his throat. As he waved his own hat in response, he said aloud, "Fool. What an utter fool I am."

The men with him carried the box coffin-style and followed him in silence. They shared worried glances and worked quietly. The body was soon uncovered, as the grave was shallow and the soil sandy. It was sewn up like a cocoon in a canvas hammock, in the sailor's traditional way of preparing a body for burial at sea. Kneeling beside it, Gresham gently brushed off the sand and dirt, then helped the others lift it gingerly into the box, nailing down the lid himself.

After he finished, he resurfaced out of the trance he'd been in. He gave the men orders to collect everything they could find on the island she might consider her personal property and to bring it all to the ship's wardroom. Then he ran as fast as his long legs could carry him back to the beach to wait for the first boat to take him back to the *Relentless*.

✳

WHEN GRESHAM REACHED the main deck, he asked where she had been taken and was directed to his own cabin. He flew down the steps of the companionway and stopped short before the stern cabin door. Trying to steady his breath and his beating heart, he swallowed hard and opened it.

She was lying unconscious on a cot near the open gallery windows at the rear of the room. Her ragged clothes were heaped on the table, and she wore one of his own nightshirts. Braxton and his mate, Mr. Lynn, were dipping cloths into bowls of water and sponging her arms and face, while Mr. Green poured spoonfuls of water between her dry, cracked lips.

Braxton looked up, and his grave expression told Gresham she was indeed in danger. He bent to one knee by the end of the cot and tentatively laid his hand on her bare ankle. Her skin was fiery hot and dry.

"I hope you don't mind us bringing her here, Captain. It is sunstroke." Braxton fanned her with a folded piece of paper, gazing at her sunburned face gravely. "The goal now is to try and bring her body temperature down as quickly as possible."

Gresham watched her thin but lovely face. His hand still rested on her small ankle, and he could feel her rapid pulse beating hard against the tips of his fingers. How frail, how delicate she looked, and yet how strong she had been just a short time ago, fighting like a wounded animal, lashing out at anyone who came near. *What have I done to her? Dear God, what have I done? Please don't let her die,* he prayed silently, desperately.

Raising his head, he found Braxton watching him. His friend's face was sad but not condemning. "She may not make it, John." His tone was soft and distant as he mopped her forehead again with the wet cloth and fanned to cool the drying moisture. Braxton's eyes went to the open windows. "There is not much you can do to help, but if we could get a better breeze in here, if we were moving, it might lower the temperature of the room and—"

Gresham scrambled to his feet. He gave Braxton a solemn, grateful nod and left.

※

FIRMLY GRASPING HIS NEW TASK, Gresham drove his men as if they were headed into an imminent battle with a deadly foe. In his mind, that was exactly what was happening. He stormed the deck, shouting orders, pointing here and there, setting his square jaw like a stone, letting fire fill his eyes. This was his fault, but he'd get this ship moving if he had to jump into the sea and tow it himself.

The dazed men were sluggish at first but soon found in the force of his voice and intolerance of any hint of hesitation that he meant business. He descended on Jameson like a hawk, demanding that he and his men double their speed. "I want that yard on the fore mast with a sail bent in the next half hour, Jameson. No excuses!"

"Aye, Capt'n!"

"Mr. Mackenzie, double, no, triple the men at the capstan and hoist that anchor!" Gresham shouted. "Lieutenant Compton! Get those boats back on board! Mr. Cooper! I want all hands ready—we sail as soon as the anchor is weighed. Look lively now!"

The frantic swarm above and below deck assured him the nearly 250 men of the *Relentless* scrambled to their stations. The sun blazed sidelong across the water, the waves flashing in brilliant alarm. Gresham rushed to the quarterdeck, taking note of the slight wind and begging for it to increase. *Come on, come on, let's get her moving, boys,* he thought between orders, willing the men to move faster.

The ship teemed with action from stem to stern, crown to hull. On the main deck stood the great, round iron capstan rising stalwart from the floor, its long bars sticking out from its top drum like the spokes of a rimless wheel, with its huge spindle belowdecks winding the anchor's cable around and around. Each bar had three men abreast pushing counterclockwise, grunting and straining against the weight. Slowly, slowly, the anchor made its ascent.

Gresham asked Compton for a status report. Jameson had just completed the installation of the new yard, and men were hauling the fore course sail. The weighing of the anchor was nearly complete as the sun dipped nearer the horizon, the breeze becoming a gusting wind.

In a quarter of an hour more the order was finally given to "Make sail!" and the *Relentless* bloomed with white snapping billows. She slowly turned on a tack with the wind, passing by the little island, the pink glow of the setting sun cast over the scene, deceptively beautiful and beckoning, hiding its dangers behind its blushing visage.

Once he set the course at the helm, he again stood at the stern cabin's door. Ignoring the smell of sweat from his damp shirt, he pushed his unbound hair back from his forehead and entered.

She had been moved higher on the cot, her head held gently over the end by Mr. Green as Braxton held a bucket beneath, her long hair swimming in the water. Gresham could feel the sea breeze on his face as he stood watching hers.

Braxton gave him a quick glance as he wrapped a towel gently around her hair and helped the others move her back down on the cot. "We wet her head. Still trying to get the heat out of her. The breeze is helpful—thank you, Captain." He gave Gresham a half smile. "She seems a bit cooler now but still hasn't broken a sweat. What I wouldn't give for a block of ice just now."

Pulling his desk chair closer to the cot, Gresham collapsed with a sigh. Now that they were underway, he was once again left with a terrible helplessness. Mr. Green rose and poured him a glass of flip. Gresham nodded gratefully and downed it, then walked to the windows and leaned out, watching the churning sea mark trailing lines behind the ship. Dejected, he rested his elbow high on the side of the window and covered his eyes with the back of his hand.

*Dear God, please tell me I haven't made a fatal mistake again. Please don't let her die too, I beg of you.* His chest rose and fell heavily, and he finally turned to look down at the frail, thin figure. Walking to her side, he knelt, propped his elbows on the edge of the cot, and bowed his forehead to his clasped hands. "The Lord is my shepherd; I shall not want . . ."

Green joined him in prayer, kneeling on the other side.

When he came to the end, Gresham did not say amen. Instead he looked over at the beautiful face, now pale in the fading light. "Forgive me. Please forgive me."

# CHAPTER
# FIVE

Gresham made his way down aft of the mess deck and opened the wardroom door. Lieutenant Compton, Mr. Latch, Sergeant Evans, Sailing Master Mackenzie, and his purser, Mr. Darby, snapped to attention. The wardroom was the domain of the commissioned and warrant officers on board. A large dining table and chairs stood in the middle of the room, with the officers' cabin doors lining each side. One had to be mindful of the low ceiling and beams.

Gresham stepped to the table and leaned on it heavily, surveying the items on display. "The lady is not faring well, gentlemen. If you are a praying man, I ask that you please keep her in your prayers." He heaved a sigh and looked down. "Now, before you are the items found on the island that one could consider the lady's property."

Taking a seat, he continued, "Here we have a worn rope, hairpins and combs, bits of clothing, a small sewing kit with no thread—just a needle and tiny scissors—and this embroidered reticule." Gresham opened the latch at the top and poured out its contents on the table. "Only a few buttons and this once lovely handkerchief."

Propping his forearms on the table, he eyed his men. "All these items in and of themselves may be of little consequence, but part of what interests me is what is not here. There are no coins, no jewelry, no books besides her Bible, nothing of any real value. She had only been on the island about four and a half months, if we go by the markings on the tree by the hut. One would think in that time there would have been more clothing left intact, but as you can see, there is little here, and what she was wearing was in rags."

He held up the small stone between his thumb and forefinger. "Now let us consider what we do find. Here is a bit of flint. Not something you would normally find in a lady's trunk. And neither is this." He set the stone down and held up the fighting knife. It had a long, much worn blade with a brass guard. Its handle was made of smooth yellowing ivory with a brass pummel at the end.

Gresham's eyes narrowed. "I have certainly never seen the likes of this in any lady's possession." Turning it around and examining it, he frowned. Squinting and holding the handle close, he gave a grunt of unexpected discovery. He passed it across the table. "What do you make of that, Mr. Compton?"

"It has been engraved, sir. 'S.G.' Seems to be someone's initials." Compton handed the knife back to the captain.

"Yes, it does." Gresham looked it over again before passing it around the table. "Has anyone ever seen a knife like this before? Mr. Darby, what do you think? Any idea where it was made?"

Darby, the ship's purser, was a smallish man with thinning hair and a constant, irritating sniffle. He examined the knife with interest, then sat back in his chair and said importantly, "There does not seem to be any maker's mark on the blade or pummel. I have seen knives like these carried by sailors and pirates. I would say it was probably made in North Africa or Turkey." He ended with a sniff and passed the knife along.

Gresham's brows raised. "Hmmm, well, who in the world is S.G., and why would he give his knife to a lady? Perhaps if someone gave it to her, they knew she would need it to survive."

The men around the table stirred. Gresham moved on and picked up the worn leather Bible and flipped open the cover. "Curious . . . the front page is missing, which usually contains the names of the family who have passed the Bible down. I wouldn't think that the owner would want something sentimental like that removed from a dearly loved book like this. Someone else ripped out the page perhaps, to keep one from discovering the identity of its owner? Hmmm."

Gresham laid the book aside. "Now, let us take a look at that hammock."

The table was cleared and the hammock laid across. "Take a good look, lads. Look for any little thing that might tell us more." Taking up the end nearest him, he studied the fabric and seams carefully, while the others followed suit.

Mr. Evans, the marine sergeant at arms, spoke first. "I say, sir, see here. Isn't that a little series of holes, like the ones made by the sail master's large needle with thick twine when a body is sewn up in a hammock for burial?" He gestured for the others to look at their sections as well.

"Yes, Mr. Evans. Quite so. All the way around." Gresham went round the table, guiding the canvas through his hands, noting the trail of little holes along the edges. When he arrived at the other side, where the person's head would have lain, he stopped and inspected it. He furrowed his brows into a questioning frown.

"No stain on either side," he mused. "No stain from the

bleeding of the nose when the needle pierced it for the last stitch." He was referring to the sailor's tradition of inserting the needle and passing the thick cord through the nose of the deceased to ensure the person was indeed dead.

Mr. Darby spoke up. "Blood stains are not easily gotten rid of."

Gresham scratched his chin. "If someone was sewn up in this hammock, perhaps the person doing the sewing knew they were still alive. Could it be that the lady upstairs was sown into this thing?"

He sat heavily back in his chair. "Now why on earth would you sew a live person into a hammock and then not bury them at sea? And why was the other poor soul in the grave buried in the ground instead of at sea if he was indeed dead? If they did not die until after they reached the island, then why not just bury them? Why sew them up in a hammock?" Gresham shook his head.

The men grew deathly silent.

Lowering his chin, Gresham looked around the group. "All right. Only one thing left. Let us get that trunk up here and have a good look."

The officers obliged, and the trunk was set center stage.

"We can see from the outside that the wood is water damaged, but only up to this salt mark here." Gresham pointed to a place halfway up the side. "I do not think it was ever submerged. It must have floated before being brought ashore."

He opened the trunk, and they all stood to peer inside. Most of the lining had been removed, but they could still see remnants of the tattered silk that had once made it lovely and feminine.

Shaking his head again, Gresham motioned for the trunk to be removed and sat down, deep in thought as he drummed the table with his fingers. The officers watched in anticipation. "So many questions and not much to go by."

Blinking, he sat up. He shot a look at Compton. "Mr. Compton, did you hear the woman speak when you were out on the boats? I do not recall her saying anything when she first appeared."

Compton looked bewildered. "No, sir, not a word. She didn't even make a sound when she was weeping."

Gresham stood, pacing in consternation. Just then, there was a knock on the wardroom door. Startled from his thoughts, Gresham called, "Enter," and Mr. Green opened the door.

"I beg pardon, Capt'n, but I've been sent by Dr. Braxton with news, sir. The lady has broken a nice deep sweat and is coolin' down," reported Mr. Green with a triumphant smile.

The men around the table sent up a cautious cheer, and Gresham flew past Green and out the door.

＊

SHE SLEPT DEEPLY while Braxton and Lynn took turns watching.

Feeling the impropriety of sleeping in his night cabin while a lady slept next door, Gresham swung a hammock over Braxton's berth in the doctor's tiny cabin off the wardroom. His mind and body had finally succumbed to weariness once he'd left his cabin after placing his own hand on the lady's cool forehead. Relief had swept over him like a wave.

Without any windows to let in the light of dawn, he slept later than usual. When he finally awoke in the darkness of the cabin, he couldn't remember where he was. He was reminded sharply when he stood and bumped his head hard on the beam above him. Now fully awake, he made his way out to the wardroom and found Mr. Darby seated at the table, examining the lady's knife. Gresham had the odd sensation that Darby was out of line, as if he were invading the lady's privacy.

"Oh! Good morning, Captain." Darby startled and stood. "Forgive me, sir. I did not know you had slept down here. Well, I shall run along to check the stores. With your permission, sir." Darby scurried out the door.

Gresham sat down and picked up the knife. After a moment, he opened the trunk on the floor and filled it with all the found items. All except the Bible and the knife.

Mr. Latch entered as Gresham closed the lid. "Good morning, Captain. May I be of service, sir?"

"Yes, Mr. Latch, you may. I want you to help me bring this trunk up to my cabin." Each man took a side, and together they bore it up the stairs.

They set it down outside his cabin, and Gresham dismissed Latch. He opened the door a crack to peek in at the cot, saw that its occupant still lay there sleeping, and silently closed the door. Mr. Quist, the marine in his red coat, stood guard in his usual place.

"Good morning, Mr. Quist." Gresham greeted him quietly. "I was hoping you could do me a favor."

"Of course, Captain. What can I do for you?" Quist was a tall, amiable chap, and Gresham was always glad he had been given the morning duty, as he was never sullen.

"Would you mind guarding this trunk for me until it can be placed in my cabin without disturbing the patient?" Gresham bent and placed the Bible, with the knife held between its pages, on top of the trunk.

"Of course, Captain. No trouble at all, sir." He gave Gresham a slight bow.

Mr. Green appeared at Gresham's elbow. "I'm sorry, Capt'n. I just took yer breakfast tray down ta the wardroom. I

thought perhaps ya were still asleep. I'll go and fetch it
for ya—"

"No need, Mr. Green. I'm returning there presently, but I
was wondering if you might do me the kindness of slipping
into my night cabin and collecting a few things for me. It looks
like I will be spending the rest of the voyage bunking with Dr.
Braxton."

THE FIRST THING she noticed was the pounding, unrelenting
pain in her head. Even her breathing seemed to exacerbate it,
so she lay as still as possible for a time before opening her eyes.
She raised her heavy eyelids just a crack. Her vision blurred,
and her aching mind could not make sense of anything
she saw.

Then her heart seized in horror as her vision cleared and
she saw a man dressed in sailor's garb open a door, drag in a
large wooden box, and place it near where she lay on a cot. The
dreaded realization that she was on board a ship rolled over
her in a wave of nausea. Still, she did not move as questions
threw themselves at her, each one increasing her terror.

*Have I been drugged again? Why am I still alive? What will
they do to me? Why has God allowed them to capture me again? Has
he finally abandoned me altogether now? I will not let them violate
me again. What should I do? What can I do?*

She allowed her eyes to take in her surroundings, and her
gaze landed on the box on the floor. Her own trunk, atop which
lay her Bible. Seeing the handle of her knife extending through
the pages of the book, her heart leaped, and a flashing thought
ripped through her mind. *I must end this. I will end this.*

GRESHAM SAT down to his breakfast tray but was soon interrupted by Mr. Green, who had not waited to knock before bolting through the door.

"What is it, Green?" Gresham was on his feet, following the little man, who had not stopped to speak but waved frantically for him to follow. As they climbed the stairs, they could hear a commotion coming through the open door of the stern cabin.

Gresham took in the scene in an instant. Mr. Quist was just inside the door, his musket swung off his shoulder, still deciding at whom he should point it. Mr. Lynn was standing with his back to the port wall, with his hands up. And Braxton, his hands also raised, was on his knees next to the cot, which had tipped over.

And there she was, crouching on the open windowsill, one hand clutching the window frame, the other pointing her knife at Braxton. She looked back over her shoulder, down into the churning wakes below.

Without hesitation Gresham reached in and grabbed Quist by the collar, throwing him backward out the door.

He sprang up the stairs and out of the aft hatch, sprinting to the stern of the ship as the men on the quarterdeck scrambled to get out of his way. Catching hold of a coil of rope, one end attached to the taffrail, used by the men who cleaned the outside of the gallery windows, he stood up on the taffrail, turned with his back to the water, and dropped off, to the exclamations of the crew.

With his feet on the stern, Gresham allowed the rope to slip through his hands as he descended until he thrust himself out over the water. He swung toward the open window just in time to surprise the lady with a quick little shove back into the room as the momentum swung him back out over the churning waves. On the return swing, he landed gracefully on his feet inside the window and slammed it shut behind him.

Green and Quist stood outside the cabin door, eyes wide and mouths gaping. Mr. Lynn had disappeared. Braxton was down on one knee, hands still raised, but he now faced the corner of the room farthest astern. She was huddled there, shaking and cowering, her knife held out before her.

Gresham's heart swelled with compassion at the pitiful sight, his chest still heaving from exertion. He motioned for Braxton to move back and Green to close the door. Seeing her Bible lying on the floor, he picked it up and sat down facing her, as close to her as he dared.

Her eyes flowed with silent tears. She stared at nothing as she trembled, her lips quivering.

*Please, Lord*, Gresham prayed, *help me reach her. Give me the words she needs to hear.*

"First, dear lady, I must give you my sincerest apologies." His voice was hushed and tender. "I am totally responsible for putting you in such distress. I admit to my lack of forbearance and not finding another means of allowing you to make yourself known in the time and manner of your choosing while on the island." Gresham warmed his tone with gentleness as he watched her intently. "It was a cruel thing to do to you, and I beg your forgiveness."

She blinked but did not move.

"I see by this much read and beloved Bible that you and I have something in common. I love this book as well, with all my heart." At this, her gaze moved to the Bible in his hands. Encouraged that her trembling seemed to lessen, he pressed on. "I have been in need of much forgiveness as of late. If not for God's grace, his love and mercy, I would be utterly lost, adrift at sea."

Her tears slowed, and her grip on her knife lessened. Her eyes drifted to the floor as she listened to his soft voice.

"I believe with all my soul that God's hand of providence

has brought us to this day. I also know that He helped you to survive your terrible ordeal for a reason, that you still have a purpose, some good work you have yet to achieve for His glory." His heart bled within him as he thought about how much she had suffered.

He opened the King James Bible and found the verse he sought. "'Blessed are the poor in spirit: for theirs is the kingdom of heaven. Blessed are they that mourn: for they shall be comforted. Blessed are the meek: for they shall inherit the earth.'"

Gresham glanced up from his reading to find her looking at him. He was held by her gaze, her lovely sea-gray eyes clear and somber. Without looking away, he closed the Bible, placed it on his thigh, and lay his left hand over the cover. "My dear sister, I know that God has seen your suffering. He will not let it be in vain."

He paused a moment, waiting to see if she would say something, but she remained silent.

"I do not know yet how I can truly help you besides bringing you safely to England and aiding you in finding your way home, but I will give you this." He raised his right hand and bent forward. "I give you my solemn promise, as I lay my hand on God's Holy Word, that as long as you are in my care, no harm shall come to you. I promise you that I, and Braxton here, and Mr. Green, and every man on this ship will treat you with the utmost kindness and respect as long as you are in our company. So help me God."

Her eyes never left his face. Fresh tears pooled and spilled over, but they did not seem to be the same tears of despair. They were the kind of tears that flow when a danger is over, not of joy but of a terrible fight coming to an end.

Gresham's own eyes misted with gratitude, that she had allowed him in, that God had given him the right words to speak to her wounded heart. He took the Bible from his lap, placed it on the floor, and slid it over to her. She placed the knife on the floor and picked up the book, holding it tightly to her chest.

"And now, dear sister, I would beg a promise from you as well. That as long as you are with us on this ship, you will not do yourself, or anyone else, any harm. For I would not be able to live with myself if any harm should come to you, even by your own hand. Please, will you give me your word?"

She looked at him with understanding and placed the Bible on the floor. She laid her left hand, as he had, on the cover, and raised her right. The steady, sober look in her eyes told him that yes, she would promise.

Reluctant to disturb the sacredness of the moment, Gresham sat still a few breaths longer, then rose to his feet. He smiled compassionately down on her as he took soft steps toward her, offering his hand. She did not flinch or recoil but laid her slender hand in his and rose, now clutching her Bible to her breast. She gazed sadly at him a moment more, then closed her eyes and leaned her forehead forward on his chest.

Shocked, he followed his instinct and put his arm reassuringly around her thin shoulders. His heart flushed with warmth as he looked over her head at Braxton. He too had mist in his eyes as he shook his head in wonder.

She stepped back from him, and her gaze turned to Braxton. She held out her hand, which he took in both of his. "I second the promise that my friend has made to you. No harm shall come to you under our watch. And I too will do all within my power to help you in any way I can. You have my word."

She rewarded his words with the slightest tug at the corners of her still chapped lips.

"Are you hungry?" Gresham asked. "Here, come sit here, and I will send Mr. Green to fetch you a tray."

The doctor had pulled the sheet from the cot and placed it around her shoulders.

"There, thank you, Braxton. That's it. Now, Mr. Green will bring your breakfast, and you shall have all the lumps of sugar for your tea your heart desires. Oh, and may I please have the loan of your, uh, dress here?" He lifted the ragged garment from the table. "Braxton will stay with you until Mr. Green arrives with your tray. I will check on you after I attend to some business."

Turning to the corner where she had been just moments before, he picked up her knife, returned to the table, and laid it before her. He looked down on her sorrowful upturned face. "Thank God, dear sister, thank God we've found you."

# CHAPTER
# SIX

Braxton sat at the wardroom table with his logbooks and personal journal and sipped his tea as he prepared to write. As a ship's surgeon, he was required to keep two identical logbooks of daily entries describing each day's events, logging patients' names, surgeries, or treatments, and the results of both. Braxton did not immediately open the logbooks but munched his biscuit, pondering his best course.

After a moment he pushed the logbooks aside. Opening his personal journal, he wrote about the events of the past few days, being as detailed and factual as possible. There was so much to record, and he didn't want to miss anything that could be helpful or important later. Tired as he was, he couldn't allow himself to lie down until he had a good start.

Just as he paused his writing, he stood to his feet at attention as Gresham entered, looking disturbed. "At ease, Paul. I checked in with our guest. Green said she ate every bite of her breakfast in tears, like a starved child, then kissed his hands with gratitude. Poor woman. She has gone to rest in my night cabin." Gresham studied his friend's face. "Looks like you could do with some rest yourself, Doctor."

Braxton threw his pencil down and blew out wearily. "So much has happened I hardly know what to do next. Sleep seems to be of the last priority."

"Hmm, yes, I know." Gresham eyed Braxton. "But if you do not get some rest soon, Paul, I fear it will be you in the sick bay next."

"I will snatch a bit of sleep before I go back up to check on her."

"Good. Now, I do have a pressing question I would like to get your opinion on before you go." Gresham's voice was low and serious as he motioned for Braxton to sit with him. "Paul, why doesn't she speak? I have not heard her make a sound, even when she weeps. Do you think she is truly mute? Is there something wrong with her voice, her throat?"

Braxton sighed, sat back in his chair, and looked darkly at his hands, clasped over his stomach. "After she collapsed and we got her on board, Mr. Lynn and I removed her garments and sponged her down before dressing her in your nightshirt." His eyes returned to Gresham with a look of foreboding. "I took advantage of that time to give her a thorough physical examination."

Gresham's eyes shadowed as he sat motionless.

"You should know, John, that she has been sorely abused. Certainly she has plenty of scarring from climbing trees and the efforts of surviving on the island, but there are other scars as well." He leaned forward on the table. "Her wrists show the scars of being bound. And"—he took a strained breath—"there are scars on her breasts. Bite marks . . . human bite marks."

Gresham's face reflected a mixture of shock and outrage.

"There is also scarring that would indicate she was raped. Probably repeatedly."

Braxton watched Gresham as he struggled against his clear outrage. His jaws clenched as he shifted in his chair, his dark eyes searching the top of the table in silence. "I had suspected something like this might have happened to her, but hearing the evidence, the violation, the violence of it all. My God, the poor soul."

"Indeed." Braxton rested his elbows on the table, rubbing his forehead over his worried brows. "She does not seem to have anything wrong, from what I have been able to observe, with her voice or throat. It is quite possible she is choosing not to speak, or that the trauma she experienced has made it impossible. I believe it is more likely the latter. I have heard of a condition called 'selective muteness'—which is only just being studied—and this could very well be what she suffers from."

Gresham shook his head. "Well, that sheds some light on it, but what kind of a man would do such a thing?" His eyes flashed. "And how on earth do you find him and bring him to justice?"

Gresham glared at the table, collecting himself. "What can we do to help her?"

Braxton narrowed a wary eye at his friend. "This isn't something that can be fixed like a broken yard, John. It will take time and a great deal of patience. She must feel completely safe and out of danger. Even then she may not be able to speak of such unspeakable things. There is also the chance she may never speak again. Only time will tell."

He squared his shoulders to face his captain. "John, you must trust this to me and promise me you will not do anything to force her in any way. Do you understand why I am asking?"

Lowering his eyes, Gresham nodded. "I promise, Paul. I know my lack of patience is one of my greatest faults, and I have seen the terrible price that others have paid for it, especially in the last few days. You have my word."

With a slight smile, Braxton laid his hand on his heart. "Thank you. Your trust in me is one of my life's greatest rewards."

"And yours mine, Doctor." Gresham heaved a sigh. "Well, there are other concerns we should discuss, but I want you to take that rest as you promised, so they will have to wait. There is just one more thing I wanted to mention in regard to the body in the hold. When you examine it, I want to know if the last stitch on the hammock was passed through the person's nose or not. I will explain later why it matters."

"Certainly. I hope to get to that very soon."

As Braxton closed his journal, Gresham picked up one of the logbooks on the table, examining the spine. "I haven't had a moment to write anything in mine for three days now. I mustn't neglect my duty, but to tell you the truth, I am reluctant to write about her. Something doesn't feel right. What about you?"

Braxton shook his head. "I am not sure either. For now I am writing notes in my private journal. Shall we talk about it later when we have had more time to consider?"

With another heavy sigh, Gresham pushed himself off the chair and turned to leave. "I have never neglected a duty before in my life, but yes, let us take some time to weigh the matter carefully."

A KNOCK on the door startled her. Mr. Green opened it to let in the doctor. She had just risen from a nap and was having a cup of tea at the table. She pulled the sheet tighter around her neck and avoided his eyes, staring out the gallery windows at the trailing wakes behind the ship.

Why was he here? Her unease grew as she fought down the queasy feeling in her stomach.

"I hope you are feeling better. May I sit down?" Dr. Braxton paused a moment before taking a chair and joined her in gazing at the sea for a time.

She sipped her tea and stole a curious glance at him now and then. Finally he spoke, but did not turn to face her, for which she was glad.

"I need to ask your permission for something. It would not be right to do this unfortunate task without consulting you."

She watched him closely, a foreboding in her chest.

"I would like to ask your permission to examine the body from the grave."

Her heart lurched, and her eyes darted around the space. She set her cup on the table and stood. She stepped heavily to the windows and grasped the frame, staring into the depths of something other than the sea.

She felt him watching her. If he examined the body, then perhaps they would understand. At last she took a laboring breath and turned to him.

Moving to the table, she picked up the teapot with a shaky hand, poured a cup, and handed it to him. Braxton took it with surprise and thanked her as she offered the sugar bowl to him.

"Oh! No, no thank you, kindly. I take my tea black." He lifted his cup to her as she returned to her seat, took a sip, and set it down. "Well, I am assuming that you are granting your consent, and I thank you. I am sure your choice was not lightly made."

None of this was easy. She gazed at him calmly for a moment, then returned to her study of the endless sea.

They finished their tea together in silence. After he finished, he rose, pushed his spectacles higher on his nose, and bowed to her. "Thank you, madam, for the company and for the tea. I should get on with my duty. I will come to see how you are faring in a little while, if you do not mind."

He looked surprised when she stood and gave him a curtsy. He bowed awkwardly again and left the cabin.

Rising to look down at the deep waters beneath the ship, she wondered what he would think about all he would discover, and she shivered.

LATER THAT AFTERNOON, Braxton emerged on the main deck and shaded his eyes from the bright sun, his vision adjusting from the dark of the hold in the belly of the ship.

Gresham saw him as he approached the quarterdeck and met him on his way. "Finished, Doctor?"

Braxton lifted the notebook in his hand. "I am ready to give you my report, Captain."

Gresham nodded. "Let us remove to the wardroom." He led the way.

Once they were ensured of privacy, they sat at the table. Gresham pulled his chair up close, his eyes full of grim anticipation. "Did you find anything unusual?"

Braxton fought down his revulsion. "Certainly unusual. Some things that I might have expected, and others I certainly did not."

He opened his notebook. "I did as you asked and gave the hammock a thorough inspection. It is identical to the one we found in the hut. It was sewn through the nose of the deceased, who is indeed a man. And so it would appear that this fellow was already dead when these two were left on the island."

Gresham frowned and sat back, shaking his head incredulously. "So she survived entirely by herself and by her own wit. Astonishing."

"Indeed. But there was something else noteworthy I found on the hammock. Urine stains. They could not have been made by the dead man inside, as they are on the area that covered the face." Braxton's lip curled. "I highly doubt that our lady upstairs would have done such a disrespectful thing, so my only other conclusion is that someone else relieved himself there as an act of defilement against the deceased."

"Dear God!" Gresham snarled. "Who would do such a disgusting thing?"

"That's nothing." Braxton eyed Gresham sideways under his knitted brows. "There's more." He glanced down at his notes and pushed up his spectacles. "Despite the decay of the body, I found two items of significance. One being a fracture of the skull near the left temple, probably from a blow from something heavy, given by a right-handed person. The other" —Braxton flared his nostrils in disgust—"no fingers. The man had no fingers. They had all been sawn off in expert fashion soon before his death, by what appears to have been a surgeon's saw, and skillfully done."

Gresham gave a look of disdain. "No fingers. You are sure they were cut off and the man was not born that way?"

"It is unmistakable. The flesh on the base knuckles the fingers were cut from showed almost no healing. I believe they were made by a trained surgeon with a saw just like the one I have in my own kit."

Gresham's eyes narrowed. "So this man was tortured before he was murdered. And it looks as if a surgeon may be the most likely suspect. Either he was acting on his own, or as an accomplice."

"And that would explain our lady's aversion to doctors,"

Braxton concluded, almost to himself, grim comprehension clouding his hazel eyes.

Gresham took the notebook from Braxton and scanned the notes. "My God," Gresham finally said, snapping the book shut. "No wonder she was terrified of us." He stood and paced with agitation.

Braxton remained seated, studying his folded hands on his stomach, remembering the look of horror on her face when Gresham had introduced him as a doctor.

"How could a man of medicine do this?" Gresham continued. "What kind of reprehensible vice would a man have to commit these atrocities? And then to leave a woman alive in such a place, almost to further her misery. Only an animal would do such a thing!"

Braxton sat glaring at the table. "And why would they do this to her?" he added. "What on earth could she have done to deserve this kind of torture and violation?"

He rose to his feet, facing his friend. "John, we have to start thinking about what happens to her after we make port. We must consider what we report to the navy about her. What will they do with her? She is utterly vulnerable. She cannot even speak on her own behalf."

"Indeed, Paul, you are right." Gresham raked his hair and took his seat again.

"I will need to start asking her about what she remembers," Braxton added with urgency. "Perhaps she might be able to write. We need to find out all we can."

Gresham gave the doctor a pointed look. "Yes, and we must anticipate what the navy will do with her if she cannot remember who she is or where she belongs." He gripped the arms of his chair. "I do not like to think of it, but they may take custody of her."

Braxton's gut seized. "Let us see what we can find out from

her. It may take some time."

"Time, Doctor? That is something of which we have a limited supply. Well, Paul"—Gresham laid his hand on Braxton's shoulder—"best get started."

✳

INSTEAD OF HOLDING the stern cabin door open when the captain and doctor knocked, Mr. Green came out, closing the door behind him. Gresham noticed the troubled look in Green's usually cheerful eyes.

"Beg pardon, Capt'n, Doctor, but I would like ta tell ye something that may be o' use," Green said.

"Of course, Mr. Green. What is it?" Gresham bent down a bit to hear the Irishman better.

"Well, sir, it seems ta me that our lady guest has a good bit o' an aversion ta blue coats, sir, officers' coats. I was doing a bit o' cleaning in your cabin, ya see, and I opened yer wardrobe and took out yer other blue woolen coat, Capt'n. She was struck with a terrible fear. She grabbed her knife and ran ta the other side o' the room, trembling and holding it out as if she were in mortal danger."

"When did this happen, Mr. Green? Why didn't you send for us?" Gresham asked sternly.

"'Bout quarter o' an hour ago, sir," Green said. "I was going ta send for ye, Capt'n, but I thought I should stay with her. I put the coat away quick as a jig. She is startin' ta calm down. She's sittin' at the window now. I believe she is prayin'."

Gresham looked hard at Braxton. "What do you recommend, Doctor?"

Braxton answered through clenched teeth. "Take off your coat, Captain." He tugged off his own.

"What? Oh." Gresham blanched but unbuttoned his coat and handed it to Green.

Braxton continued with his instructions. "Now, Mr. Green, go and stow these coats in my cabin and bring us a tea tray, and don't forget a cup for yourself. She seems to feel safe in your company. The captain and I will wait here for you."

"Aye, sir!" And Green was off.

Gresham could feel the heat of his anger rise.

Braxton's eyes flashed. "Looks like we have some confirmation that our surgeon was in His Majesty's Royal Navy."

"It certainly does," Gresham snapped. "But how on earth did he accomplish his treachery without being found out? And how in God's name was he able to have a ship of the navy anchor beside that blasted island and drop these two off without the captain's knowledge? Impossible!"

"Indeed, Captain, which proves he wasn't acting alone. He must have been aided by the ship's captain. Or he was the aid and the captain the assailant."

The revelation made Gresham want to smash something. His outrage at the thought that officers in His Majesty's service could be capable of doing anything this hideous made his blood boil. That this murdering rapist was a man of his own standing, one of his own peers, was intolerable.

"I am in no shape to keep company with a lady right now, Paul. I will return when I am fit." Gresham eyed his friend with hesitation.

Braxton took a steadying breath and let it out. "I am all right, John. I am as deeply disturbed as you, but I can hide my emotions better than you."

Gresham gave Braxton a cuff on the shoulder. "You always could." He took himself up to the quarterdeck for some fresh air.

HER HANDS WERE STILL TREMBLING as she sat at the table reading her Bible, when Mr. Green arrived with tea. He and Dr. Braxton entered the cabin. Turning to them, she shut the book with her knife in its leaves and clutched it to her chest, her heart beating hard against it.

"I've brought ya some tea, ma dear. And here's, er, Mr. Braxton, ta see ya." Green set the tray on the table and commenced pouring.

Braxton sat and gazed at her, and she thought she saw compassion in his hazel eyes. "I am sorry to disturb your reading. I understand from Mr. Green that you have just had a shock. I wish there was something I could do to alleviate your discomfort and assure you that you are safe now."

Her gaze returned to the sea. She shivered even though the room was warm. Green went into the night cabin and emerged with a blanket, laying it over her shoulders. She drew it close as Green took the chair beside her.

"I have examined the man from the grave," Dr. Braxton continued. "Thank you again for your consent."

At this she turned her face slightly in his direction. "I'm sure you are aware of what I found. I am deeply sorry." The doctor swallowed hard before asking, "Was he your husband?"

Gripping her Bible harder, she turned to him with intent, then closed her eyes and rocked slightly, her mind in a haze of remembering. She had dug his grave with her own bare hands.

Dr. Braxton leaned closer, then asked softly, "Do you know your name?"

Her eyes startled open, and she cocked her head at him. She stood suddenly in panic and tried to recall, but only confusion flooded her thoughts. Laying her Bible on the table, she gripped the back of a chair, searching her mind, feeling suddenly adrift, unable to ground herself.

*My name? What is my name?* She asked herself with alarm. *I must remember my own name, but I cannot!*

It was a new revelation. Having a name wasn't something to bother with alone on the island, but now, finding that she actually couldn't remember it, she felt unmoored, floating like a ghost, without weight.

Defeated, she crumpled into her chair. Mr. Green murmured soft endearments beside her. A full minute passed until she lifted her gaze to meet the doctor's, her heart bleeding from dismay.

"I am sorry." He spoke gently, his voice husky and low. "I understand. We will help you find out who you are. Please don't worry. Look here." His attention went to the objects in his hands. "I brought you a notebook and pencil. I thought perhaps you could write or draw something to help you communicate with us."

Dr. Braxton offered the items to her, but she was struck with panic as she pushed them from her and turned away.

Sighing, Dr. Braxton went to the captain's desk and placed them on top. "You are welcome to use these if you change your mind. I'll—"

A knock at the door cut his sentence off, and the captain entered. "I am sorry to interrupt. I can leave if you prefer."

She wished they would all just leave her alone. Her mind felt like quicksand. *God, you know my name. Please help me.*

After a few silent moments, she turned her face and rose. Captain Gresham stood just inside the door. Without his blue coat, standing tall in his waistcoat and shirtsleeves, she was not jarred by his presence as she had been before. Instead, he was only a man, and she numbly met his gaze.

He bowed. She grudgingly returned it with a curtsy, then

sat down again next to Mr. Green. Dr. Braxton sat opposite her, while Captain Gresham went to the cabinet near the desk. Rifling through stacks of charts, books, and journals, he ambled to the table with an armful of items and sat down. "Thank you, sister, for your forbearance. How are we getting along, Braxton?"

She cast her eyes downward as she listened to the doctor's answer. "Not as well as one might hope, sir. But I have promised our guest that we will do all we can to help her find her identity and where she belongs, and find justice for her and her husband, who is the man in the coffin below."

"Of course we will. I will do all I can to help you, no matter how long it takes." Captain Gresham's voice was warm and full. "You will not be left alone again. You have my word."

She shifted her gaze from the table to his face, full of sorrow and longing. *Dear God, please let their words be true.*

The captain whispered something to Dr. Braxton, who looked at him skeptically, then nodded.

Captain Gresham pulled his chair closer to the table. "There are some rather important questions we need to ask you, my dear. They may be difficult to hear. Will you allow me?"

She stiffened, bracing herself as her pulse quickened.

The captain leaned forward. "The men who did this to you and your husband, were they British naval officers?"

She flashed her eyes to his and felt the heat of rage flush through her. *Yes!*

He nodded slowly with understanding. "Was it a naval ship's captain?"

She clenched her jaws as she let her narrowed eyes bore into the captain's. *Yes!*

"Did he act alone?"

She turned her face away. *No!*

"Did he have an accomplice?"

Again she snapped her eyes back to his as she gripped the edge of the table. *Yes!*

"Was it the ship's surgeon?"

She pounded her fists on the table, flared her nostrils, and darted eyes full of fire at him.

"That's enough, John." Dr. Braxton placed his hand on Captain Gresham's shoulder.

A charged silence hung in the air. She breathed heavily as she fastened her eyes onto the captain's with indignation and fury.

After several seconds ticked by on the wall clock, the captain bent toward her, his face a mixture of kindness and sorrow. "I am sorry. I did not intend to push you. Thank you for your bravery, madam."

Captain Gresham pressed hard back in his chair. "I am appalled and infuriated that these men, my own peers, would do such evil deeds, and I assure you they will be found and made to answer for it."

They sat awhile, the air thick with emotion. She felt drained, wrung out like a damp rag, but at the same time, she felt understood. Somehow, having these men know the truth of what happened gave her an unexpected sense of peace, something she had not felt in a long time.

Finally Dr. Braxton inclined over the table and caught her eyes. "Are you all right?"

She could hear the genuine concern in his voice. Taking a long breath, she met his gaze with a faint smile. *Yes, thank God.*

Captain Gresham looked through his items on the table. "I have some maps here for you to look at when you are ready. Perhaps you will find something you recognize. Mr. Green, is that tea still warm? Let us take a break from all this and have a cup, shall we?"

Mr. Green served the tea as the captain continued. "So, well, I have a thought," he said awkwardly. "Since you cannot remember your name, what would you think about a new name, something to be called, to be known by temporarily until we can find out your true one?" He cocked his head with the slightest of smiles. "Would you like that? It would be nice for us to be able to call you something other than 'sister.'"

Tilting her chin, she looked down, considering, then her gaze returned to him steadily. *A new name? That might help.*

Looking around, her eyes landed on Mr. Green. She would trust this man with such a decision. He was so kind and respectful to her.

Finding her looking at him, Mr. Green finally spoke up. "Oh! Well, aye, Capt'n. That sounds like a lovely idea. Would ya like a new name, my dear?"

*Yes, sir,* she replied with her eyes.

"Well, yes. That would be a fine thing, I do believe, as long as t'were the right name, o' course." Mr. Green looked at the captain, who nodded that he should continue. "Well, let me see now."

He stroked his stubbled chin, and she could see the possibilities file across his face, when a gleam came into his bright-green eyes and he smiled widely. "I've just the thing!" He slapped his knee with joy. "There are initials on the ivory handle of yer knife, now, aren't there? S.G. Yes, that's it!"

Green pressed his hand to his chest. "My own dear mother's initials were S.G. Now, hers was a good, sturdy Christian name. Sarah," he pronounced proudly. "Mrs. Sarah Green. Would that suit ya, my dear?"

Her eyes grew moist, and she almost smiled as she reached her hand out to Mr. Green, who took it in both of his tenderly. "Mother would be so happy ta lend her name to such a dear lady."

"Splendid, Mr. Green! Good work!" Captain Gresham grinned brightly, stood to his feet, and nudged Dr. Braxton to do the same. "May we be the first to congratulate you, Mrs. Green." He offered his hand to her as she stood. The captain bent over her slender fingers, then handed her off to Dr. Braxton, who smiled sheepishly and did the same.

She drew the blanket close around her and meandered back to the windows. The sky was dimming as the sun dipped down beyond the silver edge of the world. Staring at her reflection in the glass, she held her hand to her thin cheek. *S.G. Sarah Green.*

# CHAPTER
# SEVEN

T he smoking oil lamps hanging over the dining table gave the wardroom a golden-gray glow. The officers had been served, and Gresham waited for the wine to be poured before he began, weighing in his mind what to share with them and what not to.

He noticed the genial, light conversation amongst the men, but knew they were not truly at their ease with him present. The wardroom was their domain, and having their superior in their midst made them stiff and overly cordial. Well, it could not be helped under the circumstances. Gresham took a bite of his salted meat and laid his knife and fork on his plate. Wiping his mouth, he sat back in his chair and asked for their attention.

"Now, gentlemen, much has happened in the last few days, and I am sure that there is a lot of gossip going around the ship about our guest upstairs. I want to assure you that the lady's demeanor has undergone a remarkable transformation since yesterday, even since this morning. And there has been some information discovered that you should be made aware of."

The faces around the table were full of curiosity, and everyone stopped eating.

"Our guest has been through a horrific ordeal, and that being the case, her fears are more than justified. It has been discovered that the body in the coffin below is that of her husband and that he was tortured and murdered. We have also concluded that he was already dead when the two were left on the island."

Low exclamations of indignation were shared around the men, genuinely dismayed.

Gresham continued. "This means that the lady upstairs survived on her own, by her own volition and wit, which is truly astonishing. She deserves our deep respect and admiration for such a feat." He added a look of steely warning to his eyes. "She does not deserve to be the subject of conjecture or ridicule, and I am relying on all of you to put a stop to anyone engaging in that practice immediately."

"Of course, Captain. You can count on all of us in that regard, sir," Mr. Compton offered.

"Thank you, Mr. Compton." Gresham looked around the table at each man as he continued. "It has also become apparent that the persons who committed these crimes, I am loathsome to say, seem to have been officers of His Majesty's Royal Navy."

Gresham's officers were incensed. He'd known they would be and felt a pang of pride and affection for these good men. "It is because of this contemptible situation that our guest has an extreme aversion to the sight of blue officers' coats. Understandable. So I am issuing an order that for the remainder of this voyage, until we are in sight of England, that no one on board, including myself, shall wear a blue coat."

Now they were surprised and skeptical. "But, Captain, if I

may ask, sir, how will the men distinguish the officers from the other men?" Mr. Latch asked.

"Well, Mr. Latch," Gresham quipped, "I am sure that by now, after a year at sea with you, the men already know your handsome face quite well." The men chuckled as Latch snapped his mouth shut.

"And now Dr. Braxton will explain to you anything else he thinks important for you to know."

Braxton explained the reason why he felt the lady was silent and that she was suffering from amnesia. The room grew deadly still. Gresham had never seen the mild-mannered, steady-minded doctor so disturbed. He was always the unflappable one, the one who was never ruffled, even in the midst of battle.

Eyes were downcast and a few whispered exclamations of sympathy were expressed. Braxton sat up straight and raised a hand to them. "Now that she has been convinced she is not in danger, she has exhibited, though still considerably sorrowful and timid, a gentle and intelligent nature. It is my hope that once she is returned to a place she knows and feels safe in, she will have a complete recovery from these symptoms."

"Yes, Doctor, we should all hope and pray for that end." Gresham had observed his friend struggle and was touched by his depth of compassion. He gave Braxton an approving smile. "Thank you, Dr. Braxton."

Gresham raised his glass. "Gentlemen, a toast. To His Majesty and his Prince Regent, and to the lady upstairs, who has been given a new name. Something to be called until her real name is found. To Mrs. Sarah Green."

"Hear, hear," they all said, and they drank to the lady's health and happiness.

BRAXTON WOKE to the sound of a voice calling. It started quietly but increased in volume and alarm.

"Meri! Meri!"

Ducking his head, he rose from his berth and lit the lamp on his small bureau. The dim light allowed him to see his friend thrashing in the hammock above his berth.

"Meri, no! Meri!"

Braxton laid a gentle hand on Gresham's shoulder. "John. Wake up, John. It is only a dream." He shook him gently.

Gresham sat up, startled. He looked around him and found Braxton's face in the lamplight.

Gresham moaned and rubbed the sweat from his face. "Oh, I'm sorry, Paul. I didn't mean to wake you."

"You were having a nightmare about your sister Meri." Braxton kept his tone gentle. "You haven't told me you still had them."

Gresham ran his hand through his hair, clearly embarrassed. "Only on a rare occasion. Certainly not as often as before."

Braxton eyed him with concern. "Perhaps you have more in common with Mrs. Green than you know."

Gresham looked at him with surprise, then lowered his eyes. "Yes, I suppose you may be right."

Braxton set the lamp down and studied his friend and his heart ached for him. "We haven't talked about what happened for years, John. Maybe it is time to bring it out in the light again, allow the memory to lose a little more of its power."

At this, Gresham shifted uncomfortably. "Oh, Paul. We've gone over it before, and nothing can change the past." He swung his legs over and dropped out of the hammock. "I think I'll go up and get some air. I forgot how stuffy it gets down here. I am sorry you have to put up with it." He pulled on his breeches and shirt and gathered his boots.

He tossed Braxton a wry smile, "Thanks, Paul. I know you only want to help, and I am indebted to you."

Braxton nodded and sighed as Gresham closed the cabin door behind him. It looked like Mrs. Green had stirred up something his friend thought was buried a long time ago.

***

GRESHAM MADE his way to the helm and relieved his helmsman. Gripping the solid oaken handles of the wheel, he let the fresh wind blow on his face. He never tired of the way the sea scented air braced him, and he looked at the canvased masts of the *Relentless* and up at the star-filled sky.

Perhaps Braxton was correct in his diagnosis and the presence of the lovely castaway asleep in his berth under his feet was stirring up the demons of his own past. He was always so mindful to keep the thoughts and feelings safely tucked away and was generally successful. The more the years washed those black memories into the past, like the storms this very ship had sailed beyond, the more he hoped he would eventually receive complete healing and forgiveness from his Lord.

But finding Mrs. Green and understanding at least some of the tragedy and trauma she had endured brought all the feelings of his earlier heartbreak back into full sail. The thought of the injustice of her plight sickened him to the core.

His mind flashed with terrible scenes, and his chest filled with the unbearable guilt of his boyhood sin. He could see again his little sister, Meredith, as he'd left her sitting on the stairs of the Clock House, where their father had placed him in charge of her while his father finished his work inside. Could remember the look of betrayal as he told her to stay on the steps while he followed an older lad, who had tempted him with a dash, to the dry dock to see the newly finished ship of the line. Could feel again the dismay of returning to find Meri had disappeared and the angry, panicked look on his father's face as they searched for her in the massive dockyard well into the night, only to find her lifeless body at the bottom of the dry dock, horrifically used and discarded like a cast-off doll.

It had all been his fault, and he had spent the rest of his life looking for any way to redeem himself for his devastating failure.

As he gazed at the stars and thought of his Creator knowing each of them by name, he could not help but allow the forbidden questions to well up again, questions he had long given up as unanswerable.

"Why, Father in heaven?" he prayed. "Why would you forsake the most frail and defenseless of your lambs to be misused by such evil men?"

The wind whipped around him as he gripped the wheel and strained to hear the answer, but the same words to his spirit were the usual reply. *My grace is sufficient.*

AFTER MR. GREEN informed him that Mrs. Green had finished her breakfast, Gresham, tired as he was in body and spirit, rallied himself as he entered the stern cabin with two men carrying white bundles. Mrs. Green's face filled with apprehension, even though Gresham knew she had been told by Mr. Green she would be having visitors after her meal. Standing, she gazed at Gresham with eyes full of questions before she dipped into a curtsy.

"Good morning, Mrs. Green," Gresham began, with a bow. "I would like to present to you some of the ship's crew, who have come bearing gifts for you. This is Mr. Huckabee, our sail-maker, and his mate, Mr. Stokes."

Each man bowed in turn as she watched warily from behind a chair on the other side of the table. Gresham saw her look down at the seat of it, and he knew she was making sure her knife lay close at hand.

Gresham continued quickly to reassure her, permitting a hint of bashfulness to his tone. "Well, you see, it had come to our attention that you might be more comfortable wearing something other than a, uh, nightshirt. And I asked Mr. Huckabee here to see what he could do for you. Now, gentlemen, if you please." He gestured toward the table.

The men stepped forward, spreading their bundles on the table before her. They withdrew the sailcloth wrappings, revealing a simply made lady's wardrobe. Her eyes went wide, and her hand flew to her mouth as she let out a little gasp.

At the tiny sound, Gresham took note. It was the first sound he had ever heard her make.

There were two shifts, one dress, and a few other necessaries, then a soft pair of small leather slippers. Her eyes misted with appreciation. She gave Mr. Huckabee and Mr. Stokes the first genuine smile Gresham had seen.

How beautiful that smile was. His heart flipped over in his chest.

Reaching her hand across the table to the sailors, she shook their hands graciously. Mr. Huckabee's crinkled round face lit up like the sun as a tear escaped his happy eyes.

"We hope that everything is to your liking, Mrs. Green," he said. "If anything is amiss, we will make it right. May you wear your new clothes in good health, and may God bless you." He sniffed loudly, withdrew his handkerchief, and blew his bulbish red nose.

She was clearly overcome as she looked over the ensemble again, then covered her face with her hands.

Gresham and Green were instantly at her sides. "Perhaps

this was too much," Gresham stammered. "Too many people in the room. Please forgive me." He waved for the others to leave.

But she caught hold of his arm and stopped him. He looked down into her tear-filled face to find her smiling up at him with a gratitude he had never seen before.

"Ah, isn't that nice now!" Mr. Huckaby chuckled. "I do believe the lady approves, Captain!"

"Now if ya please, gentlemen," Mr. Green interjected, "and that includes you, Captain, let us leave Mrs. Green alone with her new things and allow her some privacy." The small man followed the others out of the room. "That's it, yes, thank ya very much. Excellent work, my good fellows!"

THE LITTLE MIRROR in the captain's night cabin was not much help as she tried to take in her appearance. She could not remember the last time she had felt the faintest hint of happiness. It felt foreign, but inch by inch she was trusting herself to give way to it, and was cautiously glad.

She had washed at the captain's basin and slipped into a shift and her rehabilitated stays, which fit perfectly. The stockings were a bit long, but she folded them over the garters and was satisfied with the result.

Next, she found the tiny pair of sewing scissors from her trunk and snipped, bit by bit, at the sun-damaged ends of her long golden-brown hair. When she finished, she swept the tresses on the floor into a small pile near the bureau.

Using her own hairpins and combs, she pinned her hair up in a simple, dignified fashion. Then turning to the gown hanging from the hook on the wall, she studied it. The bodice had been made from an altered gentlemen's muslin shirt. The collar had been removed and the neckline opened up, with a channel sewn for a green ribbon drawstring. The sleeves had been shortened and the cuffs taken in. The skirt was attached to the shirt at a high, empire waistline and was made of damask green, which she recognized at once as the captain's own tablecloths.

Her hands slid along the silky green embossed fabric. Grateful tears fell freely as she tried it on, and in the mirror, her face shone with relief—it fit. It was wonderful to be covered, to have her modesty back, to feel like a lady again after living like a wild creature for so long. All those endless days attempting to spear a fish near the beach and gaining the strength to climb trees for coconuts had tested her in every way possible.

The thoughts gave her a moment's pause to once again reflect on how she had known, almost instinctively, how to accomplish such things, and it continued to perplex her. But she had always come to the conclusion that the Lord himself must have animated her to such activities that would help her survive. Perhaps God still had some purpose for her to have enabled her to survive as she did.

Standing to her full height in front of the small mirror, a glimmer of dignity passed over her, and for the briefest of moments, the shadow of pain left her eyes.

She had just finished tying on the little leather slippers when she heard a knock. She opened the door and found Dr. Braxton, a kind, shy smile on his admiring face as he held out to her his own remade straw hat. The crown had been replaced with the same green fabric of her skirt, with matching green ribbons.

Smiling sheepishly at him, she gently took the offered hat. She tried it on, tied a feminine bow under her chin, and tilted her head to the doctor.

"You look lovely, and I am glad my hat is able to be of

service again." He chuckled, then gave her a formal bow. "I have come to extend to you an invitation to join Captain Gresham for a stroll on the main deck, and if that is agreeable to you, I would like to ask for the honor of escorting you there."

Surprised by the notion, she bit her lip, unsure.

"Of course," Braxton explained quickly, "there is no obligation if you are not of a mind to accept. It is entirely up to you, and your decision will be honored." He watched her carefully.

Clasping her hands together, she considered for a moment more, then strode to his side, looked out the door, and took hold of his arm. "I am honored, Mrs. Green. Shall we?"

THE CAPTAIN SQUINTED into the sun as he watched the two emerge from the aft hatch into the brilliant sunlight of midday. The ship was silent but for the whip of the wind in the sails overhead and the splashing of the waves against the hull. The sea breeze played with the brim of her hat, and her dress danced around her slender frame. The *Relentless* was in her full glory, driving through the sparkling waves with strength and grace. Braxton guided her aft toward the quarterdeck.

There he waited for her, standing tall and proud by the helm, and behind him were his officers, all at attention, awaiting her arrival.

He was overcome by the sight of her. If there had been any doubt in his mind that she was indeed a lady, it was banished by her gracefulness. A pang of compassion struck him deeply at the thought of such a naturally lovely woman suffering so much indignity.

Bowing low, he greeted her as if she were royalty and thanked Braxton for his service as he passed her off to him. "We are most honored at your presence, Mrs. Green. Please allow me to introduce you to my officers." He escorted her to the end of the line of men waiting in their waistcoats and shirtsleeves.

One by one he presented his men, and they welcomed her with professional grace. However, Gresham found Mr. Darby curiously aloof and cold in his greeting. Hmmm. What would his purser, of all people, have against the lady? Mr. Darby was an odd man in general, but why did he greet Mrs. Green with even a hint of discourtesy??

Tucking the thought away, Gresham took her slowly along the starboard side and explained each function of the ship as they passed by. He was delighted to see the honest interest in her face as she looked and listened, and he was gratified to find genuine intelligence reflected in her eyes.

They made a turn around the bow, then he led her back on the port side, the entire tour undisturbed by the nearly empty deck. He felt his own tension easing as he saw her shoulders relax, and her hand on his arm grew less stiff.

As they returned to the quarterdeck, Gresham pointed out the men on the rigging above them, each man still. Just then something caught her eye, and she gripped his arm tightly, stopping midstride. Gresham looked down into her upturned face, trying to discern what she was looking at. She was transfixed by the sight of a figure on the mizzen shroud.

"What is it, my dear?" Following her gaze, he found that she was staring up at Thomas Smith, his formidable black topman. He pointed at him. "Is it him you are interested in? Mr. Smith?"

He looked over his shoulder and called back to Mr. Compton, giving Braxton a beckoning look. The two hurried to them, and Gresham asked Compton to have Mr. Smith come down to the quarterdeck. Gresham caught Braxton's eyes, jerked his chin at her, then up to Smith climbing down the mizzen shroud.

Her grip never lessened on Gresham's arm as they watched the strong, agile man make his way down to the fore of the quarterdeck near them. She let go of Gresham when Smith arrived and saluted. Cautiously she approached him, holding tightly to the brim of her fluttering hat.

Smith seemed uncomfortable under her gaze as he stood at attention. Stopping just before him, she searched his face intently, then dropped her gaze, a crimson blush staining her neck and cheeks.

Alarmed, Gresham took hold of her arm, and he and Braxton swiftly escorted her back down to the stern cabin, where they set her on a chair.

"Are you all right? Are you well?" Gresham tried to calm his pounding heart.

After a few deep breaths, she slid her hand down the side of her skirt to the deep pocket that Mr. Huckabee had created there. To the men's astonishment, she removed her long-bladed knife and laid it on the table.

Gresham looked at it, perplexed.

"Did you recognize Mr. Smith?" Braxton asked eagerly. "Was he familiar to you?"

Her shoulders dropped, and she looked down in frustration. Braxton stood and paced by the gallery windows, scratching his chin in thought.

Gresham kept his seat. They were missing something, but what? Perhaps they weren't asking the right question.

"Did you think that he was someone you knew?" he asked.

Braxton stopped short. "Yes, John, you are onto something. Is that it? You thought he was someone you recognized?"

Her eyes flew to Gresham's as a look of intense relief washed over her, and her hand flew to her chest.

Both the men breathed out relieved sighs. "Thank God!" Gresham said. "Well, that is something to mark now, isn't it? You once knew a man like Smith, a large, muscular black fellow. Is that right?"

She took up the knife in her hand and pointed to the place where the initials were carved at the top of the handle. She eagerly passed the knife to Gresham, pointing again.

He frowned and glanced sideways at Braxton. "So are we to understand that the black man you knew, his initials are S.G.? Is that right?"

Again her face flushed with relief. Braxton held out his hand for the knife and studied it. "Did this man, S.G., did he give you this knife? Was it his?"

She answered with a knowing smile.

Braxton sat down heavily in the chair across from them. "Well, now we seem to be getting somewhere!"

"Indeed so!" Gresham agreed. "Wonderful, Mrs. Green, and may God bless Thomas Smith!"

The lady's smile faded quickly, and a look of utter desperation took its place. Gresham froze as she looked at him, Their eyes locked for the briefest of moments. Her expression was a mixture of pleading and unspeakable sorrow, as if she were desperately begging him to help her. When she finally turned away, he felt shaken to the core—and the whole world shifted beneath him.

## CHAPTER
# EIGHT

Braxton insisted that she rest, and she retired to the night cabin. Gresham left the stern cabin, but Braxton lingered. His mind whirled around all that had happened in the last hour. He longed to ask the lady more but was well aware of her emotional fatigue. He was feeling it himself. He sat alone a moment longer at the stern cabin's table.

As he tried to order his thoughts, he noticed Mr. Green sweeping up tresses of the lady's hair from the floor. Green swept them onto a piece of paper and dropped them into a small pail, placing it outside the cabin door as he left.

Braxton stood, a deep, dark stirring in his chest. He wiped his suddenly sweaty palms on his breaches. The feeling was disturbing and unfamiliar to him. Yet he followed its lead and walked to the door. Closing it behind him, he looked around to see who was there. Only Mr. Quist stood guard a few steps away, with his back to him. Braxton held his breath and considered distracting him with conversation but thought better of it. Why attract more attention to himself?

Then a battle ensued within him. *Why am I doing this? Well, what's the harm?* His mind argued with his heart. *Why do I feel so guilty, like I'm some kind of thief? Because she isn't giving them to you—you are taking them without her knowledge. But she will never know, I swear it. Then what are you waiting for?*

All these arguments rushed through his mind in a moment. Then after only a slight hesitation, he withdrew his handkerchief from his waistcoat, stooped, collected the tresses from the pail, folded them up, and replaced the handkerchief in his pocket in one smooth motion.

The heat rose in his face, and his chest pounded like a drum. He quickly took the steps down to his cabin and closed the door, leaning his back on it, as if he had just committed a crime. Stripping off his spectacles, he threw them onto the bureau and sat heavily on the little chair.

What was wrong with him? Why on earth would he do something this stupid, this sickeningly sentimental? He rubbed his short hair and shook his head in disbelief. *All right now, Doctor, sort out the facts*, he chided himself, but was reluctant to follow his own advice.

Braxton had never really been in love in all his six and thirty years. He had once or twice been attracted to some female or other, but he had never met any woman with the depth of character that could engage his deeper emotions. But this woman, this lady with her tragic resilience, her inner strength, her courage and capacity to still connect with her fellow man in light of what men had done to her, had touched him to the core.

Finally allowing waves of grief and loneliness to wash over him, he slipped his hand into his pocket and removed his stolen treasure. Her soft locks felt like silk to his touch as he stroked them guiltily. They had a strangely calming effect on him.

Carefully wrapping the tresses again, he tucked them out of sight at the back of a bureau drawer. He washed his face at the bowl, cleaned his abandoned spectacles, and replaced them on his face, his eyes still misty.

With resolve, he picked up his logbooks and journal and went to the sick bay, hoping it would provide him a much-needed distraction.

⁎

THEIR LAST SHARED glance had shifted something deep within Gresham's soul. It was impossible to think of anything else. He paced the quarterdeck like a man in shock, slowly realizing that in that instant, as her eyes had locked with his, he was a changed man.

After giving orders to Sailing Master Mackenzie, Gresham stood beside the helm in silence. He was not easily distracted from his work and had always been able to focus his mind, like a spyglass on a distant ship. His work usually anchored him, gave him a sense of purpose. Even as the ship dipped and surged beneath his boots, he had always felt solid and in control. After Meri died, he had always sought control of himself as if his life depended on it.

Now he felt like his anchor line had been cut, like he was being blown by an invisible force he could not adjust his sails to. A new, gradually forming vision invaded his mind, disturbing the foregone conclusions he had about his life and his future, and hard as he tried, he could not find a way to abate it. He prayed and prayed, but the gnawing in his spirit refused to give way.

With fixed determination, he addressed his first lieutenant. "Mr. Compton, I'd like the mizzen top cleared. I would like to go up with a glass and have a look around."

"Aye, Captain." Compton set the order in motion, handing the captain his glass.

Once the mizzen top was clear, Gresham shoved the glass down the top of his waistcoat and began his ascent up the mizzen shroud. Usually he loved climbing the rigging and wore a boyish grin on his face as he reached for each line. But today in the sun's unrelenting glare, he knew that he was headed to a crossroads, a point of no return.

Seating himself on the fighting top platform, his ankles wrapped around some ropes to anchor him as the ship tipped and swayed, he wrapped an elbow around a cable and took out the glass. There was nothing to see but miles and miles of ocean, as he'd known before he climbed. It was only a flimsy excuse to obtain privacy, now that he was deprived of his personal chamber.

Replacing the glass to its place of safety, he closed his eyes as the sea breeze blew on his sweating face. To his consternation, tears spilled over, which he had not anticipated would come so quickly. *My God. How I shall miss this.*

Really, he had made his choice already. But the price was, besides giving up the air he breathed, the highest he could ever pay. But pay it he would, because he knew that his Lord required it of him.

The path was clear. He knew what would happen to the lady if she were left to the jurisdiction of the navy board or admiralty. He knew that men of power never tolerated having something nefarious in their precious command exposed, even when they weren't directly involved.

He had seen it before. During the war with France, there had been an incident with the captain of the HMS *Dynamis*, who was accused of raping the daughter of the Marquess of Mansour. Instead of the man being properly prosecuted, the navy leadership closed ranks to protect the captain and their own honor, while the woman's reputation and life were utterly destroyed.

Gresham's shoulders hung low as he rested his head on the cable. He couldn't . . . he wouldn't let that happen to her, no matter what he had to sacrifice to protect her. Tears dropped from time to time as he slowly surrendered. *I will do as you wish, Lord God. I am your servant.*

After a time, he was calm. Still hurting, but calm, and somehow hopeful. Once again he felt the substance of his faith and that the One he trusted was completely worthy of his trust. Yes, it was the Divine, and not this ship, or his career, or his status that gave meaning to his life. Above all, he knew he had a new holy calling that reigned high above all the rest.

Gresham took a deep breath and swung himself onto the shroud, and so began the next chapter of his life.

BRAXTON SAT HUNCHED over his journal, consumed by his efforts to record the latest discoveries of the day, leaving out his own self revelations. He was just finishing a list of questions that needed answers when Mr. Green appeared, clearly troubled.

Dropping his pencil and slapping the journal shut, Braxton stood. "What is it Mr. Green?"

"I'm sorry, Doctor," Green said with distress in his eyes, "but I thought ya should be aware. I told her I didn't think it proper fer a lady ta go down ta the mess deck with all those men, but she was insistent, sir."

Braxton blanched.

"She led me all the way down into the hold, searchin' for somethin'. She found it, sir. The coffin."

Grabbing the lamp from his desk, Braxton was on his way in an instant, with Mr. Green close behind. It wasn't a long way to reach the orlop deck from the sick bay and make his way down to the hold beneath its platforms. It was dark and suffocatingly dank, and he could hear the scurry of rats running from the light of his lantern. Then he found her, sitting on a barrel beside the coffin, her head bent in prayer.

Mr. Green stayed out of sight in the darkness at the top of the steps and allowed Braxton to approach her alone. She looked up when she heard his footsteps. The expected tears were not in her eyes, which Braxton took note of.

"Well, here you are. Would you like some company, or would you rather be alone just now?" He set the lamp on the coffin lid and studied her solemn face.

She sighed as she closed the Bible and placed it beside the lamp. Staring into the dark beyond the lamp light, he could not read her expression. He took up another barrel and sat down at the far end of the coffin, leaning on it with his long arm.

The hull of the ship creaked, and the dripping of the bilge water kept them company as they sat in silence for some time, until Braxton risked breaking the spell and asked one of his burning questions.

"Did they force you to remain silent?"

His soft voice brought her out of her trance. She did not seem surprised at his question. Her eyes shifted to her folded hands in her lap and then to his face. She swallowed, but her gaze was hard and steady.

Braxton ran his hand along the wood of the lid and ventured again. "His fingers are missing. Were they the price exacted if you spoke or cried out?"

She drew a long, even breath and clenched her jaws, her eyes never leaving his.

"Did they force you to watch him be tortured even if all you did was shake your head?"

At this the tears pooled in her stricken eyes, and she buried her face in her hands.

That was enough. "I am sorry. I should not have prodded you." Braxton berated himself as he reassured her. "It's all right. Let the tears flow and do not hold them back."

He thought about how ironic his words were, considering how he had pushed down his own grief for so many years, taking pride in his hardened stoicism.

Pulling his barrel closer to her, he sat there, awkwardly patting her shoulder, willing his presence to bring her some form of comfort. How could she bear such pain, such injustice, such violation? Rage surged in his veins. It took all his inner strength to resist taking her up in his arms and holding her safely to his pounding chest.

She did not cry for long. To his surprise, she took a handkerchief from her pocket and dried her tears only minutes later. He rested his hands on his knees and watched as she recovered herself. At last she looked up at him with a look of sad appreciation.

She reached for her Bible and searched through the pages. When she found what she was looking for, she pointed to a verse and turned the book around for him to read.

Braxton felt uncomfortable but took the book from her hands and read aloud. "'But what things were gain to me, those I counted loss for Christ. Yea doubtless, and I count all things but loss for the excellency of the knowledge of Christ Jesus my Lord: for whom I have suffered the loss of all things, and do count them but dung, that I may win Christ, and be found in him.'"

She stopped him there and took the book from his hands.

He stared at her, his lips curling with contempt, a frightening scorn in his voice. "What kind of God would allow such wickedness and suffering to come upon someone like you?

What kind of a God would count this kind of evil as something good?" He shook his head incredulously. "How can you believe in a God who would allow such horrible things to happen to you? I cannot, I do not accept that what you have suffered was justified in any way! I—"

He stood and clutched his head, unable to control the surging power of his anger. "I'm sorry . . . I'm sorry. I must go," and he fled up the stairs, motioning for Green to go to her as he passed.

# CHAPTER
# NINE

Gresham was alarmed when Mr. Green informed him of what had taken place in the hold. First, he checked in with Mrs. Green in the stern cabin, then he found his friend in his cabin off the wardroom, lying in his berth with his back to the door. Sitting on the small chair in the tiny room, Gresham prayed for the right words. "Paul, are you all right?"

Braxton's chest rose and fell with a great sigh. After a moment, he rolled over and stood with a weary salute. Gresham was stunned by the alteration in his friend's demeanor.

"At ease, Paul." Gresham waved his hand. "What has happened?"

Braxton rubbed the back of his neck and spoke in a rugged, bitter voice. "Forgive me, John. It seems we all have ghosts that haunt us. They are all raising their ugly heads together, encouraged by each other's company, I'm sure."

Gresham closed his eyes, understanding his friend's

despairing declaration. He opened them to find Braxton watching him defeatedly.

"All right then," Gresham prodded, "perhaps it is time for you to follow some of your own advice, Doctor, and talk about the ghost that haunts you, about your father."

Braxton drew a weary breath and scratched his forehead. "Yes, that would be the proper course of action, to be sure, but as you well know, my equally stubborn and prideful friend, it is easier said than done."

Gresham grunted his agreement and set his forearms on his knees. "Indeed. So what shall we two fools do instead? Change the subject, as usual?"

Braxton gave Gresham a wry little smile, and his face was less gray. "I'm willing if you are," and he stood, leaning his backside on the bureau. "Our lady seems to have an odd ability to draw old pains to the surface. How is she?"

Gresham sighed. "All right, I believe. She seemed anxious about you though. Sent me here with this for you." Gresham reached into his pocket and held his closed hand out to Braxton.

With a skeptical look, Braxton opened his hand and allowed Gresham to drop the small object into it. It was her little piece of flint.

Braxton's brows knitted in consternation. "Now why on earth would she give me this?" He pinched the little stone between his thumb and forefinger in the lamplight.

Gresham crossed his arms over his chest. "My guess is that it means something, represents something. What do you think?"

Braxton's face flamed. "I failed her today, John. I should have been there for her, and now she is concerned for me. I may need some time to think about this." He dropped the stone into his breast pocket.

"You, Dr. Braxton, are no failure," Gresham encouraged. "Come, my friend. Let us go to our dinner. There is much to talk over, and I need your keen mind at the table."

✳

HE AND HIS officers were gathered for their evening meal in the wardroom, when Gresham finished his plate of fish as well as the debate in his mind. He was reluctant to speak to them, as he wasn't sure if they were capable of the discretion he would need from them, but finally decided that a lack of transparency only gave speculation an opportunity, which could be even more dangerous. No, he would take his chances and pray for the best.

He sat straight and called for their attention. "Now, gentlemen, tonight I would like to hear from you regarding any thoughts you may have concerning Mrs. Green, specifically in regard to her future. Anyone?"

There was a brief silence. The first man to raise his hand was Mr. Latch. "Yes, Mr. Latch." Gresham gave him a curt nod of acknowledgment.

"Well, Captain, I have a question, sir. I was wondering what will happen to the lady once we arrive. Not knowing her family, or even her own name, it seems to me that it may be quite difficult for her, sir."

"An excellent question, Mr. Latch, and one that must be considered immediately. And what about you, Doctor? Do you have any thoughts on the matter?" Gresham noticed Braxton's brooding silence and tried to draw him out of himself.

Braxton's face was drawn. "I am afraid word will get out that we have rescued a lady castaway, and news of her will spread like wildfire through the newspapers all over England. We must prevent that from happening, if it is at all possible."

"I concur, Doctor," Gresham agreed "And would anyone have any ideas on how we might prevent Mrs. Green from becoming a national scandal?" He looked stonily around the table.

Mr. Mackenzie cleared his throat and puffed up his barrel chest. "If I may say, sir, 'tis a pity the lady's husband is not still alive to provide her his protection. An unmarried woman is most vulnerable. I fear she may be whisked off to some, well, sir, asylum, God forbid." He ended with an uncomfortable cough.

"That is quite possible, Captain." Braxton was engaged now. "She may be taken into custody by the navy board and used as a case study in some institution."

"And if that is the case, Captain," chimed in Sergeant Evans, "then what will happen to bring the men who did this to justice? Surely they would be able to claim that she is insane, which clearly she is not."

Gresham was impressed by Evans's sincere compassion. "Just so, Mr. Evans. Another valid point. Anyone else?"

Mr. Darby stirred in his chair, set his pointed elbows on the table, and touched the tips of his short fingers. "Well, Captain, there is also the fact that she is penniless. She has no means of supporting herself. How will she live?"

Gresham set his lips firmly and sat forward in his chair. Lifting his chin, he spoke in a resolute tone. "Thank you, gentlemen. You have all given voice to the same problems I have foreseen and been giving deep consideration to these last few days." He looked each man in the eye. "I believe I have a solution that might very well manage to address all these dilemmas."

They hung on his every word. Gresham's gaze landed on Braxton, startled to find a disturbingly unfamiliar look of loathing on his friend's face. Braxton's eyes blazed as his hands squeezed the arms of his chair.

*He knows*, thought Gresham in shock. His friend knew what he was about to say and hated him for it. Gresham could feel his contempt from across the table. *He suddenly hates me because of her.*

Gresham's mouth went dry. He had already suspected, but Braxton's flaring look gave him solid confirmation that he did indeed have feelings for Mrs. Green. It was in that instant that he realized there was yet one more sacrifice to be made to follow his calling, but God help him, he would make it, though it would break his heart as well.

Their eyes held for an instant more before Braxton looked away.

Gresham went on with resolve. "I will ask for the lady's hand in marriage. And if she accepts, we will be married here, on the *Relentless*, before we reach England."

Gasps of shock went round the table.

"Captain, are you sure?"

"How will this affect your career, sir?"

"That's very commendable, Captain, but what about the *Relentless*?"

Gresham raised his hand to calm the confusion. "I know, I know. I have thought it all through, prayed through every question, run through every scenario, and it has all come down to this." He snatched a glimpse of Braxton, whose eyes were on the table, looking smaller in his chair. Gresham wept internally for him. He had never meant to cause his friend so much pain.

Mr. Mackenzie's burly voice broke the short silence. "Begging your pardon, Captain, and please forgive my impertinence, but what is your plan? How will you convince her? What will happen if she does not agree?"

Gresham tried to keep his voice even. "I will need a bit of

time to help her understand the seriousness of the situation. That is why you must all keep this in the strictest of confidence. There is a distinct possibility that she may not feel this is an acceptable solution. What happens then, well, I suppose I will have to cross that bridge when I come to it." A new form of grief sank into his chest.

Mr. Darby sat up, his red nose gleaming in the lamplight. "To marry a woman whose name you do not know, Captain, whose family are also unknown, plus the fact that she cannot speak, it is all a great risk, Sir." He added, with an almost patronizing tone. "And there is the added lack of propriety in marrying a woman until her deceased husband has been dead for over a year."

"Quite right, Mr. Darby." Gresham sat and hunched over his dinner plate, studying the remaining fish bones. "It is a risk I am willing to take. I have not come to this decision lightly. Nor am I entering into this holy commitment without understanding its implications. You are all valid in your misgivings, and I am deeply grateful for your concerns on my behalf."

Gresham brightened his tone. "So, gentlemen, I hope that I might call all of you my friends." He darted another glance at Braxton, whose expression had softened. "I hope that you will all support me, and the lady if she accepts, in the next chapter of our lives." There was nothing left to say. He folded his hands on the table and stared at them.

The men, with the exception of the doctor, glanced at one another, and all had the same idea at the same time. They stood to their feet with their glasses in hand and showered Gresham with reserved praise and congratulations.

Braxton was the only one still seated, but he quickly rose and raised his glass. Taking his spoon and tapping it on the rim to draw their attention, he stood up straight and squared his shoulders to Gresham.

Gresham watched his friend's face fluctuate between remorse and affection.

"I have a toast, gentlemen. To His Majesty and his Prince Regent, and to Captain Johnathan Gresham, the best man any woman could wish to call her husband!"

"Hear! Hear!"

The expressions of joy were drowned out by the rush of gratitude coursing through Gresham's veins as he stood and reached across the table to touch his glass to Braxton's.

✳

BRAXTON REMAINED as the others left the room, supporting himself on the back of his chair, exhausted from fighting the war within his heart and mind. What was the matter with him? Of course he would marry her, but what if she rejected him because he did not hold the same deeply held beliefs? How could he truly love her if he refused to respect her faith, the very thing that kept her alive and breathing to this day?

Reality crept its way back into his mind, and it cleared.

*What kind of spell has overtaken me? How can I be angry with Gresham for wanting to help her? I am a fool indeed.*

Braxton walked around the table and shook Gresham's hand. "I wish you all success and happiness, John. I am sorry, I—"

Gresham cuffed him on the arm and held his eyes. "I am sorry too, Paul. I should have spoken with you privately first. I didn't know—"

With a wave of his hand, Braxton stopped him. "No apology necessary. I have been such a fool today. I do not know what has gotten into me."

"Wasn't it you who said we all have ghosts that haunt us?"

"Yes." Braxton smiled wryly. "I should listen to myself more often."

Gresham chuckled warmly. "As should I, my friend, as should I."

Braxton's smile disappeared. "I don't think I can sleep tonight until I've offered Mrs. Green my apologies for my horrendous behavior in the hold this afternoon. Will you go up with me?"

Gresham's brows rose in understanding. "Of course. I would like to see how she is faring myself. Shall we?" He motioned to the wardroom door.

✳

MR. GREEN OPENED the stern cabin door with a jolly grin on his weathered face. "There's been a change in the wind, Capt'n. For the better, but ya shall see for yerself!"

Gresham stopped short at the sight of her. The oil lamp cast a soft glow over her graceful form as she stood, bent over piles of charts and books from his cabinet. His heart swelled with admiration for her.

She greeted them with determined energy and gestured for them to join her on the opposite side of the table.

Braxton spoke up. "Good evening, Mrs. Green, I came to apologize for—"

She looked sharply but kindly up at Braxton and wagged her finger, cutting him off. To Gresham's great surprise, she even shook her head.

*Did I just see what I think I saw?* Gresham marveled. The winds had changed indeed.

She swept aside the books and papers and opened one large sheet in front of them—a poster of sorts. On the top of the sheet, in grand, scrolling letters, it said, "A view of the

Royal Navy of Great Britain." Below the naval crest with its golden anchor were drawings of every type of ship of the Royal Navy, in order of their ratings.

Gresham held his breath and searched her face for distress, finding only steely resolve. She looked at him with significance and then back to the chart. Pointing to the drawing of a ship in the line of third rates, she raised her chin in defiance.

The men bent close. "Third rate, Arrogant class, seventy-four guns! This is the type of ship you were on?" Gresham's eyes flashed with the implications of their foe outranking him.

Her breath shuddered and her jaw clenched as she stared Gresham in the eye and nodded slowly. *Yes.*

"Isn't that a wonderment, Capt'n?" Mr. Green piped in. "She can nod and shake her head now!" He smiled with pride at his charge.

"Indeed, Mr. Green." Gresham gave the doctor a glance before meeting her eyes again. "Thank you, Mrs. Green. This is truly remarkable, and the information significant."

Something had definitely changed in her demeanor. It was as if she were more solid in her own skin, more present with them in the room, and Gresham's heart flushed with relief.

Clearing his throat, Braxton removed the little flint from his pocket and held it in his upturned palm. "I want to thank you for your gift, Mrs. Green. I know that you want me to learn something from it, and I promise to meditate on its meaning. I also want to apologize—"

She stopped him by closing his fingers over the stone and shaking him gently. Then she shook her head and looked kindly into his sad eyes.

"Thank you, Mrs. Green, for your understanding," Braxton said softly.

Gresham fought off his strong desire to embrace her and whirl her joyfully around the room. "Well then, Mrs. Green, I am sure I speak for the doctor as well when I say that I am very encouraged by tonight's developments. May the Lord bless you with peaceful sleep, and I would like to ask the favor of being able to call on you after breakfast in the morning, if that is agreeable." Motioning to Braxton, Gresham stepped toward the door.

She gave him a suspicious look and nodded hesitantly, then dipped into a graceful curtsy.

CHAPTER

# TEN

What would the captain want to see her about in the morning?

Despite Sarah's newfound courage to communicate yes and no, she still struggled with the terrible memories of her assailants torturing her husband if she so much as shook her head in protest to their horrific abuse. Even now, when she had moments alone, she tried to speak, to make a sound, but every time she opened her mouth, the same terrifying rush would lock her chest in panic, and she'd shake with nausea.

But something had happened today. She could feel the change in her mind and body. It had started earlier that morning, when she'd thought she recognized the large dark man on the ropes above her. Something had jarred her mind from a deep stupor then, like a dense fog lifting at the edges.

She had no memories of before she and her husband had boarded the immense ship that had become a living hell to them. But she could remember her husband's handsome face as he'd escorted her to the stern cabin of that ship, could still smell the savory lamb chops and burning oil lamps, and even see the cut-glass dessert bowl filled with custard and a dot of red jam in the center. Sitting by his side, she'd tried desperately to be happy, but she wasn't.

She had searched and searched her mind for the reason, to even remember his name, but all was dark there. A black impenetrable wall.

In her mind's eye, she turned from her husband sitting beside her to the man on her other side, the captain. A sudden jolt of terror shot through her. She fought hard to remain focused on that face, but the memory was unbearable, forcing her to look away.

*Dear Lord, please help me to overcome this terrible fear and do your will, whatever that may be.*

When Gresham and Braxton reached the doctor's cabin to retire, Braxton closed the door and leaned his back on it. "John, I know that when you make up your mind to something, you will move heaven and earth to honor your decision. I want you to know, despite my own foolishness today, that I support you in this. But"—he raised his slender hand as Gresham opened his mouth to respond—"but I remember how you reacted when last we were in England and the papers were full of stories about several little girls missing from their homes. How you took it upon yourself to try and find out what happened to them. It became a sort of obsession. If you hadn't been called back to your duty on the *Relentless*, you'd still be out there looking for them, wouldn't you?"

His friend's face fell, and he hesitated before answering. "Why yes, you are probably right. Something about those stories made me feel I had a personal duty to try and find them." He shook his head. "I can't explain it. I guess I would have to admit that somehow it reminded me of what happened to Meredith."

Braxton nodded. "Yes, I am sure of it. And have you considered that perhaps you are being motivated now to save Mrs. Green for the same reason?"

Gresham groaned. "You know me well, Paul." Gresham glared at nothing for a moment as he raked his fingers habitually through his unbound hair. "I hate to say it, but you have every right to ask, and as usual, make a blasted good point. The thought had occurred to me, and I have been wrestling with it, I assure you." He looked meekly at Braxton, who was waiting for a more satisfying answer.

Gresham sat down in the little chair with a low growl, like a schoolboy about to be reprimanded by his tutor. "All right, Doctor. I'm ready to discuss. I don't want to enter into a life-long covenant with someone before that possibility has been thoroughly examined. Fire away."

Braxton did not hesitate to get right to the heart of the matter. "Do you still blame yourself for your sister's death, John?"

Gresham's defensive posture stiffened, then drooped. "I don't understand it, Paul, why this dreadful guilt still plagues me. I have prayed for forgiveness, I have reasoned my way through it, but it still lingers like a festering wound I can't keep clean."

"But you were only ten years old, John, and Meri's kidnapping and death were not your fault. Do you still think a ten-year-old boy could have prevented a full-grown man from abducting your sister if he had a mind to? Now, how could you possibly continue to hold that little boy responsible for something like that, as dreadful and painful as it was?"

Propping his forearms on his thighs, Gresham bowed his

head. "Because if I hadn't followed that fool Clarence Dooley and stayed with her on the Clock House steps as Father told me to, I could have done something, fought, screamed, anything to save her. I should have protected her. I failed her and my family."

Braxton straightened his shoulders and widened his stance, feeling like he did when he conducted life-and-death surgery on a sailor. "And what about Mrs. Green? Are you marrying her to make up for what you did back then?"

Gresham groaned softly and leaned back. "I will be honest, Paul. I do not know. I suppose it could be playing a part, but I truly believe that God is calling me to take this path, and I am committed to it." His face was open and honest, and Braxton knew he was telling the truth.

Braxton nodded. "You are the bravest man I know, Johnathan Gresham, and a much better man than I. I know I am a hypocrite, and yes, when the proper time presents itself, I will return the gruesome favor and pull my ghost out of its nasty little closet for you." He gave Gresham a rueful smile. "Perhaps you were right in saying that the hand of providence led us to that little island."

Gresham's brows raised. "Ha! I never expected to hear you say that, Doctor. Yes, I believe he did." Rising from his seat and crossing his arms over his chest, he asked, "Well, Doctor. What is your diagnosis? Is there any hope for me?"

"Hmmm, yes. I believe, as I proclaimed in my toast, that you are the best man any woman could wish to call her husband, and I meant it. But I warn you, John. You may be headed into dangerous waters. If she accepts you, her story will become yours, and there's no telling what you might be in for."

"Huh, *if* she accepts me." Gresham gave Braxton an affectionate slap on his shoulder. "If you were a praying man, I would ask you to pray with all your heart. But as you aren't, I shall have to pray doubly hard for myself."

***

THE MORNING SKY was overcast as Gresham sat with Sarah beside the gallery windows. She was grateful for the breeze, as she had arisen with a slight headache after her nightlong fight with the dark corners of her mind.

"Thank you for seeing me, Mrs. Green," Gresham began awkwardly. "Mr. Green says that you woke up with a headache this morning. Are you quite all right? I can come to see you later, if you like."

*No.* She shook her head.

She watched his handsome, strong face, full of eagerness mixed with a tenderness she had not seen before. And to think that just a few days before, she was holding a knife to this man's nose.

They sat in awkward silence a moment as they watched the watery wakes reach out behind the *Relentless*.

"I believe we may encounter some bad weather this afternoon or this evening."

She smiled slightly but knew he had not come to speak with her about the weather.

Swallowing hard, Gresham rubbed his palms on his breaches and cleared his throat. "Well, I suppose you are wondering why I asked to see you today. I felt that it was time to speak to you about the future—that is, what will happen when we arrive at Woolwich. Specifically"—he gave her a straight look—"what will happen to you once we dock there."

She raised her brows. *Ah, now we're getting to the point.* She turned her chair to face him. *Yes.* She nodded.

"You see, well, I have wanted to speak with you about the possibilities, and, uh, challenges that I foresee."

*Yes.* She nodded again, feeling the increase in her pulse.

"We will be docking at the Royal Woolwich Dockyard, and I am familiar with the place, as I grew up near there as a boy. My father worked there in the offices of the Clock House, which you will see, and we lived not far from there in Charlton parish."

She listened with rapt attention.

"Dr. Braxton and I will need to see about the navy's business regarding our commissions, the *Relentless*, and our crew, and at that time it will be our duty to give our official logbooks to our superiors."

Logbooks? She knitted her eyebrows as her mind filled with anxious questions she was unable to ask.

"Now, Dr. Braxton and I agreed that we would say nothing about you in our official logs, which, by rule, is not how things should be done. Our aim is to try and avail you of as much privacy as possible, and that being the case, we decided to write separate reports about you, with only the simplest facts. We must also report about your late husband . . ." He faltered. "Especially since you are both victims of criminal acts." He searched her face. "Do you understand?"

Her gaze shifted to the sea. *Yes, I have been anticipating this.* Nodding sullenly, she glanced to him again.

"Now your situation is highly unusual, and we have reason to believe that if your story gets out, it would be a boon for any newspaper to get hold of, and that means you would be subject to an enormous amount of public scrutiny."

*Newspapers?* This had never crossed her mind.

"Please do not worry." Gresham sliced a hand through the air. "We will do all in our power not to let that happen. In fact,

I have decided to request an extended leave in order to help you and keep these kinds of things from happening."

Her scrambling thoughts tried to keep up with what he was saying. *You would do that for me?*

He bent closer to her and spoke gently. "I am sorry, my dear Mrs. Green. I am making quite a mess of this. It is only that your situation is very serious, and we need to prepare for what may happen in the few short days we have left until we reach England. Am I making any sense?"

*Yes.* She nodded, trying to convey a look of comprehension.

"Good." Gresham gave her a half smile. "I have never met a more courageous and faith-filled woman than you, Mrs. Green. Will you be brave now, as I tell you all I have to say?"

*My goodness.* She met his gaze squarely and nodded, shifting to the edge of her seat.

"Besides the interest your story will certainly attract, there are other entities that may claim to have authority over you."

*Entities? What entities? And why would they claim authority over me?* Her thoughts raced.

Gresham continued soberly. "Since you cannot remember your name, where you are from, or if you have any family, that leaves you in a vulnerable position. You are also the victim of a crime committed by ranking officers in the Royal Navy, which means that the navy now has a dilemma on their hands. Because"—he paused, and his face darkened—"and I am morose in having to admit this, but their decisions on how to handle your case may be influenced by their need to preserve the navy's and their own collective reputations."

Her eyes narrowed and drifted to the view out of the windows. *Yes. Men have a habit of doing such things.*

"And lastly—I hate to have to mention this as well—is the fact that you are a woman."

Her eyes snapped back to his, and she laced them with

indignation—not for him, but for the unfair plight of her sex in the ways of the world. She could feel the color burn in her cheeks. *He is right to say it.* She knew. *It is another strike against me.*

"So you see, these three factors make your position most precarious. I cannot say for certain, but Dr. Braxton says there is a distinct possibility the navy will seek to take custody of you. Then they may admit you to a hospital of some sort, and you would be examined and scrutinized in ways that may prove difficult for you."

*My God!* Her hand flew to her chest, and she shook her head helplessly. Her stomach twisted as her mind reeled with the awful possibilities.

Gresham's eyes filled with compassion. "I am so deeply sorry to cause you such alarm, but I felt you have a right to know what may be coming. Was I right to tell you?"

She could hear the deep concern in his question. Looking down, she gave him a slow nod.

They sat in painful silence for a moment, then Gresham shifted in his chair. "You are familiar with the Bible text, I am sure, that says, 'Trust in the Lord with all thine heart; and lean not unto thine own understanding. In all thy ways acknowledge him, and he shall direct thy paths.'"

She closed her eyes and nodded. *Indeed I am.*

"That is what we must do now." Gresham's voice was softened with tenderness as he continued. "The Lord has been speaking to me, Mrs. Green. He has shown me the way to protect you from all of this, as he has been directing the path of my life, and that path has led me to you."

Searching his face in confusion, her heart pounded as she held the sides of her seat.

"I do not yet see the whole picture of why you had to go through the terrible things you have endured," Gresham said with honest gravity, "but God helped you to survive on that island, and then He led me to you. I believe in my very soul that we have been brought together for a reason, a purpose we have yet to understand. He has shown me that I have a new path to choose, and I am willing and most honored to choose it."

She sat transfixed by his words. *What is he saying? Is he—*

"I am asking for you to consider joining me on this new journey. I am asking you, with all sincerity, if you would be my wife."

She gasped, and her hands flew to her flushed face.

He hurried on. "Yes, I know it is a shocking turn of events, and I want to afford you as much time as possible to consider this important decision." He leaned over to her. "Please hear me out?"

She rose, shaken, and braced herself on the window frame, searching the waves and the overcast sky. *Dear Lord! I don't know what to think. Why would this man do this for me?* Her mind flashed back to the island, the long, lonely days and lonelier nights. The agony of wanting to be rescued, mixed with the fear of her assailants returning. Her terrible torment even as God was rescuing her at last, and now this?

He rose also and edged close to her. "You see, if I were your husband, I could offer you my protection. I could help you find your identity and your family, and I can provide and care for you, give you a home and place of safety. Then, if and when we find out who you are and where your relatives are, I swear to you that if you decide at that time not to"—he paused, as if his words pained him—"that you do not wish to continue to journey through life with me, then I will find a way to release you without fault from the marriage and will remove myself from your life."

Gresham dipped his head low to catch her downcast eyes and spoke with such gentleness she thought her heart would burst. "Please, Mrs. Green. Please agree to at least consider my proposal. I make it with all of my heart and with the best of intentions. Will you at least consider?"

*Dear God! How could I ever consider such a thing?* But her starving heart cried out within her, eager to grasp at the slightest hint of safety and companionship.

After a long silent battle, she lost the fight with her pride, and the stinging tears gave way. At last she faced him and nodded.

# CHAPTER

# ELEVEN

D r. Braxton was waiting on the quarterdeck when Gresham arrived. His sober yet inquisitive face asked the question without words.

Gresham trod aft with him to the taffrail, his heart still racing, and spoke quietly. "It went as well as could be expected. Explaining everything to her was a miserable task, but she took it bravely and agreed to at least consider my proposal." He gripped the railing hard. "Paul, will you go and see her in a while? I just want to make sure she is all right. She's had quite a shock."

"Of course." Braxton gave him a solemn glance. "I'll give her some time to recover, then pay her a visit." He saluted and left.

Gresham spotted Mr. Darby hanging off to the side, waiting to speak to him. "Mr. Darby?" he asked with an irritated glare.

"Good morning, Captain. I was wondering if I might have a brief word with you, sir." Darby blew his nose and sniffed, delaying the captain's reply.

"Yes, Mr. Darby, what is it?" Gresham asked stiffly, annoyed by this unusual request when he wanted time to think over his conversation with Mrs. Green.

"It is a matter of great importance, sir. Something that you may not have considered, being a bachelor and not perhaps familiar with British marital law." Darby spoke importantly, like he was a barrister arguing a case before court. "Perhaps you wouldn't mind a brief conference in this regard in a more private setting?"

Alarmed, Gresham nodded, and soon he and his purser were alone in the doctor's cabin. Gresham crossed his arms over his chest with impatience.

"Now, what is so important, Mr. Darby? I have pressing matters to attend to."

"Thank you, sir." Darby bowed slightly. "It has come to my memory that marriages conducted on board British ships are not considered legally binding. Therefore, if you do marry Mrs. Green on the *Relentless*, it may not be enough to afford her the protection you have intended to extend to her as her husband."

Gresham, rattled by this new revelation, shifted to lean heavily on the hammock. "I thank you for informing me, Mr. Darby. I was unaware of this impediment." His mind whirled. How would he manage this new dilemma?

Darby continued. "I know that part of your concern for Mrs. Green is to protect her from the eyes of the press, and that by marrying her on the ship, the entire crew would then recognize you as her husband. Then, out of their respect for you, they would be more inclined to be discreet about the events that have happened since the storm that damaged the foreyard."

Yes, he had thought about that. It was an unrealistic hope, but he wanted the crew to see them wed in hopes that they would be less tempted to spread tales about the captain's wife. "I'm listening, Mr. Darby."

Darby sniffed and patted his red nose with his handkerchief. He folded it with precision and replaced it in his pocket. "I have been looking over some of my collection of law books and discovered more. The only way a marriage is recognized by the courts is that it be performed by an official clergyman of the Church of England, in a public house of worship. The reading of the banns or a common license is required, which you may be able to obtain. However, the church chosen for the ceremony must be in a parish where either the bride or the groom currently resides."

Gresham's irritation rose. The situation was growing more complicated by the second. Gresham glared at Darby under his knotted brows.

"And then"—Darby stood his ground, seemingly undaunted by the scowl on his superior's face—"there is the added difficulty of completing the marriage registration. You see, both the bride and the groom must provide their legal names and the names of the parishes in which they currently reside. Now, you may be able to provide satisfactory information yourself, sir, but the lady upstairs cannot even remember her name, let alone where she is from." Darby paused and almost smiled. "That being the case, for you to provide false information to the registrar, your marriage would still be illegal, and you and the lady would be in danger of being guilty of perjury." And with that he sneezed loudly and withdrew his handkerchief with a melodramatic flourish.

Gresham's shoulders dropped. Dear God, if only he had known all this before he'd proposed and implied that being his wife would afford her a measure of protection.

Darby smiled smugly, removed his spectacles, and polished

them. "If I may make at least one suggestion, which may or may not be useful—"

Gresham's eyes returned to the man. "Yes, what is it?"

"There is nothing in the law that states you cannot have a betrothal celebration on a ship. You may decide to go ahead with a party on board, simply to convince the crew that you intend to marry. And I have one more thought—"

"Yes, yes . . ." Gresham was about to throttle this little man.

"You might even consider drawing up a contract of sorts, requiring the men's silence on the matter. Oh, it won't hold up legally, but it might buy you some time before the papers start hounding you." Replacing his spectacles, Darby stuck his nose up at Gresham with an official air. "I am so sorry to have to share all this tedious information, sir, but I felt it my duty to inform you."

"Yes, Mr. Darby, you have done your duty, and I am grateful to you. I have much to consider." Gresham kept his expression neutral as he gestured to the door. "I am sure you have preparations to make. There is a storm brewing on the horizon."

"Yes, Captain. Indeed there is."

AT LAST GRESHAM was allowed a few private moments in the doctor's cabin to reflect and consider. He sat on the small chair and raked his fingers through his hair before bowing his head in a short prayer for wisdom. It suddenly dawned on him that Mrs. Green knew almost as little about himself than he knew of her. How could he expect her to make a life-altering decision to marry a man when she knew so little about him and his life. Surely she would have many questions, yet he had not thought to tell her anything about himself.

*She must be told about Meri*, he thought with a surge of self-loathing. For goodness' sake, she should be allowed to know the most important things about the man she was to marry, shouldn't she?

With only a moment's hesitation, and not stopping to think of all he would say and how he would address her in this regard, he rose from his seat and marched up to the stern cabin with clenched teeth and sweating palms.

Mrs. Green answered the door herself, as she was alone.

Gresham cleared his throat and greeted her awkwardly. "I'm sorry to disturb you again, Mrs. Green. Please may I have a few more moments of your time?" He gestured to a chair at the table and they sat, her storm gray-blue eyes fastened on his with cautious expectation.

He sat stiffly with his hands clasped on the table, unable to look directly into her eyes. "Uh, I was just taking a moment to pray for wisdom, you see, and it occurs to me that you may want to know more about, well, me and my life, in general, that is, and I thought it would only be appropriate for you to be aware . . ."

He faltered when he looked up and found her studying him intently. For the first time since he was a child, he felt his face flush and broke the gaze, clearing his throat again as he considered where to start.

"Well," he began again, "you probably would like to know something about my family and where I came from and such."

He met her eyes, her face full of kind reassurance.

"I was born and raised in Charlton just to the west of Woolwich Dockyard. My mother was a woman of great faith and played the organ at our parish church, and my father"—here his father's grieving face flashed in his memory, nearly making his voice hitch—"my father was a chart maker who worked at the Clock House offices in the dockyard. I'm sorry to say that my parents passed a few years ago of influenza."

Mrs. Green nodded with understanding, and her calm countenance gave him the steadiness he needed to continue.

"I am the middle child, as I have one older sister, Penelope, who is married to a very fine rector, and one younger sister, whose name was Meredith."

Chancing a glance at her, he saw the comprehension in her face. It took him another moment to school his emotions before he could speak again.

"Yes." He unclasped his hands and wiped them on his breeches. "Meredith was murdered at the age of only eight years old."

He stared at the table but could see Mrs. Green sink back in her chair, until she pulled her seat closer to him and laid her slender hand on his forearm and caught his eye.

Gresham could barely stand the look of empathy that waited there on her lovely face, her eyes misted and full of sorrow. His stomach squeezed, and he forced himself to his feet to walk to the gallery window. He hadn't told a soul except Braxton for a long time. But he must tell her even if it meant she would reject him. She had a right to know.

A sickening trepidation seeped into his chest as he faced the window and spoke the shame-filled words. "It was all my fault."

❋

THE SKY DARKENED by the minute as Sarah gripped the sides of a tightly locked window frame to keep her balance. The view was a blur of rain, waves, and the occasional flash of lightning followed by the crack and rumbling bellow of thunder. She thought of the captain on the deck above her in his shirt-sleeves, being drenched by the deluge, and made her way to the closet where his long blue captain's coat hung out of her sight. She paused to remove her slippers and stockings, then tied on her straw hat tightly under her chin. Steadying her racing heart, she wrestled open the closet door, reached in with fierce determination and threw the coat over her arm. Besides not wanting him to be soaked through by the storm, she felt an unrelenting urgency to give him the answer she knew he was eager to hear.

When the captain shared with her the story of his sister's death and she witnessed the agony of his pain and guilt, she'd felt an alteration in the depths of her soul. Here was someone whose faith had been stretched to the breaking point, as hers had been, someone who just might understand her anguish as no one who had not experienced such a tragedy ever could. And by the time the captain had left her, she'd no longer felt utterly forsaken and alone in the world.

After much prayer and meditation in God's Word, she had heard the Spirit speak to her in the depths of her soul. *You will have beauty for ashes.* She wept for what seemed like hours with this promise reverberating in her heart, until the wind battered the ship and stirred the seas around her.

With a prayer for strength, Sarah heaved her way to the cabin door and wrenched it open, stumbling onto the steep stairs of the companionway. She could feel the familiar muscles of her tree-climbing days powering her up the steps to the aft hatch. Slinging the coat over her shoulder, she pushed with one great effort to open it, but it must have been secured from above.

Her heart sank for just an instant, when the hatch opened and she saw Mr. Latch above her. He shouted something the wind whisked away as she pushed her weight up onto the deck and lunged past the gawking second lieutenant and hurled herself sternward on her bare feet, grasping for any rope or rail she could to keep from being tossed to the deck floor.

The *Relentless* sailed down each crest and up the next like a knife. A wave breached the side of the swaying ship and doused her with a cold slap across the face, but she clenched the muscles in her belly and thrust herself toward the capstan with all her strength. Clutching the top of its drum, she peered out from under her soaking hat to see Captain Gresham driving against the rolling of the deck beneath his boots and shouting to her, but the sound never reached her over the howling wind.

At last she met him at the base of the mizzen mast, both gasping and hanging on tightly to the enormous trunk of the mast with their eyes locked.

"Mrs. Green!" he shouted above the howl. "Why aren't you below? It isn't safe up here. Let me help you back down!"

She pushed his coat into his arms, and he gave her a look of astonishment, then insisted she put it on.

*No.* She shook her head, her straw hat dripping with rivulets in front of her face. He stared at her in confusion as she stood her ground and pushed his coat back into his arms.

Grasping him by the shoulder, Sarah pulled her face close to his. Looking straight into his eyes, she nodded as vigorously and deliberately as she could and still keep her footing. Blinking back the rain, she shook his shoulder and repeated the same measured action.

"What?" the captain's eyes widened with bewilderment. "What are you saying?"

She shook him even harder and pleaded with her eyes and nodded again.

He gasped a little and shut his eyes. When he opened them again, they were filled with disbelief. "Yes? Are you saying yes, you will marry me?"

She mouthed yes with a shy smile, then grabbed tightly to his arm and buried her face in his shoulder as the ship leaped and fell beneath them. In spite of the tumult, she had never felt safer in her life.

Just then the *Relentless* lurched to starboard. They heard a great crash and a man cry out in pain. Right beside the capstan lay Mr. Thomas Smith, who had apparently lost his footing in the rigging and fallen to the deck floor. He was clenching his arm, clearly in agony.

The captain swung his coat around Sarah and threw her over his shoulder in one swift move. She could feel him put his head down as he drove toward the aft hatch door, his strong legs propelling him forward against the rolling of the ship. He dropped to his knees, opened the hatch, and carefully placed her on the steps below. She looked up as he gave her a wide grin.

Mr. Green stood at the bottom of the steep steps with his mouth gaping at her, dripping wet, and cried out, "Well, bless me soul. We've caught a mermaid."

CHAPTER

# TWELVE

"You ain't gonna take it off, Doctor, are ya?" Mr. Smith's dark eyes were wide with the thought of an amputation.

"Hmmmm, no, I think not, Mr. Smith," Braxton said, "but we will have to set it properly, bind up those ribs, and ensure you don't move for a few days. Then we'll be able to know for certain. Mr. Lynn, will you bring Mr. Smith some whiskey please?" Braxton wanted to make Smith as comfortable as possible before he had to do his worst to him.

Setting a bone in the middle of a gale on board a wooden ship bobbing like a cork in the middle of the ocean was an easy undertaking compared to subduing the internal bleeding of Braxton's broken heart. Braxton had been emerging from the fore hatch when he saw, through the rain and mist, the two of them huddled together at the base of the mizzen mast. He knew by the look on Gresham's face when she nodded her head and shook his shoulder. She had said yes.

He'd returned to the sick bay, sick himself, berating himself for not being able to control his emotions. He should . . . No, he would be happy for them. He would be a gentleman and put away these foolish feelings. *This is all nonsense, Braxton, utter nonsense.* But his internal agony begged to differ.

Smith bravely bore the setting of his broken arm, and Braxton settled him in one of the sick bay's hammocks. "Now, Mr. Smith, lie still as you can. Young Robby here will keep watch over you, and I will get you some willow bark tea to help with the pain."

"Thank ya, Doctor, sir," Smith wheezed out, gritting his teeth.

Braxton was glad the storm was letting up—nothing worse than having broken ribs on a lurching ship.

Turning to fetch the willow bark, he was caught by surprise to find Mr. Green leading Mrs. Green around the base of the foremast.

"Beg pardon, Doctor, but Mrs. Green wanted ta see if Mr. Smith is all right."

How Braxton wished she hadn't come. It was hard enough without seeing her so near so soon. "Oh! Yes, yes, of course. He is a bit worse for wear, Mrs. Green, but he will mend nicely, I think."

She was wrapped in a woolen blanket, her kind, sad eyes reflecting the dim lamplight as she approached the hammock. Smiling softly down into Smith's surprised face, she touched his hand lightly. Noticing the bowl the loblolly boy held, she gestured for him to hand it to her. Green pulled around a stool for her, and they left her there, feeding small spoonfuls of murky soup to the hulking man in his cramped and painful hammock, a sight to behold.

Once again Braxton found his breath taken away. He couldn't help it. Surely if angels existed, she was one of them.

※

WHEN THE STORM SUBSIDED, Gresham hurried to the mess deck, making his way through the swaying hammocks, the sailors' rattling snores, and the stench of unwashed bodies. His heart was full to bursting as he passed the bulk of the massive cookstove and wove around the base of the foremast to the area in the bow where the sick and wounded were given a small space to recover in peace.

In the middle of the sick bay, he stopped short. She sat, in a bundle, next to Smith's hammock, with her wavy wet hair still dripping down her back, a bowl in one hand and a spoon in the other. The contrast between the two could not have been more striking.

Mr. Smith noticed him first and attempted to salute.

"No, Mr. Smith. That's not necessary for now." Gresham stepped into the lamplight. "Hello, Mrs. Green. Are you cold? I am sure Dr. Braxton and his lads can take care of feeding Mr. Smith." His voice was hoarse from shouting orders over the storm, still soaked to the skin himself.

With a sigh, she stood and handed the bowl back to Robby, whose eyes were as wide as saucers. Then she laid a hand gently over Mr. Smith's and smiled compassionately down on his weary face.

"Thank ye, missus. Thank ye." His great dark eyes were misty and full of wonder, along with the pain.

Adjusting her grip on the blanket, Gresham led her to Braxton, standing near his desk. "Thank you, Mrs. Green. I've rarely seen such charity on board a ship in His Majesty's Navy. You have completely overwhelmed my patient with your kind attentions." Braxton smiled down on her but lifted his gaze to Gresham.

"How badly is he hurt, Doctor?" Gresham asked with real concern, as he considered Smith a dependable man.

"An upper-arm break and some badly cracked ribs. It will

take some time, but he will mend," Braxton said to them both reassuringly.

"Good. Well done, Doctor. I'll just see Mrs. Green back to her cabin." Gresham spun to leave, when Braxton stopped him.

"I'll say good night to you both then. I'll be hanging my hammock here tonight, Captain. Considering Mr. Smith's size, I doubt my lads will be able to assist him by themselves."

"Well, good night then. What's left of it." Gresham smiled wryly and couldn't help noticing the falling of his friend's face as he led the lady back around the base of the foremast. At the door of the stern cabin, he said good night to her and kissed her hand but left her quickly so she could get some sleep, something he knew he wouldn't get with his chest near to bursting with joy.

※

THE NEXT MORNING Sarah awoke with a new sliver of hope in her heart, yet her better judgment, along with the cloud of anxiety that clung to her like a wet blanket, tried to snuff it out.

Hearing a knock, she was struck with an unusual bashfulness as she opened the door, curtsied, and motioned for Gresham to enter. She could hardly believe that she was now betrothed to this roguishly handsome naval captain.

"Good morning, Mrs. Green. I, well, I hope you are well after being soaked through last night."

*Yes, I am fine.* She smiled shyly at him, feeling the color rise in her face as she gestured to the chairs she had moved beside the gallery windows.

"Thank God," gushed the captain as he sat across from her. "I, well, I was exceedingly glad to see you last night."

She couldn't help the little quiver of pleasure that raced in her heart at seeing his beaming face. *Wait! What's this feeling? This is all happening so fast. Dear Lord, are you sure?*

"I was wondering if there might be some way you could help me understand how you made your decision," Gresham asked awkwardly. "What was it that convinced you to accept my proposal?"

She had anticipated his question. She reached under her chair for her Bible. Opening it to a marked place, she pointed to a passage and handed the book over to him. *God, please speak for me, for you are the one who has spoken to me about this man and our future together.*

He gaped at her in wonder, swallowing hard. It was a passage from Isaiah 61. He read it aloud. "'The Lord hath anointed me to preach good tidings unto the meek; he hath sent me to bind up the broken-hearted, to proclaim liberty to the captives, and the opening of the prison to them that are bound; to comfort all that mourn; to appoint unto them that mourn in Zion, to give unto them beauty for ashes, the oil of joy for mourning, the garment of praise for the spirit of heaviness.'"

As he read, his voice became thick and husky. When he finished, he glanced up at her with astonishment. She looked deeply into his eyes, captured in the sacredness of the moment with him, feeling God's Spirit moving in the space between them.

She was reluctant to break the energy in the air. Surprised and confused by a powerful desire, she longed to feel his strong arms around her, to feel secure in the warmth of his embrace.

Gresham bowed his head and broke the spell. "Thank you, Mrs. Green. There is so much to talk about, so much to learn about each other, but my mind will only settle on what is most urgent." Looking up, his eyes held a hint of foreboding. "You will recall when I spoke to you that I would do all in my power to spare you from public scrutiny and help to maintain your privacy?"

She nodded readily. *Yes, I do.*

"Well, it turns out that a wedding aboard ship will not be legally binding, which will not do. With only two precious days left before we reach England, we also have a ship full of some two hundred fifty sailors who love nothing more than to swap stories in the taverns and pubs once their feet hit dry land."

She lifted her brows. *Oh dear.*

Gresham shifted in his chair. "So I have come up with a plan of sorts. It is not a great plan, but it is the only one I can think of. You see, if the men were convinced of our betrothal, I could make the case that I would much prefer for them to refrain from telling tales about my soon-to-be wife. Then I would have them all sign a document saying that they promise not to speak about you. My hope is that it may buy us some time before word leaks out, which inevitably it will. Do you understand?"

She could see the earnestness in his dark-blue eyes. *Yes. Please tell me your plan.*

"Thank God." He sighed with relief. "The idea is to have a celebration of our betrothal with the entire ship's company. There would be a few speeches, a little music, something simple that would convince the men of our intentions. We would need to have this celebration by tomorrow evening at the latest."

*Tomorrow?* She tried to convey the question with her eyes.

"I know—it is all so sudden, but we do not have the luxury of time. What do you think? Would it be something you could endure, even for just a little while? I don't want to put you on such public display, and believe me, if I thought there was any other way, I would not expose you to such an occasion." His eyes searched her face.

She looked out the window at the rolling waves trailing endlessly behind them. Folding her arms as she stood, a hidden strength welled up within her. *This is nothing compared to what I have been through.* Then with a quick spin toward him, she nodded once with a firm set to her lips, returned to her seat, and gazed at him.

"Oh! Well, all right then." He chuckled. "I am so grateful for your understanding and courage. Are you sure it won't be unsettling to you?"

She reached out and patted his hand in reassurance.

He rose with energy. "You truly are a wonder, Mrs. Green. I will meet with the officers and attend to the preparations at once."

Offering his hand to her, she rose and rested her hand in his as he brushed a kiss on her fingers. She oddly wished he would not leave so soon.

Gresham stepped to the door, but he paused with his foot halfway across the threshold, "Oh! I almost forgot. The officers and I would like to ask the pleasure of your company for dinner this evening in the wardroom. Would that please you? Or is that too many men at the table? Please do not feel obliged to accept."

She hesitated briefly, then curtsied her consent and nudged him through the door.

CHAPTER

# THIRTEEN

Gresham and Mrs. Green were greeted with cheers and applause as they entered the wardroom. The glowing lanterns filled the space with warm light reflected in the table settings and wineglasses. Gresham led her to a chair between his and a somber Dr. Braxton, who bowed to her formally.

The mood was festive, and Gresham was relieved that the officers had donned their best manners. They addressed Mrs. Green with eagerness and fawned over the lustrous string of pearls he had surprised her with just before escorting her to dinner. The men were more than happy to inform her that the captain had won them as prize for taking a pirate sloop off the coast of Jamaica just a few months before and reveled in telling her the whole tale.

Mr. Green was helping serve, and once their glasses were filled, Gresham stood and raised his in a toast to his beautiful fiancée. Then one by one the officers entertained her in their most genteel, though still sailoresque, fashion, sharing stories of their adventures on the *Relentless*.

"You should have seen the look on the pirate captain's face when Captain Gresham pulled his pistol and demanded his surrender," Lieutenant Compton boasted, grinning with the memory. "He went from a sun-scorched fiend to petrified white lamb in an instant!"

The men laughed with gusto. "And that time when we had just boarded that heathen pirate Cutless's ship when Mr. Latch was thrown overboard at the start of the fray and we had to haul him out like a flounder after the battle was over." Mr. Mackenzie's bellowing baritone chortled. "He missed all the fighting. Lucky lad didn't have to strike a single blow!"

Mr. Latch blushed a deep red but took the ribbing in stride. "Will you never let me forget, Mr. Mackenzie?"

"Not on your life, Mr. Latch, unless you ever become my captain!" the Scotsman shot back.

"There may come a day, sir," Mr. Latch retorted with a lift to his young chin. "There may come a day!"

As the stories and laughter continued, Gresham saw how Mrs. Green held herself, her posture conveying grace and good manners, with only the slightest hint of insecurity. She was attentive and generous with her smiles and nods, even laughing silently with them. My God, how had he come to be so blessed to have a woman like this in his life, let alone as his intended bride. He basked in her presence, marveling at how far she had come from the woman wielding a knife so few days before.

The main course was over, and Mr. Green brought in the dessert tray with a grin and a flourish. The cut-glass goblets tinkled against each other on his tray as he moved from place to place, setting one before each guest. Once everyone was served, they all took up their spoons and enjoyed, commenting on how wonderful it was to have such a special dish after being so long at sea.

Gresham gradually became aware of Mrs. Green's frozen gaze and stiff body and was immediately alarmed. He bent forward to try and catch her eyes, but they were unfocused, staring into space. He ventured to take her hand under the table, but it was cold and unresponsive.

He pushed back his chair and stood. "Please carry on, gentlemen. I believe that Mrs. Green has had enough excitement for the evening and wishes to retire." As he spoke, he moved behind her chair and nudged Braxton on the back discreetly.

Braxton looked up, and Gresham aimed his chin toward her. He assisted Gresham in pulling out her chair and then helped her to stand. The other men rose and bid her good night but were too full of good humor and wine to notice much amiss. Gresham and Braxton took her by the arms and out of the room. Mr. Green was out the door with them in an instant.

When the wardroom door closed, Gresham swept her up into his arms and carried her up the stairs, laying her on the berth in his night cabin. He knelt beside her, patting her hand, "Mrs. Green, Sarah, are you all right, my dear?"

She searched his face in confusion, as if trying to remember.

Braxton looked her over. "I need my medicine box." He turned to go but stopped and looked back to Gresham. "John, if she stirs, don't try to restrain her. She may believe she is on the other ship."

Gresham nodded with comprehension. "It is all right, Sarah. You are safe. You are here on the *Relentless*. Sarah, can you hear me?" What could have caused this sudden change in her? He hated feeling helpless to ease her fears.

She stirred uneasily and sat up, then stood and looked around the night cabin, dimly lit by the hanging lantern.

Gresham gave her freedom but stayed close, in case she should fall. She went out into the day cabin, searching, agitated, then paced to the gallery windows and flung one open, leaning over the sill and staring into the depths of the black churning water below. Gresham stood near but did not touch her, and he motioned for Mr. Green to bring a glass of flip, trying to distract her.

She accepted it and drained it as if dying of thirst. Just then the door flung open and Braxton entered. He swung around the wooden medical box strapped to his shoulder and set it on the table.

Seeing the box, she hurled the empty glass at it. It crashed and showered Braxton with shards. He reflexively guarded his face with his hands and drew back.

She sprang behind Gresham and withdrew her long knife from her pocket.

Gresham reached behind him protectively. "It's all right. Everything is all right."

Braxton, recovering from the shock, was bleeding from small cuts on his hands.

Gresham shot him a piercing glance. "Get rid of that box, now!"

Braxton jumped and swept the box out of the room.

Turning toward her slowly, speaking softly, Gresham pulled her trembling into his arms.

Braxton returned, the broken glass crunching under his boots. "I am so sorry. I should have been more thoughtful. I have taken it away. I promise I will not give you anything from it."

Her thin frame quaked against Gresham, and he sent Braxton a nod toward the door. Braxton's face fell, and he left the room.

"Mr. Green, would you fetch a bottle of port and three glasses, please?" He led her to the table and pulled out a chair. "Perhaps a few sips might help calm the nerves."

He could see the dismay on her face as she sat, still trembling. Mr. Green quickly produced the requested items and poured, then attended to the broken glass.

She sipped at her glass and soon seemed more calm, though subdued.

"I am deeply sorry for your distress at dinner. Was there . . . did something happen that reminded you of the other ship? Was it the dessert?" Gresham asked.

Taking a shuddering breath, she nodded.

"Did you have that same custard dessert on the other ship?"

She nodded again.

Gresham looked up, trying to remember something. "Mr. Green, what is the name of that particular dessert?"

"Well, Capt'n, cook calls it 'the lady's breast.'"

THE NEXT MORNING Braxton wearily pulled the door to the stern cabin shut behind him. He had apologized to Mrs. Green profusely about the medical box, and she was most gracious in extending her forgiveness, as he'd known she would be.

His suspicions from the night before had been confirmed during their interview. She'd recognized the dessert from the other ship and had also confirmed that the other ship's surgeon had used drugs from a box like Braxton's to keep the couple under control while he and the captain wreaked their terror on the two.

Worried that she would suffer a terrible setback, he was greatly relieved to find her only a bit tired and somber. He left with such a mixture of emotions that he had to pause and gather himself before heading up to the quarterdeck to find Gresham.

There was a great deal of activity on the main deck, as the preparations for the celebration were commencing. The ship practically buzzed with activity and the resonance of the musical men rehearsing on the gun deck below.

Braxton picked his way through the chaos to find Gresham seated at a small table, catching up on his logs with his clerk.

"Good morning, Doctor. How did your conversation go?" Gresham motioned a dismissal to the clerk and stood as Braxton approached.

"Better than I had anticipated, Captain," Braxton replied when only Gresham could hear him above the noise.

"Yes, I was very relieved to find her much calmer when I saw her earlier."

Braxton stayed silent for a moment looking at his feet, then asked gravely, "Captain, would you mind removing with me to my cabin? I have something rather personal to say."

"Certainly, Doctor. Let me get my clerk to finish this log entry."

Once Braxton's cabin door was closed, he removed a folded handkerchief from the bureau. He regarded it painfully, as if his own heart lay bleeding in his hand. Swallowing hard, he met Gresham's eyes.

"I have something here that belongs to you," and opening the folds, he revealed the strands of golden-brown hair within. "I stole them, John. I should never have taken them from the bin. She did not give them to me. I took them, and it has haunted me ever since." Shame poured over him, and his very bones ached. "Please take them from me and let us never speak of it again. I can bear it no longer."

Gresham stood aghast but opened his hand as Braxton

placed the forbidden treasure carefully in it and folded it closed.

Braxton sank into the chair. "I am sorry, John. I have fought with my feelings for her to no avail. I do not understand myself —it is like an obsession, unlike any force of nature I have ever encountered."

Gresham sighed and braced himself on the bureau. "I cannot say as I can blame you, Paul. I am familiar with the feeling myself. Good God, what a terrible dilemma."

Braxton, aware of Gresham's stiffening posture, continued. "I want you to know that I believe things are as they should be. You are the right man for her, John. You share a faith that I most certainly do not, one that you both lay as the foundation of your lives. No, I have no place to even dream of being in your position. I suppose I am destined to journey through life alone."

Gresham looked as if he wanted to shake him, but instead he turned his back and gripped the sides of the bureau. Braxton sat miserable, almost wishing Gresham would strike him, as shunning was much more painful.

With a groan of frustration, Gresham spun around and grasped Braxton by the shoulders. He spoke in a desperate, hushed tone, his eyes pleading. "Paul, God loves you and wants you to receive that love. You have this gaping wound in your soul, but he did not cause it. He wants you to give that pain to him and let him fill you with Himself. Please, I beg of you, consider—"

Braxton tore his eyes from Gresham's, raising his hand in weary protest. "Yes, yes, you have said it all before, but I simply cannot believe that if God loves me now, why didn't he love me when I was most vulnerable. No, no, this is all beside the point." He rose and pushed Gresham away. "I have to confess this to you and get it over with." He closed his eyes as he whispered, "I am so sorry."

With a heavy sigh, Gresham put his arm around his friend's shoulder as Braxton covered his long face with his hand, a single sob escaping his control.

He pulled away. "Thank you for your kindness, John. I shall never forget it."

"I trust you with my life, my friend. We will find a way to get through this paradox. We have faced greater dangers together than this." Gresham gave an ironic smile.

Braxton furrowed his eyebrows in disagreement. "I am not so sure about that, Captain. Not sure at all."

*

SHE STOOD beside her betrothed and watched from the foot of the companionway while Mr. Green went up through the aft hatch as the ship's bell rang at precisely six o'clock, and heard him greet Mr. Compton with relish. Then she heard Mr. Compton give the boatswain a command, and the tune from his pipe was followed by silence. The next tune announced the arrival of the captain on deck.

The captain escorted her up the stairs, dressed in his best blue dress coat with gold epaulets, which she had helped him into herself. He wore his best bicorn hat with gold braiding and a beautiful white flowing feather fluttering in the sea breeze. But when she emerged from the hatch, Sarah could feel that all eyes were on her.

She gasped at the sight of the men all standing silently at attention, saluting the man beside her. Delighted to see some men helping Mr. Smith gingerly up to the main deck from the sick bay and seating him at a table near the stairs to the quarterdeck, her smile deepened. He seemed in noticeably good spirits for a man who was still in great pain.

The *Relentless* stood almost motionless in the calm water, as all the sails had been furled. Sarah shielded her eyes to see the topmen waiting in the rigging and shrouds, ready for action. There were musicians and singers in place near the aft of the waist. Mr. Compton stood near the helm and Mr. Latch at the fore, near the guns. Sarah waited with anxious anticipation and clung to the captain's arm.

Mr. Compton called out to set sail. One after another, she watched in awe as the ship's sails were unfurled in a massive dance of white billows as the topmen released them in a dazzling display of strength and skill. The only sound was that of the canvas snapping to the stirring of the wind and the whirring of the ropes through their braces, the sun's evening rays lighting the ship into a blaze of golden white light.

Gresham guided her, breathless, to the quarterdeck. Above them, draping down to a table at the fore of the quarter deck forming an open canopy, were long lines of triangular flags in a bright array of colors and patterns, and behind hung the Union Jack in all its historical glory.

She smiled in awe and looked at Gresham with disbelief. He patted her hand. She was overcome at the thought that this was all for her.

As the sails were being set, an ensemble sang the old hymn "A Mighty Fortress Is Our God" a cappella. The beauty of the harmonies, the ancient truths in the lyrics, and countenances of manly grace on the singers gave the moment a sacred air. When the song ended, there was a hush, and then the fine Irish tenor voice of Mr. Green broke the silence. "Let us pray!" Each man removed his hat as their masculine voices rose with him, saying, "Our Father, which art in heaven, hallowed be thy name..."

Gresham removed his hat, tucked her hand under his arm, and bowed his head. "Thy kingdom come, thy will be done, on earth as it is in heaven . . ." Sarah could not contain the tears that rolled down her cheeks as she bowed her head and joined them in the silence of her full heart. Not until then had she fervently wished that she could give audible voice to her prayer. She felt a strong yearning to speak again, if only to give God glory from her own lips. When the prayer ended, she tucked the desire into her heart. *I will speak*, she vowed. *I will find a way to move past this paralyzing fear. God help me.*

Their attention was turned to the men in position at the guns near the forecastle. "Hold your ears, my dear." Gresham demonstrated by putting his fingers into his own.

She followed his advice just in time, as Mr. Latch, who stood with the gunner and his crews, gave the order to "Fire!" The explosion from the barrels of the foremost guns sent a shockwave through the wood beneath their feet, and a plume of smoke swirled its way before them like a frolicking cloud.

Her hands flew to her chest, and she gaped up at Gresham, her heart pounding from the power of the blast. She had never felt anything like it.

Gresham winked at her, his chest high, a look of pride on his handsome face.

He raised his gloved hand. "Thank you, good men of the *Relentless*, for your most superb welcome to me and my betrothed, Mrs. Green. Please be at ease and take your seats." Gresham's bellowing voice rang out across the deck and was answered by a roar of cheers and applause.

Sarah couldn't help herself, and she waved timidly at them. Her gaze swept the deck, finally landing on Mr. Smith, who was seated with Mr. Green at a nearby table. She gave the topman a special smile before taking her chair.

Braxton approached with his two loblolly boys, as well as

all the powder monkey boys. They bashfully handed Mrs. Green bouquets of paper flowers, each of them bowing and saying, "Welcome, Mrs. Green!"

She nodded to each with a smile and held the flowers together in her lap. Braxton led them in one more group bow and promptly herded them back to their places in the waist. Gresham chuckled, and she saw him share a wink with Braxton, and was relieved to see the grim lines had lessened on the doctor's face.

Next, Mr. Latch stood before them, saluting and bowing formally. "Good evening, Mrs. Green, Captain Gresham. Dinner is about to be served, and we have several performances by the men of the *Relentless* for your pleasure. We hope you will enjoy this special celebration of your betrothal!"

A dinner of fish, salted pork, and cornmeal mush was served, and the evening continued with songs and choruses, toasts, and laughter. After the simple meal, Dr. Braxton stepped to the quarterdeck rail, tapping the side of his glass with a spoon, settling the crowd as he stood beside the couple.

"I propose a toast." Braxton lifted his wineglass, smiled with a bow to Sarah and the captain, then turned to face the men on the main deck. "I would like to say a word about Captain Gresham, Mrs. Green, and the amazing events of the past few days." The deck hushed with anticipation. "I have had the great privilege of serving with all of you, and Captain Gresham, for several years now. I have witnessed many things that a man on the land would never be able to imagine. We have experienced together, as a ship's company, heartache and trouble, hunger and hardship, injury and death, but the past few days have been equally as adventurous."

He paused to look back for a moment, then continued. "Mrs. Green joined us under the most difficult of circumstances. Her astonishing recovery while aboard this ship has given testimony to her remarkable strength of character and her indomitable spirit. I know that I speak for all of us in congratulating her and wishing her all the best that life has to offer, even if it is spent with the likes of Captain Gresham!"

The deck erupted with cheers and laughter, and Braxton smiled mischievously at them with another bow.

He raised his hand for quiet. "Now as to my very dear friend Captain Gresham, I have never respected a man more." The agreement from the crowd interrupted him briefly, but he forged on. "This is a man who has never ceased to do his duty. He is a born leader and has led a life of integrity that is not common among men. He has never failed to rise to the occasion, meeting every situation with courage and resolve. But now"—he peered at his friend briefly—"he has once again risen to a new level of respect and admiration in my mind and heart, and I am sure the same is true for all of you." Again the exclamations of agreement rose and fell.

Then the doctor raised his glass. "Please join me in drinking a toast to the King, to his Prince Regent, and to the two most extraordinary people I have ever met, Mrs. Green and Captain Gresham!" And he stepped aside to touch his glass to theirs with mist in his eyes as the ship erupted with cheers of "Hazzah! Hazzah! Hazzah!"

The musicians struck up a happy shanty tune, and Sarah watched with amusement as some of the men jumped up on their benches to dance, including Mr. Green, who danced a jig, much to the astonishment of Mr. Smith.

The captain stood, helping her to her feet as he wrapped his arm around the doctor's shoulders. "Thank you, Paul. I am forever in your debt," she heard him say to his friend over the noise.

"It is I who needs to thank you, Captain, for not throwing

me overboard." The doctor gave an ironic chuckle and took another gulp of his wine.

Gresham cuffed his shoulder and laughed aloud, only to be silenced by the sight of Mr. Compton hurrying his way. "Captain, the main top watch has just spotted land, sir. The coast of France. We should be entering the English Channel by midday tomorrow."

CHAPTER

# FOURTEEN

Gresham cut the party short, much to the chagrin of the crew. After delivering Mrs. Green to the stern cabin, he set about making ready to moor the *Relentless* next to the pier at the Royal Woolwich Naval Dockyard, built by King Henry VIII in the sixteenth century. The *Relentless* herself had been built there and put into service in 1810, under his command.

A sinking dread replaced his happiness. He was at one with the *Relentless* and knew her every wooden board and iron brace, her voice in the creaking of her hull and the whisper of the wind in her sails. She had been his wings, like riding the back of an eagle over the countless waves of the seas, giving him a freedom and autonomy that few men who walked the earth would ever know. He knew that this could be his last farewell, the last few hours in communion with her as her master, and the pain of his grieving heart became almost unbearable.

In the midst of his agony was the need to think clearly, to plan and orchestrate not only their mooring at Woolwich but getting his betrothed secretly through the massive dockyard, out the main gate, and to the Lee Side Inn in Charlton in the next parish to the west.

Because he had grown up there as a boy, he had many old acquaintances in the area, and one of his most beloved was Mrs. Eliza Yates, a widow and the keeper of the Lee Side Inn, just on the main road from Woolwich toward Greenwich, which led on to London. Mrs. Yates had been a family friend and attended the same parish church as his family, St. Luke's. She always made room for him when he was in need of one, and her kitchen prepared a very nice chop.

She was the exact person to leave Mrs. Green with until he had things sorted out and could take her on from there to Hatfield in Hertfordshire, where his elder sister Penelope lived with her rather successful husband, Rev. Henry Keate, the rector at the prestigious parish church St. Etheldreda's. They lived in the comfortable old vicarage. Indeed Gresham was blessed to have a few faithful and trustworthy friends left in England.

Early the next day, he spent time writing letters, one for Mrs. Yates at the inn and one for his sister, Penny, in Hatfield. How utterly astonished Penny would be to read it. His sister always tried her hand at being his matchmaker but had given up the idea of her brother ever marrying when he was assigned to the *Relentless*. She joked with him during his visits, calling the ship his wife. How he longed to see her and her amiable husband. *They will understand*, he thought as he sealed his letters. He left them on top of his stack of logbooks and journals on Braxton's little bureau, ready to take with him on the first boat to cross to the pier.

Gresham asked for Dr. Braxton, Mr. Compton, and Mr. Green to meet with him and Mrs. Green in the stern cabin, as much would need to be planned in order to be ready to depart the ship. They sat together over steaming cups of tea at the captain's table, with rapt anticipation.

"My first priority, of course, is to get Mrs. Green off the ship and safely to an inn in Charlton without being noticed. There, she will be in the very kind and capable hands of a dear old family friend and one I trust completely. Mr. Green, I will need you to pack for us. We will take small traveling bags to the inn, and the rest will be sent on up to Hatfield ahead of us. I will also need you to travel with me and Mrs. Green to the inn and stay with her until I am able to secure the *Relentless* and disperse of my duties. I'll then rejoin you with Dr. Braxton. Does that suit you, Mr. Green?"

"Aye, Capt'n! I would like nothing more!" Mr. Green's eyes twinkled with delight over his cup.

"Thank you. I am sure your presence will be a great comfort to Mrs. Green." He gave the lovely lady sitting silently beside him an admiring smile.

She nodded, relief showing in her anxious eyes.

Gresham gave her an awkward side glance "Now, Mrs. Green, I will have to ask you a rather odd question."

She tilted her head and nodded for him to continue.

"Well, I have tried to think of a better solution, but it seems there is no other way to get you out of the dockyard without drawing attention. You will need to be dressed as a sailor— specifically, a midshipman."

Her brows popped up in surprise, but she seemed amused. Nodding that she was up to the challenge, she set her cup down decisively.

"Well, that was easy." Gresham gave a brief chuckle.

Even Braxton's eyes lit up.

"Now," Gresham said with a smile, "that being decided, we will not be able to treat you as a lady from the time you disembark the *Relentless* until you are safely tucked away in one of Mrs. Yates's tidy rooms. Will that be acceptable to you?"

*Yes* was the nodded answer, and she directed at him a smug smile of her own.

"I knew I could count on you." He flicked his eyes to his first lieutenant. "Mr. Compton, I understand that you and Mr. Latch have been canvassing the crew for signatures on a document, something to ensure their discretion concerning Mrs. Green, is that correct?"

"Yes, Captain," Compton replied with confidence. "We decided it might be best coming from us, sir, as we have more direct interaction with the men, and they know they will be answering to us as well as to you if they decide to go spreading tales, sir."

Gresham patted the table twice. "You have done me a great service, Mr. Compton. I have no idea how successful such an agreement will be or for how long, but I am deeply touch by your efforts, and I am sure Mrs. Green feels the same."

She nodded her sincere agreement.

"And now, to an even more delicate matter. Dr. Braxton and I will request an audience with the admiral of the dock, Admiral Warwick, to make our separate report to him regarding Mrs. Green. He is the highest authority at Woolwich and will know how best to proceed. Dr. Braxton has agreed to arrange to have the remains below examined by the proper authorities. Then he will escort them to Hatfield, where we hope they may receive a proper burial."

He fixed a sober gaze on the doctor. "It is very good of you to do all of this for Mrs. Green, Doctor. We will be extremely relieved to know that this matter is in your capable hands and will look forward to you joining us in Hatfield."

"I will do my best." The Doctor gave them both a reassuring tap to his chest, just over his heart.

"Very well then. Mr. Compton, I will need all the help you can provide in regard to the crew. I have already settled my accounts with Mr. Darby, and he knows what his duties are as far as the ship's stores are concerned. Let us make ready. I would like to have things in order by the time we drop anchor."

SARAH WAS unable to hide her nervous excitement at finally seeing civilization again. She had gone with the captain just after dawn to see the shoreline of France at a distance off to starboard. He'd explained the journey so she could anticipate what she would see as they progressed toward the dockyard. They would be in the mouth of the English Channel in just a few hours, where they would see England on the port side as they made the turn to the northeast, then snaking their way around to head west into the mouth of the mighty River Thames.

Her heart leaped as England came into view. Seeing the towns and villages on the shoreline to starboard, the church steeples, and hearing the distant ringing of bells sent a marvelous thrill through her as she leaned out of a gallery window to take it all in. Even though none of it stirred any memories, the bustling was familiar to her in general, and she smiled wistfully as the land edged closer. They passed many ships and boats along the way, and she was glad the weather was fair, as her view from the *Relentless* was full and clear.

Impatient to do something useful, she went into the night cabin and pulled her dilapidated trunk away from the wall and opened it. It was a miserable sight. Her stomach turned with memories as she sorted out beleaguered piles of what she should keep and not. When she was finished, the pile of things to keep was pitifully small.

*Not much to pack,* she thought, *but at least I shall travel lightly,* and she mused on how she would hide her hair when she became a midshipman.

Soon after, Mr. Green came in with a bundle of clothes and a carpetbag. "Here are some items ta try on, ma dear. Oh, I see you've been gathering your things—very good. Here is a bag ta pack them in. Are these items on the floor here ta be discarded?"

She confirmed, and Mr. Green gathered them and departed, leaving her to try out the midshipman garments. A sickening wave washed over her. *What if I draw attention to myself? What if someone asks me a question I cannot answer?* She grasped the edges of the table and prayed for God to give her the wisdom and calm she would need to get past this first challenge.

With this prayer she tried on the items heaped on the table. After several comical failures, she was able to laugh silently at how ridiculous she felt in a pair of white breeches. Finally she settled on a pair that would do.

When Mr. Green returned, he was delighted to find his new charge, Midshipman Green, dressed and ready for orders. The only foreseeable problem with her costume was her long brown tresses that insisted on falling out from under her bicorn hat. After much stuffing and pinning, she finally felt they would not betray her.

If she could only have fun with this charade and not be hobbled with fear, she would be all right.

Mr. Green tutored her in the ways of saluting and whom to salute. This she would have to pull off if they were to be able to navigate their way out of the dockyard without incident. She committed in her heart to be brave so that she would not be a burden to all these fine men who were moving heaven and earth to help her. *Now, if only I could speak.* She vowed that she would.

✳

THE *RELENTLESS* ANCHORED beside the great Woolwich Dockyard, where hundreds of seafaring craft, a forest of masts, and a cacophony of sounds surrounded them. The boats were lowered into the Thames, ready to convey the captain and his landing party to the base of the ramp that led up to the little office shed on the side of the long pier. She stood beside him, a fresh-faced midshipman, saluting and nodding and sneaking in a glance his way when no one was looking.

"My God, you are a brave one," Gresham said as they descended the stairs on the outside of the hull. Then she saw a grimace of agonizing pain cross his visage when he looked up at the ship as his foot left the hull of the *Relentless* and his hand released the manrope.

She searched his face as he took his seat. A devastating realization dawned on her, what he was sacrificing for her. She wanted to stop the boat, to jump into the river, to remove the burden he had taken upon himself on her behalf, but Mr. Bowling had pushed them away from the *Relentless* and was rowing them swiftly to the ramp at the pier.

Helpless to act, she knew that putting up a fuss now could put them all in a precarious situation. No, she would have to see this part of the journey through. Just get out of this dockyard, teeming with a confusion of men, carts, horses, cranes, and cables, and when the immediate danger was passed, decisions would be made.

She capably jumped from the boat to the ramp and followed Gresham up to stand beside the little office building at the top, where he was addressed formally by the dock agent. She couldn't concentrate on their conversation. All she could hear was her pulse surging in her ears. *I cannot let him do this!* She clenched her fists and dug her nails into her palms. *This is all my fault.*

They were moving on now, picking their way through the mass of movement on the walkway. Her senses were bombarded from all sides by the swarm of humanity, the cries of the seagulls, shouts, swearing sailors, the smell of unwashed bodies and dead fish, and the crunch of her borrowed boots on the weathered boards. She shadowed Gresham's every step, followed by Mr. Green carrying their bags, who would casually call out encouragement to her. "Yes, that's it, just ta the right now. Mind that rope there, that's it."

She kept her eyes open for any superior officer headed their way, anticipating the need to salute. Her heart pounded like a drum against her ribs, and she was thirsty. Licking her lips and gritting her teeth, she told herself to keep walking.

"Now here we are. Here is someone who needs our respect," Mr. Green coached from behind as a lieutenant headed in their direction. She saluted him a bit too soon, but he didn't even glance her way. Gresham had only turned to check on her a few times, always with a reassuring nod, then continued to forge the path forward.

He stopped for a moment to point to the tall Clock House down the way on their right and turned in that direction. Just then a voice called out from the crowded gangway on the left, and they halted.

"Captain Gresham! I say there, Captain Gresham!" A man in a captain's uniform darted his way toward them and arrived at Gresham's side. "Don't you remember me? It's Reed! Phillip Reed from the *Undaunted*."

"Well, I say, is that really you, Phil?" Gresham shook the

man's hand heartily. "It looks like congratulations are in order —the last time I saw you, you were a second lieutenant!"

Gresham gave Sarah and Mr. Green a warning glance as she saluted and kept her eyes on Gresham. "Mr. Green, you and the lad carry on. I will meet you on the far side of the Clock House presently," Gresham casually ordered with a gesture to keep going.

Her heart sank, but Mr. Green gave her a smile and led the way. She wanted desperately to stay where she was but forced her feet to move. *He will join us soon*, she made herself think. *He will only be a moment and then we will be on our way.*

They waited near the steps of the Clock House, and she jumped when the booming bells in the tower rang out the hour. Mr. Green chatted with her about his first time to Woolwich and how impressed he had been with the enormity of the place . . . anything to fill the time. But when the clock struck the half hour, he stopped. A look of concern clouding his jovial face increased her own sense of alarm.

"Now, I'm just going ta look down the side o' the building here ta see if I can see the capt'n. I'll return presently."

She nodded and went to stand with her back to the brick wall next to the stairs, as out of sight as she could manage.

Scanning the people who walked up and down the steps, she focused on being ready to salute if the need came. She was desperately thirsty and needed to relieve herself badly, but she clenched her jaw, trying not to think of it.

With her back hard against the cool brick of the building, the sting of tears behind her eyes came on sharply. *Dear Lord, you've brought me back! I am here. I am truly back in civilization! Thank you, God. Help me find my way home.*

Suddenly she was aware of someone speaking to her. "Boy. I say, lad, are you all right there?" A gray-haired man in a green felt hat and civilian clothes was climbing the steps and had seen her distressed face. Even though she could not identify him as a naval officer, she stood to attention and saluted.

The man laughed and reversed his steps, coming around to stand a few feet from her, backed into the corner. "That's not necessary for me, young man. Now, I asked if you were all right —are you?" And he took a step closer.

She nodded, a bit too swiftly, and felt a tendril of silky hair slip out of its place over her right ear. *Dear God! What should I do?*

She was just about to make a run for it, when the captain rounded the walkway and came to stand behind the man. "Ah, there you are, Mr. Green. Our carriage is waiting—hurry along now," and he gestured toward the main gate.

The man whirled when he heard Gresham behind him. "Oh, pardon me, Captain. I thought your midshipman here had lost his way. Good day to you, gentlemen." He tipped his hat and made his way back up the stairs and into the large doors of the Clock House as the next hour rang out.

The captain paused. She noticed him staring at the steps the man had just taken, his countenance gray as a dreadful war played out on his face while he stood frozen to the spot. Casually she bumped his arm, trying to break the spell he was under. He startled and looked down on her in confusion, but she smiled up at him with a salute, and he came to himself, swallowing hard. He led her to where Mr. Green waited beside a cab on the street outside the gate.

Gresham entered first, then pulled her in beside him. Mr. Green sat up top with the driver, and they jerked into motion.

❋

GRESHAM TOOK her hand as they started. "Oh, my dear, I'm so sorry for my horrendous delay. Are you all right?" He resisted the temptation to crush her to him. "First, I was accosted by that old acquaintance, and then, as if on cue, Admiral Warwick himself stopped me on his way to his offices and insisted on speaking to me. I am terribly sorry you were left alone to fend for yourself. Can you ever forgive me?"

She nodded, but he could see the threat of tears in her eyes.

"We are only a mile and a half away from the inn. We will be there soon, then you can take off this silly hat and stop pretending."

As instructed, the driver did not stop at the main entrance to the inn but drove around the back to the kitchen. Mr. Green hopped down to open the cab door.

Gresham paused before stepping out. "You will only have to pretend until we get you up to the top level and close the door behind us. But first I must greet Mrs. Yates and make sure she received my letter in time for our arrival."

Mr. Green managed their few bags, but before he reached the door, it flung open, and he was nearly knocked over by the swift exit of a rather tall, middle-aged woman in an apron and cap, who flew straight to Captain Gresham, exclaiming excitedly, "Johnny, my boy! My dear Johnny! I am so glad to see you!"

Gresham caught her in his arms and swayed with her in an exuberant embrace. "My dear Mrs. Yates, it has been far too long!" Gresham kissed her soundly on the cheek, and she stood back, looking him over from head to toe.

"Oh, how your parents would be proud of you, Johnny, God rest their souls. You look so well, so fit, and so very handsome." Her white cap had nearly come off her gray curls, and she set it to rights as her eyes took in the shy midshipman standing to the side. "And this must be the young man you told me about! Welcome, welcome!" She winked at Sarah, then up at Gresham knowingly. "Now let us go in and get you all settled. Ah! And this must be Mr. Green. Hello to you, my good fellow. Yes, let us not tarry out here longer. Fred!" Mrs. Yates called loudly at the kitchen door. "Fred! Come quickly. Here is an old friend to see us. Fred!"

Bursting out the kitchen door came a young man in his late teens, tall and lanky with a good speckling of pimples on his fair face. "Captain Gresham! How wonderful to see you again, sir!" Fred shook Gresham's hand amiably.

"Fred!" Gresham exclaimed. "My how you've grown! You are taller than your grandmother now!" Gresham gave the boy a cuff on the shoulder. "Let's get inside and up the stairs, where we can speak more freely."

Fred took up the luggage from Mr. Green, and Mrs. Yates led the way from the kitchen to the narrow back stairs. She found the key for the attic door on the jangling set tied to her apron and opened it, revealing a tidy and comfortable sitting room furnished with a settee, a table and chairs, a small desk, and a fireplace. There were two dormer windows, one on each side, and a door on each end of the room, leading to two small bed chambers.

"Mrs. Yates, you will know from my letter that this is no midshipman but Mrs. Sarah Green in disguise." He placed a hand on Sarah's shoulder. "You may take off that hat, my dear, but I'm afraid you must remain in breeches until we are on our way to Hatfield, just to be safe."

Mrs. Yates extended her hand to Sarah with a charitable smile. "I am most pleased to make your acquaintance, Mrs. Green. Johnny wasn't long in his letter, but I trust there is some reasonable explanation for the need for such a ruse."

Turning to the confused Fred, Mrs. Yates said, "Now, Fred, I am sure Johnny will explain it to us in time, but run along now and fetch them some tea and toast and make sure that cook is preparing their dinner."

Fred dashed out, and Mrs. Yates closed the door behind him. "Now then, Johnny, let us have a chat until Fred comes back with your tea. Are you all right, Mrs. Green? Would you like to join us at the table?" She hesitated at the look of weariness on Sarah's face. "Hmmm, no, I think perhaps you had better have a lie down. Come this way and let us make you more comfortable in this back room, shall we?"

Mrs. Yates and Gresham took her to the back bedroom, and Sarah stopped short in the doorway with a gasp. Mrs. Yates looked at Gresham with confusion, but he smiled at her. "Mrs. Green has been a very long time at sea and this is the first lovely room with a real bed she has seen in many months. Am I right, Mrs. Green?"

*Yes.* She nodded, then shook her head with a look of disbelief. With tears in her eyes, she looked at Mrs. Yates and fell directly into the sturdy woman's arms.

"Well, well, my dear Mrs. Green, you poor thing!" Mrs. Yates patted Sarah's back affectionately. "There, there now. I am sure you have been surrounded by smelly sailors with no female company, and it is a great relief to be back in a civilized place again. Let us leave you to rest, and I will bring you a cup of tea when it comes." Mrs. Yates gave Gresham a little push, and they left her.

※

As they sat at the table with Mr. Green, Mrs. Yates searched Gresham's face. "Now, Johnny. What do we have here? Why all this intrigue?"

"It is much too long a story to tell you everything, but I will

149

give you the gist of it. Though I must warn that you may find it extremely hard to believe." Gresham raised his brows at her.

After a knock on the door, young Fred came in with a tea tray. Mrs. Yates took it and asked him to hurry back with their dinner. She poured for them and took a cup to the back room, where Sarah lay on the ruffled counterpane, fast asleep.

"That poor girl is all in, Johnny." She sat again and bent close to her cup, ready for the tale.

"I will have to keep it short, for as soon as I have eaten, I will have to return to the dockyard." Giving Green a dubious look, he began.

Mrs. Yates didn't react at first. But then, blinking in confusion, she asked, "I am sorry, Johnny, but did you say that you found Mrs. Green and her dead husband on a deserted island? You must forgive me, my dear. I think I must be losing my hearing."

Gresham smiled in amusement. "Yes, Mrs. Yates, you heard me right, and what's more, her husband was murdered." He waited for that one to sink in.

"What? Dear Lord in heaven! Is this true, Mr. Green?" She kept her voice low.

"Aye, Mrs. Yates. I've witnessed it all meself and still have trouble believing what has happened in the last few weeks. Besides, I've never known the captain ta tell a falsehood, have you?"

"Oh, of course not. I mean, not since he was a boy, that is. But, Johnny, that still doesn't explain why you've brought her here dressed as a lad. Pray continue!"

"All right," Gresham said. "We believe that she and her husband were victims of some very powerful men in the Royal Navy—"

"The Royal Navy, you say?!" interrupted Mrs. Yates. "Well, I have never heard of such a thing!" Her eyes widened in horror.

Gresham's eyes narrowed. "Nor I, madam. So you see, we have three serious concerns. One being the need to protect Mrs. Green from the press, another to protect her from being found by the men who perpetrated these crimes against her. On top of that is the very real concern that the Royal Navy may seek to take custody of her, and since she is suffering from amnesia and is unable to speak—"

"What? No voice? No memory? Oh, the poor girl."

Gresham's voice softened, and he explained.

Settling her large frame back in the small chair, the woman shook her head. "You were right to bring her here, Johnny, but surely word will get out about her. Your crew must know how you found her. The navy will start looking and—"

"Yes. We have taken every measure to slow this inevitability, but you are correct. We must get her out of the vicinity as quickly as possible. I have plans to take her on to my sister's home in Hatfield and try to buy as much time as possible. We must find out her identity and where she came from before the navy or her attackers catch up to us."

"You mean, her name isn't Mrs. Green? She does not even remember her name?" Mrs. Yates looked from one to the other with great perplexity.

Another knock came at the door, and Mrs. Yates let in Fred and a house maid carrying in the dinner trays. "Set them on the table, dears, and I will sort things out, thank you."

Gresham tapped on the back bedchamber door and was grateful that Sarah answered, her sleepy eyes smiling softly as she re-pinned her tousled hair. His heart melted with the sight. He led her to the table, where Mrs. Yates set out their meal and Mr. Green poured the wine.

Gresham held out Sarah's chair as she pleasantly sniffed at the lovely chop and roasted vegetables set before her.

Mrs. Yates smiled down on her with deep kindness. "I am

most honored to have you in my humble home, Mrs. Green. Now if you need anything at all, you simply give the bellpull a tug and either Fred or I will be up in a jiffy. Perhaps you might be interested in a nice hot bath, would you? Yes, I thought you might, so after you have finished with your dinner, I shall send Fred up with the tub. Now"—she fixed her gaze on Gresham— "is there anything else you require, Johnny?"

"No, my dear lady. You have been more than helpful. I cannot tell you how grateful I am to be under your roof again, Mrs. Yates. Oh! Did I mention that Dr. Paul Braxton will be joining us for the night as well?"

"Yes, you did. I so look forward to seeing him again. He will have the room just below you here, and Mr. Green will be well situated downstairs by the kitchen with Fred. In my mind, it is the best room in the house. You will awaken to the lovely smell of freshly baked bread in the morning, Mr. Green. Does that suit you?"

"T'will remind me of me home in Ireland, Mrs. Yates. I can think o' no better felicity." Mr. Green gave Mrs. Yates a wink and a bow.

"Oh! Beware, Mr. Green. I have been known to fall for such charming gentlemen as yourself, sir. I'll bid you all good night then," and she left them with a troubled smile.

MR. DARBY BLANCHED at the sudden entrance of Captain Gresham to the wardroom. He had just finished with his book of accounts for the night when the door opened abruptly.

"My apologies, Mr. Darby. I didn't mean to startle you."

"Oh, no, Captain. I did not expect to see you again this evening." Darby saluted Gresham with an odd look of suspicion in his eyes. "Is there anything I can do for you, sir?"

Gresham seemed not to notice how stiff his purser was in his addresses. "Uh, no, thank you, Mr. Darby. I just need to finish up a few things here before returning to shore. I'll send for you if need be," and after a short moment in the doctor's cabin, he said good night and left.

Darby's shoulders sagged, and he scanned the room with darting eyes. He took up his books and retired to his cabin, sitting at his little desk and lighting a smoking lamp.

He pulled open a little drawer and removed a folded paper. He opened it and read the addresses he had written there that morning, copied from the letters the captain had left on top of his logbooks on Braxton's bureau, which Darby had found while snooping around the officers' cabins. One was the address to the Lee Side Inn in Charlton, the other to a Mrs. Henry Keate in Hatfield, Hertfordshire.

He placed the paper back in the drawer out of sight. Dabbing at his dripping nose, Darby sat back in his chair to polish his spectacles, thinking about the events of that afternoon.

He had watched from the main deck as Gresham had escorted the disguised Mrs. Green to the pier, then caught the next boat across. Following at a distance, he was impressed by Mrs. Green's performance and smirked as she picked her way through the mass of people and obstacles on the walkway.

He'd paused when the other captain intercepted them and Mr. Green turned left up the busy roadway, leading Mrs. Green toward the Clock House. Pacing as the two captains conversed, Darby then froze in happy astonishment when Admiral Warwick himself dismounted a nearby carriage and stopped to greet them.

*What luck! This could not have been more fortuitous!* After the other captain left, the admiral gestured for Gresham to walk with him toward the administration building ahead, and

<br>

Darby could see his captain's hesitation, then acquiescence. *Huh, what choice did he have? Poor Mrs. Green will have to wait a little longer.*

He considered her as he followed the two. He really had nothing against Mrs. Green or the captain, certainly not. They were both quite agreeable, but Darby was strictly a business-man, not at all sentimental, and business was business. Money was also money, and Darby was always in pursuit of it, especially when it came without much effort. He also liked being in business with important people. He was especially pleased to have important people beholden to him. There was no better felicity to his calculating mind than to be indispensable to those in power.

At last, pausing at the steps of the administration building, Gresham saluted the admiral and sped his way back toward the Clock House. Darby did not hesitate to seize his opportunity. Just before the admiral reached the entrance, Darby opened the large door for him and greeted him with an affable smile. "Good afternoon, Admiral Warwick. How providential that we should cross each other's paths just now." Darby saluted and gave the admiral a formal bow. Producing his calling card, he held it out to Warwick, who was obviously annoyed. "May I offer you my card, sir? I believe it may be of great benefit to you. You never know when the services of a well-informed purser may be of use."

Warwick took the card with an irritated snatch, then Darby saluted again and made his way out the door.

✳

"So much impertinence, these blasted pursers. Scoundrels, all of them," Warwick muttered as his secretary held his office door open. Flinging the card onto a pile of reports on his desk without a glance, Warwick turned his attention to his secretary and told him to add an appointment with a Captain Gresham onto his schedule for five o'clock the next day, and for God's sake, fetch him some tea.

# CHAPTER
# FIFTEEN

Hot water, lavender-scented soap, clean hair, clean towels, and a sweet little fire to sit by all felt like sheer bliss. As Sarah sat drying her hair by the warmth of the fireplace, her emotions fluctuated between grateful gladness and doubtful sorrow. Overwhelmingly thankful to God for returning her to civilization, to the comforts of a warm bed and meals she did not have to find and kill to eat, her heart soared with prayers of deepest gratitude one moment, then fell again from the terrible realization of all that Johnathan Gresham was sacrificing for her sake.

*How can I let him do all of this for me? He even proposed marriage to protect me.* She felt the Lord had spoken to her heart to accept his proposal, but how could she take advantage of his chivalrous intentions?

He'd never mentioned love. Plenty of people married without being in love, but was this what he truly wanted for his life? Was it what she wanted for hers?

Her mind had been so muddy before, but now it was clearer. Somehow she must remove herself from him before it was too late, for his sake, if not for hers. But how? Where would she go? How would she manage? She owned nothing and didn't have a half penny to her name. She didn't even know her name. She had tried and tried but had yet to be successful in forcing her voice to move. *Dear Lord, what shall I do?*

As her turmoil battled within, her eyes fell on the small desk in the niche of the dormer window. Tossing her damp hair over her shoulder, she took up the lamp from the table and pulled the window curtain closed. She sat on the little upholstered desk chair and opened the lid, revealing the little nooks and shelves within, a stack of writing paper, and a quill and bottle of ink. Her heart raced as she held up the ink bottle and opened the stopper. Remembering the last time she wrote anything was a desperate plea for help aboard the first ship, which had been found and dearly paid for. Would she be able to hold back the rising panic long enough to try?

She grasped the edge of the desk, feeling the solid wood beneath her fingers. *I am here now. God has brought me up out of the pit, out of the miry clay. Doesn't that mean he still has a purpose for me? The very desk I sit at now is proof enough that he has set my feet on solid ground. I am here now, and like the psalmist, I will sing a new song.*

She bit her lip as she took a sheet of paper and picked up the quill. *Just do what comes naturally*, she told herself and dipped in the tip. That was easy enough, but when it came to placing the tip on the paper, her hand trembled. *Keep it simple.* She fought back the urge to close the desk and return to the fire. *Just write one letter now. Let's start with A*, she coached herself. Then she began. *A. B. C. D. E. . . .* She wrote on until the whole alphabet was traced out on the page.

She sat back with a surge of relief. *Thank you, Lord. I can do this! And now, to write a word, just one word. Let me see now . . .*

*What about the first word of my favorite Bible verse? Yes, that's it!* She wrote the word *And* with success. She continued, one word at a time, until once again she sat back with tears in her eyes as she read, "And we know that all things work together for good to them that love God, to them who are called according to his purpose."

Her hand flew to her mouth. *I did it! I can write! Now I can communicate and converse! I will write them all letters of gratitude right now!* She could hardly control her fluttering hands as she reached for more paper. She licked her lips and tossed her damp hair. Her progress was slow but sure, with only a few blotches of ink smudging away from her. Soon she was blotting her first full page, a letter of heartfelt thanks to her dear friend Mr. Green.

As she folded the letter and wrote his name on the blank side, she smiled to herself as she imagined the little man's face when he read it. Drawing a deep breath, she noticed how open her usually tight chest felt, like being freed from a cage, and she eagerly reached for another page.

It was late when she finished the last of her three letters of thanks. She left them on the table, all folded with the names for whom they were intended: Mr. Green, Dr. Braxton, and Captain John Gresham.

*Good night, dear messengers,* she bid them, knowing her next letter would not be as sweet to write.

Mr. Green tapped softly on the door of the attic sitting room before entering. All was dark and quiet but for the lingering embers of the little fireplace. Green tiptoed to the back bedchamber door and opened it a crack, satisfied that his charge was safe and sleeping. Closing the door, he turned to glance over the room for any stray teacups and such that needed clearing, when he came to the table and spotted the three letters, one addressed to himself, his name written in a beautiful lady's hand.

He looked back at the bedchamber door, filled with solemn wonder. Picking up his letter, he sat next to the fire and held the paper to the light. His hand shook as he carefully unfolded it, gasping to find the page filled. His eyes went straight to the bottom, where there was a signature, *Mrs. Sarah Green*.

Tears rolled down his wrinkled, unshaven face as he sent up a prayer of deepest gratitude. *The dear girl. She has remembered how to write, and she has written ta little ol' me.* He was impeded from reading by tears but at last was able to wipe them away and focus on the words.

He had just finished reading her letter of thanks and dried his face with his handkerchief when there was a quiet knock on the door, and in came Captain Gresham and Dr. Braxton.

Green sprang to his feet, his finger to his lips, pointing at the bedroom door. "She is sound asleep, Capt'n," he whispered.

"What is it, Mr. Green?" Gresham asked. "Are you all right? What has happened?"

"I am fine, Capt'n, I assure ye, but ya must come ta the table, sir, and see for yerselves," and he led them by the light of the lamp to the table.

Gresham and Braxton both gasped at the sight of their names on the letters waiting for them. They exchanged unbelieving glances, and Gresham looked at Green with astonishment. "You mean . . . she . . . These are from her?"

"Yes, Capt'n. I have just finished reading the one she wrote fer me, sir." He held up his refolded page so Gresham could read his name.

Braxton sat down and picked up his letter. "Well now, this is a very fine development indeed."

Gresham reverently lifted his letter to his chest . "I believe, gentlemen, that I would like to read mine in private, if you don't mind. I shall bid you good night. Mrs. Yates has arranged an early breakfast for us up here in the morning." He nodded meaningfully to Braxton, then went to the front bedroom with a candle and closed the door.

Green held a lamp to guide Braxton to his room on the second floor, where they said good night.

⁕

BRAXTON WENT out the kitchen door just after dawn with a warm, buttery bun in his hands and a letter in his coat pocket. He'd had a restless night and didn't feel like wasting anymore time in bed waiting for Mr. Green to wake him.

He ate his roll as he walked, enjoying the freshness of yeasty bread after so many months of stale, hard ship's biscuits. The dewy grass sprang softly beneath his boots, and the sky grew lighter with each step, taking him closer to the river.

Once he reached the small road that paralleled the Thames's shoreline, he stopped to lean on a nearby tree, licked his buttery fingers, and withdrew the letter from his pocket.

He had read it a dozen times already and nearly knew it by heart. But he would read it again and let the words wash over his lonely, parched soul.

My Dear Friend Dr. Paul Braxton,

I must beg for your forgiveness for the way I treated you that first day. I want you to know that my reprehensible behavior had nothing to do with you. My terror and contempt were all buried within me by another. My troubled mind and unreasonable fears blinded me to the man I now know. Please accept my deepest apologies for treating you in ways you did not deserve and for not accepting the great compassion you offered me. I am ashamed and promise to make amends to you in some way, someday.

You have been a steady hand, guiding me back into the light from a very dark place. I know that God brought you, along with the others, to save me, not just in body but in soul as well. There is too much to thank you for on this small page, but I will thank you, from the bottom of my confused and broken heart, for all the kindness, dignity, and understanding you have shown me. To be known, Doctor, to be understood, is the most powerful of medicines, and now, dear sir, please allow me to do something of the same for you.

I have seen you, Dr. Braxton. You are a loyal friend and an honest man who considers the needs of others above his own. You sacrifice little pieces of yourself every day, offering your fellow man more than just medicine and cures, but a balm for the soul.

I have also seen your loneliness, and it is a fearful thing to see. But I will tell you this, that you are not alone in this world, and I will tell you why.

You have the best of friends in John Gresham. His love and respect for you is to be envied. There are few men in this weary world who can claim such a bond. You, dear Doctor, you are the man who has such a friend.

You have my friendship as well. How could you not? And our friendship will last because it was forged in the fires of great adversity. It has already been tested and shown to be sound.

And yes, dear friend, you have the friendship of God,

whether you like it or not. His love for you will never end because it cannot. God's love is eternal and one that you will never win the fight against, no matter how hard you try to lose yourself to despair. No, he will win, and you will know it when he does. Do not fear him, for he is the one who brought us together.

There is much more to say, but for now, I have spoken my gratefulness to you at last.

Sincerely,

Mrs. Sarah Green

PS: How and where is Mr. Thomas Smith?

Braxton blew out a slow breath at the end. She was right. To be seen and known was the most powerful medicine known to man.

He tucked the letter into his breast pocket and turned his steps back toward the inn. Today he would prove his friendship to her once again, and the course for the next chapter of his life would be set.

GRESHAM BARELY NOTICED when Braxton entered the room. His focus was completely consumed by the very solemn Sarah presenting him with another letter. Mr. Green stood by in confusion beside Mrs. Yates, who had arrived greatly disturbed a few moments before with a note in her hands from Sarah, asking her for a position at the inn.

Gresham's chest pounded in alarm as he took the letter from Sarah's hand. "Do you want me to read it aloud?" he asked, his heart full of dread.

She nodded sadly.

He unfolded the paper.

"'My Dear Gentlemen,

I wish I had the time to write to you all that is in my heart, but since time is short, I will get right to the point.

I know that you are all making tremendous sacrifices for me, to ensure my privacy and safety. I have become an enormous burden to you all, and I simply cannot allow you to continue to risk your careers, your livelihoods, and your reputations on my behalf.'"

Gresham stopped and shook his head. "No, no, my dear, this is not right. You must not think of things this way. We are all—"

The look of desperate determination in her eyes caught his heart like a vise. She shook her head at him and motioned for him to continue.

Gresham pleaded with her. "No, I will not continue. You do not understand,"

He was stunned as she took the paper from him and handed it to Braxton to finish reading.

Braxton's face was grim, but she shook his arm pleadingly. Braxton swallowed hard and continued.

"'Therefore, I must take my leave of you today and find my own way from here. Now that I have remembered how to write, at least I have some form of communication to aid me. I will be asking Mrs. Yates if she will take me on as an employee so that I may earn my way and perhaps save enough in time to venture forth toward finding my identity and my family, if I have one.'"

Gresham listened in disbelief and agony. She wanted him to leave her, but how could he leave her now? The thought of separating from her was impossible—she had become his life, his heart, even, he was surprised to realize in that moment, his love.

His heart bled as he watched her looking down at the floor. Braxton read on.

> "I cannot tell you how heart breaking it will be for me to be separated from you all. You have become my safe harbor, but no more. I will trust my future to God and be a burden to you no longer.
>
> You are all the most excellent men that anyone could ever have the privilege of knowing. I will write to you and keep you informed of my progress. Please do not try and convince me to do otherwise. I would not be able to bare it.
>
> The Relentless needs you, and you need her. Be free and go back to her, knowing that you have done all that you can to help me.
>
> Sincerely,
>
> Mrs. Sarah Green"

"Oh no, my dear Mrs. Green!" Mrs. Yates exclaimed. "You cannot mean it. Can you not see how much these dear gentlemen care for you? Do you not understand the true nature of your situation and how impossible it would be for you to separate yourself from the very friends God has put in your life to protect you?"

Mrs. Yates took Sarah by the hands as she spoke, her face bent to catch her downcast eyes. She then turned to Gresham with a pleading glance. "Johnny, have you not told her? Should you not tell her now the true condition of your heart?"

Gresham jolted inside, but before he could respond, Sarah pulled free from Mrs. Yates. She tried to retreat to her bedchamber, but Gresham caught her in his arms and would not let her go.

"Gentlemen, Mrs. Yates," he asked quietly, "would you mind giving us a private moment?"

When they were gone, Gresham guided her to sit with him on the settee and offered her his handkerchief. He sat facing her, silent for many moments, then spoke in a quiet tone. "I understand why you have written this goodbye, and I honor your choice. However, there is something that you must be informed of before you make your final decision."

She was quiet and still. At last her eyes met his, full of questions.

Gresham had never felt such desperation. "Perhaps I should have told you this before and not have waited. I . . . I didn't want to frighten or pressure you."

Her face filled with alarm as he struggled for the right words. "Dear God." He groaned in frustration, wiping his hand over his face. "How I wish I could call you by your true name in this moment."

He shook his head. "What you need to know is this—that I love you, Sarah Green. I need you like the air I breathe. You are part of my soul now. I want you, not a ship, not a career, nothing but you. Please, Sarah, even if you cannot, do not return my love, do not force me out of your life. At least until you know your whole story."

Time stood still. He could hardly bear it as she stared at him without moving. Then she stood to peer out of the window over the desk. He could not stand the suspense.

Standing, he prayed a fervent prayer in his heart, then stepped toward her. She faced him, tears streaming down her face.

"I will honor your choice. But please, Sarah, choose not to send me away. God will give us beauty for ashes."

Her breath caught at his words. She closed her eyes and turned away from him for what felt like an eternity. Finally she swung around, locking her eyes with his, full of surrender, and she held out her hand to him. His clenched chest gave way to an audible moan as he took her hand, then held it tightly to his heart.

"May I stay with you?" His voice cracked with the depth of his emotion.

She lifted her face to him, and looking deeply into his eyes through her tears, she nodded.

"Thank you, God," he cried softly, fighting with everything in him not to take her in his arms and kiss her tears away, "and thank you, Sarah. We will find our way. We will find it together."

# CHAPTER
# SIXTEEN

Gresham and Braxton traveled back to the dockyard from the inn in a hired cab, followed by young Fred, driving his grandmother's wagon.

Braxton expressed his relief when he heard that the talk of Sarah's separating from them was over. "I want you to know something, John, that I have committed to seeing this through, for both of you. I'd had my own thoughts of letting the two of you go your way and finding another path for myself, which will need to happen eventually, but I want both of you to know that I consider you as my family and I am with you, come what may."

Gresham had hardly recovered himself from the events of the morning, and Braxton's statement made him emotional all over again. "My God, Paul," he said with a heavy sigh, "I am terribly glad to hear it. What would we do without you? But are you sure? This could be the end of our naval careers, or worse."

Braxton sat back with a sigh. "I am now, but I will admit

there have been times when I thought I could not bear to go forward. But that has all changed." He waved his hand in front of him. "I can't quite explain it . . . I just feel like myself again."

"Thank God!" Gresham said. "This may prove to be a challenging day to be sure, but we have each other's backs, and that means a lot. I must admit that I am more than uneasy about our meeting this evening with Warwick."

Braxton sighed. "As am I. But let us take one challenge at a time."

Once at the pier with Fred and the wagon, they continued to the ramp across from where the *Relentless* stood anchored. Gresham had promised the lad a tour of the ship, and he took him across in the boat with them. Leaving the boy in the capable hands of Mr. Latch, Gresham and Braxton went below to the wardroom.

Their first item of business was to check in with Mr. Compton on the status of the ship. "Everything is in order, Captain. And this is for you, sir." Compton handed him a thickly folded parchment tied with string. "Here is the confidentiality agreement signed by the crew. I thought you should have it, sir."

"Thank you, Mr. Compton. Your service to me has been exceptional, and I will put in a good word for you with the admiralty. You will make a very fine captain, and I think it will not be long until you get that promotion. I shall be glad to see it."

He did not say a final farewell to Compton, the officers, or crew—or even to the *Relentless*. He didn't want any talk about the fact that he may be prevented from returning, and they could plead ignorance if anyone asked about him.

After collecting the excited Fred and the coffin from the hold, they loaded the box onto Fred's wagon. The next item on their agenda was to engage the services of a doctor qualified to make a legal report regarding the man's remains. Dr. Braxton had once been acquainted with a doctor at the dockyard hospital and had found him the day before to still be employed there.

The only information they gave the examiner was that they had found the body when stopped at an island to make repairs.

Dr. Onslow's findings were much the same as Braxton's. As Onslow washed up in a basin of water, he said, "I'll have a copy of my report ready for you in the morning, Braxton. I don't feel it is necessary to store these remains here so long as the authorities are able to get to them if they deem it necessary."

Once they had the coffin loaded back on the wagon, Gresham informed Fred of the grim contents, then sent him to take it as inconspicuously as possible to his grandmother's stable. Fred left them wide eyed, with a promise not to let Gresham down.

"I am glad to have that business over with." Gresham felt a weight lift from his shoulders.

A young boy selling papers stood along the roadway as they walked back across the grounds toward the administration building. Gresham noted the headline—"London Girls Still Missing"—and bought a paper, tucking it into his coat pocket.

"John, you must not allow yourself to be caught up in all that again. Sarah needs your full attention." Braxton gently but firmly admonished his friend.

Gresham patted his pocket. "Yes, Paul. I only want to see what is happening in the case. I promise you I will not allow myself to be distracted." He meant his promise, but something about these missing girls had touched his heart deeply ever since he'd first heard of their plight.

Pausing on the way, Gresham asked Braxton if he would mind if he said a prayer for them before they went in. He didn't mind, so Gresham bowed his head and quietly, humbly asked the Lord to help those girls, and to give Braxton and him wisdom and discernment as they met with the admiral. Then they marched up the steps of the intimidating brick building.

Gresham felt like he was walking to his own hanging but tried to keep the image of Sarah's lovely face before him. *Please, God, grant us favor with this powerful man.*

✳

ADMIRAL WARWICK's office was a heavily furnished, thickly carpeted room. The walls not covered by large paintings of ships in battle were lined with bookcases and displays with model ships, antique swords, and pistols. Warwick sat in an enormous leather-bound chair behind an equally imposing oak desk, looking over the documents in his well-manicured hands.

Gresham and Braxton stood at attention and saluted as he waved at them without looking up. "Yes, good evening, gentlemen. Do sit down."

They took their seats.

The admiral heaved a dramatic sigh, placed the documents on a stack of papers to the side, and pulled his chair close. "Well, now, Captain Gresham, good to see you again. And this is?"

"May I present to you Dr. Paul Braxton, ship's surgeon for the HMS *Relentless*, Admiral. He has also brought a special report for you, sir. We thank you for your time and attention to this unique and troubling matter."

Warwick propped his elbows on the desk, the gold brocade on his cuffs gleaming as he touched the tips of his fingers in front of his aging face. "Well, Captain, you have my attention. What is this troubling matter?"

Gresham sat forward on his chair, "Well, sir, I received orders while anchored at Port Royal, Jamaica, to return to England immediately. We sailed from there to the north and were just passing the Bahamas, when a sudden squall in the dead of night caused us considerable damage. The next day an uncharted island was sighted, and we anchored there to collect the necessary timber and make repairs."

Warwick was attentive but blinked his eyes as though unimpressed.

Gresham hurried on. "It was on the tiny island, sir, that we made a very unusual and distressing discovery."

Warwick eyed Gresham soberly.

"We found a grave, sir, with the remains of a man sewn into a Royal Navy–issue hammock and buried in the ground, a small cross at the head of the grave."

The admiral crossed his arms over his blue gold-trimmed coat and motioned for Gresham to continue.

"Yes, sir. Dr. Braxton here has made a thorough examination of the remains and found some interesting anomalies."

Gresham looked to Braxton to continue.

He sat forward and cleared his throat. "Yes, Admiral. If you please, sir, I have it all written here," and he offered his report to the silent man behind the desk.

Warwick took it and flipped over the first page. Pursing his lips and grunting occasionally, he scanned the pages, stopping now and then to read in detail. "Well, it is an interesting find indeed, gentlemen." The admiral grunted. "Clearly this man was murdered, from what I see here. And the hammock, urine stains, yes. Fingers missing, blow to the head, curious indeed. But it will be next to impossible to solve the mystery of this man's strange death and burial with no clues as to his identity." Warwick opened a desk drawer and dropped in Braxton's report with a nod of approval before turning his attention back to Gresham. "I take it that the body is not all you found, Gresham?"

Gresham sat up straight and set his face like flint. "That is correct, Admiral. We also found the dead man's wife." Gresham paused. "Alive."

Warwick bent forward and cocked his wigged head. "Excuse me, Captain, but did you just say you found a woman, this deceased man's wife, alive on this island?"

"Yes, sir. She had been victimized as well, sewn alive into a seaman's hammock, and left there to die." Gresham laid his report on the desk as he kept his tone informational, trying not to betray his inner turmoil.

Warwick tapped a finger to his lips and huffed. He leaned on the leather arm of his chair in contemplation. Gresham and Braxton exchanged a quick glance. Finally Warwick opened yet another desk drawer and withdrew a whiskey bottle, then produced three small glasses. He said nothing as he poured the golden liquor into each glass, setting one before each of them and taking up his own, sipping with narrowed, distant eyes.

When Gresham and Braxton hesitated to take their glasses, Warwick broke his silence. "Please, gentlemen, I am sure that bringing me such a tale has put you in as much need of a drink as I am in hearing it." He motioned for them to take up their glasses.

Gresham, who preferred wine to hard liquor, sniffed at the pungent alcohol, then took one sip and swallowed, feeling the heat travel to his stomach.

After a few moments, Warwick asked, "And in what condition was this woman when you found her?" He swirled the golden liquid in his glass.

Braxton spoke up. "She was extremely thin, malnourished, but remarkably well in spite of the circumstances, sir."

Warwick gazed at the doctor from the corner of his

narrowed eye. "And her mental condition? Was she in her right mind?"

Gresham spoke up. "She was frightened of us, of course, as her assailants were also officers of the Royal Navy." And there it was, the dangerous truth, shot like a cannonball across the admiral's bow.

Warwick set his glass on the table and leaned forward on his forearms, clasping his hands before him on the desk. A menacing cloud fell over his stern face, the curls from his long gray wig swishing forward, casting shadows. "Do you mean to tell me that the man or men who perpetrated these hideous crimes were officers of the Royal Navy?"

"Yes, Admiral," Gresham answered. "We believe they were a naval ship's captain and the ship's surgeon of a third-rate Arrogant class, seventy-four gunner, sir."

"You 'believe,' but you do not know for certain?" Warwick sat back, glaring. "Gentlemen, these are most serious accusations to be making against your fellow officers. Let us be extraordinarily careful of not stepping out of line based solely on conjecture." Warwick's face was hard and full of warning.

"Indeed, Admiral. As to the assailants being a ship's captain and surgeon, the lady has confirmed that is the case, sir, but as to the exact identity of the men, that is still in question."

Warwick's patience was clearly waning, but Braxton interjected before he was able to speak. "You see, Admiral, the lady has suffered from amnesia and has not been able to remember the name of the ship or the men who assaulted her and her husband. In fact, she does not currently remember her own name or where she is from, sir. She has been through a terrible ordeal."

Warwick returned to sipping his whiskey, ruminating. "And where is this lady castaway now?"

"She is staying with a family friend in Charlton, sir. We thought it best for her privacy to keep her out of the public eye. She does not deserve to become a newspaper scandal. She is a very well-mannered and religious woman who desires only to find and be safely reunited with her family." Gresham felt his edges fraying under the pressure to make this powerful man understand her plight.

"Well," Warwick said decisively, "she must be brought to the dockyard hospital at once and examined by the naval doctors. The navy should take custody of her until she can recover her memory and her family are found. And if what she says is true and these men do turn out to be officers of the Royal Navy, then the navy must take on the responsibility of finding them and bringing them to justice." Warwick plunked his glass down firmly.

The admiral ignored Gresham's move to speak. "I see that the two of you have requested a four-month furlough. Have you any thoughts as to what will happen to the *Relentless* during your absence?"

*This is an interesting change of course*, Gresham thought. "Well, sir, as I have yet to be informed of why I was requested to return to England, I am not sure what the admiralty has in mind for her."

"There have been issues with Barbary pirates attacking merchant ships in the Mediterranean, and the thought was to send you there to help clear them out, but seeing as you have requested this leave, and from our records, you are due the time, I have in mind to send the *Relentless* under another's command." Warwick was playing cards, and the *Relentless* was his ace.

Gresham felt a knife twist in his gut. "That is very reasonable, Admiral. May I suggest that you keep her current complement intact, sir, and promote my first lieutenant, Mr. Timothy

Compton, to command her in my absence? He is able and worthy and knows the *Relentless* by heart, sir."

Warwick sighed impatiently. "Hmm, yes. I will take that into consideration. Your furloughs have already been granted. I signed the paperwork earlier today. Did my secretary give you the documents when you came in?" His tone had become almost too amiable, and Gresham took note.

"Yes, Admiral, thank you."

"Well, gentlemen." Warwick rose from his chair with a forced smile, and Gresham and Braxton followed suit. "Thank you for your reports. I should like to meet this castaway of yours when you bring her to the hospital tomorrow. I assure you that everything will be done to help her," and he rounded the desk to shake their hands.

"There is one last thing that you should know, Admiral." Gresham ever so slightly resisted being hurried out, and Warwick paused before opening the door.

"Yes, Captain, what is it?" Warwick glowered at Gresham.

"The lady and I are engaged to be married, sir." Gresham braced himself but was undaunted. His commitment had been made, and he was unmovable.

Warwick's jaw dropped. "Dear God, man, have you lost your mind? Marrying a woman with no name and no family? For all you know, she might be mad!" Warwick's professional demeanor had completely left him.

Though jarred by his superior's rebuke, Gresham played his last card. "I am convinced that she is not, sir. She has accepted my proposal. So you see, sir, there will be no need for the navy to take custody of her, as she will be well cared and provided for."

Warwick's eyes narrowed as he jerked the heavy door open. "Well then, Gresham, I see that congratulations are in order. I wish you and your betrothed all the best, of course."

"Thank you, Admiral. And thank you for your time. I will send you news if there are any further developments, especially if the identities of these criminals come to light. I personally would like to see them pay for what they have done."

"Oh, indeed, Captain," Warwick growled. "So would I."

# CHAPTER
# SEVENTEEN

The vase of Mrs. Yates's yellow roses brought a splash of color and lovely, sweet scent to the attic sitting room. Sarah sat basking in their beauty at the little desk, in her midshipman's uniform. Her eyes turned to the dormer window, as a new reality pulled at her heart. Gresham's confession of love had sent a thrill through her, and she certainly had great affection for him, but she did not trust herself to claim she was in love. She was much too apprehensive, and she wanted to know that he loved her for who she was, not only because she was a woman in distress.

So too, she wanted to be sure that she was not consenting to marry Gresham only out of desperation. Still, something deep inside her had changed with the knowledge that someone loved her, and she sat for a moment and let her heart pour out her gratitude to her Lord.

She remembered the day of John's proposal and how fervently she had prayed for wisdom and discernment. Hadn't she heard God's still, soft voice whispering the answer to her soul? Indeed, he had spoken, and his answer was clear. "It will be difficult, but it will also be good. I will give you beauty for ashes."

What joy had filled her aching heart at those words! *And now,* she thought, as she looked down on the blank page before her, *I must trust in the Lord and lean not unto my own understanding.*

When she finally dipped her quill in the ink, a new question came to her. *What can I communicate that would be most helpful? I know—I shall write everything I can remember. Perhaps there may be more clues to find in what I already know.* She began with her first memory, being greeted on the poop deck of the tall ship of the line by its terrible captain.

✳

It was after six in the evening when Gresham and Braxton rushed in the door. Gresham hurried to Sarah as she whirled from her chair at the desk.

He laid his hands gently on her shoulders, his face full of urgency." I am sorry to startle you, my dear, but we must gather our things and leave at once!"

She shook her head questioningly.

"There is no time to explain, but Braxton and I met with Admiral Warwick, and as we left Woolwich, we doubled back and discovered we are being followed by a couple of brutes."

Her eyes went wide, but without hesitation she gathered her pages from the desk and ran to her little bedchamber to pull out her carpetbag. Gresham had done the same, but instead of placing his items by the door, he came barging into her room and threw them onto the bed. She watched in surprise as he took a chair and stood on it, reaching to the ceiling over the wooden wardrobe. He found a latch and opened a hatch over his head.

Braxton, Mrs. Yates, and Mr. Green had all crammed into the little room as Gresham reached behind the wardrobe and produced a narrow wooden ladder and attached it to some hooks on the opening, resting its bottom on the floor. Finally he stood, panting, looking bleakly at the faces before him.

"I've been such a fool," he whispered, shaking his head in regret. "I should have anticipated this. I am so sorry."

Sarah shook her head and offered him her bag.

"Just a moment, my dear. We must wait for a signal from Fred before we go." He turned to Mrs. Yates with sorrowful eyes. "My dear Mrs. Yates, I assure you I had no idea our coming to you might put you at some kind of risk—"

"Oh shush, Johnny. This is nothing. I am only sorry that you and Mrs. Green must leave me so soon." Mrs. Yates hugged him tightly with a firm kiss on his cheek. "You must write me and keep me informed. I shall be worried sick until I hear from you."

Gresham nodded. "I promise to send word as soon as I can. Mr. Green, I suppose this is goodbye for now. You have your instructions and the money I gave you? Are you sure you are up to the task?"

"Aye, Capt'n. We'll see this thing through now, won't we, Mrs. Green?" His eyes misted with affection when Sarah took his hand. "I will miss you so, ma dear. I shall see ya as soon as I am able, and we can write ta each other now, can't we?"

Sarah abruptly opened her carpetbag. She held out her ivory-handled knife to Mr. Green with a wistful smile.

"Oh, no, ma dear," Green protested. "Ya must keep this—it may be important or come in handy!"

"No, Mr. Green," Gresham said. "I think it a brilliant idea that you should have the knife if Mrs. Green is willing to part with it. It may be of help as you search for its original owner." Gresham nodded to Sarah with appreciation.

"All right, but if ya should ever require it, I shall return it to ya posthaste." Mr. Green accepted the formidable knife from her and held it securely to his chest.

"Braxton," Gresham said, "Mrs. Yates will hide you tonight until you can be smuggled out with the coffin. Send messages ahead and let us know how things are. And don't forget to collect that report from Dr. Onslow."

Sarah took the doctor's hand.

"I shall miss you as well, Mrs. Green, but I will join you soon, I promise." Braxton bowed, and Sarah patted his shoulder affectionately.

She dug into her bag again and withdrew the folded pages she had just placed inside, handing them to Braxton.

Scanning them, Braxton shot her a look of comprehension. "You've been writing your memories?"

She answered with a knowing nod.

Mrs. Yates once again engulfed Sarah in a warm embrace. "Farewell, my dear Mrs. Green. I am sorry to part with your delightful company so soon, but we shall meet again, I am sure of it! Go with God, my dears."

"Since we are still waiting for Fred's signal, I would like to ask the Lord for safety." They all huddled in a circle, even Braxton, and Gresham prayed, "Lord God in heaven, we beseech you for your favor and divine intervention. Please, Father, grant us your angels to protect us and give us safety as we leave this good place, and keep those who remain safe as well. Amen."

Just then a pebble was thrown into the hatch opening—Fred's signal it was time to depart.

Gresham climbed up the ladder and lay flat on the shingled roof. Braxton handed up the bags and thrust his hand out to Gresham, sharing a knowing look, then helped Sarah ascend.

She grasped his hand tightly. His eyes filled with shiny tears as he helped her up.

Looking back down the hole, they waved goodbye, and Gresham closed the hatch.

She gave him a firm little nod, and he led her crawling along the roofline, then dropped down onto the kitchen roof and helped Sarah down. Gresham glanced around and saw Fred at his post at the corner of the stable. He led her stealthily to the edge of the inn's roof and stood. Tossing the bags over the gap to the stable roof, he knelt and whispered in her ear. "We will have to jump, Sarah. I'll go first and help you catch your balance when you land."

She looked at the distance, calculating, then nodded with confidence in her eyes.

Turning to stand on the roof's edge again, he winked back at her and lunged, but a broken shingle came loose under his foot upon landing, causing him to lose his balance, his arms flailing as he fought to keep from falling.

"John!" Sarah cried out, then clasped her hand over her mouth.

Gresham righted himself and stared over at her in astonishment. Their eyes locked in amazement, mouths gaping, then smiling in wonder as they remained still, listening to see if Sarah had been heard.

A moment passed, and Gresham planted his feet and motioned for her to jump, which she did without hesitation, flying over the gap and landing light as a bird.

He embraced her quickly, then crawled again to an open hatch in the stable's roof and assisted her down the ladder. Gathering their bags, he hurried her to the open window in the back stall, where Fred waited to help them into the closed carriage outside.

CHAPTER

# EIGHTEEN

The air from the open windows grew heavier as they traveled west. John pointed out the way to Sarah through Greenwich, then north into the East End of London. She concentrated hard to see if anything seemed familiar, to no avail, but she tried not to let her frustration ruin her relief at being away from the dockyard.

The late-summer sky dimmed as they rode, and Sarah was disappointed to lose the enjoyment of the scenery. Though there were dim streetlamps, there wasn't much to be made out in the inky darkness as night fell.

The lack of light was made up for by their conversation. Sarah sat beside John, feeling both relief and awe of her new ability to speak, though every time she opened her mouth, there was still a flash of dread she would have to push past. Her voice was weak and broken from disuse, and she could barely talk above a whisper, but the fear subsided more with every word or phrase she pushed out.

A wide mix of subjects were covered, some happy and

some utterly disturbing. Sarah would shut her eyes hard, clenching the side of the seat as she told John the memories she had written on the pages she'd left with Braxton.

"Sarah"—John met her eyes with gentleness—"you do not have to share these things with me now. Perhaps it is too soon yet."

"No, John," she responded. "Please, I need to get all this out in the open between us. I . . . I hope that it will be helpful somehow."

John took her hand. "I am listening. But there is no rush. Only tell me what will make you feel better for me to know."

Each sentence grew a bit easier to speak, if more painful to tell.

John stirred in his seat as he listened, clenching his jaw. "Dear God in heaven, Sarah, how could you endure it all? What terrors you have known. It is a marvel you not only survived but have not gone completely mad." He turned to face her. "Is there another woman in the world like you?"

Sarah sat back in her seat, her gaze falling to her lap. She felt what must surely be a crimson stain from her neck to her cheeks. "I am afraid, John. My feminine dignity has been wrenched from me." Flooded with embarrassment, she asked meekly, "What if I am incapable of fulfilling my . . . my wifely duty to you? What if I am unable to . . . to—"

John squeezed her hand. "Hush, my dear. We will leave that in God's hands for now, and when we are married, you will find me a patient man. I shall not force myself upon you, nor ask for anything you are not willing or able to give. We must trust the Lord to be our great physician in all things, even this." He tilted her chin up and held his face close to hers. "Sarah, promise me you will not be ashamed of yourself because of what was done to you."

She tried to push back in protest, but he insisted on an answer. "Promise me, Sarah. Promise me now."

Tears sprang to her eyes as she relented. "I promise, John. God has promised me beauty for ashes. I will choose to believe him, even in this, but, John, would you be willing to wait for me, at least until we know my real name?"

His brows rose, but he answered easily, "Of course, my love. That would be very appropriate, but I will wait even longer if need be. I promise not to touch you until you are ready, but I will also let you go if that is what you wish in the end."

***

AFTER SENDING his men to follow Gresham and Braxton, Admiral Warwick poured himself another whiskey and put his feet up on his desk. He sniffed the malty liquor and took a large sip, swirling the smooth vanilla liquid around in his mouth before swallowing its heat. "Well, well, now. What a peculiar situation we have on our hands." He spoke aloud to himself, resting the cool glass against his sagging cheek. "And what shall we make of this, Admiral? Yes, what shall we do?"

He pursed his lips before taking another swig. Swinging his legs down and placing the glass on the desk, Warwick pushed his chair back and opened the door. He found his secretary still sitting at his tall desk. "Mr. Wilson!"

The young man jumped. "Aye, Admiral."

"I want you to find out where the HMS *Peleus* is immediately." Warwick thumped back into his office, slammed the door, and returned to his glass.

"So, my dear captain, it looks as though the winds have changed." He sat forward and tapped the tips of his fingers. "Now we shall see who has the advantage—you or me."

There was a knock on the door, and he sat up. "Enter!"

His secretary entered with a document. "The HMS *Peleus* is on its way to England, Admiral. Returning from the West Indies. She is due to dock here and should arrive within a week, I should say, if the weather holds, sir."

"Capital, Wilson, that will be all. I'm heading home now."

"Good evening, Admiral," and with a salute and a formal bow, the man left the admiral poring over the document with satisfaction.

※

THE JOURNEY to Hatfield required them to stay at a coaching inn on the outskirts of London overnight. The next morning Gresham told Sarah she no longer had to wear her midshipman's uniform, and she arrived at the breakfast table in her green-skirted gown and an eager look on her face. Before long they were on the road again. How he was enjoying her company and learning more about her.

Gresham noticed that after she had told him the details of her horrific ordeal, she seemed lighter, freer. He was mesmerized by Sarah's voice, her laughter. How good it was to hear her laugh after all she had been through.

"Do you realize," she asked, "that we have never really had a proper chaperone?" But before he could answer, her face shadowed with a different question. "John, you were so troubled when we were leaving the Clock House yesterday. Is that where Meredith was when you last saw her? You were lost for a moment, and your face was full of a terrible sadness."

Gresham dropped his shoulders.

"I killed her, Sarah. I should have stayed with her and watched over her that day instead of leaving her alone on theOse steps. I have lived with the guilt of that day and have been searching for a means to make it right ever since."

Sarah lifted eyes full of compassion. "But you did not kill her. You must believe that. Oh, John, please. You must forgive yourself and give this terrible burden over to the Lord. If God does not condemn you, then you go against his will in condemning yourself."

He stiffened and sat up straighter, a multitude of thoughts racing through his mind. After much consideration, he said, "I have never thought of it that way before. You have expressed a different way to view my self-condemnation, and you are right." The profound revelation startled him. "How is it that this has never occurred to me? Have I really spent all these years fighting against God's will?"

She smiled up at him. "You must give this to the Lord and let him carry it for you. Besides, is it not God who holds the number of our days in his hands? You did not have the power to change the number of Meri's days on this earth. She is in the loving arms of her Lord now. Be at peace, for she is resting in the arms of Peace himself."

He gazed at her, stunned, then out the window. The sting of tears smarted his eyes, and a lump grew in his throat. A few hot drops escaped as he released his burden with silent prayers. Finally he wiped his face. "Forgive me, my dear, for crying like a child in front of you."

She shook his arm. "No, John, you have cried the unspent tears of a little boy whose heart has just been freed from a terrible pain."

He looked at her with new appreciation. "God knew, Sarah . . . he knew I needed you to give me this word of wisdom. Thank God for you!"

"And thank God for you, Captain Gresham, for without you I would surely not have lived to see this blessed day."

✳

It was dark when they reached the ancient village of Hatfield. Gresham told Sarah what he knew of its rich history and the church where his brother-in-law, Mr. Henry Keate, was the rector.

"St. Etheldreda's church has been here for centuries. It is named after an Anglo-Saxon saint. And then there is Hatfield House, once the residence of Queen Elizabeth, and part of the old palace still stands to this day." Gresham pointed out locations he knew as they turned off the Great North Road and started down the hill on Fore Street, the steep main street of the town, lined with shops, all dark and quiet. Near the top of the street, on the left, stood the stately church, and next to it the old vicarage. The carriage stopped on the gravel drive outside the front door of the house.

The lanterns by the entrance were lit, and Sarah could make out the outline of the large and welcoming country house. She was surprised at how grand it was for a rectory, with its lovely gabled roofs, white stucco walls, and well-kept grounds. She smiled at the sound of crickets humming. Light streamed out the large windows, and the smell of the rose bushes and freshly cut grass added to its inviting aspect.

They had barely left the carriage when the door was flung open, and a tall lady and not-quite-so-tall gentleman came out to greet them.

"Oh, John! You are here. You are really here at last! We received your letter this afternoon, and I could not believe it!" The lady was just shy of Gresham's height, with glossy brown hair, slightly touched with gray at the temples. Under her white cap, her dark-blue eyes were the twins of her brothers', glowing in the lamplight. She wore a pale-peach cotton gown and white muslin chemisette over her stately figure, and an embroidered shawl draped over her arms. She embraced her brother exuberantly and kissed his cheeks, then stepped back with a mixture of concern and pleasure on her lively face.

Gresham took Sarah's arm and brought her forward. "Penny, Henry, may I present to you my betrothed, Mrs. Sarah Green. Sarah, this is my sister, Penelope, and her husband, Reverend Henry Keate."

The gentleman offered Sarah an amiable smile and outstretched hand. "Welcome, welcome to Hatfield, Mrs. Green. We are honored to have you here. John has told us about you in his letter. We have so much to talk about!" He was neatly dressed in black breeches, with a white shirt and cravat, charcoal waistcoat, and black tailcoat. His pale-blue eyes twinkled at her from behind his round spectacles, and his balding head was rimmed with graying hair.

Sarah gave him her hand and curtsied, "Thank you, Mr. Keate. I am most happy to be here." Sarah spoke as loudly and smoothly as she could.

"Oh! Oh my goodness!" Penny exclaimed. "You can talk! But, John, you told us Mrs. Green was unable to speak!" Her eyes were wide and wondering.

"It is a brand-new miraculous development that has only just happened late yesterday, Penny. Isn't it wonderful?" Gresham's eyes shone with pride in the dim light.

"Well, that is very good news indeed! My dear Mrs. Green, it is my greatest pleasure to meet you. You are most welcome, most welcome." Penny shook Sarah's hand warmly. "Please do come in out of the night air. John, did you get this poor girl anything to eat on your way? You must be famished!" Penny escorted Sarah by the arm into the entryway and paused. "Now, let us take you up to your rooms and let you freshen up —no need to change if you are not inclined. I can help you get settled, and we'll go down to the sitting room and get better acquainted, shall we?"

They were led up the wooden staircase and down the hallway on the right. Penny brought Sarah into the last bedchamber on the left, followed by Gresham and Henry carrying their bags. "I call this the Blue Room. I thought you might enjoy being in the corner with the view from two sides. In the morning you will see the church behind the house and the field to the south, between us and Back Street."

Sarah stood at the foot of a beautiful four-poster bed with a blue satin coverlet and ruffled pillows. She reached out to touch the smooth cloth. She stared as if in a dream. Also gracing the space was a large wardrobe, a desk under the east window, and two chairs with blue-striped upholstery and ornately carved wooden arms.

She heard Gresham speaking to her and came back to herself.

"Mrs. Green has been so long away from civilization. Are you all right, my dear?"

"Oh, Mrs. Keate," Sarah said wistfully. "What a beautiful room! Please forgive me . . . I can hardly believe I am here,"

"My dear Mrs. Green," Penny cooed. "How much you have gone through. Run along, gentlemen, while I help our honored guest get settled." Penny waved the men out and took Sarah by the hands. "Mrs. Green, I want you to know that the rector and I, once we received John's letter, went straight to our knees to pray for you. It is incredible to know only some of your story, and even more astounding to know how the Lord has orchestrated everything and brought you to this very house. What a miracle!"

Sarah's heart warmed. How sweet to hear these kind words.

Penny's age was only betrayed from time to time when she

furrowed her brow. "I offer you my sincere friendship and hope that you will feel completely at home here." She squeezed Sarah's hands. "May God continue to bring you comfort."

Sarah sighed. "Oh, Mrs. Keate, I—"

"No, my dear, let us dispense with formality. Please call me Penny, or sister, if you like."

"And you shall call me Sarah, until we find my real name." She returned Penny's squeeze.

"Thank you. I shall. Now let us unpack your things. Oh! I forgot to tell you that your other luggage arrived today. Is there anything you would like to have brought up?"

"No, thank you. This is really all I have in the world." Sarah took the carpetbag from the floor beside the door and placed it on the bed.

"Good heavens! But this is nothing!" Penny gaped at the pathetic bag.

Sarah smiled shyly as she opened it and drew out its meager contents.

"But, my dear girl, how have you gotten along with so small a wardrobe?"

"Well," Sarah said uncomfortably, "when John found me, I had very little in the way of clothing, and he was kind enough to have his sailmaker make me what I am wearing now. I was exceedingly grateful to have something, anything to wear."

Penny looked Sarah over carefully. "Good heavens! Well, that was very nice indeed, essential that these were made for you, but this will never do, Sarah. We must go to the shops tomorrow and get my dressmaker, Mrs. Dunham, to make you something immediately! We have much to do!"

Penny's mouth turned down, and she paused in awkward silence for a moment. Finally she said in embarrassed tones, "Oh, forgive me, Sarah, but, well, a thought has just occurred to me. How long has it been since your late husband passed, my dear?"

Sarah blanched. "Oh! Well, I am not exactly certain. I was on the island for over four months, that I know, but . . ." Her voice dropped off as heat suffused her cheeks.

Penny's face softened. "Please forgive me, my dear, for my impertinence, but it is custom for widows to wear mourning black for the first year after their husbands have died, and I was just thinking about what would be appropriate in your case—"

"Oh!" This thought had never crossed Sarah's mind, and she was ashamed of herself for not thinking of it before. "I . . . I had forgotten all about that—"

"Well, let us give it some thought, and we can discuss it later. For now"—Penny plopped her hands on her hips—"let us go down and have our little meal and make our plans, shall we? Are you ready?"

"I am. Thank you, Penny." As they left the Blue Room, Sarah's heart filled with misgivings. What else had she forgotten about such things?

Just as Penny stepped out of the room, she stopped and paused, then slowly turned around to Sarah with another look of deep concern.

She looked down at her clasped hands and said softly, "There is one more important issue I . . . I am, that is . . . has my brother told you anything about what happened to our younger sister, Meredith?" Her eyes raised to meet Sarah's, full of worry.

Sarah's heart squeezed with empathy. "Yes, Penny. Your brother has been completely forthcoming about Meri's death and what he feels his role was in it." She offered her hand to Penny, which was warmly taken. "I am terribly sorry for your loss and believe God is helping John to forgive himself for what happened. It seems to have haunted him all these years since."

Penny patted Sarah's hand affectionately. "I am glad to hear it, Sarah. I have been praying for him for years now to allow God to heal that awful wound." She let go of Sarah's hand and stood straighter. "I am proud of him for revealing himself to you. It was a horrible tragedy, but my brother was only a boy." She shook her head regretfully. "Our family was never the same afterward, but God is our healer. I hope that John will finally be able to allow God to take on his guilt."

Sarah gave Penny a small smile. "I believe he may be doing just that." She hoped with all her heart it was true.

THE FOUR OF them sat comfortably at the round table near the open windows of the well-appointed sitting room. The scent of flowers wafted in on the cool night air from the garden outside. The upholstered furnishings, the wooden mantel with a beautiful painting of a country landscape, the heavy brocade curtains with their lacy sheers, and the plush carpets spoke of the artistic sensibility of its occupants. There was a depth of comfort without being pretentious, and Gresham had always found himself at home here.

There were platters filled with cold meats and cheeses, fruit and warm bread, and the red wine had been poured. Gresham filled his plate and lifted his glass, "Thank you, my dear sister and brother-in-law, for your generosity in welcoming us under such hasty and unusual circumstances. May God bless you for your kindness."

Henry's eyes crinkled with affection at Gresham behind his spectacles. "The pleasure is ours, I assure you, John. You know this is your home when you are on land, and we are always happy to have your company, but to meet your lovely betrothed, Mrs. Green, now that is a delight beyond words. We had lost all hope in ever seeing you wed."

Penny touched her husband's hand. "Now, Henry, Sarah and I have already agreed to forgo formalities and be known by our Christian names, isn't that right, Sarah?"

"Indeed, Penny. And I would be ever so grateful to you, Rector, if you would call me Sarah as well." She gave the man across from her a shy smile.

*How lovely she is, and how blessed am I to have her sitting at my sister's table beside me.* Gresham was still in wonder about his spiritual experience in the carriage. Where did Sarah's incredible gift of wisdom and insight come from?

"But of course," Henry agreed. "I am quite happy to be a part of this arrangement. Besides, I am sure we will all be intimately acquainted before long. Now, John, you had much to say in your letter, but I am sure there is much more to tell. Please proceed, as your sister and I are sitting on pins and needles."

Gresham finished a slice of peach, relishing its sweet juiciness. "I have already written to you all the major points, so I will tell you what has happened since yesterday," and he filled them in about having the body examined and the meeting with Admiral Warwick.

When he informed them about being followed and how they had escaped, Penny's eyes went wide. "Good heavens, John! I remember that hatch in Mrs. Yates's roof, and the distance between the inn and the stable. Are you telling me that you actually made Sarah climb up there and jump like a schoolboy? Sarah! How could you face the height, the expanse?" Penny frowned disapprovingly at her brother. "John, how could you possibly put a lady in such a position?"

Gresham smiled and laughed, half at the familiar look on

his sister's face, but the other for how little she knew about his beautiful fiancée's abilities. He held his hands up in surrender. "I will let Sarah explain it to you, sister! I am not the cad you make me out to be."

Sarah's smile dimmed. "It was no trouble at all, Penny, for you see, in order to survive on the island, I"—the smile faded completely, and her eyes fell to the table—"I had to climb trees, and so, you see, the roofs and jumping from one to another—"

Gresham saw her falter and regretted making light of her terrible ordeal. "I am sorry, my dear," he said softly and then turned to Penny. "Sarah has been through more than we can imagine. She had to fend for herself, relying purely on her own wit and physical abilities, with the help of God, just to make it from one day to the next." He took her hand. "She is the bravest, most intelligent and wise woman I have ever known."

Henry bent forward and spoke tenderly. "My dear lady, please forgive us for our presumptions. Surely yours is the most harrowing story we have ever heard, and we hope you will be patient with us as we try to understand—"

Sarah interrupted him, "No, please do not apologize, sir. I mean, Henry. I—"

Gresham could see the color rising on her face and took over. "It is all right, Sarah. I am the one who needs to apologize." He set his half-eaten plate aside. "This is a very serious situation, as you can see. The crimes perpetrated against Sarah and her late husband are of the most severe nature, and I am determined to do all I can to protect her from any further harm."

Henry took Penny's hand. "Yes, and we will join you in that effort, won't we, my dear?"

"Yes, yes, of course." Penny's eyes moistened as she gazed at Sarah. "I am so sorry, Sarah. The Lord has brought us all

together, and we must rise to the task he has set before us."
She switched her gaze to her brother. "So tell us, John—what
needs to be done?"

Gresham set down his wineglass and pulled his chair in
close. "We must be married immediately, before the navy or
these horrible men have a chance to find her. I explained to you
in my letter what might happen if Sarah is taken into custody
by the navy. Our meeting with Admiral Warwick and his
subsequent surveillance confirmed my suspicions in that
regard. I believe it is only a matter of days before they find out
where we are, and if Sarah is not my wife by then, it might be
too late." John tried to convey his urgency to them. "We
desperately need your help, Henry. I will need to obtain a
license here in Hatfield tomorrow and ask that you marry us on
Sunday morning at the church after the service."

Henry gaped. "My, my, that is soon indeed, John, faster
than I had anticipated, for Sunday is the day after next. Have
you stopped to consider? You cannot supply Sarah's real name,
and there are grave consequences for registering a marriage
license with false information. It would not only compromise
you and Sarah but also myself and your sister's reputations,
perhaps our livelihood."

Penny faced her husband with troubled eyes. "But, Henry,
have we not just this moment promised to do all we can to
help them? We must not make decisions based on mere
reasoning alone. No, we must pray, Rector. We must seek God
first, mustn't we?"

Henry smiled and gave a low chuckle. "Once again, my
dear, you have preempted me. Of course you are right, and we
will ask for God's wisdom and guidance, but we must also
count the cost of our actions and be prepared for the consequences."

Gresham nodded, grateful for his brother-in-law's insights.

"I have considered all of the possible consequences on my part, and I am resolved. Please, Henry, will you consider? I hate to put you and Penny in any danger, but I have no one else to turn to."

"Of course, John, but there are also more concerns." Henry tilted his face toward Sarah. "You will please forgive me, Sarah, for any discomfort I may cause you by this discussion," then he sat back and focused again on Gresham. "There is also the fact that Sarah's late husband has been gone less than a year. She has been through a terrible ordeal to be sure, but propriety would dictate that she be in mourning for a full year before remarrying."

"Of course, Henry." Gresham's frustration grew. "But this whole situation has been well outside the bounds of propriety and social norms the entire time. Besides, Sarah must be protected. What will become of her if we do not marry?" Gresham continued in earnest, "Thank you, brother-in-law, for your wise counsel, but I feel it is well past the point of discussing what would be proper in the eyes of a world that has no claims on us at all."

Henry sat back quietly and gazed with concern at his wife.

Penny joined in. "Well, yes, dear, Sarah and I were just discussing whether it would be more appropriate for her to dress in mourning black, as her station as a widow would require, but this is a rather unusual circumstance, is it not? Perhaps considering the danger Sarah is in, we should forgo these man-made obligations and do what is best for Sarah's safety."

Gresham's insides tied in knots as he looked at his poor fiancée. "Sarah, what are your thoughts, my dear? I am anxious, as you know, to guard you from harm, but you must be free to choose what is right by your own conscience."

Sorrow and confusion played across her beautiful face. "I

. . . I am not sure what to think. I—" She turned desperate eyes to Gresham. "Oh, John, I am so sorry to be so much trouble to you all. I don't know—"

Tortured by her distress, Gresham asked her, "Will you let me decide for you, Sarah? I will tell you, if it were up to me, I would put aside all of this nonsense and not waste another thought on it."

"Hear, hear, John!" Penny cried. "I must agree. We must not forget that even our Lord Jesus did not pay attention to such ridiculous rules in his day." Standing, she marched to Sarah's side and took her hand. "Sarah, please forgive me, us, for putting this false virtue before your safety. Henry, do you not agree?"

John stood as the rector rose and joined them. Henry offered his hand to Sarah, now in tears, and helped her to her feet. "I too ask your forgiveness, my dear, for my thoughtlessness and vanity. We are in agreement. You should not be required to submit yourself to the rules of society in light of the terrible abuse and loss you have suffered at the hands of evil men."

Gresham's heart nearly burst as Henry leaned over to catch Sarah's eyes. "I am ashamed to have added to your sorrow in this way. Will you forgive me?"

A small sob escaped as Sarah fought to speak. "Yes, Rector, of course. Thank you," she whispered.

"It is a very difficult situation, Henry," Gresham said. "Your reactions are understandable."

"Dear Sarah, my poor girl." Penny moaned, wringing her hands. "What pain you have suffered, and to think we have added to it. I am so very sorry."

Sarah wiped her tears with her handkerchief. "No, please, you must stop apologizing. Your intentions were only good and proper." She gave them a tender smile. "God has been so kind and generous to put me in the company of such caring people."

Henry shook his head, his eyes distant. "The ways of the Lord are most mysterious. I promise you both that Penny and I will fervently pray for his guidance and will give you our answer about performing your wedding in the morning."

Penny rallied. "Now dear family, it is getting late, and we have much to do on the morrow. Let us retire now and have an early breakfast, for we must plan our strategy."

# CHAPTER
# NINETEEN

Sarah placed the fragrant red apple into the pocket of her pettifore, then tossed her long, wavy brown hair back over her shoulders. She grasped the top railing of the fence and stood up on the lower, bending over and calling to the shaggy Shetland pony on the other side. Removing the apple, she held it out to him.

"Come on, boy. Come and get this lovely apple I have for you," but the pony was not enticed and swished his tail as he offered her his backside.

"What a stubborn pony you are!" she called after him, laughing.

Hearing the chatter of other children, she turned to see a heavily laden apple tree with a dark-haired boy sitting in its branches. He was picking the best of the apples and tossing them down to a beautiful little girl, her blond curls swaying down her back to her waist, giggling as she tried to catch the tossed apples in the lap of her upturned pettifore.

Sarah's heart leaped when the little girl turned to her, a

dazzling smile on her smooth, young face, her clear blue eyes dancing with delight.

Then Sarah woke up.

She bolted upright in her bed and tried to remember where she was. Her heart pounded as she searched the dawn-lit room. Feeling the silky-smooth satin of the bed coverlet and smelling the scent of lavender brought her back to the old vicarage in Hatfield. She threw off the covers and tried to calm her heart as she splashed her face with water from the wash bowl.

Feeling somewhat recovered, she pushed open the curtains, revealing the green field beyond, lit pink and blue by the soon-to-rise sun. She sat at the desk and gazed out at the beauty, trying to remember the details of her dream.

Inspired, she took a blank page from the stack on the desk and drew out a pencil from the little drawer. Closing her eyes, she sought out the lovely child's face smiling at her, then she popped her eyelids open and began to draw.

It was only minutes before she sat back and held up the sketch to the increasing light. Looking at her from the page was the very likeness of the little girl from her dream. Sarah almost sobbed out loud, and tears filled her eyes. "I know you! I feel it in my heart. Somehow I know your face!"

Sending up a prayer of gratitude, she dressed quickly. The night before, Penny had slipped some of her own items into the room to add to Sarah's sad little wardrobe. She found a hair-brush, stockings and garters, ribbons and sashes, a pair of short white gloves, a lacy white cap, and a lavishly decorated green bonnet with pink satin rosebuds. Two lovely shawls now hung from the hooks inside the wardrobe, along with a satin beaded reticule. Penny would have given her some gowns to wear as well, but their differences in height and stature precluded it.

Sarah dressed up her gown with a rose-colored sash and paused, grateful yet still feeling guilty about not wearing black. *Why?* she asked herself. *Why do I not want to wear black to honor the death of my husband? Shouldn't I? Why do I not feel like the grieving widow I should be?*

It was a perfectly honest question that she needed to find the answer to, but when she glanced again at the drawing of the young girl, she forced the question to the back of her mind for later.

She swept up her hair hastily, donned the white cap, then threw a white shawl over her shoulders. Taking a quick glance in the long mirror, she smiled at her glowing image as a tingle of warmth raced through her limbs. *Lord, is it wrong for me to feel this way?*

Pushing the thought further back, she took the drawing from the desk, rolled it carefully, and tucked it into the deep pocket of her skirt. Then she tiptoed down the hall and was surprised by her groom-to-be, shaved and dressed, pulling on a bottle-green tailcoat as he stepped into the hall.

"Good morning!" John whispered, giving her a wide smile. "You look like an angel!"

"Good morning, and what is this? Where is your captain's coat?" She straightened his cravat and tugged on his collar.

"I am on leave now and not required to wear it all the time. Besides, I think it best not to be immediately identifiable as a naval captain just now." He gave her a wink and tucked her hand under his arm, steering her toward the stairs.

"What are you doing up so early?" he asked.

Sarah smiled up at him in excitement. "I had a dream! A beautiful dream. And I have something to show you."

"That's wonderful! Let us go out the back and take a little stroll, and you can tell me all about it."

They greeted the cook on their way past the kitchen and

opened the back door to the garden. The air was fresh and smelled of dew and damp earth. He guided her through the gate, then into the churchyard, and they slowed their steps, gazing up in admiration at the ancient gray-stone building.

John pointed out the intriguing aspects of the church, but Sarah stopped and tugged his arm. "I would love to hear all there is to know about this place, John, but I am afraid I am just too excited to wait."

Releasing his arm, she stood before him, full of earnestness. "I had a dream, John. I can't remember the last time I had one!"

He looked down at her with new interest. "Oh! I didn't know. Forgive me. Tell me all about it," and he led her to a stone bench.

They sat together, and she told him about the dream in detail.

When she finished, she removed the paper from her pocket and unrolled it. "Look, John, I was able to draw her exact likeness. Isn't she wonderful?"

John took the paper, his mouth dropping. "Sarah, you drew this? It's exceptional." His voice was soft with admiration.

"Yes, just after I woke up. I know this face, John. I don't know how or why, but I recognize this sweet little girl!" She beamed at him.

"Well, then . . ." He stood and gave her his hand. "We shall have to find her, won't we? Come, let us see what the Lord has spoken to my sister and Henry, and show them this fantastic drawing of yours!"

✳

WARWICK PACED BEHIND his leather chair. His hands behind his back held a crushed piece of paper. He had just received a message that Gresham had outwitted him and was nowhere to be found. Eyes full of fire, he threw the message into the bin and walked to the window facing the River Thames.

Throwing open the sash, the sounds of the teeming dockyard burst upon his ears as the briny air caught in his flaring nostrils. Looking over the ships anchored near the pier, his eyes rested on the HMS *Relentless* at the western end of the dock. "I will give you something to think about, Captain Gresham," he murmured to the world.

Shutting the window roughly, he strode to his desk. Removing Gresham's and Braxton's reports, he slammed them down on top, drumming his fingers on them.

He then opened the office door. "Mr. Wilson! I will speak with you."

The young man came with his notebook in one hand and saluted with the other.

"Aye, Admiral. How may I be of service, sir?"

"I want you to send a message to the *Relentless*. Get me her first lieutenant, Mr., uh, I don't remember the name. Just bring him to me at once. I wish to speak with him."

"Aye, Admiral, at once, sir." Wilson rushed from the room.

Warwick growled as he shuffled through the pile of papers in the box on his desk. Just then, there was a knock at the door. Looking up with hot irritation, he paid no heed to the calling card that fell from the side of the papers in his hand onto the floor and under the corner of the desk.

"Enter!" Warwick threw the papers back into the box and flipped the reports over.

"Captain Baker is here for his appointment, Admiral."

Warwick lowered himself impatiently on his chair and waved his hand. "Show him in. But I want to know as soon as the lieutenant from the *Relentless* arrives."

"Aye, Admiral," and the captain was shown in, much to Warwick's chagrin.

✳

GRESHAM BEAMED as he handed Sarah's sketch to his brother-in-law at the breakfast table.

"This is a marvelous drawing, Sarah," Henry said between bites of toast. He and Penny had already said they'd had full confirmation in their prayers and would do all they could to help the couple, much to Gresham's relief

"Isn't it amazing, Henry? And she drew it from memory just this morning." Penny tapped the shell of her soft-boiled egg with a little silver spoon. "You have some talent, my dear! And you say that this girl is familiar to you?"

"Yes! I am sure that she means something to me." Sarah sipped her tea with a far-off look in her eye. "I only wish I could remember why, or at least remember her name."

"You say you were also a child in your dream, and there was a boy as well. Perhaps they were childhood friends, or even siblings," Gresham offered as he enjoyed his salty ham and eggs. He was greatly pleased to see Sarah so happy and hoped this dream would be the beginning of her memories coming to the surface.

"Perhaps they are. I wish I could tell for certain." Sarah took the drawing Henry passed to her and smiled down on the child's image.

"I am sure that the Lord will reveal it all to you in his time." Penny's faint crow's feet crinkled as she smiled and patted Sarah's hand. "I still say that you have shown yourself a gifted artist."

"Oh, it is only a simple sketch." Sarah laid the page carefully aside and helped herself to more strawberry jam.

Shaking his head in amazement, Gresham remarked, "I'd say it's a great deal more than that. I cannot draw anything! You are full of surprises this morning, my dear."

Gresham's mind was already at work, wondering about his fiancée's newfound skill. "I know we have much to do in town today, but the shops will not open until ten o'clock. Sarah, would you be willing to try your hand at another sketch before we go?"

"Of course, John. What would you have me draw?" Her eyes twinkled at him.

Gresham had someone in mind but did not want to ruin her happy morning by mentioning him. No, he'd start with something less disturbing. "Braxton will be arriving today. What about surprising him with his portrait?"

Sarah set down her fork and wiped her mouth. "Why, what a splendid idea. Won't he be surprised. I don't know if I shall succeed at capturing his likeness, but I shall try."

"Wonderful. That's the spirit!" A safe subject to see how she would do.

In a quarter of an hour, they had adjourned to the sitting room, and Sarah sat at the table, paper, and pencil before her, and her eyes closed. John sat on the settee with his back to her, and his sister and the rector sat on the divan opposite him. He exchanged suspenseful glances with them as they waited, quiet and still.

Gresham was strangely nervous. He fought the strong urge to watch over her shoulder but had promised he wouldn't. He looked at the clock on the mantel—ten minutes passed nine o'clock. He could hear the clock ticking and the sound of her pencil scratching against the paper.

"All right, I think I am finished. It is the best I can do for now. Perhaps I can work on it a bit more when we return from our errands." She ambled to Gresham and handed him the page.

He peeked at the clock—twenty passed nine. Only ten minutes. He looked with amazement at Sarah and motioned for her to sit beside him. When she was seated, he aimed a glance at Henry and Penny, then flipped over the page.

There he was, his stalwart friend Dr. Paul Braxton. "This . . . this is remarkable, Sarah," he said incredulously . "It is not only his likeness, but you have captured his personality as well. I . . . I am—"

"Oh, John, how can you leave us in such suspense!" Penny made her way behind the settee to stand behind her brother, and Henry joined her, peering at the drawing over Gresham's broad shoulder.

They gasped in chorus. Henry took the paper carefully from Gresham's hands. He and Penny studied it with open mouths and wide eyes.

"But this is astonishing, Sarah!" Henry looked both over and through his spectacles with raised brows. "It is Braxton to the tee!"

"I can hardly believe my eyes!" Penny laid her hand on Sarah's shoulder and smiled down on her. "God has given you a gift, Sarah!"

Gresham, sat sideways and stared at her. "It seems that I am about to marry a talented artist on the morrow." He shook his head. "You are a walking wonder, my dear. A walking wonder."

*

THE QUARTET EMERGED from the old vicarage in fine form. Gresham had admonished them, especially his sister, to be discreet and not to draw any undue attention. He had also supplied Sarah with a substantial roll of notes, much to her surprise. "You are not marrying a poor man, Mrs. Green, and I want you to buy anything, and I do mean anything, you like today. You need so much, Sarah, and I am grateful and glad I have the means to take care of you in some amount of comfort and fashion."

From the drive of the old vicarage at the top of the hill, they stepped out onto Fore Street and started down the walkway. The town was alive with activity. Shoppers and businessmen bustled along, coming and going, and carriages and carts made their way up and down the steep, narrow street. Hatfield was a charming town, and its main shopping lane shone in the morning sun.

Sarah held tightly to Gresham's arm and shivered with nervous anticipation. "I am so anxious, John. I cannot remember how things are done at drapers and dressmaker shops." She was grateful to have the loan of Penny's green bonnet, both to shield her eyes from the sun and to hide her embarrassment.

"Do not worry, my dear. You are in the hands of the best shopper I have ever known, Mrs. Penelope Keate." Gresham winked at Sarah and covered her hand with his.

Penny pulled Henry with her as she neared them. "What's that, John? Did I hear my name mentioned?"

Gresham chuckled. "Yes, dear sister, I was just extolling your virtues to Sarah."

"Oh really? And what virtues might you mean, may I ask?" Penny smiled mischievously under her bedecked yellow hat.

"Only that you are the best shopper I have ever known, with the best taste I have ever seen, and that Sarah need not feel awkward with you in charge." He gave Sarah a playful grin.

"Well, John! I do believe that is the nicest compliment you have given me in quite some time. I humbly thank you, brother," Penny chirped. "We have much to accomplish today. We have a wedding in the morning to prepare for as well as taking care of Sarah's wardrobe. Oh, here we are already." She stopped in front of the next to the last shop on the south side of the street. "Now, Sarah, this is the shop of Mr. Sharp, the draper. We are most fortunate in Hatfield to boast of two excellent drapers. Come, dear—you shall judge for yourself."

A bell over the door jingled as they stepped in, and Sarah blinked, waiting for her eyes to adjust from the brightness outside. When her sight cleared, she gave a slight gasp. The shop had a high ceiling, and the walls were covered in shelves and cabinets. There were rolls and bolts of colorful fabrics, gauzy white muslins, heavy satins, delicate silks, and flowing lace panels. Here and there fabric was draped from the higher shelves in waterfalls of color, texture, and light. To Sarah's great relief, there were no other customers in the shop.

GRESHAM AND HENRY kept their distance, allowing the expert to take charge. Henry stood close to Gresham and spoke quietly. "She is the most intriguing woman I have met, besides your sister, of course. But I wonder, John. Why on earth would any man wish to harm such a lady? I am still struggling to make sense of it, as I am sure you are."

Gresham nodded in somber agreement. "Let us see if Sarah feels comfortable enough for us to leave the ladies here and be about our business. It will not take long. We can gather them from here and escort them for the rest of the day."

He cleared their plan with the ladies, then stepped with Henry back out onto the street. By the time the gentlemen returned, Gresham found Sarah bewildered from all the decisions to be made, and shocked at the amount of fabric it took to dress one average-sized woman. Gresham paid the bill, then led their ladies out into the sunshine again.

After fulfilling Penny's list of necessities at the haberdashers across the road, they moved up the street toward the boot maker's shop. Halfway there, Sarah halted and was drawn to a shop window. Inside was a display of antique jewelry lying on red velvet, surrounded by an assortment of hanging lamps, brass candlesticks, and gold-framed portraits in miniature.

"Oh, Sarah, that is just the pawnbrokers, my dear. They will not be any use to us for what we are shopping for today," Penny said as she and Henry continued to stroll up the walkway.

Gresham wrapped Sarah's arm around his again and peered at the display with her. "See anything you like, my dear?"

She smiled shyly, blushing under her bonnet. "Look at all of these wonderful old treasures, John. Aren't they glorious? I just love old things. They have stories to tell, you know. Can you imagine what tales that pocket watch would tell if only it could speak?"

Her eyes were shining like gems when their eyes met. "I know we don't have any time to go in today, but will you bring me here again, John, when time allows? Just to look around?"

"I promise, my love," and he fought hard against the temptation to kiss her long and deeply, right there on the sidewalk. "Now, let us see about getting you some proper shoes, shall we?" They advanced toward the boot maker's shop.

As they turned to enter, Gresham looked back. He took note of the sign above the door and its symbol of three gold balls hanging from the iron hook above the door. S. G. Lawrence, Pawnbroker and Antiques.

# CHAPTER
# TWENTY

Braxton entered the old vicarage with Gresham that afternoon. Gresham called for Sarah and the others, and Sarah came lightly down the stairs, looking lovelier than ever. Braxton held out his hand to her with a grin, but she kissed him on the cheek instead of taking it. He blushed with pleasure. She looked so well and happy, and he was glad to see it. He was relieved to be with them again and had much to tell them.

"I am exceedingly glad to see you, Dr. Braxton," Sarah said with a smile. "We have missed you, haven't we, John?"

Braxton didn't even here Gresham's answer, he was so caught up with the sound of her voice, speaking to him and saying his name.

"It is good to be with you both, and Mrs. Green, to hear you speaking! It is music to my ears!"

They were interrupted by Penny and Henry greeting him with an affectionate welcome. "Now, my dear doctor," Penny chimed. "Soon you will have tea and catch your breath a bit before we get you settled."

Braxton nodded. "Thank you, Mrs. Keate. I will readily accept your refreshments, but I am afraid there is a rather pressing matter outside that John, the rector, and I will need to address before partaking. Gentlemen, would you mind? Please excuse us, ladies."

They went around to the stable, where a man with a wagon stood holding the reins of his horse. They helped unload the plain wooden box from the back and placed it in the corner of the stable. After Gresham paid the driver, the three men gathered beside the box.

"So this is the poor fellow, Sarah's late husband." Henry placed his hand on the top and shook his head. "What a tragedy. How terrible to wind up like this, a young married man, a beautiful and talented wife, to be so brutalized and treated with such outrageous indignity."

Braxton leaned against a wooden post and crossed his arms. "Indeed, Rector. These two have suffered unspeakable things, to be sure. The question now is, what shall we do with him? Have you made any plans, John?"

"I would like to see him get a proper burial as soon as possible and was hoping that Henry might be able to help us find a place for him." Gresham looked questioningly at his brother-in-law.

"I am afraid it is not a simple matter," Henry replied. "I must apply for permission with my superiors in such a case, if he is to be buried here, because he is not a resident of the parish, but that will take some time."

"Time is definitely a problem on many fronts." Gresham rubbed his neck in frustration. "What if there were a place his remains could be stored, a safe place where no one would be able to disturb him until we can find the proper place and time?"

"Hmmm, that could be the answer for the short term, John.

I have an idea, but it will have to wait until after the wedding tomorrow."

"I am much obliged to you for everything, Henry." Gresham shook Henry's hand.

"God works in mysterious ways, my dear brother, and this is mysterious indeed!"

⁕

TIMOTHY COMPTON RETURNED to the *Relentless* after a disconcerting interview with Admiral Warwick. He had never been interviewed by an admiral before and felt like the meat had been picked off his very bones. In addition, he had made a disturbing and providential discovery while sitting in front of the admiral's rather intimidating desk. It made his blood boil even more than Warwick's interrogation.

As soon as his boots landed on the main deck of the *Relentless*, the officers on board saluted him as the boatswain piped out the tune informing all on deck that the captain of the ship had come aboard. Compton stopped, startled, and a cheer went up from the crew as the officers saluted and offered him their hearty congratulations. He waved an unsure hand in reply, then turned back to the group of officers, noting that Mr. Darby was not among them. "Well, gentlemen, I see that news has spread rather quickly. I would like to have a conference with Lieutenant Latch, Sergeant Evans, and Master Mackenzie in the stern cabin, immediately, if you please."

They saluted as one with a chorus of "Aye, Captain," and the three requested followed him on his way to the gun deck.

The men stood in the stern cabin, solemn and hushed, as they awaited their first orders from their new captain.

Compton threw is bicorn hat on the desk and motioned for the men to take a seat. "I have just had an interview with

Admiral Warwick." He paused, considering his words. "First, well, you already know that I have been named captain of the *Relentless*, and we have orders to sail to the Mediterranean immediately."

The men around him exchanged glances but remained silent. "Admiral Warwick was most curious about Captain Gresham's whereabouts and peppered me with questions about Mrs. Green. As I am not privy to all of Captain Gresham's plans, I was able to avoid revealing too much, thank God, but he was adamant that I should have no further contact with him. A strange request. He has ordered that every single man in the crew's complement before we docked should be returned and that we are to sail for the Mediterranean on Tuesday."

At this, the men gasped, and Mr. Mackenzie was the first to speak. "Tuesday, Captain Compton, but how will we be stocked and the men returned in time to leave with on such short notice, sir?"

"We must do all we can to be ready and sail no later than noon. If we are not sufficiently supplied when we sail, then we will be able to complete our stores at the Port of Malta." Compton turned to Mr. Latch and held out his hand. "And now, congratulations, Mr. Latch, on your promotion to first lieutenant."

Latch stood to attention and saluted. "Thank you, Captain Compton. I am deeply honored, sir."

"Very good, Latch. And now, do any of you happen to know where Mr. Darby is?" He searched their faces in turn.

Mr. Latch spoke up. "He is due to return anytime now, Captain. He has been making purchases at the dock warehouse and having his goods loaded, sir."

"Thank you, Mr. Latch. I want you to locate Mr. Darby at once and bring him to me. It is a matter of great importance."

"Aye aye, Captain!" Mr. Latch saluted and left the room hastily.

Looking grimly at the others, Compton spoke with a low growl. "There is a traitor among us, gentlemen, and I'll be damned if I will allow him to continue to serve on this ship."

❋

THE GENTLEMEN FOUND Penny waiting alone in the sitting room when they returned from the stable. "Sarah has just run upstairs for something, gentlemen. Now here is our tea. Please come and sit here, Doctor."

Braxton sat and sighed with relief. "I am terribly glad to have that part of the adventure over with." Reaching into his breast pocket, he pulled out a folded paper and handed it to Gresham. "I was able to obtain that list for you, John. Perhaps you would like to show it to Sarah after tea?" He was apprehensive about showing Sarah the document, as it contained the names of all the Royal Navy ships' captains currently serving on Arrogant class ships. How he wished they could all have a few days to rest and recover without every hour having to rush into the next.

Sarah returned with something wrapped in her hands and a shy smile. Braxton felt his heart flutter briefly, but with a brotherly kind of affection.

"Sarah has a surprise for you, Paul." Gresham smiled with anticipation.

"A surprise? For me? Well, I can hardly imagine," Braxton gushed, feeling awkward.

"Yes, my friend. This is for you." Sarah laid the package before him.

"Well, I am indeed surprised, Mrs. Green. It looks to be the size of a book—is it?" He was so unaccustomed to receiving gifts, he hardly knew what to do or say.

"It is not. Now please call me Sarah and open your gift."

He pushed his spectacles higher on his nose, darted a quizzical glance at Gresham, then shook his head in bewilderment as he pulled off the brown paper.

It was a picture frame, and the back was toward him. When he turned it over, he froze, full of shock and disbelief. He was looking through the glass at himself, accurately captured, his features, his typically serious affect, even his spectacles were perfect. Sitting back in his chair, he fumbled for the right words.

"I am utterly, completely . . . to tell you the truth, well, where on earth did this come from? This is amazing!" He tore his eyes from the portrait and looked around at the happy faces watching him.

Penny burst forth with the answer. "Sarah drew it for you just this morning. Isn't it wonderful?"

Braxton's wide eyes flew to Sarah's. "You drew this? From memory? I am indeed impressed. Sarah, you have real talent." His head fairly whirled at this new development. "When we were on the ship, you would not even attempt to draw or write, and now, in just two days, you can write, speak, and draw. It is extraordinary!"

"Yours is not the only portrait she drew this morning. Show him, Sarah," Gresham encouraged.

"John was kind enough to run out and purchase us these nice frames," she said, holding up the portrait of the little girl. "I had a dream last night, the first I can remember, and this little angel was in it. I know her somehow. Not her name or who she is to me, but I know her face. Isn't she lovely?"

Sarah offered the picture to him, and Braxton marveled over the face peering back at him. She was perfect, the very idea of a beautiful child. Her eyes had the slightest hint of Sarah's, and the shape of her young face made him want to reach into the glass and touch her cheek. "I am speechless." He shook his head in awe and handed the frame back to Sarah.

As she placed it back on the table, a dark shadow crossed over her face, and she shifted in her chair toward Gresham. "John, there is something that I must do. I will need some time alone in my room. Do you mind excusing me?"

"Are you all right, Sarah? You are suddenly serious, my dear." Gresham directed a look of concern to Braxton.

"I am quite all right, but there is something I would like to do that may be of some help." She gathered the picture of the little girl and excused herself.

"What could be troubling her, John? Do you think I should go to her?" Penny asked anxiously.

"Would you, Penny?"

"Certainly. If you will excuse me, gentlemen, and please, finish your refreshments."

DARBY STOOD BEFORE A SMALL DESK, facing his new captain with his hat in his hands. Compton did not immediately look up from his writing but eventually sat back and looked Darby over with a cold eye.

"You may leave us, Mr. Latch, and please close the door behind you." Compton tossed his quill onto the desk. "Excuse me, Mr. Darby, but I do not recall receiving your salute when you entered my quarters. Perhaps you have already forgotten that I am the captain of this ship now."

Darby resented the condescending tone in Compton's voice. He had never heard him speak so before. After he saluted, he ventured, "Yes, I just heard. I congratulate you,

Captain Compton. I am sure that Captain Gresham will be relieved to know that his beloved *Relentless* is in such capable and familiar hands," and he gave the young man a short bow.

"Yes, thank you, Mr. Darby, and now, you will be wondering why I sent for you so urgently." Before Darby could answer, Compton continued. "I have recently returned from an interesting interview with Admiral Warwick, and I have something rather distressing to discuss with you." He reached into the pocket of his waistcoat and withdrew a small card and handed it to Darby.

Darby's face fell as he recognized it at once. "Oh, well, yes, this is my card. If you please, sir, where on earth did you find it?" He shoved the offending thing into his breast pocket and took out his handkerchief reflexively.

Compton bent over hard on the desk and glared sideways at him. "In Admiral Warwick's office, that's where."

"Oh, well. That is surprising. I wonder how in the world it got there?" Darby's mind swirled. *He has nothing on me, this ignorant upstart.*

"You gave it to him yourself, Mr. Darby, and told him he might be interested in the services of a well-informed purser." Compton's eyes narrowed, and he stood, shoving the chair roughly under the desk.

"I beg your pardon, but I did nothing of the sort! I have no idea how the admiral came to be in possession of my card!" Darby's red nose ran in earnest, and he blew it with a loud vengeance.

"That is not what *he* said," Compton said coolly. Reaching into the desk drawer, he removed a folded paper and again handed it to Darby. "I'd like to know why you happened to have this piece of paper with this information written in your own hand in your desk drawer, Mr. Darby. You have no right to have this private information in your possession."

Darby was still shaken by what the admiral himself had told Compton. Seeing the note with the two addresses was completely unacceptable. Darby felt the red from his nose spread to the rest of his face, and he puffed out his chest.

"You took this from my private cabin! You had no right to look in my desk for anything, you . . . you arrogant welp!" Darby was stunned by his own words. "Oh, no, I didn't mean that, Captain. I am terribly sorry. I don't know what came over me—"

Compton glowered down on him as he strode to the door. "Mr. Quist, I want you to take Mr. Darby down to his cabin and have Sergeant Evans post a guard. I do not want Mr. Darby to leave his quarters until I give further orders, is that clear?"

"Aye, Captain. Perfectly clear, sir!"

JUST BEFORE DINNER, the ladies emerged from Sarah's room and came down the stairs together. The men rose when they appeared at the sitting room door.

Gresham saw Sarah's face was pale and somber, and she carried a stack of papers in her hands.

"I am so sorry to have kept you waiting, but I hope these will prove to be useful." Sarah placed four drawings onto the pale-yellow tablecloth. "If you do not mind, I would like to show them to you here before we go in to dinner."

They gathered around.

"These are the faces of the men who attacked me and murdered my husband." She pointed to the two drawings labeled "Captain" and "Doctor." "And this is the man who gave me the knife. I have much more to tell you about him. And this"—she picked up the last page with a sorrowful glance—"this man was my husband."

Gresham's gut clenched as he took the page from her hand. His heart stilled as he took in the handsome young man with thick, wavy, dark hair and long sideburns. His brows were dark and thick as well, and his light-colored eyes were rimmed in black lashes, his lips full and unsmiling. He had the look of a gentlemen, but though his jawline was strong, something in his expression bothered Gresham, something weak and spoiled.

He said nothing as he laid the portrait back on the table. Braxton had picked up the doctor's portrait and was studying it intently. Henry held the drawing of the black sailor, and Gresham took up the portrait labeled "Captain."

His blood ran hot in his veins as he held up the man's image. So this was the savage who'd ravaged and tortured, killed and left for dead this innocent woman and her husband. *This is the face I shall see when he meets his Maker, hanging from a gallows.* Gresham's body tightened as he studied the face. *I will find you, Captain. Oh yes, I will find you, and you will know the taste of justice.*

"John!" Penny said loudly, and the spell was broken. "John, Sarah is speaking to you—did you not hear?"

"Oh, I am sorry, Sarah. What were you saying?" He was sweating and had to force his fingers to loosen their grip on the page.

Sarah took the picture from him and set the drawings aside. "I said, I would rather not look at them anymore tonight, if you don't mind. I am hungry after all that concentration." She smiled softly and took his arm.

"Yes, of course. Henry, will you lead the way?"

THE CARRIAGE PULLED up to the darkened doorway of an old warehouse just west of the London Dock on the River Thames. The dimly lit alley smelled of brine and fish, the light of the few streetlamps reflected in the black puddles on the road, and the sound of men arguing made its way around the smoke-stained buildings on the street above. The driver hopped down from his seat and placed a wooden step under the carriage door before opening it.

Admiral Warwick would hardly have been recognized to anyone not intimately acquainted with him. He wore civilian clothes, and his balding head, rimmed with graying stubble, looked too small for his body without its curled wig. Stepping hastily from the muddy road, he ducked into the shadow of the doorway, removing a shiny silver key tied to a crimson red ribbon from his coat pocket. After several tries and many ugly words, the door finally opened, and he shut it securely behind him.

Feeling his way to the shelf inside the door, he found the tinderbox and lit a taper. Holding it out before him, he found an old, dirty lamp and lit it. The light revealed a large room filled with old pieces of furniture covered in dust, broken barrels, and coils of thick rope in piles here and there. The smell of must and dead rodents filled the admiral's flaring nostrils.

Holding a handkerchief over his nose and mouth, he picked his way to the back of the room. There he set down his lamp to push aside a large broken bookcase standing against the filthy wall, revealing a narrow staircase leading below. Warwick coughed, wiped his sullied hands on his coat, and retrieved the lamp.

He proceeded down the steps to stand before a locked door. Here he brought forth his key again, this time having quicker luck with the lock. Entering the dark and deadly quiet space beyond, he locked the door behind him.

The dim light revealed something quite different from the space upstairs. Warwick gave a sardonic half chuckle and moved easily toward a carved wooden table. He lit the lamp there, doubling the light, which further illuminated what was a clean and well-furnished drawing room. Tables and chairs for card players, plush red leather couches and chaise lounges, elaborately patterned Persian rugs, and a well-appointed dining table adorned the area. Gold-framed paintings hung beside rich tapestries on the walls, but there were no windows to be seen.

On the wall to the left was a large, menacing door with iron hinges and a small barred window, but Warwick turned to the right, lighting more candles along his way, to a small room enclosed in the corner of the space. Its door had a lead glass-beveled window, and Warwick cursed when he found it locked. "Blast you, Granville." He growled. He retreated into the parlor, looking here and there. His narrowed eyes landed on a pair of tall, heavy brass candlesticks standing beside the dark fireplace on the far side of the room.

His boots left clumps of mud on the expensive carpets as he made his way there. He grasped one hefty candlestick and carried it back to the door in question. First he used it like a club on the lock, with no success. Then he held it over his head and smashed it with all his strength against the leaded-glass window. This showed greater promise, and he slammed the window again and again, weakening the leading between the glass planes, and finally, with one last mighty swing, sent the candlestick clean through the smashing glass and metal. Using his handkerchief to shield his hand from the shards, he reached his arm over and turned the knob on the other side of the lock.

SYDNEY F. GREY

Warwick paused to wipe his sweaty brow and take up a lamp before opening the door with defiance. At last he was inside the small office. Ignoring the crunch of the glass under his boots, Warwick set the lamp on the desk and went behind it, muttering to himself. "Now I shall find you out, you filthy scoundrel. You cannot hide from me."

He searched the desk drawers thoroughly. He ignored the pistol and ammunition, the collection of odds and ends, but looked long and hard at every scrap of paper he came across. He then turned his attention to the tall cabinet against the wall.

The cabinet was locked as well, but Warwick picked up his abandoned candlestick and attacked it until the doors flung open with the force of his blows.

The boxes of glass medicinal bottles tinkled when moved. More boxes were filled with surgeon's tools and leather restraints, some stained with the dark brown of old blood. Warwick threw these boxes down with disgust. "You sick animal," he snarled through his clenched teeth. "I knew you were a demented man, but I had no idea how much and to what lengths you would go to satisfy yourself."

Warwick turned his attention to the drawers below. There he found, under a pile of other papers and charts, a large leather satchel tied with a leather thong.

"Ah, what do we have here?" Warwick held the leather to his nose and sniffed the edge. "I believe I smell the sweet scent of victory." He chuckled low as he sat behind the desk.

He unwound the thong and opened the case. Inside were many pages and letters, which Warwick removed and fanned out over the top of the desk. There were invoices and receipts, ledgers and calling cards, but the thing that interested him most were the letters of correspondence.

He opened the bottom desk drawer again and brought

222

forth an amber bottle of Scottish whiskey. He broke the seal and pulled the stopper out with his teeth, spitting it across the room, then drank long and hard.

One by one he read each letter and studied every envelope and postmark. He sorted them out into different piles as he progressed through them, snorting and chuckling now and then. Though he took a draught from the bottle between pages, his patience waned. He went from reading every word to merely scanning the pages as his frustration mounted. "No, no, no!" he shouted at the desk. "These are all well and good, but I want something personal, something that will make him squirm."

Shuffling through the remainder of the unread letters, he came to the last few and stopped. Placing them triumphantly before him, his eyes glimmered in anticipation. The first letter he lifted before his smirking face had come from Jamaica. The return address was from a Reverend Horace Bunting in Queen's Town, which Warwick knew to be in the heart of many major sugar plantations. "Now, what on earth is a man like you doing with a letter from a Jamaican rector?"

He unfolded the page.

Dear Captain Granville,

I am happy to write you that I would like to offer your brother, Mr. Robert M. Granville, a position in our Queen's Town parish missionary organization and will look forward to accepting him and his new wife into our community, as we seek to help the Negro slaves in our care. With the Prince Regent's recent approval and the new directives given by the Church of England allowing for the teaching of Negro slaves to read and write, I am sure that your brother's added efforts in this endeavor will not only increase the number of slaves we are able to teach but also the number of souls we may reach for the glory of God and his kingdom.

I am in your debt for recommending your highly qualified brother and look forward to seeing you again when you bring him and his wife to our fair island.

May the Lord bless you with safe travels and a speedy return from England.

Sincerely,

Mr. Horace Bunting

Rector, Queen's Town Parish, Jamaica

Warwick laughed out loud, rocking with delight in his seat, the rector's letter in one hand and the bottle of whiskey in the other. "Now this is more like it!" Laying the letter aside, he turned to the next envelope, which was larger and thicker than the others. Reaching in, Warwick muttered, "Hmmm, oh, lovely, lovely indeed."

He held in his hand a black notebook, a record of debts owed to many accounts by a Mr. Robert M. Granville. The corners of Warwick's mouth rose as he turned the pages and read the names of those to whom the debts were owed. At the end of the last page was a large totaled sum. "Well, well. The little brother you despised had a terrible gambling problem, thanks to your influence. Ha-ha! Now I see his desperate need to flee from England to a more tropical climate. You are a clever man indeed, Granville."

Laying aside the notebook with the rector's letter, Warwick studied the broken wax of the seal on the last letter. "Oh yes, and this will be from your beloved father, I presume." Warwick sat back and planted his mud-stained boots on the desk. Drinking the last swig from the bottle, he threw it hard onto the glass-littered floor with a satisfying crash and opened the letter.

224

Dear Felix,

I am overcome with disappointment at your brother's recent marriage, and even more so by the news from you of his scandalous accumulation of gambling debts. I was not aware that he had developed such detestable habits while attending seminary at Cambridge, which you know I disapproved of from the beginning. I would have called him home at once had I known before.

He has shown an egregious lack of character, not only by his disreputable actions and marrying a woman beneath his station, but even more so in his deception of me and your stepmother, who is beside herself with the shame he has brought upon us and the family name.

I am grateful to you, son, for your efforts to find a solution to this dire situation and have enclosed herein the sum you requested for financing your plan. May you arrive safely in Jamaica and deliver your brother and his wife to their deserved destiny. As per your stepmother's fervent request, I ask that, if by some chance of fate, they should perish on the journey, that you should give them a proper burial on land and not bury them at sea. She has a queer superstition about such things, and I ask you to honor her wishes in this.

Sincerely,

Father

"So!" Warwick laughed. "This is why you didn't just dump them overboard. Poor daddy was terribly upset. First you ruin your rival by introducing him to gambling, then devise the perfect plan to be rid of him forever. How cunning!" Warwick thumped the letter triumphantly.

He again scanned the other documents on the desk and chose a few more to add to his collection. Looking around smugly, he took up the lamp, then left the office. He snuffed out the remaining lights and paused before the door leading to the stairs. Turning to the large door with the little barred window, he lifted the light to try and see inside, but all was inky black. He shrugged and made his way back up the stairs, through the upper room, and out to the waiting carriage.

"Back to Woolwich, and make it quick," he yelled to the driver and took his seat, looking back on the dark old warehouse with a self-satisfied grin.

CHAPTER

# TWENTY-ONE

At the end of a delicious dinner, Sarah leaned over to Gresham while dessert was being served. "John, would you mind taking me to the stable after dinner? I would like to visit him, and I have something I need to tell you before our wedding tomorrow."

Alarmed by the concern on her face, he agreed immediately.

The others retired to the sitting room to further examine Sarah's drawings, and Gresham and Sarah excused themselves. Their shoes crunched on the gravel drive as Gresham held a lantern and led her silently to the stable door. The smell of horses and hay wafted over them as they entered, and Gresham hung the lantern on a wooden post. He showed her where the coffin was, covered with straw and harnesses.

"Would you like me to clear it off for you, Sarah?"

"No, thank you. That will not be necessary." She walked over the hay-strewn floor and laid her hand lightly on the corner of the lid, bowing her head.

Gresham studied her face in the dim light. He sensed that

something was amiss but didn't want to disturb her silent thoughts.

She removed her hand and faced him. "John, I have a confession, and I must make it now, as it may mean something to you." Her voice was low and steady, and she met his gaze evenly as she spoke.

"A confession? What do you mean?" He reached out his hand to her, but she raised hers and continued.

She paced as she began. "I do not remember much about my first marriage, but there is something I do know, though I do not remember why." She stopped in front of him, eyes full of desperation. "You see, I did not love the man who lies in this coffin. I feel I was fond of him, but I know I never loved him. I have been trying hard to understand why, but the answer evades me. Do you think I am a terrible person?"

The distress in her honest face nearly shattered him. "Oh, my dearest, how could I ever think so? Many people marry without love, and they are not at fault for doing so if the reason is noble and God has ordained it. Please, Sarah, you must not think less of yourself for having made your decision. I am sure that time will help us to understand the reason."

"Yes, I know, and you are very good to say all of this to me, but I had to make you aware of it all the same. Do you understand?"

Not giving her another opportunity to hold him at bay, he strode to her and took her by the hands. "Of course I do, and I love you all the more for your consideration and honesty. I am glad to know you and your heart better, but this does not change the way I feel about you in the slightest. Do you believe me?"

"I believe you, John," she said softly, "and I thank you with all my heart."

Gresham released her. "Sarah, can you tell me anything

more about him? What was he like?" He struggled between the need to know and the desire to leave this man completely in the past.

Sarah resumed her pacing. "He was handsome and charming, but that is not why I chose to marry him, I am sure. I know that there was something lacking in his character. When I think of him, I feel a sense of betrayal, yet how can that be? Did he not lose his life because of me?"

His chest tightened with anger as she described the man in the coffin next to them. "I cannot say. But there is one thing I know for certain—that you must not feel responsible in any way for what happened to him or yourself. Whatever the motive was for these horrific men, there is absolutely no justification for their actions."

"Yes, you are right, I know, but why do I feel as though I . . . I walked into a trap? Yes, that's it, as though somehow this man could have prevented what happened but failed to protect us both. I also feel I should have done more, said more, protested . . . Oh, I don't know how to explain it—I was such a fool."

Gresham took her by the shoulders and drew close to her, looking intently into her stormy gray-blue eyes. "It is right for you to try and understand these things, my dear, but I want you to know that no matter what the circumstances were surrounding your marriage to this man, it does not change the way I feel. But I must ask you this, Sarah"—John's heart thudded as he posed his question—"do you feel trapped now? Do you feel that you are in a powerless position, with no other choice but to marry me?"

She shook her head and pulled back again. "Oh, John, I don't know. Our situation is so different. A woman in my position has few real choices. I only know that by marrying me, without knowing my real story, I . . ." She shook her head in consternation. "I just hope that neither one of us will regret it after—"

Gresham took a deep breath and stepped close. "Do you remember what I promised you the day I proposed, that if at any time you no longer wished to journey with me through life, that I would release you without fault?"

"Yes, but what about you? What if you are the one who no longer wishes to journey through life with me?" Her words were full of sincerity as she raised her chin and looked into his eyes.

"That, my love, will never happen, and when I make my vows to you tomorrow, I will make them with all of my being. I do not expect you to do the same—"

"But, John—"

"No, Sarah, I never want you to feel trapped by me. Never. I love you too much to do that to you."

Her eyes brimmed with tears, and she took his offered hand. He held it reverently and felt as if his heart would burst.

"Pray, John," Sarah whispered. "Pray that we will both do what is right in God's eyes in the morning."

"With all my heart, my love. With all of my heart."

IT WAS CHRISTMAS MORNING, and the house was alive with activity. Sarah could smell the spiced cakes and puddings baking in the kitchen and the fresh pine scent of boughs on the mantel over the burning hearth. Hearing a knock, she ran to the front door. There on the step was a dark-haired boy, about her age, holding a large box in his arms.

Sarah gasped and asked, "Oh! Is this for me?"

The boy's face was half hidden behind the box, but she could see the top of his head nod vigorously.

She giggled with delight as she lifted the lid, full of joyful anticipation. But when the lid was off, she looked into the box and screamed, her hands flying to her mouth in horror, and the boy dropped the box and ran away sobbing.

Stooping down, she pushed the open box aside, revealing a dead puppy, its neck wrenched.

Then she awoke.

Sitting upright in the bed of the blue guest room in the old vicarage, Sarah's heart pounded, and she was covered in sweat. She grasped a bed pillow to her chest and tried to calm herself. "It was only a dream. Only a very bad dream," she whispered, then prayed. Still distressed, she went to the desk and lit the glass globed lantern. Pulling back the curtains, she found that it was barely dawn, and she sat on the chair with a shiver.

She briefly wrote out a description of the nightmare and folded the paper over, tucking it into the desk drawer.

She returned to the bed and knelt beside it. "Dear Father in heaven, I am confused and upset, but I know that you are speaking to me and will reveal things to me in your time. Please help me to face my past, knowing you will see me through and will be faithful to me in all of your ways. I want only your will to be done today. Please show me the way, Lord. Speak to my heart now, Father. I am desperate to know what you would have me do. Should I marry John Gresham today or not?"

She quieted her heart, listening in her spirit. *Beauty for ashes*, she heard, like a whisper from a still, small voice. Warmth flooded her body, and she surrendered to the brush of the Lord's Spirit passing over her. Finally she spoke to the coming light of dawn increasing over the sky. "I will make no false vow before you today. Your will be done."

S<small>T</small>. Etheldreda's church stood nobly on a spur of high land at the top of Fore Street, with the London Road passing behind, running between it and the arched gateway to the old palace and gardens visible over the half wall to the east. It was surrounded by ancient headstones and flowering trees and bushes. Its high arched windows, tall bell tower, and ancient churchyard gave it a grand and storied aspect.

Penny insisted that her brother not see his bride until after the service. She made him sit on the front row with her in order that Sarah could sit in the back of the church with Braxton, who had been asked to escort her down the aisle. Penny also expressed her disappointment in Gresham's decision that the church bells not be rung nor the organ played for the wedding after the service, so as not to draw attention.

Braxton escorted Sarah into the well-lit nave to the back pew behind the rest of the congregation, almost directly under the great pipes of the organ. Gresham and Henry had shown him the inside of St. Etheldreda's on a previous visit. He marveled again at the Tudor architecture of the high, arched wooden ceiling and the diamond-patterned marble floor.

He couldn't remember the last time he had been inside a church for an actual service. Among his travels there had been the occasional opportunity to see a cathedral in some port city, but his resentment of his father, who'd been a deacon, and the beatings he had received from him as a child in the name of religion had put him off any type of religious practice.

As he sat beside Sarah, dressed in Mr. Huckabee's green-skirted dress, rose-colored sash, Gresham's pearls, embroidered silk shawl, and green bonnet, his vantage point felt entirely different. He took note of the rise of an unexplained foreboding seeping into his bones. Were his old childhood experiences creeping to the surface because of being in a church, or was it because of his irrational infatuation with

Sarah on the ship rising up again to protest the wedding ceremony to come?

The organ rang out the introduction to a hymn, and the ancient walls reverberated with a majestic resonance. Then the voices of the parishioners joined the song. Sarah joined her voice to theirs, joyful tears rolling down her angelic face.

He felt a strange surge of tingling energy run through his limbs. Tempted to dismiss his experience as religious manipulation, as he always had in the past, he found that he was unable to lean on that old, insensitive reasoning while standing beside this particular woman. Keenly aware of all she had suffered, he fought to understand how she could go on believing in this so-called Savior, Jesus. Yet he knew that Sarah, and Gresham for that matter, were honest in their faith and not the kind of people who were readily deceived.

As the hymn reached its climax and the last notes hung like a spirit in the space above them, Braxton was disappointed the music had ended. They took their seats as Henry, dressed in black robes, mounted the pulpit and asked the congregation to join him in prayer. Sarah bowed her head immediately, as did the others, but Braxton was reluctant. Instead his eyes drifted from Sarah to Henry as he made a concerted effort to listen to the words and not analyze them before the prayer was finished. He knew the prayer well himself.

"Our Father, which art in heaven, Hallowed be thy name . . ." When they reached the line saying "and forgive us our trespasses, as we forgive those who trespass against us," something in Braxton's gut twisted and he could no longer pay attention. A familiar rage rushed to the surface of his heart, and he shifted with indignation. Fighting the potent temptation to stand up and leave, he looked down again at Sarah's bowed head and caught himself.

*This is it,* he thought. *This is the foundation of my anger and*

233

*the impenetrable wall I have built upon it for myself, stone by stone, trying to protect myself from these very words.*

He stared at the back of Sarah's head incredulously. How could she speak them after all she had been through? Surely this woman was no trespasser. Why should she forgive those who had trespassed against her? Why should he?

The prayer ended, and Sarah whispered, "Do you remember what I told you in my letter, my friend?"

She might have shaken him, for how her question jarred him. He looked down into her confident face and nodded.

"God loves you, Paul Braxton. Why not let Him?" She sat back and turned her attention to Henry again, speaking from the pulpit.

Braxton rubbed his sweaty palms on his breeches as he repeated the question to himself. *Why not let Him? What did that mean?*

Henry continued his sermon, and Sarah listened intently. Schooling himself not to let his mind wander, he turned his attention to Henry's words.

"And so, my beloved brothers and sisters, when we come to this point in the Lord's Prayer, are we merely reciting words, or do we consider their true meaning? Someone might feel that he is not as bad a transgressor as another man, and so might be inclined to think that he is not a transgressor at all. Well, if that were so, then we might all be able to make that claim, for even an evil man might find another more evil than himself and claim the same."

Henry grasped the railing and gazed over the crowd. "And what about forgiving those who have trespassed against us? Surely if we feel that we are without sin, then why must we forgive those who do so against our own person? Do you see how very easy it is to fall prey to our own sense of pride and refuse to look at ourselves in the light of

Christ's perfection, instead of comparing ourselves to other people?"

Braxton's heart pounded. Henry continued to speak, but Braxton could no longer hear him. Was it true? Was his pride in comparing himself to others preventing him from comparing himself to Christ's perfection? *God loves you,* Sarah had said. *Why not let Him?*

For the rest of the service, he grappled with the thought. *Let God love me? What if? What if I let go of my pride and asked God to forgive me, not thinking about what anyone else had done, even my father?* Braxton looked at Sarah as he battled in the pew beside her.

*Is that the difference between us? Am I full of unforgiving pride, while she wasn't too proud to ask for forgiveness for herself? Is that what made it possible for her to forgive others?*

They stood for the closing hymn, and again the exalted sound surrounded him like the waves of the sea. Again he felt a rush of power move through him, but this time he chose not to explain it away. To his amazement, it did not leave him, and it was still there when the last notes faded away.

AFTER THE SERVICE, Braxton took Sarah into the far back of the sanctuary, where they stood waiting behind a partition. Sarah shifted and could not seem to stand still. She smiled up at Braxton, sometimes fidgeting with her shawl. After some time, Penny peered around the screen and handed Sarah a bouquet of frothy white roses with daisies and baby's breath. She gasped with delight and kissed Penny on the cheek. The scent of the blooms reached Braxton and helped to calm his racing heart.

"Are you still sure about this, Sarah? It is not too late to run away." Braxton smiled nervously down on her with a twinkle in his eye.

She hesitated a moment before saying evenly, "Yes, Doctor, I am sure."

They were interrupted by the sound of singing coming from the far end of the church. Sarah gave a little gasp as Braxton offered her his arm. He guided her around the screen, and pausing for half a moment, they saw Penny and Henry singing the hymn "Love Divine, All Loves Excelling" in the center of the transept in the soft white light of the arched windows. And before them, tall and serious, stood Captain Johnathan Gresham in his dress uniform, his white feathered blue-and-gold bicorn hat under his arm.

Braxton's heart welled up with love for the two as he brought them together. When Penny and Henry finished their hymn, he took Sarah's hand from his arm and passed it with joy to his friend, then proudly stood to Gresham's side.

The ceremony was simple. When Henry asked if there was a ring, Braxton reached into his breast pocket and produced the sapphire-studded golden sphere. The light from the windows caught on the gems with a flick of blue fire as he handed it to Gresham. Sarah's eyes widened as Gresham repeated Henry's words of promise and placed it on her finger.

Sarah also repeated her vows but added something at the end no one had expected. "With all my heart, so help me God."

Braxton noticed the tender look of surprise on Gresham's face.

"You may now kiss the bride!" Henry announced, and Gresham took Sarah's hands and kissed her gently. The others clapped and cheered, their voices echoing in the breadth and height of the sanctuary.

There were embraces and kisses, handshakes and laughter as the newlyweds left the beautiful church. They walked together through the gate at the side of the house and went to the little porch where their abundant celebratory breakfast awaited them.

No sooner had they taken their seats when the maid came in with a sealed letter on a tray. "There's a letter for you, Captain," she said with a curtsy.

Gresham glanced with concern at Sarah, then at Braxton. "It's from Mr. Green. It might be urgent, my dear. Should I read it now or leave it until after we've enjoyed our breakfast?"

"Yes, do, brother. Leave it until after—" Penny pleaded.

"No, John," Sarah interrupted. "Read it now. It could be something important that you should respond to presently and will be remiss if postponed." Sarah's face clouded as she met Gresham's gaze.

"All right. I will excuse myself for just a moment. Please carry on without me. I shall return presently."

He returned moments later and handed the letter to Braxton, his face shadowed and grave.

"What is it, John? What does Mr. Green say?" Sarah asked anxiously.

"The *Relentless* has a new captain, and she is set to sail for the Mediterranean Sea the day after tomorrow before noon." Gresham shared the news flatly and sat down.

Henry reached over his still-full plate as Braxton handed the letter on to him. "You had assumed that would happen, John. Who is the new captain?"

"My first lieutenant, Timothy Compton, has been promoted to the post. I am glad for him. He is a fine fellow and knows the *Relentless* almost as well as I do."

Sarah touched his arm. "But, John, it still must be distressing to let her go on without you. I am so sorry."

"I am sorry as well, brother," Penny said sympathetically. "A chosen loss is still a loss. Did the letter say anything else?"

Gresham stiffened. "Yes, and this is what is more distressing to me than the news of Captain Compton and the ship. It is about Mr. Darby, my ship's purser."

"Mr. Darby?" Sarah asked incredulously. "What has happened to Mr. Darby?"

"He has betrayed us, Sarah, or at least attempted to." Gresham's face grew harder by the moment.

Sarah shifted in her chair to face him. "How so? Please tell me all of it."

"Compton was summoned to meet with Admiral Warwick and found Darby's card on the floor by the admiral's desk. Warwick gave Compton his promotion and his orders to sail immediately. He was insistent the entire ship's complement that was on the ship when we docked, be on the ship when they sail. An unusual and curious request. When Compton returned to the ship, he made a search of Darby's cabin and found the addresses to the Lee Side Inn and to this very house in his desk."

The ladies gasped in unison. "But how did he get this information?" Sarah asked urgently. "Do you think he meant to give it to the admiral?"

"I am not sure." Gresham looked about him for an answer. "Perhaps I was careless somehow. But I never thought that one of my own officers would betray me." He slapped his hand hard on his thigh and drew his lips tight.

"None of us would have guessed it, John," Braxton offered. "Perhaps Darby, being a purser, after all, looked at it as a money-making opportunity?"

"In any case, we cannot be certain he didn't share what he knew with Warwick, or perhaps others. Compton has him locked up on the *Relentless* but is not sure if he can hold him there when they sail." Gresham sat upright and sent Braxton a grim look. "Paul, would you be willing to go back to Woolwich as soon as possible and see what more can be learned?"

"Of course" was Braxton's immediate reply.

"Now, please, gentlemen, let us not think of them for at least the next hour. Then we will go to our knees and seek the Lord's wisdom. Until then"—Sarah rose, her lemonade glass lifted high and a warm smile on her face—"I propose a toast to my new husband, Captain Johnathan Gresham. May the Lord bless him for all of the ways he has blessed me!"

They all stood and joined the toast, but a shadow had been cast over the party.

CHAPTER

# TWENTY-TWO

After the wedding breakfast, Gresham took Braxton and Henry to the study for a conference. "That jackanape Darby! How could he betray us when he knows what Sarah has been through? What would he possibly have against her?" Gresham paced the room, allowing his anger to express itself freely.

Braxton sat in front of Henry's desk and rubbed his high, creased forehead. "I do not think it has anything to do with Sarah personally, John. Darby is a businessman. His only possible motive would be to sell information for money. Compton has related that Darby insists he did not actually divulge any information to Warwick. Perhaps he is telling the truth."

"Money? The man knows I have money. Why not black-mail me?" Gresham braced himself on the back of the empty chair beside Braxton. "Compton will either have to hand him over to the naval authorities with some provable charge, or he will have to let him go free. It sounds like he is guilty of insubordination, but that would only warrant a temporary punishment. Compton can have Darby replaced, but Warwick has ordered that everyone who came into port with the *Relentless* is to leave with it. Which brings me to more questions."

He took a seat and sat forward. "Mr. Green mentioned that Thomas Smith was released from the infirmary and has been helpful in trying to find Mr. S.G., but though his injuries preclude him from working as a topman, he will be given other duties and required to leave, as will Mr. Green and you, Paul."

Henry folded his hands on his desk. "What would be the consequences of Dr. Braxton not leaving with the ship? The navy has granted him leave, have they not? What if he never receives word of these orders? Is he still responsible for obeying orders he has never received? It seems to me that as long as the doctor and the others stay unavailable until after the ship sails on Tuesday that their positions should not be compromised. Or am I missing something?"

Gresham shook his head. "No, Henry. You are correct as far as Braxton is concerned, but if it can be proven that Green and Smith have received word, they would have no other choice but to sail, which leaves us without eyes on the ground in Woolwich."

Braxton sat up straight. "Then as soon as I arrive, I will find out if they have had official notification. If not, I will encourage them to remain unavailable as well." He glanced at Gresham. "I should be off then, if I am to intercept them. The sooner the better."

"A moment more, if you please, Doctor." Henry turned his grave eyes to Gresham. "It seems to me that you indeed have a problem with this Admiral Warwick. I am convinced he is acting outside his line of authority by his maneuvers to cover up what these evil men have done. Why hasn't he made any attempt to interview more of your crew than just Captain

Compton? He seems to have an unusual lack of curiosity, if you ask me."

"Hmmm, yes, Henry, you make an interesting point." Gresham frowned. "His behavior is rather odd on many fronts. If only we had a way to find out what he is up to. Someone who might be close enough to him to look for clues on our behalf."

Braxton raised a hand. "It is another thing I shall investigate. My trouble is that Warwick knows my face. Otherwise I might try to spy on him myself." He gave a halfhearted chuckle. "I have never imagined myself to be the spying type, but I will do what I can to be good at it."

Gresham stood and cuffed Braxton on the shoulder, then reached to shake his hand. "Dr. Braxton, if there were any man in the world who presented himself any less a man of intrigue, it would be you, which may be exactly what is needed. Wait, I have another thought. I must retrieve something from my room before you go."

Gresham dashed upstairs and brought down the document that Mr. Compton had given him with the signatures of the crew. "Look for Darby's name," he asked as he unfolded the document on the desk. He flared his nostrils, and heat infused his face. He slammed his fist down on the paper.

Braxton stood straight, his hazel eyes flashing, "It is not there. He never signed it."

"And he is the one who told me to have this paper drawn up and signed by the whole crew. Blast! What a fool I've been!" Then catching sight of his brother-in-law's distraught face, he lowered his voice. "I am sorry, Henry. Please excuse my language."

"No, John, there is nothing to excuse. This is indeed troubling. His deliberate act of not signing this document confirms his intentions. But the ladies will be worried by now, and Paul should be off. Shall we?"

They emerged from the study to find the ladies waiting for them in the sitting room. Braxton retrieved his bag and set it just inside the entryway, where Sarah approached him, her Bible in her hands.

"I want you to have this, Paul. I want you to have it with you as you go out into difficulty and possible danger on my behalf. I would feel much better knowing you had it with you."

Gresham added his encouragement. "Yes, Paul. We will all feel better knowing Sarah's Bible is with you. Besides, you never know when you might need some good reading as you slink around alleys and watch people from park benches." Gresham smiled affectionately, taking the Bible from Sarah and shoving it into Braxton's bag on the floor. "But do not lose it. That Bible is incredibly special, you know."

"Sarah, this is your Bible. I can buy my own. I couldn't possibly—"

"It is yours now. May it bring you as much comfort and strength as it has given me," and she pulled his face down and kissed his cheek. "Always remember that you are not alone. You have us. We are your family."

Gresham pulled him into a bear of an embrace. "Thank you, Paul. Your selflessness is unequaled. If there is any trouble that would put you in harm's way, then get yourself back to Hatfield and we will face it together." Gresham picked up his bag. "I'll walk you to the post."

WHEN GRESHAM RETURNED, they gathered at the sitting room table. "This precious day has been clouded by the never-ending challenges that continue to plague us." He looked longingly, sorrowfully at his new wife. "My dear Sarah. I am terribly sorry. There never seems to be a moment's peace for you."

Sarah's face looked pale. "It is I who should be sorry. Look at the trouble I have brought upon you dear people," she answered painfully.

Gresham's heart twisted, but Penny jumped in before he could reassure her.

"No, no! My girl"—Penny laid her hand on Sarah's arm—"you are my sister now, and we will face this together as a family. I am so very sorry that your wedding day has been spoiled, but I know there is not a challenge in the world that God is incapable of seeing us through. And you, my dear, know that better than any of us."

Henry concurred. "That is true, Sarah. Now please do not trouble yourself with this needless guilt any longer. We must turn our attention to what is needed next." He pulled his chair closer. "I may have a temporary solution as to where to keep your late husband's remains until he can receive a proper burial. I have thought of a place that might be more secure to hide them than our stable."

Gresham was grateful to both of them for their insight and compassion toward his bride. He studied Henry's face eagerly. "Please continue, Henry."

"There is a bit of space tucked just below the highest floor of the church tower, next to the carillon. The only means of entry is by a narrow set of spiral stairs leading up from the room behind the organ's pipes. As far as I know, only Mr. Caie, the church warden, and myself have the keys to the door leading to those stairs. If I inform Mr. Caie that I am storing something there that must remain confidential for a time, then it would not be easy for just anyone to find it out, unlike the possibility of someone snooping around my stable, which could be easy enough to break into if someone had a mind to."

"That sounds perfect, Henry. Perhaps we should wait until it is dark before we take him there." Gresham felt a small piece of weight lift from his shoulders.

"Indeed," Henry agreed. "So that issue will be settled tonight, but I am not as hopeful as the doctor that this Mr. Darby is telling the truth about not giving any information to that admiral. What say you, John?"

Gresham heaved a sigh, reluctant to say what he knew needed to come next. "I agree. It looks like we shall have to go over Admiral Warwick's head if we are to see any justice done, and I am afraid that Sarah and I will have to leave Hatfield as soon as possible."

Before Penny could interject, Henry slapped his hand gently on the table. "Yes, my thoughts exactly. We shall begin immediately to make our preparations. Penny, we will need to be packed and ready to travel as quickly as possible. We must make the house ready to close up behind us as well. The servants will need to be instructed and places found for them until we can return."

Penny took advantage of her husband's need to breathe. "I agree, Henry, of course. We can go around the shops tomorrow morning and collect what we can of Sarah's wardrobe and have the rest sent, but we have not yet discussed where we are going. And, Henry, what about the church? I'm sure your curate will be happy to stand in for you, but shouldn't you do Lord Salisbury the courtesy of letting him know before you just up and leave? He is expecting us at the manor house to attend his wife's sporting event next week."

Sarah sat forward to speak but was preempted by her new brother-in-law. "I will speak to Lord Salisbury as quickly as can be arranged, but as to the question of where we shall go, I should like to know John's thoughts on that concern."

"We must go to London to see what can be done at the

admiralty, but it must be somewhere inconspicuous. I cannot readily suggest a place, but—"

Henry smiled. "I may have a place for us to consider, my boy. I will write to the seminary I attended in London, as it may be just the place for us. I am still acquainted with the dean. If I can gain permission, then we might stay at one of the faculty houses not currently occupied. We would be tolerably comfortable there for some time, if need be."

"What a capital idea, Henry." Gresham smiled down on Sarah.

"I will write the letter presently, but we have not given Sarah a chance to submit her opinion on our plan. Now, Sarah, what say you, my dear?"

She nodded slowly. "Well, I believe it is a good plan. My only concern is, what shall we do if the seminary cannot take us in?"

"You are right, and so we must also come up with another plan in case the seminary is not a possibility." Gresham kissed her hand and stood, as did Henry.

"Well now, Captain, we have a battle plan. Ladies, I know this is a wedding day and a day that should be spent in merriment and cheer, but we shall have to postpone that for another day. We have our orders from the captain himself, and now it is time to pack."

GRESHAM AND HENRY made their way to the stable after dark. Uncovering the box, Gresham looked it over. "Just how narrow is the staircase to the tower? Perhaps we will not be able to get the coffin up it."

"We are not going to take the coffin up, John, only the

body." Henry handed Gresham a hammer and winked. "Shall we?"

Gresham felt uneasy about hiding a dead body in the tower of a church, no matter how well it was wrapped, but once they were up the narrow spiral stairs of the tower and had tucked their burden in the small room under the level where the bells hung in silence, he felt more comfortable.

"I think our poor friend will be safe enough here for now." Henry led the way back down the steps and locked the door behind them. They left the church and strode back to the vicarage. "We have made great progress today in our preparations. It may be possible to leave within the next day, depending on when I can have an audience with His Lordship."

Henry stopped short before opening the back door of the house. "And now, dear brother-in-law, you have a brand-new bride waiting for you. I suggest that you put aside the concerns of the moment and give her your full attention." His light-blue eyes twinkled in the reflection of the light from the hallway as he opened the door and motioned for Gresham to enter. "I bid you good night."

Gresham paused outside the door of the Blue Room. He had promised Sarah he would wait for her and intended to live by it. They had even agreed to sleep separately until she was ready, but his heart and body ached for her. "Help me, Father," he whispered as he turned to the room across the hall.

"John," Sarah whispered from her open door.

He turned to her, her dressing gown flowing over the curves of her body, her lips soft and eyes searching.

"Thank you for waiting for me. I do not think you will have to wait forever."

He smiled as he nodded, taking her hand and kissing it. "Thank you, Sarah, for this and for the promise you made me today."

"I meant it, John, with all my heart. Let us keep our doors open, shall we?"

# CHAPTER
# TWENTY-THREE

Gresham was deeply asleep in the room across from Sarah's and was jolted from his slumbers by Sarah calling out. "No, Michael! No!"

He bolted into the room and could just make out the look of terror on his bride's face as she sat in the dim early light of dawn. "Sarah, Sarah, are you all right?" He sat beside her and stroked her arm, speaking in a soothing tone. "Sarah, wake up, darling. It was only a dream."

Sarah startled and came to herself. "Oh! John! Is it you? Oh, I am so very glad!" She buried her face into his chest.

"Yes, dear, it is me, your husband. I am here." He held her gently to him and kissed the top of her tousled head. She clung to him for a few more minutes, and he felt the tension slowly release from her body.

In time she let go and sat back to face him. "I am so sorry, John. I did not mean to wake you so early."

He held her hand, circling his thumb on her soft skin. "Do you want to tell me about your dream? You were very upset by it."

Her shoulders eased, and she squeezed his hand. "Perhaps I should. It may help." She shifted to look at him directly.

He reached up and tucked a long, wavy strand of hair behind her ear so he could watch her expressions. "I am listening."

"I was standing outside beside a lovely grove of trees. The evening sunlight was casting beautiful shadows and streaks of light among them, and I was inspired by the patterns of light on the grass beneath. I turned and saw an artist's easel beside me, and in my hands were a pallet and a paint brush."

"I have suspected that you might also be able to paint as well as draw. We must get you some materials and have you try," Gresham said in a low, husky tone as he trailed his finger along her wrist.

"Yes, well, perhaps. But"—she sighed and swung her legs off the bed to better face him—"on the easel was a small painting, the exact image of the grove captured on the canvas. It was a lovely little painting, and I was very pleased with it.

"Then I was aware of someone watching over my shoulder. I turned and saw him. At first I could not see his face clearly. He pushed me aside and took the painting from the easel. He smiled down on me with a terrible look in his eyes. He said, 'Thank you, my dear. This will fetch a pretty penny.'"

Gresham sat upright. "This man took your painting to sell it without your consent?" He was indignant on her behalf.

Sarah sighed. "Yes. I didn't want him to sell it—I desperately wanted to keep it." Her chest rose and fell as her voice became more urgent. "He took it and walked away. I pleaded with him not to take it. Then he turned to me with the same awful look on his face, and I recognized him."

Gresham took both of her hands in his. "Can you tell me who he was?"

"It was him, my late husband," she said, "and his name was Michael."

Gresham narrowed his eyes, searching her face intensely. "Are you sure, Sarah? Your own husband did this to you? Do you think your dream is a vision of something that actually happened?"

She breathed heavily and looked painfully into his eyes. "Yes, I do." She hung her head and wept.

Enfolding her in his arms, he comforted her. "Oh, my love. I am sorry. So very sorry."

As he held her there and felt the waves of sorrow pass through her to himself, a multitude of thoughts clamored for his attention. Michael. Michael who? What kind of man would do something so heartless to his wife? How could he steal her work and use it for his own gain? If he were capable of this kind of betrayal, what else had he done to her?

He thought about the man's body lying hidden in the church tower. Because of the evidence of his torture and murder, Gresham had always pictured him as a victim, as a man undeserving of his fate. But now Gresham saw him in a different light.

As he held her, it was all he could do to keep from lifting her chin and comforting her with passionate kisses. *Waiting for her is going to be much harder than I anticipated. God help me.*

✳

JOHN LED Sarah down to the breakfast table. The hall mirror told her that she was still a bit pale, but she felt she had mostly recovered from her nightmare. Still, she felt the weight of memories yet to be revealed and hoped she would have enough courage to face them when they rose to the surface of her mind.

Penny poured their tea. "Sarah, my dear, are you feeling well?"

"I am quite well, Penny, thank you. I had another dream, but I suppose I should tell you of the one I had the night before. I wasn't able to tell you about it yesterday because of church and the wedding." She smiled weakly at John and took a sip of tea.

"Another dream?" John asked. "Perhaps you would like to wait until after breakfast to tell us. We have a bit of time before we go and collect your things from the shops at ten."

She looked up and smiled more brightly. "Perhaps we can talk about it after our errands and I've had a bit of fresh air."

At ten o'clock sharp, John escorted Sarah and his amiable sister out of the house. The weather was warm but the sky was a bit overcast, and John predicted rain sometime later in the day.

Their first stop was the dressmaker's shop. Penny chatted with Mrs. Dunham as John whispered to Sarah. "I believe Penny has everything in hand here. What would you say to heading to the boot makers, and then we can take a look inside the pawnbroker's shop, like I promised you?"

"Oh yes, let's. I am just dying to have a look there." Sarah's heart gave a little leap as her husband went to tell Penny their plan.

"But of course, my dears. You two run along and come fetch me here when you are finished," Penny said with enthusiasm.

Their visit to the boot maker's was a bit of a disappointment. Nothing was ready there, which was a shame. Sarah was in dire need of some real shoes.

They stepped out of the shop, and Sarah smiled up at Gresham and tugged on his arm. "May we go to the pawnbroker's now?"

"Of course." He returned her smile just as a newspaper boy passed them on the walkway, calling, "'New Reward for Missing Girls'!" waving a paper over his head.

Sarah watched as John bought a paper, showing the headline to her with knitted brows.

"What is it?" she asked, alarmed by the headline.

"It is a case I've been following. Several girls between the ages of eight and fourteen have been taken from their homes in London for a few years now, never to be seen again." A cloud passed over his face as he folded the paper and tucked it into his coat pocket. "I've been praying for them and their families, but we can talk about it another time."

He led her to the door under the three golden balls hanging above the next shop and entered.

No one was there, but Sarah heard the bell ring and knew someone would show themselves presently. John let go of her hand and bowed to her with a wide smile. "Please, madam, enjoy yourself. The shop is yours."

Sarah shivered with delight. In front of her were tables and open shelves full of glimmering dishes, crystal, china, and vases. The store fairly sparkled with the sun from the windows dancing off the gold leaf, brass, and cut glass. A chandelier hung from the ceiling, and its crystals showered the walls with little rainbows.

Making her way to the glass counter, she examined the trays of gold watches, coins, and jewelry. "Look at that lovely cameo, John. I have always marveled at how delicate the workmanship is that goes into creating such a tiny masterpiece on a bit of shell." Moving down the counter, she paused and studied with appreciation as John watched her from the side.

In the section behind the tableware, she found herself surrounded by richly carved, deeply upholstered chairs and chaises, wooden side tables, and bookcases. There were pedestals with ornate statues and candelabras, and Sarah strode slowly through the maze, caressing the pieces now and then with her gloved hand.

Her eyes were caught by an especially striking, large china cabinet against the back wall. She started toward it, when she froze and caught her breath, her hand flying to cover her mouth. John was by her side in an instant, his hand supporting her at her waist.

"What is it, my dear. What is the matter?"

She could not turn her eyes to him. They were fixed on something on the shop's dimly lit back wall beside the china cabinet. She withdrew her hand from her mouth and pointed a gloved finger.

John looked, squinting his eyes. "What is it, Sarah?"

Followed closely by John, Sarah cautiously made her way through the last of the furniture and stood before a small painting on the wall. It was framed in wide, gold-gilded molding, and within its borders was an exquisitely rendered image of a grove of trees, the evening light shining on the green grass in stark contrast to the dark shadows cast by the tree trunks. And in the lower right-hand corner was a tiny signature—S.G.

Reaching out to touch the frame, she whispered, "There you are!"

John's eyes widened in astonishment. "Is this . . . this is your painting, Sarah?"

"Pardon my delay in attending to you. I was hindered by an issue with one of my clients delivering a rather large armoire to the back door."

Startled, Sarah turned to see an old shopkeeper, his wrinkled face reddened by recent exertion. She stood blinking, unable to speak.

John addressed the shopkeeper. "Oh, it is no trouble at all, really. We were just looking at this rather amazing little painting here. Yes, uh, can you tell us anything about it?"

Sarah hardly trusted her own eyes. There it was, the very painting from her dream, hanging on the wall before her. She couldn't make sense of what the men near her were saying. Their voices sounded distant and disconnected. Her mind was a whirl, but one thing was clear. She told the painting silently, in her heart, *God has brought us together again.*

Turning back to John, she could contain herself no longer. "It is a miracle," she said in awe. "John, this is a miracle from God!"

A wave of warm energy passed through her, and she swayed. John caught her by the arm and led her to a chair, facing the painting on the wall. He knelt beside her and patted her hand. "Yes, my dear. A miracle indeed."

She could discern what they were saying now. The excitement in her husband's voice rose by the moment, as did the shopkeeper's. "Really, sir, you mean to tell me that this lovely lady, your wife, is the artist that painted this little gem?"

"Where did you get it? Who sold it to you?" John's tone reminded her of him giving orders to his officers on the *Relentless.*

"Why, I bought it at an auction, sir, a while back. Goodness, let me see. Just let me fetch my records and you shall see for yourselves." The man retreated behind a curtained door.

John knelt beside her again and searched her face. "Are you all right, my dear? I do not know if you are pleased or ill. Please tell me."

"Oh, I am most pleased but also struck with the wonder of it. I am overcome, but I assure you that I am very well indeed."

He sighed and kissed her hand quickly. "As am I. If we can only find out more—"

"Here we are now." The shopkeeper placed his books on

top of a large pedestal and moved it near Sarah's chair. She stood beside the man as Gresham looked over her shoulder. The man thumbed through the first record book and tossed it onto a nearby chaise, where he promptly tossed two more.

"Ah! Here it is! You see, here is a description of the painting, and here is the place it was purchased! Shefford, Bedfordshire. Why yes, I remember now. I purchased it along with some other items at the auction house in Shefford."

Sarah read and reread the painting's simple description and the record of where it was purchased. Then her eyes fell on the date of purchase—March 30, 1818. Her head swam with new thoughts and questions as she took her seat again. Staring up at her handiwork on the wall, unbidden tears spilled onto her cheeks.

Suddenly she was aware that John asked about the cameo she had admired in the case as well and was handing the shopkeeper several bills. The man went back behind the curtain, and John resumed his place by her side, carefully pinning the cameo to her bodice. "We are taking your painting home, my love. Where it belongs. He is just going to wrap it up for us—"

"Oh thank you. How can I ever thank you enough?" She kissed his cheek just as the shopkeeper returned with some string and folded cloth.

In a few minutes they were back out on the street, John carefully carrying their precious bundle in his arms. They hurried up the walkway to the dressmaker's just as Penny emerged.

"Well, there you are! I was just coming to find you. I have sent the packages from Mrs. Dunham to the house with her assistant. Oh! I see you have a new cameo, Sarah. It's lovely, and what have we here?" Penny lifted the corner of the fabric wrapping and tried to peek inside.

"It is a miracle, Penny, a real miracle!" Sarah felt her face flush, and she was sure her eyes danced. "Hurry—we must show you. Come quickly!" And she started off, laughing and motioning them to follow.

✳

Captain Timothy Compton opened the wardroom door and entered. "Ah, Mr. Quist. I am here to see Mr. Darby. Please stay, as I will need your assistance."

"Aye, Captain." The tall marine saluted and stepped aside.

Opening the purser's door, Compton found Darby sitting at his desk, frowning and wiping his spectacles. "We are about to sail, Mr. Darby, and I have decided that you will not be coming along."

Darby's eyes shot up to Compton's face. "But what about my stores, my merchandise? You cannot simply sail away with my property!"

"Watch me," Compton snapped. "Once again you have failed to show me the respect due a ship's captain." At this, he caught the little man up by the collar and stood him on his feet. "I should have you flogged twice now, Darby, but I will show you how merciful I can be by escorting you off my ship."

Compton nodded to Quist, who took Darby by the arm, and they emerged from the aft hatch on the main deck just as Mr. Latch came aboard. "Mr. Latch, is everything in order?"

"Aye, Captain." Latch saluted with a wide grin.

"Very well then." Compton nodded. "Mr. Evans, read the declaration, if you please."

The sergeant at arms cleared his throat and held a paper out before him.

"'My dear superiors of His Majesty's Royal Navy Board and Admiralty:

I am submitting to you my recommendation for the court martial of Mr. Daniel Darby, once ship's purser for HMS Relentless. Mr. Darby has shown an egregious lack of respect for authority, is guilty of insubordination, and has been negligent in his duties as ship's purser. He has also been found to be in possession of confidential information and caught in the attempt to sell this information for his personal financial gain.

Let it be known that Mr. Darby has been relieved of his duties on HMS Relentless as of September 4, 1818, by my order. Custody of Mr. Darby is being given over to the Woolwich Port Authority, as HMS Relentless is under orders to sail on this same date to assist in addressing His Majesty's concerns in the Mediterranean.

Mr. Darby has been paid a fair sum for the goods he had already stored on the ship prior to his detainment.

Sincerely,

Captain Timothy Compton

HMS Relentless"

Darby's face matched his red nose. "But you haven't paid me anything! You have not even allowed me to pack my private possessions!"

Compton held out his hand to Mr. Latch. who placed in it a sealed envelope. "This should be sufficient to cover the cost of the goods you have already stored. As to your personal possessions, they will be given to the port authority. And just so you know, this is a copy of the letter I have already submitted to the admiralty. Goodbye, Mr. Darby, and good riddance."

CHAPTER

# TWENTY-FOUR

T he two couples bent over the painting on the sitting room table with expressions of awe and wonder. Gresham spoke up. "Please let us sit and listen to Sarah tell us about her dreams, and I for one could also use a cup of tea. Penny?"

Penny rang for tea, and Henry and Gresham placed the painting on top of a low bookcase, where everyone could view it. They sat in stunned silence until the tea tray was brought in.

Gresham's head spun, knowing that Almighty God himself had been guiding them all to this very day. From that freakish storm near the Bahamas, to the pawnbroker's shop in Hatfield, the Lord had been directing their footsteps all along. The revelation that even the most common of details, like using the lack of dresses and the need for new shoes, was not beyond the concern of the God of the universe had left him feeling small and humbled.

"I suppose I should begin with my dream from the night before, but I must warn you, Penny, it is a bit unpleasant." Sarah's voice was soft and solemn.

"I have a very sturdy constitution, dear sister. You need not worry on my account." Penny patted Sarah's hand affectionately, though she watched Sarah with concern.

"All right then." Sarah told them in detail of her dream about the boy and the dead puppy in the box. Gresham sat still, staring at the tablecloth. He remained silent when she finished, but he covered her hand with his.

"Oh, my dear, that is distressing," Henry said as he gazed at her from over his spectacles. "But I should like to hear about your latest dream before we discuss this one, if that is all right."

"Yes, I agree." Sarah stared at the painting on the bookcase, her voice hushed and sad as she told them about her dream of her late husband. "His name was Michael. I remember it now."

Sarah stood and looked closely at the tiny initials painted at the bottom right corner. "S.G.," she said, and turned to Gresham, shaking her head. "Isn't it astonishing John? These really are my initials!"

"Indeed," Gresham agreed, his whole being reverberating with awe. "The Lord has orchestrated everything. Just think, Sarah, if you had not come to Hatfield, you might never have found your painting."

Sarah smiled at him with deep gratitude. "And if God had not sent you to rescue me, I would have never come to Hatfield." Then she quickly set her gaze back to the painting. "Wait a moment . . . wait." She held up her hand, studying the signature. She paced beside the table a few times, then stopped beside her sister-in-law. "Penny, help me. What are ladies names that begin with *S*, other than Sarah?"

"Well now, let me see. There's Sandra, and Sally, and Scarlett, hmmm."

"Sabrina and Sheila," Gresham added.

"And Sessily and Sade," Henry threw in.

"Hmmm, no, no, none of those. Keep going, please." Sarah bit her lips and rubbed her hands as she paced some more.

"Sage! I once knew a woman named Sage!" Penny nearly shouted.

"What about Sylvia or Sissy?"

"Sapphire!"

"Susan or Susanna?"

"Savanah? Or how about Samantha?"

"Oh!" Sarah stopped still. "Samantha. Samantha." She said the name over and over again under her breath. "Samantha, Samantha, Sammie, Sam, Sam . . . That's it!" Facing them with wide eyes, she declared brightly, "My name is not Sarah. It is Samantha. Mrs. Samantha Gresham!"

AFTER THEY CELEBRATED the miraculous discovery of her painting and her given name with a glass of sherry, they were called to an early luncheon by the cook. Before taking her seat, Samantha paused in front of the large mirror over the mantel and smiled back at her reflection. "Samantha, Samantha Gresham," she whispered with content.

"Now that we know your true Christian name, Samantha," Henry said. "I feel much better about registering your marriage with the records office, and we should be going there before we leave town to sign the papers. John, where is that note you obtained from the pawnbroker about the auctioneer in Shefford? I should like to see it again."

John retrieved the note from his pocket and read it aloud before passing it to his brother-in-law. "Mr. Charles Blyde, auctioneer, Shefford, Bedfordshire. I believe we should go there and see where it may lead. What are your thoughts, Samantha?

Goodness, but it is so wonderful to be able to call you by your proper name."

"And it sounds so very nice to hear you say it, John! Yes, we should go to Shefford as soon as possible. How far is it from Hatfield, Henry?" Samantha's heart was so full of joy she could hardly eat.

"It is not far at all, only about half a day's carriage ride in good weather, I should say. I would recommend leaving just after luncheon today and making a stop overnight if I were not still awaiting a response to my request for an appointment with His Lordship."

"Oh, Henry, do you really think we would be able to start for Shefford today?" Penny shared an excited glance with Samantha. "It would be wonderful to find more clues about Samantha. We might find out more about her family, where she lived."

"Yes, my dear, but you know I must wait until I have heard from Lord Salisbury. He may even grant me an interview yet this very day. We must trust the timing to God and proceed accordingly, my dear."

As the Keates were conversing, Samantha's enthusiasm was marred by a fleeting bolt of fear racing through her, startling her with an icy warning.

Henry must have seen the change in her demeanor. "Samantha, if you are not up to traveling to Shefford, we do not have to go. We have no idea what we might find there, good or bad or nothing at all. Perhaps you would like some time to adjust to all the new discoveries of the day before you are ready to explore new ones."

"Oh yes, indeed, my dear. Forgive me for getting ahead," Penny said. "We will not go a moment before you are ready. In fact, we might even allow our husbands to make the trip for us if you think that would be better."

"Thank you, Penny." Samantha sighed. "I am not quite sure what to think just now. I do feel a bit uneasy. If I could just have a little time to think about what has happened this morning, I—"

She was interrupted by a knock at the front door, and the house maid entered with a curtsy and an envelope on a tray. "Message for you, Rector. From Hatfield House, sir."

"Ah, that will be from Lord Salisbury." Breaking the seal, Henry read the short communication. "Very good. His Lordship will grant John and me an audience the day after tomorrow at three o'clock. Well, I'd say that gives us just enough time to make for Shefford today, stay the night, and return tomorrow morning—that is, if you would like to do so, Samantha. As I am still waiting for word from the seminary, it may be a good use of time."

John searched her face. "It can still wait, Samantha, if you would like to have more time to think it over."

"Yes, John." She sighed again. "But I do believe Henry is right. It would be a good use of time, and besides, we may learn things that might prove useful to us as we decide what to do and where to go next." Samantha gave John a weak smile. Taking a deep breath, she addressed them all. "Let us leave for Shefford presently. I am sure the Lord will help me to face whatever is waiting for me there."

❋

SHEFFORD WAS A MARKET TOWN, situated beside the River Ivel. Gresham had never been there, but the Keates had visited once or twice. It had a few wide streets filled with shops, pubs, and trades, and they might have enjoyed wandering the town if not for their urgent quest to find Mr. Charles Blyde.

They stopped at the livery stables and went into the traveler's pub next door to inquire as to the location of the auction house. Gresham then hired a coach to take them to the other side of town to the address.

Gresham watched Samantha's face as they traveled the short distance. She gripped his hand tightly, and he could read anxiety in her eyes, despite her brave smile. He'd had misgivings ever since they'd left Hatfield that perhaps this was happening too soon for her. He prayed for wisdom as his mind raced ahead, anticipating what they might find.

When the coach stopped before the large auction hall, he paused before stepping out. "Samantha, are you sure about this? It is not too late to say you are not ready."

"No, John," she said. "We have come all this way, and we shall see this through together. I will be all right," and she touched his cheek with her gloved hand.

He helped her and his sister out of the coach and retrieved Samantha's well-wrapped painting.

"May the Lord be with us," Henry said, and they entered. The hall was large and the ceiling high. There were tables and partitions, shelves and displays, some empty and some full. In the center was a raised platform surrounded by empty space, where the auctioneer would conduct his business on auction day.

Gresham spotted the office sign hung high in the front corner of the hall, and they made their way down the aisle between lots of furniture and farm tools. At first there seemed to be no one present, but after knocking, they heard a voice from the back of the hall shouting, "I'm coming . . . I'm coming!"

A tall man with a rather black mustache appeared in the aisle, wiping his hands on his long apron. "Good afternoon, ladies and gentlemen. Auction day isn't until Saturday, unless you have come to inquire about selling something?" He took his place behind the counter and leaned on it.

"Actually, we have come to inquire about something else." Gresham placed the painting on the counter. "We are seeking a Mr. Charles Blyde, sir. Might that be you?"

"At your service, sir." The man's smile made his mustache grow even larger. "And what may I do for you good people?"

Giving Samantha a questioning look, Gresham waited for her approval before unwrapping the painting. She nodded, and he carefully removed the string and fabric. He placed it before the auctioneer, and Mr. Blyde looked it over carefully.

"Do you recognize this painting, Mr. Blyde?" Gresham watched the man's face intently.

"Hmmm. It seems a bit familiar, but you must understand, sir. I have many, many paintings come and go here, and I cannot remember them all."

"Yes, of course." Gresham nodded. "You see, this painting was bought from you by a Mr. Lawrence, a pawnbroker in Hatfield, Hertfordshire." Gresham removed a paper from his pocket and showed it to Mr. Blyde. "He says he bought it from you around six months ago. We found it in his shop just yesterday."

"Hmmm, yes, I am familiar with Mr. Lawrence. Give me a moment, if you please, and I shall search my records."

"We are especially interested in who brought you the painting, sir. It is a matter of utmost importance," Gresham said as Mr. Blyde unlocked the office door behind the counter.

"Yes, of course. A moment, please." The man disappeared behind the door.

Gresham felt the suspense in the air and tucked Samantha's hand protectively under his arm. At last Mr. Blyde emerged with a few record books and placed them on the counter.

"Let me look through these now. I assure you I keep meticulous records and am sure to find the information you need." Mr. Blyde ran his finger down one page, then another. "Here it is. Painting, eleven by fourteen inches, landscape, grove of trees in evening light, painted by S.G." Blyde turned the book around for the group to see. "Just there. Sold to me by a Mr. Richard M. Granville of Campton, Bedfordshire. You can see the address here. Shall I copy it down for you?"

Gresham read the entry over Samantha's shoulder. "Yes please. Is there anything you can tell us about this man, Granville? Do you remember him?"

"Hmm, vaguely. Tall but not quite my height, I should say. And I would guess the ladies would find him to be rather a dandy, sir. Well dressed, if I remember correctly."

Gresham turned to Samantha, whose eyes were fixed on the name on the page. She had frozen stiff, and he gently turned her toward him. "My dear, let me take you to the coach with Penny while Henry and I finish up with Mr. Blyde."

She nodded slightly and readily allowed him to escort her back outside. She paused before entering the coach and faced him. "John, it is him. He was known to his family and friends by his middle name, Michael. My name was Samantha Granville, and—" She faltered, and Gresham lifted her into the coach.

"Penny, look after her. I will only be a moment!" He hurried back into the auction hall. Henry had rewrapped the painting and was headed to the entrance, motioning for Gresham to go back out. "I have asked many more questions, John, but the man seems to know nothing more about Granville. Here is the address he copied down for us. He says that Campton lies but a few miles southwest of here."

CHAPTER

# TWENTY-FIVE

G resham and Henry joined the ladies in the coach but did not yet give the driver instructions as to where to go next. Samantha's face was full of confusion, and she rocked in her seat, her eyes distant and sad.

"Samantha, are you all right? How can we help you?" Gresham's stomach knotted, and he chastised himself for not waiting longer before coming to Shefford. "I am sorry for bringing you here before you were truly ready. Henry and I should have come alone and spared you this . . . this—"

"No, John, no." Samantha waved her hand. "I . . . I just need to think, I . . . Where is the notebook I brought with me? I should like to write some things down." She searched urgently around her seat.

"It is with our bags on the back of the coach, John," Penny said.

Gresham dashed out and back.

Samantha took the book and pencil with shaking hands. "I am not sure I can write just now. Henry, would you mind taking things down for me?" Her voice trembled as she handed the items across to him.

"Of course, my dear. Just take your time now. I am ready."

Gresham's heart raced. He held her hand tightly, waiting with bated breath.

"Michael Granville. I vaguely remember our wedding inside a brick church, a bit like St. Etheldreda's, only smaller and less grand. I can only make out his face, and no one else. Everything is cloudy. I wasn't happy, though I tried my best to be. Mostly I was afraid."

Her body tensed, and a flush of anger blew through him. "Can you remember what you were afraid of, Samantha? Were you afraid of him?"

"I cannot tell you exactly. I was afraid of him, but it was more than that. I was, I—" She paused as a new thought crossed her pale face. "I did not want to leave. I was afraid of going abroad with him and leaving my home." She looked up into Gresham's face with understanding. "He was taking me away, because . . . because, he was running from something, someone."

She tugged on his hand with pleading eyes, "Oh please, John, let us go to the address the man gave you. We might find my family! Please!"

"If you are sure, my dear. We can go, but I am deeply concerned for you." Gresham battled with his own opposing forces, wanting to go and find what they could but anxious not to expose Samantha to any potential heartache that might be waiting for her there.

"Yes, hurry. Let us go now and see!" Samantha pleaded

Gresham nodded reluctantly as Henry addressed the driver.

At Gresham's insistence, Samantha lay her head on his shoulder and closed her eyes. He exchanged worried glances with Penny and Henry, and they rode mostly in silence the few miles to the village of Campton. The evening sky grew darker as heavy clouds gathered, threatening rain.

Samantha sat up and watched out the window as they came into town, still holding tight to Gresham's hand.

"Oh!" she suddenly exclaimed. "Stop, please stop!"

Henry ordered the driver to stop, and they all peered with her out the window. "That is it!" she exclaimed. "The church where we were married."

Henry instructed the driver to pull onto the lane, and they climbed out in front of the churchyard gate. The sign on the brick wall read, *Church of All Saints*. Samantha gasped, her gloved hand flying to her mouth.

"Are you sure you want to go in?" Gresham asked.

She nodded.

Holding firmly to her elbow, he opened the gate and guided her down the gravel walkway to the entrance at the side of the church. He twisted the doorknob and opened the heavy wooden door.

They found the church utterly silent, lit only by the fading light from the arched windows. Gresham felt a prickling run down his spine as he looked down the archways of the nave to the space in front of the wooden pews, where marriage ceremonies were held. Samantha trod slowly into the center aisle, her face pale and her eyes full of old shadows.

Gresham stayed close behind her as Penny and Henry followed. To his surprise, she turned at the front pew to stand just under the high pulpit. She stared intensely at the space above her, where the rector would stand to give his sermons. Without moving, she reached a trembling hand toward him, and tears fell from her softening eyes.

Gresham took hold of her, gently sat her on the front pew,

and knelt beside her, as Henry and Penny sat on each side. "What is it, my love? What do you see?"

"Father . . . I see my father," she whispered and turned a teary smile to him. "I see my dear, dear father. He is the rector of this church."

"My heavens, Samantha, how wonderful." Penny raised her gloved hand to her heart, mist filling her eyes.

Gresham's heart leaped in his chest. "Oh, my dear, this is amazing!"

She smiled happily, grasped his shoulder, and shook him urgently. "Oh, John, John! What if he is still here? We must find him!"

She stood, and they rose with her with renewed energy.

"Samantha, listen to your heart," Henry softly encouraged. "Where does it lead you?"

She smiled at him, her eyes sparkling, and led them back down the aisle and out the back doorway. It had begun to rain lightly, but Gresham hardly noticed. Samantha looked around her, then pointed to the stand of trees to their right, behind the church. She ran toward the grove, hoisting her skirts, laughing like a child.

Gresham ran after her. The scene was somehow familiar to him, and it came to him as he ran.

"This is the grove in my painting!" Samantha shouted back at him in delight. He caught up to her, smiling as she took his hand and swung his arm playfully. "Can you see it, John?"

"Yes, yes I can!"

She laughed again and led him into the trees, weaving in and out under their stately branches. He had never seen her so happy, so beautiful, so whole. She halted behind a large pine and faced him, pulling him close.

"Kiss me, John, my love. Kiss me," she said breathlessly, her chest rising and falling, full of life and vitality.

Gresham's body surged with longing for her as he drew her into his hungry arms and kissed her deeply, passionately. "Oh, Samantha, how I love you."

A flash of lightning and burst of thunder startled them, and they could hear Penny's concerned voice calling.

The rain was increasing by the moment, and they ran laughing back to Penny, who had sent Henry to the coach for umbrellas. But before he returned, Samantha's smile faltered. She moved slowly, cautiously across the wide churchyard toward a gate in the tall wall to the west—there were too many trees behind it to see what lay beyond.

Gresham's heart sank with a new foreboding as he followed her to the gate. Once there, they peered together and tried to make sense of what lie behind the tangle of unkept bushes and branches. He opened the gate, checking her face for signs of distress. "What is it?"

She held tightly to his arm as they picked their way through the brush, and then they saw it. Samantha screamed and ran without him toward the hulk of a blackened, burned-out building.

He caught her just before she stepped into the charred, wet rubble. "Samantha!" he cried as her legs gave way, and they crumbled to the blackened ground beneath them.

Henry came running, followed by Penny under her umbrella. They huddled over them as Gresham knelt in the wet ashes with Samantha on his knee. "Oh no! Oh no, John! This was our house. This was where we lived. What has happened to it?"

The only thing left of the house were a few bits of standing brick and collapsed roof beams lying like enormous black bones around the edges of the ashen interior.

"Henry, would you ask the coachman to come around?" Gresham asked, lifting his wife into his arms.

THEY DROVE BACK the way they had come, to an inn Henry had seen on their way into Campton. Henry went in to arrange for rooms and dinner. Gresham helped Samantha, whose wet clothing was streaked with black soot, like his own, inside and up the stairs to their rooms. Penny and Henry traipsed after them, and the innkeeper set their luggage just inside the door.

Gresham took Samantha to a chair and bent to take off her wet slippers.

"Your dinner will be ready shortly," the bearded innkeeper said. "I will let you know—"

Gresham looked up when the innkeeper paused and saw the surprise on his face. "Why, is that you, Mrs. Granville? What a wonderful surprise to see you back in Campton!"

Samantha stood, as did Gresham. She stared at the man. "I . . . I know your face, sir. You are—"

"Ivan James, madam. You would remember me and my wife, Hope, surely. She is just downstairs in the kitchen. She will be right glad to see you, Mrs. Granville, indeed she will!" The man smiled broadly, showing a few missing teeth.

Samantha slowly stepped toward him. "Oh yes, Mr. James. Of course I do remember you."

Henry stepped between them and encouraged the man out into the hall. "It is very nice to meet you, Mr. James. And we will be delighted to meet your wife as well, sir, as soon as we come down for dinner. Now if you will excuse us, we can all do with a bit of freshening up. Thank you for your assistance," and he closed the door.

Penny nodded with approval at her husband and took over with Samantha. "Now, gentlemen, if you please, you can use the other room, and I will help Samantha out of these wet things."

GRESHAM AND HENRY did not wait for Mr. James to call for them before heading down to the dimly lit pub. There were no other guests there, so they asked the innkeeper for a pint each and invited him to join them at a table in the corner by the window. The rain poured down in sheets now, with flashes of lightning and rumblings of distant thunder over the countryside.

"Thank you for giving us a moment of your time, Mr. James," Gresham began, his face grim. "We would like to ask you a few questions, if you don't mind."

"Oh, I don't mind, sir, but begging your pardon, might I first know who you are?"

Gresham darted Henry a wary glance. "My name is Johnathan Gresham, and this is my brother-in-law, Reverend Henry Keate. We have come here from Hatfield in search of information regarding Mrs., uh, well, her name is no longer Mrs. Granville, you see. It's—"

"Oh really!" interrupted the innkeeper. "Now that is some news, sir, indeed. And may I ask, what has happened to Mr. Granville?" He tilted his head and eyed Gresham under his shaggy gray brows.

"He has passed away, you see—"

"Passed away, you say? Already? Why, he was still a young man in his prime when last I saw him, which would have been just a few weeks after their wedding. How came he to be dead so soon, sir, if you don't mind my asking?"

Irritated at the man's constant interruptions, Gresham took a sip from his pint and tried to renew his patience. "He was murdered, Mr. James, and we have come to—"

"Murdered, you say!" His voice rose in pitch and volume, and he rose from his seat. "Well now, Mr. Gresham, I should like my wife to join us for this conversation, if you don't mind. Hope, my dearie, come quick! There is something you must hear. Come quickly."

Hearing the shuffle of footsteps, he winked at Gresham and Henry. "Aww, there she is, my bonnie lass."

Gresham and Henry stood as she approached, an apple-cheeked woman no taller than Gresham's elbow, wiping her hands on her apron and adjusting her white cap. "This is Mr. Gresham and Reverend Keate, my dear, the gentlemen who have traveled from Hatfield with our dear Mrs.—oh yes, Mr. Gresham was just telling me—"

"Yes, pleased to meet you, Mrs. James," Gresham interrupted this time. They were seated once again, and Gresham took another sip of his pint, considering what to share and what not to. "Please let me explain." He held his hand up as James took a breath to speak. "Mrs. Granville's late husband, Mr. Granville, is deceased, madam, and—"

"Murdered, my dear. The man has been murdered." James looked at his wife from under his bushy brows.

"Oh! You don't say!" the woman exclaimed. "Well, thanks be to God, I say! Oh, forgive me, Rector, that was not a very Christian thing to say, I'm afraid—"

Henry shot Gresham a wide-eyed glance. "No, madam, indeed not, but you must have good reason to say such a thing. Please tell us what it is."

With a slight hesitation she said, "Oh, well, I don't mean to be uncharitable, sir, especially to Mrs. Granville, dear girl, but being that the man is dead—"

"I'll tell you, Rector," James said. "The man was a lout, sir. A lout and a scoundrel," and he slapped his hand on the table with a whack.

"How so, sir?" Henry asked. "Pray, enlighten us."

James continued. "Word had it that he was in terrible debt

when he married Mrs. Granville. He married her and ran off to Jamaica with her to flee from his creditors, he did. Even though he had studied for the church, he was a terrible gambler." He nodded stiffly to his wife, who then took up the tale.

"He and his brother, they were quite the pair of them, sir. His brother helped him by getting him a place as a missionary in a Jamaican mission. The way I saw it, serving the good Lord was the only way that man could convince her to marry and go away with him, poor girl. And now you have brought her back here? I can hardly believe it. And I will tell you, gentlemen, it don't surprise me one bit that man met his fate the way he did. Not one bit."

Gresham's mind whirled, trying to absorb all he was hearing. Henry had taken out the notebook from his coat and was scribbling as fast as he could.

"You are not surprised? Why? And what about this brother of his? Who is he?" Gresham asked.

"Well, sir," James answered, "if you don't mind me giving you my honest opinion . . . I don't mean any disrespect to Mrs. Granville, you understand—"

"Please, Mr. James, speak freely," Gresham encouraged.

"All right then." James narrowed his eyes. "As I understand it, there was three brothers. We never saw the eldest. He's to inherit, you see, and wouldn't have nothing to do with Mrs. Granville. Their father, the Marquess of Pommeroy, never approved of his youngest son's choice for a wife, even though they grew up just next door to each other in Cambridgeshire and were longtime friends. But his half brother, Captain Granville—"

"Captain Granville?!" Gresham nearly shot out of his chair. "His brother is a naval captain?" His mind was wild with the implications.

"Yes, sir. And he is the one who took Mrs. Granville and his brother off to Jamaica not but a month after the wedding."

A hideous revulsion filled Gresham's belly, and his veins felt like they ran with a black poison. He looked at Henry, whose face blanched with alarm. It was her late husband's own brother, his own flesh and blood, who did this to him, to her. Gresham wanted to vomit but swallowed hard and asked his next terrible question.

"And what of her family? She was completely undone when we found the vicarage in ruins just before we came here." He dreaded to know but forced the question out of his clenched mouth.

"Oh! You mean you don't know?" Mr. and Mrs. James went silent. Mrs. James looked with worried brows up at her husband's long face and pulled a handkerchief from her apron pocket. "I can't tell them, Ivan. Please . . ." She wiped a sudden tear from her round cheek.

Gresham's heart sank. "The rector and his lovely wife, sir, they passed away in the fire. They couldn't get out in time, but Mrs. Granville's sister, Miss Josephine, she was rescued, though badly burned, they say. We don't know how bad, as we haven't seen her since she was taken to a hospital in London just after the fire."

Gresham sat back in stunned silence and gazed out the window. Nothing could be seen but the occasional flash, followed by the low roll of thunder. *Dear God*, he prayed, *dear God in heaven, how will I tell her.*

"How long ago was the fire, Mr. James?" Henry's voice was low and sad.

"'Twas only around a month and a half after Mrs. Granville left, sir. Did no one tell her?" The innkeeper patted his wife's knee as she quietly wept at his side.

"Do they know what caused the fire?" Gresham asked.

"Well, the constable had a man from the London court up to take a look, and they said it started in the front parlor, sir."

"And the rector and his wife, were they found?" Gresham could barely speak the question.

"Not much of them, I'm afraid. The man from London said they should have had time to get out. He thought maybe somebody locked all the doors and windows from the outside somehow, though he couldn't prove it, but that's what they say Miss Josephine told him. She only got out from the window of the sitting room after the fire brigade broke it open, sir."

"Oh dear, oh dear," Mrs. James said between sniffles. "She doesn't know any of this yet. How terrible it will be for her."

*Indeed it will.* Gresham's body was drained and limp, but he still thought to ask one more important question. "What were their names?"

Mr. James's face grew sorrowful. "Mr. Edmond and Geraldine Hollingsworth, sir, and they were the finest folks I ever knew."

# CHAPTER
# TWENTY-SIX

Braxton sat on a bench near the walkway to the administration building, observing all who came and went. Wearing civilian clothes and a brown tricorn, he hadn't shaved and looked as scruffy as any of the tradesmen roaming the docks.

He sat reading Samantha's Bible, his hand in his pocket holding her little piece of flint and had just finished reading the Sermon on the Mount, when he heard a familiar voice coming up the walk. Pulling his hat lower over his face, he recognized the voice of Mr. Daniel Darby, frantically speaking to the marine hurriedly escorting him to the doors of the administration building.

Braxton's pulse quickened as he rose to follow at a distance.

"I am so very glad that the admiral has read my letter and agreed to see me. I have been most unjustly treated by that Captain Compton, and the admiral should know that his orders were defiantly disobeyed."

The silent marine opened the large door and followed

Darby, still rattling on, inside. Braxton tucked the Bible under his arm and paused only long enough to allow his quarry a little headway, then entered the large hall himself. He saw them head up the large staircase, which Braxton mounted calmly. Darby and the marine turned to the back of the second floor, toward Admiral Warwick's office.

Braxton leaned casually against the wall, where he could peer under his hat at the office door. The admiral opened the door, and Darby was escorted in.

Braxton's lips tightened. If only Gresham were here—he would know what to do. Aware he couldn't simply stand where he was, he strolled the other way and peered over the side of the staircase at the people going and coming below. *How I wish I could be a fly on the wall of the admiral's office just now*, he thought, still not sure what his next move should be.

Finally he went down the stairs to wait for Darby to come back down. A rather thin, gaunt-looking man in an officer's uniform passed him going up. His face seemed somehow familiar, but try as he might, Braxton couldn't place him.

Pacing the lower hall, he listened for Darby's voice and kept an eye on the stairs.

He waited for an hour before heading back outside to watch from the bench. There he waited another hour, as his backside flattened. He crossed over to the east steps of the Clock House and watched yet another hour, until he was finally spotted by Mr. Green entering the dockyard gate.

"Mr. Smith and I have some interesting news for ya, sir. Perhaps ya would like ta join us for an early dinner." Mr. Green walked away before Braxton answered.

Braxton pressed to his feet with a heavy sigh, and they caught a cab to the Lee Side Inn.

⁕

THEY SAT at the table in the attic, and Braxton told Mr. Green, Mrs. Yates, and Mr. Smith about seeing Mr. Darby and what he had overheard.

"Oh, dear me, Doctor, will that man ever stop causing trouble?" Mrs. Yates lamented as she poured the wine.

"Not yet, it seems, Mrs. Yates." Braxton took a long sip from his glass and eyed Mr. Green. "You said you had something interesting to share with me, Mr. Green?"

The steward cleared his throat and gave Mr. Smith a sideways wink. "Yes, Dr. Braxton, indeed. Mr. Smith has proven ta be most helpful, sir. Ya see, he can speak with people who would never dream o' disclosing anything ta me, isn't that right, Mr. Smith?"

Mr. Smith sat quietly, and Green didn't wait for his silent friend to answer. "Ya see, I gave Mrs. Gresham's knife ta Mr. Smith ta take around ta the Negro sailors here at the dockyard, asking around fer its owner. And low and behold, if he didn't come up with a name."

Braxton bent forward over his plate, his fork in midair. "And what is this name, if you please?"

"Tell him, Mr. Smith. This is yer good deed, not mine," Green encouraged.

"Samuel Gardner, sir" was the base-toned reply.

"Samuel Gardner! Well, congratulations, Mr. Smith. You have done us all proud." Mrs. Yates gushed over the shy giant.

"Yes, thank you so much for your help, Mr. Smith, and did you find out anything about this Samuel Gardner?" Braxton was eager to pull more out of the man.

"'E's a sailor, sir, and word 'as it the ship he sails on, the HMS *Peleus*, 'as just docked 'ere at Woolwich."

"The HMS *Peleus*?!" Braxton could hardly believe his ears. He dashed to his room and dug through his papers, returning quickly with a copy of the list of third-rate Arrogant class ships and their captains. He skimmed through the names, mumbling to himself. "Aha! Captain Felix Granville! We've got him!"

✳

IT WAS STILL RAINING LIGHTLY as they rode back to Hatfield the next morning. Samantha lay cradled on Gresham's lap, completely drained by her grief. He wished he did not have to take her from Campton so soon, but there was nothing left for her there besides a few family friends. Henry had interviewed the constable and the new rector, but not much more had been learned.

Once they arrived at the old vicarage, Gresham helped Samantha up to the Blue Room and Penny took over from there. It was already half past two, and he and Henry were due for their audience with Lord Salisbury at three.

Henry's man, Edward, hitched up his small carriage, and they drove down the Great North Road south to the entrance gate for Hatfield House. The rain stopped and the clouds were lifting, and the fresh air gave Gresham a much-needed respite.

He hardly noticed the extensive gardens and groves as they rattled up the long, straight drive. He was equally as unaware of the magnificence of the massive mansion as they dismounted and were led by a servant into the enormous entry doors. Turning right, they marched past the lattice-filled archways and through a large door at the end of the walkway.

Mounting the grand wooden staircase, Gresham noticed paintings of Adam and Eve as he climbed the steps to the ante-room above. There, they were asked to wait. He felt small under the richly paneled ceilings, standing next to a life-sized portrait of King George III reviewing the troops on the lands of this very house.

"Hmmm, yes," Henry said softly beside him. "His Majesty was here in 1800, before he became ill."

"His Lordship will see you now," said the servant behind them, motioning toward the library door.

Gresham's breath caught in spite of him by the splendor of the place. There were bookcases full of books, from the richly carpeted floors to the high ceilings paneled in white with gold relief. All the chairs were upholstered in red leather, and above the white marble fireplace was a mosaic painting of a man of importance. They were led in the other direction, where a well-dressed gentleman in his later years sat behind a great wooden desk.

"Ah, and here is my favorite rector, Mr. Keate. How are you, my dear fellow?" The Marquess of Salisbury stood and offered Henry his hand.

"I am well, Your Lordship, and most grateful that you would grant me and my brother-in-law here, Captain Johnathan Gresham, an audience at such short notice." Henry bowed, then shook the man's hand.

Gresham bowed, and Salisbury shook his hand as well and returned to his seat.

"Please, gentlemen, make yourselves comfortable. May I offer you some sherry? Adams, please, fetch us a tray, will you." Henry and Gresham took their seats in the plush red chairs in front of the palatial desk. "And now, Rector, there was an urgent quality to your request. Tell me all about it."

Gresham was relieved to find such an important man to be so considerate.

"Yes, thank you, my lord." Henry gave a side glance to Gresham and swallowed. "It is rather a complicated matter, so I will spare you as many details as possible. The gist of it, my lord, is to notify you of my need to be absent for a time in order to deal with some grave and pressing family concerns. My brother-in-law and his new wife require our assistance and support presently, and we have need to take some time in London."

"Oh, I see." Lord Salisbury raised his brows. "Well, Mr. Keate, I appreciate your informing me. Is there any way in which I can be helpful to you? How much time will you be in London, do you know?"

Adams came in with a tray and poured each of them a small crystal glass of sherry.

"Thank you," Henry said as he took his glass. "The length of our stay is still in question, my lord. I would rather err on the generous side and say we will need at least a month, if not two. I have already put my curate, Mr. Faithful, in charge."

Gresham sipped the sherry as if it were liquid gold. He had never tasted better and was glad for the wine's calming effect on his frayed nerves.

"Well, that is not such a very long time to be away, Rector." The marquess turned to Gresham. "I wish you all the best with your family matters. But how distressing for you and your new bride, Captain Gresham. Do you gentlemen have any family or friends to stay with in town?"

Gresham cleared his throat and sat up straighter. "My brother-in-law has been kind enough to make inquiries of his seminary in London, my lord. We are still waiting to hear if they will accommodate us."

Lord Salisbury did not immediately respond to this news but turned his chair to look thoughtfully out the window, his thinning lips pressing together, his fingertips touching in front of his chest. Henry gave Gresham a questioning look.

Salisbury turned back to them. "If you do not mind, Captain, may I ask, to what purpose do you travel to London?"

Gresham was startled by the directness of the question. "Well, my lord, there is a delicate and urgent matter concerning my wife, you see. She has been the victim of a crime, and we are in the midst of trying to find justice for her, sir." Gresham's hands grew sweaty, and his pulse quickened. He didn't want to lie to the marquess, yet neither did he want to say anything that wasn't truly necessary.

Lord Salisbury set down his glass and pulled his chair closer to his desk. "You mean to say that Mrs. Gresham has been victimized? By whom, sir? Do you know?" His voice was low and indignant.

Gresham replied simply. "Yes, my lord, we do."

Salisbury's long nose flared, and he blinked. "Well then, if you know who it is, why do you not notify the authorities immediately?"

"That, my lord, is a very long story," Henry declared. "We do not want to take up any more of your valuable time, Lord Salisbury—"

The marquess lifted his hand to Henry and kept his focus on Gresham. "Please, just one more question, Captain. Forgive me for prying, but will you not tell me this criminal's name?"

Gresham felt a flush of panic, but his hesitation was short. "He is Captain Felix Granville, sir, of His Majesty's Royal Navy."

Salisbury's eyes lit instantly with anger as he slapped the desk and stood. Henry and Gresham went to their feet, exchanging wide-eyed glances, and placed their glasses on the tray.

"Felix Granville? The detestable second son of that scoundrel the Marquess of Pommeroy?"

"You know of him, my lord?" Henry's mouth hung open, as did Gresham's.

"Sit down, gentlemen." He motioned for them to be seated as he poured another round from the sparkling bottle. "We have much to discuss. I knew there was a reason why I felt I had to know. It is like you say, Rector—the Lord works in mysterious ways." And he sat down heavily in his chair, taking up his glass.

Their conversation lasted another hour, as Lord Salisbury shared his story, and Gresham and Henry told theirs. They learned that Lord Salisbury's daughter, Caroline, had been accosted by Felix Granville at a ball at Hatfield House. When Lord Salisbury confronted him, he denied the charges and ran back to his father's estate in St. Ives. Salisbury followed him there and confronted Pommeroy concerning his son's behavior toward Caroline, only to be threatened with the spreading of lies about her and the ruin of the family's good name.

Gresham told what he could of Samantha's story, concluding with the revelations from the evening before about the suspicious death of her parents and of her missing wounded sister, Josephine. In the end, much to Gresham's and Henry's surprise, Lord Salisbury insisted that he join them in their quest and that they all travel with him that very evening to his house in St. James's Square in the West End of London.

"Now, gentlemen, I must conference with Lady Salisbury about my departure, and you must make haste back to the vicarage and make ready. It is terrible indeed to impose this bit of travel upon Mrs. Gresham, but she will be most comfortable once she is safely tucked up in my townhouse. Please, Rector, make sure that Mrs. Keate does not have the vapors worrying about dresses and such. I will instruct my coachman to collect you from Back Street behind the church, which I hope will provide you more privacy than gathering you from the front of your house. Now if you will excuse me."

Henry and Gresham rode back to the vicarage in a state of shock and awe. "Henry," Gresham asked, still shaking his head in disbelief, "what just happened?"

"A godsend, my boy, an honest to goodness godsend!"

※

PENNY SAT in the chair beside Samantha, who lay in the bed of the Blue Room. Gresham's heart oozed with pain for her as he sat at Samantha's feet. She lay pale and spent against the satin pillows. "How are you, my dear?"

"I am not doing very well, John, but God is carrying me through one breath at a time." Her voice was weak from sobbing and her eyes swollen from crying.

"You are my brave one, Samantha. I need to tell you that we have a difficult time ahead, my dear. I can hardly bear to say it, but we must be ready to travel to London within the hour, and before we leave town, you and I will need to go to the clerk's office and register our marriage license."

"Good heavens, John. We leave within the hour? Has Henry heard back from the seminary?" Penny's eyes flashed back to Samantha. "Oh, brother, how can we put this poor girl through all of this? She needs peace and rest."

"I am most painfully aware, sister." He nearly moaned. "And I would give anything not to make Samantha move from this place, but it cannot be helped." Reaching over to take her hand, he kissed it and continued, the lump in his throat making it nearly impossible to speak. "God has sent us another miracle, Samantha. He has provided a very safe place to stay in London and a powerful new ally to help us. We are being taken by Lord Salisbury to his house in St. James's Square, and he has pledged to help us in any way that he can."

Penny's mouth dropped open. "Lord Salisbury? We are . . . he is . . . What are you saying, John?"

"It is true, Penny. Now, we do not have the luxury of time to discuss it more. We must hurry and have everything ready to close up the house immediately. In the meantime, Samantha and I will walk down and sign the marriage registration."

Gresham's eyes misted over, and he lowered his head. "I am sorry, my love. So very sorry."

✳

BRAXTON SAT at the little desk, writing an urgent letter to Gresham, when Mr. Green entered the attic sitting room with alarm. "Hurry, Doctor, pack yer things. Capt'n Gresham has sent his brother-in-law's man, Edward, ta fetch ya. Mrs. Gresham is in a bad way, and they need ya at once."

Without hesitation Braxton gathered his papers from the desk and went to the bedroom. In moments he returned to the table with his bag packed and stacks of papers and letters. Sorting through them, he came across the drawings Sarah had given him and stopped short. Picking one out, his eyes flashed with anger. "You! It was you on the staircase yesterday!"

"Who, sir? Did ya see one o' those scoundrels?" Mr. Green rushed to his side and looked at the drawing labeled "Doctor."

"Yes, Mr. Green. I saw him yesterday for only a moment on the staircase in the administration building." Braxton gathered the rest of the drawings and handed them to Green. "You may need these. Keep them out of sight."

"Aye, Doctor. Are ya ready, sir?"

They went out the back door of the inn, made their way to the roadside of the stable, and found Mr. Smith, Mrs. Yates, and young Edward waiting in the shadows.

Mrs. Yates kissed his cheek. "Oh, my dear Doctor, please be safe and give them all my warmest greetings. Tell them I will pray for Mrs. Gresham, and please keep us informed."

"God speed, Dr. Braxton." Green and Smith saluted him and shook his hand.

"Keep up the good work, gentlemen, and keep an eye out

for Darby and Mr. Gardner. I will send word back as soon as I arrive and know more."

Braxton turned to Edward. "What has happened, Edward? Is Mrs. Gresham hurt?"

"No, Doctor, but she has had some terrible news, sir."

"What news?" Braxton paused on the step of the carriage as Edward went to his seat up top.

"They have discovered so many things. Her real name is Samantha Granville, and her poor parents were killed in a terrible fire. Hurry, Doctor, we are off to London!" Edward motioned for Braxton to get in.

"London? Where in London?" Braxton's head was in a whirl at all the new developments.

"To St. James's Square, sir. To the house of Lord Salisbury."

AFTER SEEING Dr. Braxton off and returning to the pub inside, Mrs. Yates was approached by a strange, gaunt man in a naval officer's uniform. Mr. Green recognized his face immediately and motioned for Smith to follow him out the back door. They hurried around among the shadows, where they viewed the man mounting a horse. But before they could rush out of hiding, the man rode away heading west, the same direction Braxton and Edward had taken but a few minutes before.

Mr. Green ripped his straw hat from his head and slapped it against his thigh. "Blast!" He spat, then motioned for Smith to follow him back to the kitchen.

"What did that scary-looking chap have ta say ta ya, Mrs. Yates?" Green asked her in a panic.

Mrs. Yates's eyes were as grave as Green's. "He was asking who the man was who just left in the carriage."

"And what did ya tell him, me dear?"

"That he should never come to my inn again if he was only here to ask questions that were none of his business—that is what I told him!"

Green's face expanded into a wide, appreciative grin. "That's ma girl!"

※

PENELOPE KEATE HAD ACCOMPLISHED a heroic feat. She had everything packed, the servants taken care of, the dressmaker and boot maker notified of the forwarding address, and had placed an order for proper mourning clothes for Samantha. She'd convinced her husband to send Edward with their carriage to the Lee Side Inn for Dr. Braxton, and she'd even packed a basket of refreshments for the drive to London.

At any other time in her life, her head would have turned completely around with the thought of being the house guest of the Marquess of Salisbury in his home in St. James's Square in the most fashionable part of London, but something had been altering her view of society and propriety since her brother and Samantha's arrival at the old vicarage.

She had known grief herself, when her little sister, Meredith, had died tragically at the dry dock at Woolwich and when her parents had passed away together ten years ago from influenza. But she had never truly experienced the kind of violation, the unspeakable cruelty and grief that her sister-in-law had, and was still enduring. In light of Samantha's suffering, everything else seemed like vanity, and she had become keenly aware of how far she had succumbed to vanity's temptations over the years.

She and Henry had never been blessed with children, but she could feel her maternal instincts forging to the surface as she cared for Samantha. Her capacity for empathy had grown much in the last few days, and though there was deep pain in the stretching of her heart, she felt she was a better woman for it.

It was in this mindset that she entered the marquess's exquisitely grand and palatial house in London. Her head was not turned but was steady, focused on the ministry God had set before her, as she kept her mind on all that was genuine and true.

Braxton arrived only a short time after them, and when he entered Samantha's bedchamber, Penny flew into his arms and held on to him with relief. "Oh, Doctor! We are so glad you have come!"

## CHAPTER

# TWENTY-SEVEN

Darby was exceedingly relieved when Admiral Warwick sent for him the next morning. He felt small in his chair in front of the great desk as he explained how badly Captain Compton had treated him, the measly amount he had been given in compensation for his goods, and the fact that Compton had deliberately disobeyed the admiral's direct orders to ensure that every one of the *Relentless*'s crew that had arrived with her at Woolwich should also leave with her for the Mediterranean.

Darby also delicately probed to see what Warwick knew about Mrs. Green, her late husband, and the actions taken by Captain Gresham, all of which the admiral indicated he had already been informed. Darby thought he had impressed Warwick by telling him of the Lee Side Inn and Hatfield, which the admiral took note of.

But then, much to Darby's surprise, the tide turned.

Warwick sat behind his desk and glared down at Darby for several minutes. He shifted uncomfortably.

At last the admiral broke his silence. "I received a copy of

Captain Compton's letter requesting that you be court-martialed. You have only proven the spirit of his accusations by your own behavior here today. What makes you think I am interested in the affairs of Captain Gresham, that I would take your word over those of a captain, Mr. Darby?" Warwick steepled his fingers in front of his aging lips and eyed Darby

"Well, sir, I . . . did not suppose, Admiral," Darby stuttered. "I was not trying to act dishonorably, sir—"

"Tell me why, Mr. Darby, I should not throw you out of my office and have you clapped in irons for your indiscretions," Warwick shouted, slamming the desk hard.

Darby was shaken. He had completely underestimated the admiral and had nothing left to use as leverage. "Well, Admiral, I was only trying to be helpful, sir. Captain Compton—"

"Captain Compton is a very long way from Woolwich by now. But as far as being helpful, or, rather, useful, that is still in question. Yes . . ." Warwick went to the wall and tugged twice on a long bell pull. "I will give you a chance to prove how useful you can be, Mr. Darby. But I warn you, if you do not pass the test, then I will see to it that a court-martial will be the least of your concerns."

*

DARBY ARRIVED in Hatfield just before dark, escorted by two strapping men under the employ of Admiral Warwick. He was still enraged by the treatment he had received but saw no way around doing the admiral's bidding.

He had been sent to spy on Gresham and Mrs. Green and to find out if their marriage had taken place. If so, under what name did the bride sign the registration? If the marriage had not taken place, or if the registration was made with false information, he was to bring both Gresham and Mrs. Green back to Woolwich and had within his possession the legal documents that gave him the power to ensure they complied.

Their first stop was at the registrar's office. Darby found that the marriage between a Captain Johnathan Gresham and a Mrs. Samantha Granville had been registered but a few hours before his arrival. He made a note of the names and felt a bit of relief. Good for them. He had no desire to cause them real harm but now needed something else to appease Admiral Warwick.

After a brief interview with the barkeep of the Eight Bells Tavern, he found he had not far to look for the rector and his place of residence. He and his escorts walked up Fore Street, passed the old vicarage and the church, then doubled back again. The house was dark, so Darby felt safe enough to lead his companions around the house, checking the doors and windows, all of which were locked.

Darby paused at the back of the stable and could see a gap between the door and the frame. He tried the latch, but it wouldn't move. However, the door was loose on its hinges. "Can you get me inside please?" he asked the brutes politely, stepping aside.

Within a moment the latch was broken and the door swung open. Darby found a lamp hanging on a hook near the door with a tinderbox and lit it, holding it up to the dark. No horses were in the stalls, and if there had been any means of transportation, it was now gone as well.

He let out an irritated sigh as he made it to the front of the stable and turned around to go back, then paused at the site of something oddly familiar against the wall to the side. Moving closer and wiping the straw from the top, Darby smiled with great satisfaction. "Congratulations, Mr. Darby. We shall bring the admiral a little gift to show our esteem."

SYDNEY F. GREY

Gresham sat with Lord Salisbury, Braxton, and Henry in yet another expansive library in the marquess's house on Bury Street in St. James's Square. After spending half the night before exchanging developments and information with Braxton, he was tired and wanted only to go to Samantha and comfort her. But their formidable new ally was determined to move forward with his plans to go over Admiral Warwick's head, indeed over the heads of the entire admiralty, to the very top of the chain of British Naval Command, to First Lord Admiral Melville himself.

The thought of it made Gresham's head spin like a top. Melville was the highest authority in His Majesty's Royal Navy, second only to the Prince Regent himself. He kept seeing a vision of Samantha when she'd stood in pleading prayer in the little dinghy beside the hulk of the *Relentless*, and he tried to make sense of how they had come from there to here.

They had just received word from Mr. Green regarding the appearance of Dr. Hugo Fletcher at the Lee Side Inn. Knowing that Granville's ship had docked, and he and his butcher were now on the loose in England, gave Gresham a renewed drive in the face of his fatigue.

Lord Salisbury proceeded. "I hope to receive a response to my urgent letter to Lord Melville no later than tomorrow morning. In the meantime, I have set a guard around this house and sent word to place one at the vicarage in Hatfield. Dr. Braxton, your letters to the London hospitals with the description of Miss Josephine Hollingsworth have all been dispatched, and I have sent a man to find the person who was assigned to investigate the fire at the vicarage in Campton. We might anticipate him answering my request for an interview as early as this evening."

Salisbury pressed back in his high-backed leather chair behind the desk and drummed his fingers on its marble top.

294

"Now, gentlemen, is there anything else we should be doing that has not already been initiated?"

Henry raised his hand. "We spoke to you before leaving Hatfield regarding the body we hid in the tower of the church. Since we have had no opportunity to retrieve it and provide a proper burial, perhaps something more suitable than the church tower could be arranged for its storing until things can be sorted out in that regard."

"Ah yes! I will make arrangements for it to be removed, and with Mrs. Gresham's permission, I will have it sent to his father's estate in St. Ives."

Gresham felt a tremendous load lift from his mind. "Thank you, my lord. I am sure she will agree that is the most appropriate place for him." He glanced at Braxton before adding, "But I am still very puzzled as to Admiral Warwick's connection to all this, my lord. At first I was convinced he was only out to save face for the navy. Now that we know he has spoken with Darby, and possibly this murderer Dr. Fletcher, I feel there has to be more to it, that somehow he has a personal stake in the game. I am uncomfortable not knowing, but not sure how to find out more."

"Hmmm, yes, indeed, Captain." The marquess sat forward. "There is a missing piece to the puzzle there, to be sure. Warwick's behavior is strange." Salisbury reached for another sheet of paper. "I will send a man to Woolwich to keep an eye on him for us."

CAPTAIN FELIX GRANVILLE sat in front of Admiral Warwick's desk, his feet on top, a lit cigar in one hand and a glass of whiskey in the other. His blue captain's coat was unbuttoned and his cravat untied. His thick dark hair hung loose over his broad shoulders, and he casually regarded Warwick with a sardonic smile on his uncommonly handsome face.

Warwick wanted him feeling comfortable and off his guard when he sprang himself from the trap Granville had put him in and happily reversed their positions. "How was your last tour, Granville? Anything interesting happen?" Warwick sniffed his whiskey and took a slight sip. He wanted to be sure of a clear head as he danced with the devil in front of him.

"Nothing really. The same rot and nonsense as usual. I did have a rather satisfying time with a few little Negro girls while docked at Port Royal, but other than that, there was nothing truly remarkable. What about you, Andrew? Made many trips into town lately?" Granville blew a series of smoke rings skillfully toward Warwick.

Warwick waved irritably at the foul-smelling cloud and gave a little cough. "Hmmm, perhaps. I wanted to speak to you about your last bill, Felix." Warwick pulled out a drawer, removed a letter, and flung it on the desk beside Granville's feet.

Granville begrudgingly lowered his legs, placed his glass on the desk, balancing the cigar on top, and opened the paper. "Yes, Andrew. It is far past due, you know. Not like you at all. I am here to accept payment, of course, and to invite you to my next soiree. I have my men looking for merchandise exactly according to your taste, young and fresh." Granville's handsome mouth curled in a lustful smile. "Who knows? I might even join you again."

Warwick resisted the man's titillating invitation and pulled his chair in close. "I am not going to pay you, Felix, not now, not ever." He waited, excited to observe the man's response.

Granville retrieved his cigar and settled back in his chair. "Well then, you would give me no choice but to expose you and your nasty little habits to some very influential people,

296

Andrew, you know that. Are you growing forgetful in your old age, my friend?" His lips pursed in a mocking smile, and he drew another long draft from his cigar.

"No, Felix. This time you will be paying me.' Warwick opened the desk drawer again and tossed over the letters and notebook he had taken from Granville's lair.

The captain shuffled the papers before him and was dead silent for a moment. He raised his narrowed eyes and glowered at Warwick, then slammed the papers back down on the desk and laughed, loud and hard, slapping his thighs and rocking in his chair. Warwick even saw tears come to his eyes.

*What kind of reaction is this? Well, let us see how he acts when I give him the next bite of bait.*

Warwick sat back in his chair annoyed. "I am glad to have made you so happy, Felix, but I should like to inform you that your brother's dead body was found, you see, found and brought to this very dockyard. It seems that he had been tortured and murdered. All his fingers were missing. Gruesome really. And there was someone else found—his wife, Mrs. Granville, and she was not dead."

Granville stopped laughing and rose from his seat. Crossing his arms over his chest, he stared down at Warwick, his face blank and devoid of emotion. His eyes did not blink, and Warwick was startled by the man's empty gaze.

After a deadly moment of silence, Granville took his seat again. "Very interesting."

Warwick was highly disappointed at this lack of reaction. Granville asked no questions but passed the news over completely. "You know, Andrew, I really hate to disappoint you, but I have some news for you as well." Reaching into the interior pocket of his coat, Granville produced his own packet of papers and laid them on the desk in front of Warwick. "You must have been so completely distracted by the letters you found in my office that you stopped searching once you found them. You see, you neglected to open the lowest drawer of that cabinet and failed to discover these." Granville casually collected the stolen documents that Warwick had carelessly left within his reach and placed them securely in his coat pocket.

Warwick's face reddened with rage. "What is this Felix, more rubbish? You don't have anything more on me than I already know." He slid the papers back in Granville's direction.

"Oh, but I beg to differ. Humor me, won't you, and have a little look." Granville went back to puffing and sipping.

Warwick's mind flamed with horror as he took up the papers and scanned their contents. The documents contained records, all under the heading of his own name, with dates and times and detailed descriptions of his activities at Granville's secret chamber in the basement of the filthy warehouse in London. But that was not what rocked Warwick to the core. Beside these details were the names, ages, addresses, and physical descriptions of every young girl he had ever encountered there, and when and how they had been killed and disposed of.

"My God, Granville, I never knew you butchered them afterward! You never told me that you murdered them! You disgusting, evil—"

"Now, now, Andrew, don't upset yourself so." Granville downed the rest of his whiskey and put out his cigar in the glass. "Dr. Fletcher does have rather peculiar tastes, but he must also be accommodated, just like everyone else. So you see, Andrew, if you try to take me down, then you are going with me—not only for the crime of raping all these children but for murdering them as well."

"But I had nothing to do with killing them! You and that sick butcher of yours—"

"Oh yes, I am afraid that we will testify against you, and you will hang from the yard between us. And now"—Granville sighed as he snatched the papers from under Warwick's hands, then held out his palm to him—"I will take your key, Admiral."

Warwick stormed from his chair, reached into his coat pocket, and threw the key on the scarlet ribbon at Granville. It hit his arm, raised in defense, and bounced off, landing somewhere under the chairs before the desk.

Granville laughed again, not even looking for the key. "I bid you a good evening, Admiral. You can expect to see me again very soon."

MR. DARBY WAS NEARLY KNOCKED over by the captain exiting the admiral's office, but he regained his balance and hurried to the secretary's desk near the door. "Now would you please tell the admiral I am here about something extremely urgent."

Mr. Darby found the admiral in a terrible mood when he approached his desk. "Well, Darby, what did you find in Hatfield?"

"Good evening, Admiral. I found that Captain and Mrs. Green, and the captain's sister and her husband, had already left Hatfield. Unfortunately, it seems that their marriage has taken place and that it has been registered with the proper legal information. However, I think you will be very pleased with what else I found." Darby paused for effect. "I have brought you the body, sir. The one we found on the island. It is waiting for your inspection just outside the back door."

Darby triumphantly withdrew his handkerchief from his pocket and dabbed at his nose.

Warwick glared at him, then stood and walked around his desk. "We shall see, Mr. Darby. We shall see."

Darby led the way to the waiting wagon. A swarm of star-lings clamored noisily in the trees above them, and the last light of dusk made it just possible to make out the shape of a coffin-sized box on the wagon's bed. Darby instructed his escorts to take the box off the wagon and set it on the ground.

Lighting a torch, he then produced a hammer from the wagon. "Shall I open it, Admiral, or would you like to do the honors?"

"Get on with it," Warwick spat.

Darby went to work prying up the wooden lid. He slid the top off the back of the box and stood aside, fighting the urge to smile broadly.

Warwick took the torch from one of his men and held it over the box. Darby watched with inner glee as Warwick bent over, but his heart sank when the admiral's face blazed with rage. "What body, you fool? There is nothing there! You have come all the way from Hatfield with an empty box!"

"What?" Darby looked in the box with dismay. "But I was certain. I—"

Warwick took hold of Darby by the collar and shook him hard. "You worthless little rodent, you come with me!"

A few moments later, Darby stood with his knees knocking before the admiral's desk, trying not to relieve himself in his breeches, berating himself for not looking inside the box before bringing it all the way to Woolwich for nothing.

Warwick paced behind his desk chair, muttering and spewing. Finally he turned sharply to Darby and hissed at him through clenched teeth. "I should have you flogged and hung out to dry, you sniveling idiot. You deserve nothing less. But I may have need of you later, so I will show you how merciful I am and have you thrown into confinement until I have use for you." He strode to the wall and jerked the bell pull. "Sit down,

Mr. Darby, until my men come for you," and Warwick left the office, slamming the door.

Darby, shaken to his core, sank down. He looked around him in a panic, desperate to find a way of escape, but there was none. At last he dropped his face in his hands and sobbed out loud. "What have I done? Dear God, help me. What have I done?"

Withdrawing his hands from his wet, snotty face, he reached for his handkerchief. Just then his eyes were caught by something shiny under the chair next to him. After giving his nose a good blow, he reached down and retrieved the object. Dangling it from his shaking fingers, he saw it was a silver key tied to a scarlet ribbon.

Hearing footsteps outside the door, he reflexively dropped the key into his waistcoat pocket and stood as his captors entered, licking their lips.

❖

BRAXTON SAT in the marquess's library with the other men speaking with Mr. Cromwell, who had arrived after dinner. Gresham posed his questions and listened to their answers as if in a trance. As Braxton listened, images of the burning house and the people suffering and dying inside was almost more than he could take. Henry sat beside him, taking copious notes, and Lord Salisbury asked again regarding the possibility of the fire being set on purpose.

"I have investigated many fires, my lord, and after time you get to know how fire behaves. I still believe the fire was set on purpose because of where it started and how it traveled throughout the house, sir. However, I was not able to substantiate my conclusion with enough evidence to support it."

"And you still feel that Mr. and Mrs. Hollingsworth had a

good chance of getting out and surviving but were prevented in some way that would point to someone deliberately trapping them inside, is that correct?"

"That is even more difficult to prove, my lord, but there were signs that someone had recently been there, including a small pile of fresh nails I found in the yard next to the house."

Braxton sat forward and took over the questioning, "What more can you tell us about Miss Josephine's condition and where she was taken?"

"I am sorry, Doctor," the man stated flatly. "I am unable to provide you with that information, as I did not arrive on the scene until a few days after the fire. Miss Hollingsworth had already been taken to London, but the constable in Campton shared his report with me. All I can do is repeat what you have already been told."

"If you don't mind, Mr. Cromwell, would you please repeat what the constable reported to you about the injuries Miss Hollingsworth suffered?" Braxton glanced at Gresham and saw that his eyes were closed.

Mr. Cromwell opened the satchel on his lap. "Let me see . . . ah yes. Here we are."

Braxton braced himself and trained his eyes on the patterns on the Persian carpet beneath him.

Mr. Cromwell read aloud. "'Miss Josephine Hollingsworth was rescued by way of breaking a ground-floor window of the home's sitting room, where a heavy curtain rod, its fabrics in flames, fell on her just before being pulled through the opening. Her head, hair, and right cheek were burned, as were her right arm and both hands. Her clothes caught fire, but the flames were put out before causing further injury.'"

Gresham stood suddenly, his face ashen gray, his eyes distant and unfocused, and he strode with determination out of the library. Braxton excused himself and followed him down the hall to the front door, calling after him, "John! John, are you all right?"

Gresham did not stop to answer. Opening the front door of the grand house, he went quickly down the steps, through the gate, and into the street. The dark pavement shimmered with recent rain as he turned right up Bury Street. Braxton followed him at a distance and watched him turn right again onto Jermyn Street.

Pausing, Gresham crossed to the other side after a passing carriage, where Braxton saw him stop and gaze at the tall iron gate at the back of St. James's Church. Finding the gate locked, he made his way to the corner of the wall and up Church Street, stopping again at the corner of Piccadilly.

Ignoring the heavy traffic, Gresham came to the main gate of the church and found it open. Braxton called out to him as he entered, but the noise of the street covered his voice.

The church was dimly lit when Braxton saw his friend near the front of the nave. Gresham shrugged out of his tailcoat and threw it on the front pew, then fell hard onto his knees at the step of the platform.

Not wanting to interfere, Braxton took a seat on the back pew and watched his friend in agony. Gresham's sobs could be heard as they echoed off the white marble-and-gold-gilded arches of the cathedral ceiling. He could just make out the images of the towering stained-glass windows rising above Gresham on the back wall, the central scene being that of Christ hanging on the cross.

Gresham almost writhed on the floor with his grief. Braxton gripped the back of the wooden pew before him, not knowing what to do. *I wish Henry had come. He would know how to console him.* And then he heard Gresham's voice rising up between moans.

"How could you!? How could you allow all this evil to

happen to them? To Meri? To her?!" Gresham shouted at the image in the window, shaking his head, and sometimes his fist. "These monsters! You let them run free, raping and killing at will!"

Gresham curled into a ball on the step then, his hands clutching his head, giving one last horrible cry. "How could you?!" Then his sobbing continued.

Braxton felt helpless. Then looking up at the figure on the cross in the window, he prayed, *Show me what to do.*

He made his way up the aisle until he stood behind his strong, brave, undone friend on the step. Kneeling, he laid his arm over Gresham and looked again at the image above them. Quietly, reverently, he began, "Our Father, which art in heaven, hallowed be thy name." Gresham's head rose, just enough for Braxton to catch his swollen eyes. He nodded to Gresham, then looked up again at the image and continued. "Thy kingdom come, thy will be done, on earth as it is in heaven."

Braxton found himself fighting his own tears, struggling to get air passed the rock in his throat. "Give us this day our daily bread, and forgive us our trespasses, as we forgive those who trespass against us."

Gresham's body shook with a groan from the depths of his being. Braxton gripped his shoulder and went on, "And lead us not into temptation, but deliver us from evil. For thine is the kingdom, and the power, and the glory forever. Amen." His prayer ended in a whisper, and he sat back on his heals, still gazing at the suffering man on the cross.

After some time, Gresham pushed himself up on his knees and faced his friend. "I am so sorry, Paul. Please forgive me. I never truly understood before."

Braxton sniffed and smiled weakly, "Neither did I, John. Neither did I."

# CHAPTER
# TWENTY-EIGHT

After Gresham returned to the town house with Braxton, Lord Salisbury and Henry informed him that they had apprised Mr. Cromwell of the story regarding Samantha and her late husband. They'd given him all the information regarding Captain Felix Granville and Dr. Hugo Fletcher of the HMS *Peleus*, even though Mr. Cromwell insisted that the matter was entirely under the authority of the admiralty. However, he said he would keep Lord Salisbury informed of any further information that came his way.

The first thing the next morning Lord Salisbury received word from First Lord Admiral Melville and needed to leave for his appointment by ten o'clock. He announced he had decided to go by himself first to see how Melville would respond to hearing all that had happened.

After breakfast and a brief consultation with their host, in which they had supplied him with copies of their reports and Henry's notes, Gresham mounted the stairs, relieved not to go. After his episode in St. James's the night before, he was utterly exhausted and wanted desperately to be with his wife and rest for an hour, though they were still sleeping in separate rooms, out of Gresham's respect for Samantha and her time of mourning.

Penny, who kept faithful vigil with his grieving wife, left them for an hour's peace together.

"John, you look exhausted, my dear." Samantha's voice was thin but calm. "Please come and lay here beside me and rest.

"Truly? You would be comfortable with me beside you?" His weary heart leaped for a beat.

She nodded and patted the bed. Gresham lay his bone-weary body down on top of the covers and fell instantly asleep holding her hand. He awoke an hour later, feeling her stroking his head gently as she whispered prayers over him.

"Thank you, Lord God, for this faithful man you have sent to love me and protect me. He is my miracle in the midst of so much pain and sorrow. Please, Father, give him rest. Bless him with your spirit of peace and give him strength. Help us, Father, to find the end of this struggle and move on with our lives together."

He shifted and caught hold of her hand, kissing it. "Thank you for your prayers. That you should pray for me at this time is beyond me. It is I who should be praying for you."

"But you, Johnathan Gresham, you are the answer to my prayers. You are my gift, my beauty for ashes."

"Ashes," he repeated. "We are surrounded by ashes."

"It does feel that way. Oh, John, please pray for my heart. I am struggling in a way I never have before." Her face was drawn and pale.

"Of course you have my prayers, my love. Tell me what troubles you so."

She held his hand tightly and swallowed hard. "I . . . I am finding it impossible to forgive Felix Granville or Hugo Fletcher after what they have done to my family. I just can't."

She looked at him with such a desperate sorrow it almost burst his heart.

"I share your struggle. My faith has been challenged like never before in light of your suffering, and I am angry. I have questioned God to his face. But we must trust that God understands our grief. Surely he will be patient with us, and you must be patient with yourself, Samantha."

After a long, silent moment, she steadied herself and met his eyes. "You are right, John. We are surely in the midst of the fire, but if God has seen others through such things, then we must trust he will see us through as well. It will take time."

He pressed his face against her hand. "I am with you, Samantha. We have each other."

"Indeed. God knew I would need you." She kissed his hand and sat up. "I have so much I want to tell you about things I have been remembering the last two days. You have been so busy that we have had no time to talk."

He sat up against the carved wooden headboard beside her. "Tell me everything." Gresham focused on her face, the face he had come to love so well.

"I remember my sister, Josephine, of course. She was the little girl from my dream. We were very close, and it nearly broke my heart to leave her after I married Michael, who was the boy in my dreams. My father had been the rector for the parish, under Michael's father's charge, and we grew up at the vicarage next to his father's manor in St. Ives, until our fathers had a falling out and we moved to Campton. It was his brother Felix who killed the puppy and put it back in the box without Michael knowing." Samantha looked down at their clasped hands. "Felix was a very disturbed child, like the man he has become. He hated Michael from the moment he was born. I recognize that now."

Samantha shifted, and Gresham's heart warmed as she lay

her head on his lap, looking at him with endearing trust in her face.

"After Michael finished his studies at Cambridge, he came to Campton and frantically proposed to me, telling me he had always loved me, and convinced me that I should marry him and go with him to the mission in Jamaica. It wasn't until after the wedding that I learned of his gambling debts and the true reason he was running away from England. By then it was too late, and I stepped into Felix's trap at Michael's side."

Gresham opened his mouth to speak, but she hurried on.

"And then there is the sailor Mr. Sam Gardner. He was badly treated by Felix and Dr. Fletcher. He had only half a tongue, John. Someone had cut it out long before we met. He was their slave. But he pitied me, perhaps because we shared the same name. My family called me Sam from the time I was a child."

"Perhaps that is why they used him, my dear. Because he could not betray them."

"Yes, I believe you are right. It was he who placed his knife, the flint, the rope, my Bible, and the ship's biscuits in my trunk and set it on the waves to land on the island. I never would have survived without the gifts he gave me."

Gresham looked down into her worried eyes. "May God bless Samuel Gardner, and may we find him soon."

WHEN LORD SALISBURY returned from his interview with Lord Melville, he urgently called the men into the library. "I am happy to inform you that my meeting with Lord Melville went rather well, considering, though he seemed to have some reservations regarding Mrs. Gresham's reliability." He raised his hand as Gresham protested. "However, he expressed his desire to meet you, Captain Gresham and Mrs. Gresham, in person. There are only a few difficulties with this proposition." Salisbury focused on Gresham. "Lord Melville is leaving for Scotland the day after next and will be gone for some months, which leaves little time between now and then for a meeting to take place." He shifted in his leather chair and knitted his gray brows. "The other impediment is that His Lordship is to attend a ball being given in his honor tomorrow evening at the Banqueting House at Whitehall."

Gresham tried to listen patiently but felt his irritability rising. Lord Melville was his ultimate superior next to the King, yet he was incensed at the man questioning his wife's reliability.

"And so," continued the marquess, "Lord Melville has extended an invitation of sorts, or rather an order, for you, Captain, to accompany your wife and myself to the Admiral's Ball tomorrow evening in order for him to meet you in person before he leaves or executes any orders concerning the crimes that have been alleged against officers in His Majesty's Royal Navy."

Gresham rubbed his forehead in confusion. "Excuse me, my lord, but are you saying that I must escort my grieving wife to a ball tomorrow evening? Why, that would be impossible, sir. How can I put Samantha through such an ordeal? It is unthinkable." He shook his head at the very thought.

"Yes, yes, Captain, I did mention the fact that Mrs. Gresham is just newly mourning the death of her parents and her missing sister, but Lord Melville said it couldn't possibly be helped. He has no time before the ball to give you a private audience and reminded me of how fortunate it was he could even give me a hearing today." His gray eyes softened, and he bent over the great desk toward Gresham. "I am sorry, Captain. I do not see that there is any way around it. The only consolation is that he extended the invitation to those whom Mrs. Gresham might find a comfort to have in her company at the ball, so all of us, even Dr. Braxton and Mr. and Mrs. Keate, will be attending."

Gresham looked at Braxton and Henry with dismay. "Dear God, how will I tell her?"

Braxton's eyes were tired and sad as he scrutinized Gresham. "Mrs. Gresham is the bravest woman I have ever known. God will help her, John. And may God help us all."

---

THAT AFTERNOON SAMANTHA stood in front of the mirror for the first time since she had arrived at Lord Salisbury's London house. She hardly recognized herself. Touching her cheek, she thought she had aged a century in the last few days. Her face was drawn, the circles under her eyes from expressing her grief were dark and pronounced in a way they never had been before. She had also lost what weight she had gained after being rescued from the island, leaving her looking frail as she stood on the little pedestal, waiting for the seamstress to complete her measurements.

Her beautiful new wardrobe had arrived earlier that day from Hatfield, but there was little in it suitable to wear now in her time of mourning. She didn't care what she wore to the Admiral's Ball, but Lord Salisbury had insisted a gown be made for her, and for Penny too. He thought it best for her not to wear black, but a dark navy blue. At another time, and for another reason, she might have enjoyed the occasion to dress up, but she felt numb about the whole affair, something to endure. She would endure anything if it would bring them closer to finding Josephine and keeping her safe from the terrible men who'd tried to destroy them both. She was convinced that the fire had been set to prevent her family from ever questioning what had become of her.

Penny had been a godsend, as well as Gresham and Braxton. Even Henry had made several calls to her chamber and spent precious time reading to her from God's Word. Lord Salisbury had visited her once and provided an easel for her painting, to be displayed in the corner of the room. She marveled sorrowfully at how God had used it to guide her to the truth.

Gresham and Braxton returned to the room after her fitting, and a servant brought in a tea tray with cakes and biscuits.

"Please, Samantha," Braxton urged, "sit here and have some tea and cakes. You are not eating enough to keep a bird alive." He made her a little plate of sweets and placed it before her. "I must insist you eat all of this. Doctor's orders." His tone was kind, but she saw the worry in his eyes.

Penny poured Samantha a cup and placed it on the table. "Yes, my dear. We are all terribly concerned for your well-being. And now to have to attend a ball at a time like this, it is simply outrageous. What on earth could Lord Melville be thinking? I cannot think of anything crueler to do to a lady in mourning."

"I am beside myself." Gresham covered Samantha's hand with his. "I wish I could think of a way out of this ridiculous situation, but to actually have the First Lord Admiral order us to attend a ball is . . . is . . . ."

"Is a tremendous opportunity," Samantha said quietly. The others looked at her in disbelief. "If a man such as Lord Melville is convinced to take up my sister's cause, then God is providing us an extraordinary opportunity." She took up her cup with a little nod.

Finally aware of them watching her, she turned to

Gresham with a weak smile. "John, we have already come through so much. It is only a ball. That is all."

"You never fail to astonish me." He lifted her fingers to his lips. Sighing, he nodded in agreement. "You are right. It is just a ball."

❋

Mr. Darby had been taken to London by Admiral Warwick and his thugs in the middle of the night. He was still in excruciating pain from the flogging the two guards had given him after his embarrassing performance with the empty coffin.

They dragged him roughly from the carriage and into a dimly lit building in a dark alley. *Not far from the river*, he thought, as he could smell the dank, humid air. He only saw the dust and overturned furniture for a moment before he was hurried down a small staircase.

"Let us in, Granville!" Warwick pounded on the door, which evidently was locked. "You know I no longer have my key!"

Darby's mind flashed to the silver key in his waistcoat pocket.

Soon he heard the lock being turned from the other side and was shocked to find himself pushed into a large, well-lit, and elaborately furnished room.

For an instant Darby could not believe his eyes as they whisked around the room and landed abruptly on the tall, dashing figure of a man in a captain's uniform leaning on the fireplace mantel. The man's face was turned to the blaze within, and he held a lit cigar in his hand.

"Put him in the hold, if you please," the man said without turning.

Darby's heart sank as the guards pushed him toward a

large, foreboding door with a small, barred window to the left. His wrists were quickly chained to the wall next to the door, and he could hear the scurry of rats in the darkness beyond as the guards slammed the door and shot the bolt.

He slunk onto the floor, as close to the door as his bonds would allow. He was sore, tired, hungry, and desperately thirsty, but he forced himself to concentrate, training his ears on the voices of Warwick and the captain speaking in the other room. He could not make out all their conversation, but he heard enough to make his blood run cold.

"My spies have located them. They are the guests of a Lord Salisbury at his house in St. James's Square. It is under guard, but my men have found out they have plans to attend the Admiral's Ball tomorrow night at the Banqueting House in Whitehall."

The admiral scoffed. "How on earth did they receive an invitation? It is a very exclusive event. I have my own invitation with me, but under the circumstances was not planning to go."

"Oh, no, Andrew, you will be attending."

The captain murmured something more, but Darby could not make it out.

"Are you out of your mind?" Warwick roared. "You cannot abduct a woman from a ball in plain sight! First, they will catch you in the act, and second, if you are successful, they will find you and hang you the next day."

Darby was for once glad that Warwick's temper increased the volume of his voice.

The other man laughed nonchalantly. Darby's skin crawled.

"You are funny, Andrew, very funny indeed. I will not be the one abducting Mrs. Gresham—you will." The man snickered again, then the room fell silent.

"So it has come to this, has it? And what if I refuse?"

Darby could make out the slightest bit of fear in the admiral's voice.

"Then I will hang you myself, Andrew. Here in this very room."

Darby froze against the cold wall. There was dead silence, save for the pounding of his heart in his small chest. *And if he hangs Warwick, he will certainly do no less to me.*

Suddenly the cell door flung open and Warwick himself pulled Darby off the floor by his collar. "Come along, you dog. I have a job for you."

# TWENTY-NINE

M rs. Yates stood outside the back door of her inn in the bright, crisp morning light and watched as Mr. Green and Mr. Smith climbed down from the wagon. On the back sat a dark muscular man, so close in size and stature to Mr. Smith they could have been brothers. The newcomer moved cautiously off the wagon, and she felt his dark eyes taking her in suspiciously.

"Good morning to ya, Mrs. Yates! 'Tis a fine morning, a very fine morning indeed." Mr. Green turned and motioned for the stranger to come closer. "I would like ta introduce ya ta Mr. Samuel Gardner. Mr. Gardner, this is me very dear friend Mrs. Yates."

Not waiting for him to speak, she smiled at him warmly and greeted him. "I am most happy to meet you, Mr. Gardner. Thank you so much for coming. You are welcome here, and I have your meal waiting for you all in the kitchen. Please, sir, come right this way."

Gardner stood still until Mr. Green encouraged him to follow. "We must make haste, Mr. Gardner. Mrs. Yates's cook makes a very fine spread, and ya'll be glad ya partook o' it before we reach London."

While Mr. Smith and Mr. Gardner ate their meals, Mr. Green took Mrs. Yates aside for a conference. "He is a peculiar sort, Mrs. Yates, ta be sure. Half his tongue was cut out some time ago, and he can only grunt and shake his head. 'Tis difficult ta learn anything from him. But ya should a seen his face when we told him that Mrs. Samantha Granville had been found on that island alive. Glad ta the core, he was."

"Oh, Mr. Green, how can we be sure he wasn't party to the terrible crimes that took place? He has a rather frightening look about him. What happened when you showed him the knife? Did he recognize it?"

Mrs. Yates had to bend down in order to hear Mr. Green's hushed voice. "The man held it as if it were a priceless relic, and tears came ta his eyes. I told him how it was he who had helped her ta survive till we got there. That Mrs. Gresham gives him her highest regard. I am sorry ya weren't there ta see his reaction, ma dear."

"Well, Mr. Green, shouldn't you be getting on your way? Captain Gresham will not be happy. Oh my goodness! I almost forgot to give you this." Mrs. Yates plunged her hand into the pocket of her apron and pulled out a sealed letter.

Mr. Green opened it immediately and held it so Mrs. Yates could read with him over his shoulder. He looked up at her with wide eyes. "We must make haste! I da not like the sound of Mrs. Gresham being in such a public and vulnerable position! Please, Mrs. Yates, may we have use o' yer carriage and two horses? I fear the wagon will travel too slowly."

He darted back into the kitchen before she could answer. "Come quickly, gentlemen! We have a ball ta attend!"

✳

THE LATE-SUMMER EVENING WAS CLEAR, but there was a chilling hint of the coming autumn in the air as the party from Lord Salisbury's house boarded the carriages for the short drive to the Banqueting House in Whitehall. Gresham took Samantha's hand and wrapped it protectively around his arm as they sat across from Lord Salisbury in his grand carriage. The Keates and Braxton followed them in another carriage as they drove the few blocks to Charing Cross, through the Admiralty Arch, and on to Whitehall.

The Banqueting House was the one remaining building of the Palace of Whitehall, which had once been the residence of British monarchs in centuries past. Most of the palace had been destroyed by fire, but the stately Banqueting House remained intact, which was most fortunate, Gresham mused, not only for the history of the building itself but for the priceless Ruben paintings that covered its gallery ceiling.

Gresham assisted Samantha from the carriage, dazzled again at the sight of her. Samantha's lovely face was like that of an angel's sculpted in marble in the moonlight. Glints of gold highlighted the curls of her brown hair, entwined with navy-blue ribbon and silver combs. Her gauzy white chemisette, tucked into her exquisitely decorated navy-blue gown, lay over her smooth skin, where the pearls he had given her shimmered in the light of the streetlamps. She wore long white evening gloves, and over her shoulders hung a loose robe of black silk, adding to the striking contrast between her complexion and her dark garments.

He stared at her in awe, not only of her beauty but of her courage. She tucked her hand firmly in the crook of his arm and smiled up at him sadly.

"I love you," he whispered so that only she could hear.

The others joined them, and Lord Salisbury, dressed in a fine costume befitting his station, led them through the iron gate and into the entrance of the long building. Gresham could feel Samantha leaning on him as they made their way through the gathering crowd inside the hall and toward the cloak room under the grand staircase ahead.

Lord Salisbury himself assisted Samantha out of her wrap and handed it to the attendant, and Gresham handed in his hat. He wore his captain's dress uniform and felt out of place among all the admirals and other dignitaries.

He dreaded taking Samantha up to the main hall. Looking solemnly down into her gray-blue eyes, he asked, "Are you sure, my dear?" for the hundredth time that day.

"Yes, John," she said with a nod. "As long as you and the Lord are with me, I can face anything."

Lord Salisbury smiled at them and motioned toward the stairs. They were joined by the others and took their turn in the growing line of elegant attendees and made their way up the red-carpeted steps. Samantha paused when they reached the doorway to the hall. Gasping himself, they entered the hall with its massive white stone columns and the soaring ceiling covered with the enormous paintings, with gold-gilded moldings glimmering in the light of the massive brass chandeliers.

The hall was lined with windows, both on the main floor and the gallery balcony above. At the opposite end of the room sat an ensemble playing lively tunes. Tables and chairs awaited at the sides of the hall, and Lord Salisbury led them through the groups of excited guests to a set of unclaimed chairs.

"I will leave you all here, if you don't mind," Lord Salisbury announced. "I will spare you the myriad of introductions that would need to be made were I in your midst. Please don't hesitate to collect me if I am needed. I shall keep an eye on you, and promise to return before the dancing begins."

Gresham was glad to have Samantha safely in a chair by the window and pulled his near, as did the rest of them, making a protective knot around her. But once in his seat, his heart quickened in his chest.

Was he nervous to meet Lord Melville? If he were honest with himself, he would have to say yes. Who wouldn't be? It was the next best thing to meeting King George and the Prince Regent themselves. He had never dreamed of being in such a position. *God in heaven, please help us. Help me to be alert and on guard in the midst of all this distraction*, he prayed, scanning the room for faces he might recognize.

A servant came by with a tray of sparkling champagne. Though he would rather not have any alcohol, he was terribly thirsty and took two, one for Samantha and one for himself. She smiled at him and touched her glass to his lightly, then took a slight sip.

"Oh my," Penny said discreetly, "It is very nice champagne."

They must have seemed a somber lot compared to the rest of the gaily chattering guests. Then the music stopped, and the sound of a ship's whistle could be heard piping over the hushing of the crowd.

Everyone in the hall stood to their feet. All eyes were fixed on the doorway, and the guard stepped forward, announcing the arrival of the guests of honor, First Lord Admiral and Lady Melville.

Samantha stood close to Gresham as he and Braxton saluted with the rest of the officers while Lord Melville led his wife into the center of the hall. The couple looked exactly as Gresham had pictured. Lord Melville was a dignified man with snow-white hair and an air of calm confidence, and Lady Melville was a stately woman, with a beautiful face and elegant manner. He was relieved to find them so for Samantha's sake. If they had been disagreeable and arrogant in their demeanor, it would have made the coming introduction less pleasant than it already would be.

Lord Salisbury returned to them as a toast to Lord and Lady Melville was made, followed by the opening dance. They returned to their clutch of seats and sipped silently at their glasses, watching the dancers as they whirled by. Gresham longed to take his bride out on the floor. He might not have grown up as a gentleman's son, but his mother had insisted her children learn a few of the finer dances. How marvelous to take Samantha and float with her across the floor in such a beautiful place.

The first few dances went by as the group sat waiting for their invitation to meet their esteemed hosts. Gresham kept a close eye on Samantha, but her face was calm as she watched and listened.

She touched his knee lightly and whispered, "It is lovely to see, isn't it? And the music is like balm for the soul." She squeezed his arm and smiled, her eyes looking like sapphires in the glittering light.

How he longed to take her away, far away, where there was no more danger, no more mystery, where they could finally rest in each other's arms and make their own memories together. *Dear God, how much longer must we have to endure this evil cloud that hangs over us?*

At last a servant came to address Lord Salisbury, who held out his hand to Samantha. "It is time, my dear. Will you allow me to escort you?"

She glanced at Gresham, who nodded soberly, and took the marquess's hand. The others stood and promised to pray for them as Gresham followed the pair to the other side of the hall, where Lord and Lady Melville sat on a red-carpeted dais.

Gresham's body tensed as they approached, remembering this was the man who had questioned his wife's reliability. He worked his jaw, trying to calm himself, and held his hands behind him to keep from clenching his fists.

Exchanging a sober glance with Lord Salisbury just before reaching the dais step, Gresham stood at attention and saluted.

Lord Melville rose and helped Lady Melville to her feet. "At ease, Captain," he said as his wizened eyes swept the three, assessing them. "Please come forward." Melville motioned for them all to ascend the step and stand before them.

"Thank you, Lord and Lady Melville, for your kind invitation." Salisbury bowed, as did Gresham, while Samantha dipped into a graceful curtsy. "May I present to you Captain and Mrs. Johnathan Gresham."

Lord Melville's eyes barely left Samantha's during the introductions. Gresham watched as the First Lord Admiral studied Samantha's every move and expression. Once again Gresham fought back his anger.

"We are pleased to meet you, Mrs. Gresham, Captain," Melville said with smooth dignity. "I have told Lady Melville some of your story, and she has found it to be quite fascinating, haven't you, my dear?"

"Indeed, my lord. So this is the lady who survived all alone on a deserted island. You must have a very strong constitution, Mrs. Gresham."

Gresham detected the slightest note of condescension in the lady's voice, which sent his blood heating in his veins.

"I am not worthy of such a kind assumption, Lady Melville," Samantha replied graciously. "It was only by the grace of God that I survived. I cannot take any credit for myself."

*Brilliant*, thought Gresham with pride.

Lord Melville turned to Samantha. "I understand that you have just recently learned of the death of your parents, Mrs.

Gresham. Lady Melville and I extend to you our condolences and thank you for accommodating our schedule in attending our party at such an inconsiderate time. Please accept my apologies for insisting on meeting you tonight."

Gresham suspected Melville's smooth manner hid a deeper agenda and prayed that God would continue to give Samantha wisdom in answering.

"There is nothing to forgive, Lord Melville. You are an important and busy man, and it is I who am exceedingly grateful for your generosity in hearing me and my sister Josephine's case. It is no inconvenience to me to do anything that might help me find her and put an end to the danger these men pose to us and others."

"Hmm, yes." Melville narrowed his eyes and pursed his lips. "In regard to these men, I understand that Captain Granville is your late husband's brother. Is that so?" He finished by raising his chin and looking down his nose on Samantha.

Gresham felt the perspiration popping out on his brow, and his hands were sweating inside his gloves. How helpless he was to aid her in the presence of such a powerful man.

"Yes, my lord. That is correct." Samantha straightened her shoulders ever so slightly.

"Strange and terrible," Melville continued, "to be treated so by one's own brother. And you are sure that it was Captain Granville and not someone else who perpetrated these crimes against you and Mr. Granville? I understand that you have suffered from amnesia." Melville suddenly turned his gaze on Gresham, just long enough to take in the look in his eyes, then looked back down on Samantha.

"It is true that I lost my memory for a time, but I now remember perfectly, and as God is my witness, my lord, I am absolutely sure."

Though Samantha's voice was clear and steady as she stood her ground, Gresham could take it no more. He stepped closer to his wife's side and cleared his throat. "If I may speak, Lord Melville, Mrs. Gresham has been through the most horrific ordeal imaginable. It is our greatest hope, my lord, that you will find it within your purview to bring about justice for my wife and her sister and put an end to the suffering these men have wreaked upon them, as God has placed you in a position of power, setting you in authority over His Majesty's Royal Navy." Gresham barely took a breath before continuing, unheeding the warning in his head that he was stepping too close to the edge of propriety.

"I am personally, deeply incensed that men of the Royal Navy could be capable of such atrocities, and I am highly aware that their deeds might shed a questioning light upon the navy's leadership, but that need not be the case, my lord." Gresham glanced at Samantha. "My wife and I desire, as much as anyone, all the discretion and privacy that can be managed in this situation. I promise you, Lord Melville, that Mrs. Gresham and I have no desire to bring the integrity of the navy under public scrutiny and will do all we can to keep these matters in the strictest of confidence."

When he finished, he found it odd to still find the music playing and the dancers swirling behind him. Lord and Lady Melville frowned on him uncomfortably in silence.

Samantha looked up at him and squeezed his arm. "My husband has seen me through all this like a guardian angel, my lord, and he speaks for both of us. You have my promise for discretion as well."

After an awkward moment, Lord Melville whispered to Lady Melville, who nodded and returned to her seat. Gresham glanced around and found that most of those not dancing were watching the tête-à-tête on the dais and whispering behind their fans. How long had they been standing there waiting for a response, he wondered. It felt like a torturous eternity. Finally Melville came closer and offered his hand to Gresham.

"You have spoken with conviction, Captain Gresham, and I congratulate you. You have also shown yourself a loving husband at the risk of your own career, and that I admire."

Gresham could hardly believe his ears as he shook the man's hand. Melville turned to Samantha with serious eyes. "You have my sincerest apologies, Mrs. Gresham, for the way you have been treated by men in my command, and you have my promise to do all I can to help you and bring them to justice."

Samantha's eyes brimmed with tears as she smiled sweetly up at Melville. "Thank you, my lord. I thank you also on my sister's behalf. You and Lady Melville have given us the greatest of gifts. The gift of hope."

Melville extended his hand to her, and she laid hers in his. He bent over her fingers slightly as she curtsied. "Pray God she can be found." Melville straightened. "I do not believe I shall ever forget meeting you, Mrs. Gresham, Captain. Good night."

As they hurried back to the others, Gresham could feel the eyes of the entire room on his back. Lord Salisbury reached over and shook Gresham's hand with a respectful nod. "Well done, my friends, well done. And now I believe it is time to depart, is it not?"

They all followed Salisbury as he made his way to the door. The music still poured through the entrance of the hall as they traveled back down the grand staircase to retrieve their belongings from the cloak room beneath the stairs. Gresham finally allowed himself to feel the slightest sense of relief.

The entrance hall was nearly deserted where they stood by the wall of curtained windows beside the cloak room door, waiting for the attendant to return. But before the man came back to the counter, they were surprised by the sudden, menacing appearance of Admiral Warwick. Gresham's stomach clenched as he and the group instinctively stepped back from the man's looming presence, caught between the admiral and the wall of curtained windows.

Gresham saluted, but was on guard and moved Samantha behind him protectively. Braxton had stepped in front of her as well, and together they shielded her from Warwick's searching gaze.

Warwick smiled and swept his arms dramatically before extending his hand. "Ah! Lord Salisbury. It is my great pleasure to finally meet you, sir. And Captain Gresham, this must be your lovely sister, Mrs. Keate, and her good husband the rector. Yes, yes, and what a fashionable company you all make." Warwick was loud and boisterous.

Gresham's mind raced. Where had he come from? He suspected the man was drunk, by his grandiose behavior.

Lord Salisbury stood firmly in front of his entourage. "Good evening. Admiral Warwick, I presume?" Salisbury did not take the offered hand.

Gresham wanted to retrieve their things and be off, but Warwick stood firmly in their way. Gresham could see the distress on Penny's face and could only imagine what Samantha was suffering behind him.

"I have been looking for you, Captain Gresham. You have been a very difficult man to find, you know." Warwick shook his finger at Gresham, his mouth curled in a mocking smile. "And here is Dr. Braxton. You are completely out of place, Doctor. You should be on board the HMS *Relentless* on duty in the Mediterranean Sea. But no. How odd to find you both here, at the Admiral's Ball, no less."

Gresham saw Braxton stiffen. He dared not push forward and leave Samantha unprotected.

"If you will excuse us, Admiral Warwick, we were just leaving." Lord Salisbury tried without success to move past the man.

"Oh dear, have I been keeping you? I do beg your pardon." Warwick smiled widely and bowed low to them, then spun and disappeared under the archways of the undercroft beneath the main hall above.

Gresham reached behind him and turned, but Samantha was not there. His face fell as his heart jolted. "Samantha!" He searched the faces of those around him. "Samantha!" he called again, with no answer.

The other's looked around them. "Where is she?" Braxton asked urgently.

"She's gone!" Gresham shouted. He dashed toward the windows and swept the curtains aside in a panic, but there was nothing there. The windows had no sashes to open.

Just then came a terrific scream from the cloak room. Gresham and Braxton rushed to the counter and flung themselves over it. They found a female servant shaking and screaming, pointing to the body of the cloak room attendant on the floor under the coats, the sash of the cloak room window standing wide open.

Gresham sprang out of it like a cat and ran, searching the alley behind the Banqueting House. He strained his eyes in the dark, running up and down the back of the building, then back to the open window. "Samantha! Samantha!"

Braxton came running, followed by Salisbury, with a constable. "We looked around the front and asked the cab drivers if they had seen anything, but they saw nothing," Braxton said.

"We have to find Warwick at once!" Gresham yelled, but then stopped short.

"Captain Gresham." They heard a man's pained voice

calling from somewhere in the black shadows behind the Banqueting House. "Please, Captain, I may be able to help."

They followed the voice into the shadows. The voice came from a man sitting in the inky darkness of the alley's gutter. Gresham and Braxton gasped when they came close and could make out his face.

"Darby!" Gresham didn't know whether to be repulsed or dismayed. Clearly the man was injured. His leg stuck out sideways in an unnatural manner. "Who did this? Where have they taken her?" Gresham took Darby by the collar in spite of his injury and shook him.

Braxton intervened and pried Gresham off the sobbing little man moaning in agony.

Darby's voice trembled as tears rolled down his drawn face. "Warwick. He made me stand guard as he killed that poor man. He tried to force me to go with him again, but I jumped from the carriage. I am sorry, Captain. So very sorry."

"What have you done?!" Gresham shouted, "Where has he taken her?!"

"I do not know, Captain. It is a terrible, hidden place in the bottom of an abandoned warehouse. I don't know where, somewhere close to the river, but . . ." Darby's voice cracked with pain. His hand shook as he reached for his waistcoat pocket. "You will need this," he whispered hoarsely as he drew out the silver key on its scarlet ribbon. "Please, please ask her to forgive me."

Gresham held up the key on the ribbon in horror.

"You must find her quickly, Captain," Darby moaned urgently. "I fear for her life."

"Take this man into custody at once," Lord Salisbury barked to a constable who ran up to them.

In no time, more men had arrived, and they picked up Darby and took him away.

Gresham looked around helplessly. "An abandoned warehouse near the river? But there are thousands of them!" He shook his head in desperation. "Where do we even begin to look?!"

"Capt'n! Capt'n Gresham!"

His despairing thoughts were interrupted by a familiar voice calling from somewhere behind him.

"I am here," he shouted, turning to see who it was. He had not seen the crowd of onlookers that had silently gathered. Then he saw a small man with a straw hat pushing his way through the crowd, running toward him. "Mr. Green!"

Green emerged from the onlookers, gasping for air. "Capt'n, I have heard. Hurry, sir. We must go!" At that moment a carriage came barreling down the alley as Green pulled Gresham toward it. "Hurry, Capt'n! We have found Sam Gardner! He knows where they have taken her and is already on his way there. We know where to go, sir. Hurry!"

"Paul!" Gresham called. Just as he reached the carriage, Braxton and Lord Salisbury crowded in behind him.

"The pistols are under the seat, sir!" Mr. Green shouted as he and a constable climbed onto the back of the carriage.

Mr. Smith snapped the reins. They were off at top speed, the constable blowing hard on his whistle.

# CHAPTER
# THIRTY

S amantha woke up to find herself on the floor of a fast-moving carriage. Her mouth was full of a foul taste, and she coughed hard, trying to clear her lungs. Her mind was groggy, and she shook her head, blinking her blurry eyes. Her gloved wrists were bound and aching, and she was slowly aware of someone laughing above her. A man somewhere, cackling in delight.

"I bet you never thought you'd see the likes of me again, now did you, pretty Mrs. Granville." The voice came to her thickly, like it was traveling through water. "Ha-ha! I can't say as I've ever been happier in my life to see you again, my dear, ha-ha!"

She struggled to her knees and leaned against the side of the seat. Her head was clearing, and her vision as well. "Where am I?" she asked the dark shadow on the opposite bench.

The man laughed again, slapping his thigh. "You are with me, Mrs. Granville, your favorite doctor of all. Dr. Hugo Fletcher."

All at once the blood rushed to her head and she fell back

SYDNEY F. GREY

hard on the door. *Oh no!* She screamed silently, her eyes darting in panic. *Oh no!*

Fletcher took hold of her roughly and threw her up on the seat to face him. Suddenly he jumped on her and straddled her lap, breathing heavily into her face, running the back of his finger down her cheek. "The captain wouldn't let me have any of you the last time, wanted you whole so you could suffer longer. He only let me have the fingers of that spineless husband of yours. Oh, don't get me wrong, Mrs. Granville. They were a nice little treat, but you were the one I really wanted."

Samantha answered the man by vomiting in his face. He slapped her hard as he jumped back, spitting and flinging the vile from his shirt. This time she was the one laughing.

He slapped her again, and she went silent. He went back to his seat and glared at her. "Just you wait, you little tramp. I promised the captain he could have his way with you first, but he promised me I could do whatever I please with you afterward this time, and believe me, I shall have my satisfaction."

She tried to clear the rest of the fog from her mind. She must think. He had not meant to aid her, but the slaps he gave her had helped. She was surprised she was not more frightened. Perhaps it was the effects of Fletcher's drugs. *This time,* she thought as her numbness gave slightly to her budding anger, *you will not silence me. This time you will have to kill me to keep me quiet.* And with that thought in mind, she screamed.

Fletcher rushed to cover her mouth, but she kicked him as hard as she could, and he fell backward. She screamed again, and he came again, this time avoiding her legs, but not the blow she struck him with her bound hands. He fell to the floor, and she tried with all her strength to hold him down while screaming at the top of her lungs.

He flung her off and smashed her against the carriage

330

wall, knocking the wind out of her. He straddled her once more, this time with a knife to her throat. "You scream just like your mother, Mrs. Hollingsworth. But scream again and I'll cut your heart out." Then he shoved a rag from his pocket into her mouth and sat on the seat with his foot on her chest.

Her whole body filled with a burning rage at the mention of her mother. Her recent grief had left her weakened, but her wrath filled her with new strength. She found it hard to draw the breath back into her chest through her nose. For the moment he had won, but not for long. While she wheezed, she threw up a prayer. *God help me. Give me strength or give me death.*

She sat still, waiting for her lungs to expand again, watching Fletcher's every move, but the carriage stopped before another opportunity arose. The door opened, and Fletcher forced her out, his knife at her throat, into an alley way in front of an unlit building. The door opened, and Admiral Warwick himself approach them. Warwick took her on one side and Fletcher by the other, but before they could push her through the door, she gagged out the rag and let go another bloodcurdling scream, struggling like a wild animal to break free.

Warwick gripped her face and squeezed her jaw. Pain shot through her head like a bolt. "Shut up, you witch, or I'll let Fletcher cut your tongue out while I watch."

Warwick held his hand over her mouth as they shoved her into the darkness of the warehouse. Fletcher stifled his laughter. "That would be delightful, Admiral, delightful indeed."

"Get on with it, you fool!" Warwick snapped, and they pushed her, still struggling, behind the filthy bookcase and into the tiny stairwell. The door at the bottom was locked, but Fletcher withdrew a silver key hanging from a red ribbon around his neck and unlocked it while Warwick held her tightly.

The door opened, and the stairwell flooded with light just as Samantha was able to bite down hard on the inside of Warwick's thick fingers.

"Blast!" He slammed her onto the carpet inside the door.

Fletcher giggled with glee.

"Lock the door, you fools!" roared a voice from the other side of the den.

Samantha knew immediately who the voice belonged to. She did not need to see the man's face to know that it was her former brother-in-law, Felix Granville.

Fletcher, still giggling, locked the door while Warwick pulled Samantha harshly to her feet and propelled her toward the man waiting by the fireplace. There he thrust her onto the carpet at Granville's feet and held her there, his booted foot on her back.

"Here. Here is your wench, Granville. Now I have done my part and I am finished. If you ever so much as send me a letter again, I will have you court-martialed and hung. Whatever debt I owed you has been paid many times over. I am done, Granville, do you hear? It is over."

Warwick took his foot off Samantha's back and strode toward the door. She stole a glance in Granville's direction and noticed he was not even paying attention as Warwick shouted at him. He casually sipped at his glass of whiskey, then took a long draw from his stinking cigar.

"Fletcher! Come and open this blasted door!" Warwick shouted.

Samantha jerked when she heard a loud slap and a short cry of pain. She wriggled around just in time to see Admiral Warwick's lifeless body collapse in front of the locked stairwell door, a gaping wound on the side of his wigged head.

Fletcher held a bloodied cudgel and laughed hysterically. Granville sat and crossed his legs, flicking the ashes from his cigar into the fire. "All right, Hugo, all right. You've had some fun now. Drag him to your room and leave me alone with my beloved sister-in-law."

Samantha's stomach wrenched with nausea. Warwick was dead.

Granville rose and stretched, yawning, then seized her by the upper arms and pushed her onto a red leather chaise lounge across from the fireplace. To her surprise he withdrew a penknife from his sleeve and cut the cords binding her wrists. Taking up his chair beside the blaze again, he barely looked at her as he poured himself another whiskey.

She quickly stripped off her long gloves and rubbed her wrists, watching him warily.

"Well, Sam, our sweet little Samantha. How nice it is to see you again, my dear. My goodness, how long has it been now, six months? Seven?" His tone was smooth and condescending.

Samantha's rage crescendoed, but she would play his game —just until she figured out what to do next. "Why did you hate Michael so much, Felix? Was it because he had a heart and you never did?"

His eyes still avoided hers as a sardonic smile curled his lips. "You have guessed it, little sister. I am so very proud of you, Sam. You and that sharp little mind of yours. So unbecoming in a woman, you know."

"Oh, that is nothing, Felix," she retorted. "I also know that you hated him because he became your father's new favorite when he was born. Dear old Lord Pommeroy kicked you out of his heart as well as his house, didn't he? I wonder what he would think of you now that you have killed his favorite son?" She took advantage of his lack of attention and surveyed her surroundings.

"But you have forgotten, Sam. Michael fell out of father's favor because of you." He took another drag from his cigar and blew the smoke her way. Finally his eyes met hers. "You were a great gift to me, Samantha, you know. It was only because of you that I was able to ruin my little, good-for-nothing brother and then pretend to be the hero by taking him out of father's way. Hmm . . ." He chuckled quietly.

Samantha felt her outrage emerging to the surface like bile. *I will hold nothing back now.*

Standing slowly, finally unable to keep back her contempt, she took a step toward Granville and spoke in a low growl, "You, Felix Granville, you are nothing but an animal. You killed my parents and hurt my sister. What did they ever do to you, Felix?"

Granville sat perfectly still as he listened to her, staring emotionless into the fire.

Samantha couldn't contain her rage. "You just can't stand people who are capable of love, can you, Felix? Because you are nothing. Nothing but an empty shell."

Granville took a deep draft from his cigar and blew the smoke into the fire. Then as if she had said nothing, he smiled and sat back. "What a wonderful time we had, Samantha, on my ship, don't you think? I remember it like it was yesterday. Let's do it again, shall we?"

Tossing his cigar in the fire, he stood and stepped toward her, eyes blazing. Samantha rolled over the back of the chaise in an instant, taking hold of the heavy brass candlestick from a nearby table, ready to strike. He stood still and thrust his hands into his pockets, like a young boy, sniggering.

Samantha stood her ground. "It will not be so easy this time, Felix. You do not have another victim to torture to make me do as you please." Her knees shook with fatigue under the skirts of her gown, but she was determined not to give in to it.

She kept an image of her mother screaming, surrounded by leaping flames, in her mind's eye and let her rage fill her veins with its power.

"Don't you know that is why I unbound you?" Granville chuckled. "I am relishing a fight, Sam. Fight me, my dear. The resistance makes it more exciting." Granville's handsome face darkened. He easily stepped over the chaise with his long legs as she stepped back, falling onto the settee she had not known was behind her. She brought down the candlestick with both hands as he came for her, narrowly missing his head but cracking down on his broad chest. Raking the weapon out of her hands, he threw it away, landing on top of her with the full weight of his body.

His chest crushed hers as he reached for the flap of his breeches, stifling the scream she tried to release. She fought him with what strength she had left, scratching at his face and kicking with her legs.

Over his shoulder she saw the long tapestry beside the fireplace move stiffly and felt a sudden draft of cool air. Then a large dark hand reached around Granville's neck as he suddenly pushed back off her, raising his hands. Her chest heaved as she scrambled backward. Grabbing a glass ashtray, she stood on the settee and swung her arm back, ready to throw, but froze.

There, behind Granville, stood a large black man in sailor's garb, holding a long knife with an ivory handle to Felix Granville's throat.

Samantha's grip on the glass ashtray slipped, and she jumped when it crashed on the marble-topped table beside her, shards of glass scattering around them. "Is it you?" she whispered. "Thank God it is you!"

"Ah. Welcome back, Mr. Gardner," Granville said. His voice strained as Gardner pulled his chin up with one hand and slowly scraped the knife like a shaving blade over Granville's Adam's apple. "I wasn't expecting you so soon, uh—" Gardner let the blade nick Granville's white skin, and a trickle of red blood ran down onto his white cravat.

She held Gardner's gaze as he held on to Granville. His eyes grew bright with tears, and his nostrils flared. She felt like he stared into her, trying to make her understand something, but then there was a loud bang from her left. Samantha screamed as Gardner fell onto the carpet behind Granville, who had managed to remain on his feet.

"No! No!" she screamed at Fletcher, who held a smoldering pistol in one hand, with a second one in the other.

Fletcher doubled over and howled. His eyes watered as he stumbled to Granville's side, looking hungrily at the man on the floor. "There you are, Captain! Your ole friend Fletcher has come through again." Then he offered a pistol to Granville. "Thought you might like one of these yourself."

Samantha had crawled off the back of the settee and was stumbling slowly, slowly backward toward the door to the stairwell.

"You will not be able to get out that way, Samantha," Granville said in an exasperated tone, buttoning up his breeches. "You must have a key to get in and out of that door, my dear." He pushed his thick hair back from his forehead, then shoved the settee aside. Taking the second pistol from Fletcher, he stepped toward her, giving her his most dazzling smile and pointing the gun at her face. "Come now, Sam. It will be just like old times, and then I will finish the job I should have finished long ago."

A surge of new fury ripped through her. Widening her stance, she stood defiantly, trying to light him on fire with a blaze from her eyes. Raising her arm straight in front of her, she pointed at Granville and spoke in a loud, measured voice,

"I rebuke you, Felix Granville, in the name of the Lord Jesus Christ! Get thee behind me!"

Instantly she dropped to the floor and rolled as fast as she could to the side of the doorway, over shards of glass littering the floor. She was aware of a hundred stinging cuts on her arms and hands but didn't care, for she had heard what the men had not been able to over their laughter and conversation in the middle of the room. The turning of a key in a lock.

Granville watched her curiously as she rolled over the glass, then stiffened when he heard voices as the door burst open. He raised his pistol too late as two shots rang out almost simultaneously. From her vantage point on the floor, Samantha saw the bodies of Fletcher and Granville fall in thudding heaps onto the oriental carpets beneath them.

"Samantha!" Gresham cried, from behind the door where he could not see her on the floor.

"I am here, John! I am here!"

✦

BRAXTON, Salisbury, and some constables rushed in with Gresham into the chaos of the disheveled room. Tossing his smoking pistol to Mr. Green, Braxton heard Samantha answer Gresham's calls from where she lay on the floor in a heap of broken glass, her arms bleeding.

Gresham threw down his pistol. "My God! Samantha, you are hurt!"

Braxton hurried over as Gresham carefully took her up in his arms and placed her on the nearest chair.

"I am all right, John. I am only scratched. Please, Paul, Sam Gardner—he has been shot! Over there!"

Braxton ran to the black man and touched his fingers to his neck. "He is alive!" He pushed the man onto his back and examined the wound above his left temple. Ripping his cravat off his neck, he held it to the gash, sponging away the blood, trying to see the wound more clearly.

Salisbury ensured that Fletcher and Granville were dead. Then men were everywhere, searching and shouting. One discovered the passageway behind the tapestry, and another found the chamber behind the hold. Warwick's body was found there, his fingers already removed.

To Braxton's relief, the bullet had been prevented from entering far into Gardner's head by the hard, thick bone over his brow, the sure sign of a poorly loaded pistol. "Good God in heaven, you must have had an angel in here too," Braxton said over the man in great relief.

Braxton called out to Samantha as Gresham lifted her and headed for the stairwell. "He will live! Thank God!"

He remained with Gardner and tended to the unconscious man until transportation was arranged, then traveled with him to the charity hospital on the north side of the city, oversaw his surgery, and was still there to greet him when he woke up just before dawn.

"Hello, Mr. Gardner. My name is Dr. Paul Braxton, and you, sir, are my hero."

CHAPTER

# THIRTY-ONE

"Murder and Abduction at the Admiral's Ball" was the main story in the London papers the next few days, but as she read the articles, Samantha was relieved to find that the mystery lady who had been abducted was referred to only as Mrs. Miller, who had been found in good health that same evening by her husband, Captain Miller.

Lord Salisbury was inundated with requests for interviews but was able to keep the reporters at bay. With the help of the admiralty and Lord Melville's connections, he was able to quell the curiosity of London with simplistic answers and explanations.

A few days later, Mr. Cromwell sat sipping his tea and rereading the notes he had just taken. "It is quite a story, Mrs. Gresham. Quite a story indeed. But"—he placed his cup on the saucer—"one that shall never be told, I understand. I will tell you that Mr. Darby has proven to be a wealth of useful information, making our initial investigation a bit easier. I believe the admiralty will be more lenient with him because of his cooperation."

He sighed and rose to his feet. "Well then, I hope not to bother you further, as the court has agreed to continue the investigation in full cooperation with the admiralty. There are, as you may have guessed, several more clients of Granville's, and the deaths of many possible victims, that still need investigating. However, you need not be involved with all that. I promise to keep you informed."

John stepped forward, his face grave. "Do you believe that some of the victims may be the little girls that have been disappearing from their homes in London?"

"Why, yes, Captain. We have already found there to be a connection between Granville and the missing girls. Thank God you all have put a stop to that at last."

"Yes, thank God for that," Gresham echoed, relief and awe in his voice.

Samantha took John's arm and smiled up at him, understanding the meaningful look on his face. "You have finally been able to help them, my dear. Be at peace now."

Gresham looked down at her with glistening eyes. She was overwhelmingly grateful for his sake that God had used him to bring them justice after all.

"Thank you, Mr. Cromwell," Lord Salisbury said, shaking the man's hand. "I will see you out."

Samantha rubbed the back of her neck. Although the danger from Granville and Fletcher had passed, her heart still ached to find her missing sister. She was grateful Mr. Cromwell had promised to keep looking for Josephine, but in a city as large as London, it was an almost hopeless pursuit.

"Are you sure you still want to go and visit Mr. Gardner today, my dear?" John looked down on her with concern. "You are tired now. Why not wait until tomorrow to see him again?"

"No, John, I really do want to go, just for a little while. He comforts me even more than I comfort him, I am afraid."

John shook his head with a slight smile. "Nonsense, Samantha. You can see how grateful he is in the tears that run down the man's cheeks when you hold his hand. Just like a mother with a child. It is truly a sight to behold."

※

AFTER A TOUCHING VISIT with Sam Gardner and Braxton at the charity hospital, the Keates and the Greshams returned to Lord Salisbury's house in time for tea. As had become their custom while the marquess was out, they took their tea in the sitting area of Samantha's large chamber. They gathered there, waiting for the tray to be brought.

Samantha gave John's hand a squeeze. "Have you had any more word from Mr. Green and Mr. Smith, John? I am glad to know the navy agreed to extend their leave, but what will happen to them after that?"

"It is a good question, my dear. However, Mr. Green hinted something to me before returning to the Lee Side Inn, that he had a great desire to retire from the navy, as he had found a pressing new interest he wished to pursue." He smiled at her with a twinkle in his eye. "I have my suspicions that his new interest may be none other than Mrs. Yates herself."

"Really!" What a delightful surprise. "How wonderful! And I am sure Mr. Smith would be glad to work at the inn for them. If only they could find such happiness."

Penny looked at her brother pleadingly. "Oh, that would be splendid! John, isn't there anything you can do to assist them?"

"I shall see what I can do, sister. In the meantime—"

The loud clack of the knocker on the front door interrupted him.

Before long, a servant entered with the tea tray, followed by the butler. "A letter for you, Mrs. Gresham." The man bowed, offering a sealed letter on a silver tray to Samantha. He bowed again and left.

"Why, it is from Lord Melville, John! He has written to me from Scotland."

"Lord Melville?" He pulled his chair closer to hers.

"Yes, look here." She let them all see the return address before opening the seal. Holding it so John could read it with her, they read silently, glancing at each other in awe between sentences. It was not long, and Samantha laid the page on the table beside her plate, shaking her head in wonder.

Penny set her cup down loudly on her saucer. "Oh, sister! Do not keep us in such suspense. These last several days have been taxing enough. Is it good news?"

Henry patted his wife's hand. "Patience, my dear Penny. They are both obviously speechless. I would assume by their reaction it is good news indeed."

Samantha handed the letter over to Henry. "Please forgive me, my dears, and read it for yourselves."

"GOD WORKS IN MYSTERIOUS WAYS INDEED." Henry broke the awed silence as they rode back from the First Lord Admiral's house just down the street from the Banqueting House. It had been two weeks after Samantha received Lord Melville's letter of invitation. Samantha's arm was wrapped around John's, and she leaned on his shoulder.

She sighed lightly. "Indeed he does, Henry."

That night as she lay in her bed, she tried to remember every moment, every word that was spoken at the small but formal presentation that evening at Lord Melville's London home. He and Lady Melville had made a special trip back from Scotland just for the occasion. A lavish dinner had been served afterward, and they had even brought in the beautiful Italian soprano Angelica Catalani to sing in the music room afterward.

Samantha felt like she had walked into a dream and had stayed unusually quiet the whole evening. It was almost too much to comprehend, and over and over she heard the words *beauty for ashes* whispered to her still-grieving heart.

The results of the evening had been monumental. Lord Melville announced to her that Lord Pommeroy, the father of Felix and Robert Michael Granville, had been found dead from an apparent suicide at his estate in Cambridgeshire just two days after receiving the body of his youngest son and was informed that he had been murdered by his elder half brother, Felix, who was also dead. Lord Melville, in light of this development, had petitioned the Prince Regent himself to allow for all of Lord Pommeroy's estate to be granted to Captain Johnathan and Samantha Gresham, to be disposed of in any manner they saw fit, as a means of restitution for the crimes perpetrated against Mrs. Gresham by that family.

Next, Lord Salisbury was awarded the Royal Guelphic Order Gold Star, given to both military and civilian men displaying heroic acts of chivalry. Lord Melville apologized that the Prince Regent could not present it to Lord Salisbury himself, but their priority of secrecy regarding the whole affair prevented such a public demonstration.

Then Captain Gresham was also pinned with the Royal Guelphic Order Gold Star and offered a new commission with His Majesty's Royal Navy as commander of the new ship of the line, HMS *Ilios*, a seventy-eight gunner, at double his former salary. Samantha saw a wave of uncertainty pass over her husband's face at the news but decided it best to wait until they were alone to ask him why. Lord Melville shook John's hand and personally thanked him for helping to put an end to the child abductions and murders that had plagued London for the last two years. Samantha could not have been prouder and happier for her husband.

And finally the good doctor was called forward. Samantha squeezed John's arm in anticipation. This man deserved as much as any of them, she thought, and hoped he would not be disappointed.

Braxton received a special citation and medal recognizing his acts of service beyond the duties of a warrant officer and ship's surgeon, and he was offered a new commission as well, though not on board a naval vessel. After receiving a thorough report on his excellent treatment of Mrs. Gresham in her recovery, the admiralty ordered that Dr. Paul Braxton be given a special position at the Royal Naval Hospital in Greenwich, to head the treatment and research for those sailors afflicted with the effects of trauma and amnesia. He would be offered a home on the campus of the hospital and full support for his work by the Royal Navy.

Samantha thought she heard her friend gasp slightly at the offer of such a position and was delighted that his reward was so very fitting his abilities.

Tears of gratefulness ran down onto her pillow. "Thank you, Lord God in heaven," she prayed. "Only, please, Father, help me to find Jo, and help me to forgive, Lord. I am so grateful for your patience with me."

# THIRTY-TWO

T wo quiet days had passed since their dinner with Lord and Lady Melville. Braxton, who had been volunteering at the charity hospital after the administrator had seen his skill in treating Mr. Gardner, asked to meet with Gresham and Samantha after his morning attendance with his patients. He sat with them in Samantha's sitting area after luncheon, sipping his tea and smiling in spite of himself.

"Mr. Gardner is doing much better," he announced with a sense of relief. "We have been able to avoid infection in his wound, and he will be able to leave the hospital tomorrow."

"Oh, Paul, that is wonderful news! Did you share with him that we would like to offer him a position if the navy will release him from service?" Samantha passed him a plate of biscuits.

Braxton set down the plate. "He has requested to be allowed to work on the docks at Woolwich instead of returning to sea, but would much rather come and work for you, of course. I will put in a good word for him, and I know John will do the same."

"Of course." Gresham grinned. "With pleasure. I will stay in touch with him through Mr. Green."

"Capital. And that brings me to my purpose in asking to speak with the two of you." He sat up straighter. "First, Samantha, I wanted to speak with you about this," and reaching into his coat pocket, Braxton brought out something and placed it on the table between them. It was the little piece of flint she had given him weeks ago on the *Relentless*.

"So much has happened since we all came together." Braxton changed his tone to somber. "When you gave me this gift, I was a very different man. I had no idea what your intent was in giving me such a present, Samantha, but I hope I have come to understand the message you meant to convey when you bestowed it upon me."

He paused, picking up the little stone, considering it a moment. "A flint is only a piece of rock by itself. It has no real function without the addition of something else to give it a purpose, to make it useful and give it value."

He set the stone back on the tablecloth and leaned heavily on the arm of his chair. He creased his forehead as he looked meaningfully at his friends. "I was like this little stone. I was, except for my friendship with you, John, a lone piece of flint, cold and utterly alone."

Samantha and Gresham sat motionless, as if holding their breath. "But you two, you were like blades of steel, striking against me with your faith in God, bidding a spark to ignite."

A mist of tears gathered in Samantha's eyes.

"Your faith, Samantha, in the midst of all you have suffered and endured is irrefutable, and I found it impossible to continue to deny its merit, that you had placed your faith in something with substance, not just a fantastic wish. Oh believe me, I had already been challenged many times by John. We had many an argument about God and the question of suffering, as he can attest to." He smiled at Gresham. "If he had not engaged in those discussions with me, I would not have been able to see any of the light that shone from you, Samantha."

She retrieved her handkerchief and dried her sweet tears.

Bending forward, Braxton said, "Oh, my dear, I do not wish to make you cry so. I—"

"No, Paul, I am crying happy tears, my friend. Go on . . . go on." She wiped away another tear that had dropped to her cheek.

"I guess what I am trying to say is, a spark has indeed ignited within me, because of the two of you, and also the echo of Henry's sermon on the morning before your wedding. Do you remember? He spoke about the folly of comparing ourselves to other men, when we ought to compare ourselves to the perfection of Christ."

Gresham chuckled. "I remember it well. I was praying hard for you to hear those words from the front pew. I am exceedingly glad you did."

"Yes I did, and it finally dawned on me why Jesus taught the prayer he taught to his disciples, that we ask for forgiveness for our trespasses while we continue to forgive those who trespass against us. Christ suffered unjustly on our behalf but extends his forgiveness just the same, and if he can forgive us, then who am I"—he aimed his finger at his chest—"that I should not forgive others, even if I was wronged unjustly."

Braxton sat back in his chair, taking up the stone again in his fingers. At last he set his gaze back on them. "Thank you, my friends. I give you my sincerest gratitude for your love and faithfulness and for not giving up on me."

They were out of their chairs and pulling him up into a

group embrace. "Thank you, Jesus!" Gresham shouted to the ceiling.

Braxton nodded. "Yes, yes, but there is more I wish to discuss with you. Please stop fussing over me and let me finish."

❋

THE LEAVES on the trees of London were turning, and it was time for the party from Hatfield to finally make their way home. Braxton was there to see them off and bid them a bittersweet farewell. He was to be at his new post at the Royal Naval Hospital in Greenwich by the end of the next week and wished to stay in London to finish up with his final patient at the charity hospital before heading to Charlton to visit Mr. Green and Mrs. Yates, who had announced their betrothal after Mr. Green and Mr. Smith were both granted their retirements from the navy. Then Braxton would make his way the few miles to the west of Charlton to Greenwich to start his new life at the hospital there.

As the carriages rolled away from Lord Salisbury's grand townhouse on Bury Street, Braxton waved at them until they took the turn onto Jermyn Street, then entered the carriage that waited to take him back to the charity hospital. He allowed himself a few private tears, but only a few, for he had promised, as had they, to write often and to visit as much and as soon as possible.

Sitting back in his seat, he put his feet up on the opposite bench, lacing his fingers over his stomach. Gresham had chosen not to accept the navy's offer of a new commission, which had not surprised Braxton. Instead he and Samantha would sell off Lord Pommeroy's estate and take up an offer made by Lord Salisbury to join him in creating a new merchant shipping business and were in discussions about where best to set up their operations.

The situation suited his friend's new married life well. Gresham would have command of his own time while being able to sail on his own ships. Braxton was happy for them but still felt a pang of loneliness, hoping they would choose a location not far from Greenwich.

When the carriage pulled up in front of the hospital, he stepped down and retrieved his bag. Mounting the steps of the building, he paused, reminding himself that he was not alone. That God would be with him, and he must learn to trust in him more.

He stowed his bag in a storage closet in the hallway before entering the ward where his last patient rested. He made his way along the row of beds against the wall of the large hall and gently touched his patient's hand. Mr. Worsley had been recovering from a broken leg that had been amputated from below the knee, and Braxton was pleased he had been able to prevent an infection that would have resulted in more of the poor man's leg being removed.

"Well, Mr. Worsley, it looks as though you are mending nicely, thank God." Braxton was keenly aware of his newfound vocabulary and meant what he said.

"I cannot thank you enough, Dr Braxton," said the old tradesman earnestly. "I was so afraid I might lose the whole leg altogether, but you have proven yourself a skilled surgeon, sir, and a most considerate man. I just may be able to go on providing for my family because of your handiwork, Doctor. May God bless you for it."

"Thank you, Mr. Worsley. He already has." Braxton stepped aside to allow an orderly to take the man's plate and cup to her cart and tidy up the man's blankets and pillows. Braxton smiled and raised his hand, "You have my consent to go home to your family as soon as tomorrow. I will be leaving in the next day or two to visit some friends in Charlton, so I bid you farewell."

As Braxton turned to leave, he ran right into the cart that the woman had begun to push toward the foot of the next patient's bed, causing a clamor of dishes, which he caught just in time before the whole lot fell over. "I am terribly sorry, miss! How clumsy of me. Let me help you," and he went about straightening the stacks of plates and bowls that had tipped out of place.

He stopped short when he saw the plumb-colored, burn-scarred hands of the woman putting the items to rights. Standing up, he tilted his head to see her face, but her white cap covered her head completely, the brim lowered so far that he could only see the tail end of a burn scar trailing down the side of her right cheek.

He gasped. "Wait, please, miss, wait." He went to the other side of the cart and tried to catch her eyes. "Please, miss, could you . . . would your name possibly be Miss Josephine Hollingsworth?"

She stopped and looked up at him in alarm from under her cap. She took a step back, obviously frightened. "Why no, of course not. My name is Jones, Doctor, Geraldine Jones. Now if you will excuse me." She dropped her head, taking hold of the cart handle and hurrying on.

Braxton had seen the likeness in her visage to that in Samantha's drawing of her younger sister. Not wanting to frighten her more, he followed her a few steps to the side. Remembering that Samantha's mother's name was Geraldine, he was even more convinced that he was indeed looking at Josephine Hollingsworth herself.

"Please, Miss Jones, I . . . may I . . . that is, after you . . . No, it can't wait." Taking hold of the cart from the front, he bent over it to catch her eyes again, "Please, miss, come with me." He turned the cart around, pushing it noisily back down the row of beds and out into the hallway.

"Please, Doctor, I need to finish my work, sir," the lady begged in a loud whisper as she followed him out the door. "I have my duties, sir, please!"

They stood on either side of the cart for a breathless moment. Braxton felt desperate, searching for the right words to say without alarming her more.

"Please, miss, please allow me to speak to you. I have news from your sister, Samantha."

The young lady's eyes were barely visible under her brim, but Braxton saw her mouth widen in surprise, and she stepped back in confusion. "What, uh, who did you say, sir? You have news from my sister? I . . . I do not have a sister, sir, I assure you—"

"I know it must sound terribly strange, but I have just seen Samantha not an hour ago, here in London. She is searching for you desperately. Please, miss, please allow me to take you to her!" Braxton spilled out the words in spite of himself.

The lady hesitated and protested weakly. "No, sir, you must be mistaken. I—"

She stopped when Braxton suddenly dropped to his knees beside the cart and raised his eyes to the ceiling. "Please, God, please help me to convince this dear lady that I mean her no harm! Please help her to understand that I am her friend and only want to reunite her with her beloved sister, Samantha."

He looked at her again and begged, not knowing what else to do. "Please, Miss Hollingsworth. Your sister has become one of my dearest friends, and she has been heartbroken since she learned of the fire at the vicarage and about your parents. She has been beside herself with grief and her longing to find you. I beg you to believe me!"

He stayed on his knees, breathing heavily, watching her battle with indecision.

"Is it . . . is it really true?" she whispered, stepping closer, placing her trembling, burn-scarred hands on the side of the cart. "Samantha is here? In England? But how can that be?"

Relief poured over him as he rose to his feet. "I was on the ship that brought her home from the West Indies." Braxton spoke more calmly. "She has just left London on her way to Hatfield in Hertfordshire. I can take you to her."

"But who are you, sir? I know that you are a doctor, but how do I know that what you say is true?"

Braxton caught a glimpse of her sister's strength in the flash of her pale-blue eyes as she lifted her chin slightly in defiance.

Braxton searched for a means of proof, but his mind came up short. Then as if from a whispered inspiration into his heart, he knew what to do.

Taking a step back from the cart, he looked at her with a shy smile. "Ask the Lord, Miss Hollingsworth. If you have anything like the faith your good sister possesses, then pray and ask God. I know that He will attest to the truthfulness of my words, and while you pray, I will just go and retrieve some things from my bag." A wave of warm energy flushed through him, filling him with awe.

Daring to leave her and hoping desperately that she would not flee, Braxton stepped quickly down the hall to the storage closet where he had stored his belongings.

His knees went weak when he reached his bag. He felt dazed and found it remarkable that no one had entered the hall while he had pleaded with God and the lady on his knees. Then he laughed, covering his mouth with his hand to muffle his joy. Lifting his eyes to the ceiling, he sent up a prayer of gratitude, then pulled out the items he sought and walked back to where the lady stood clutching the cart handle.

Josephine had pushed her sap back a bit, exposing her face to the light. Braxton caught his breath. She was beautiful, like a porcelain doll.

He approached her, holding out a book in his hand. "Here, this is Samantha's Bible," he whispered. "She gave it to me to help me understand God's love. Do you recognize it?"

She took the book with a little gasp. "Perhaps," she whispered back, opening the front cover reverently.

"Oh, someone tore out the page of family names, which I can explain, but there is also this—" He handed her the portrait of himself in the gold frame and held his breath.

Placing the Bible on the cart, Josephine took the picture, and her voice wavered. "S. G . . . Samantha . . . she drew this of you?"

Her eyes flew to his, filled with tears.

Braxton could hardly contain himself, and his voice cracked with emotion. "Your sister will be so very, very happy to see you again, Miss Hollingsworth. Shall we go?"

After explaining the situation to the hospital administrator, who had been gracious enough to allow Josephine to remain there under an assumed name after her recovery, they collected her few possessions and arranged for a carriage. Braxton found himself seated across from Samantha's own sister, still shaking his head in wonder.

"I can hardly believe it." Josephine clung to the bag in her lap, her voice wobbly. "Please, Dr. Braxton, how is she? And how is her . . . her husband, Mr. Granville?" She hesitated as she mentioned her brother-in-law, her eyes dropping to her bag.

"Oh, she is well, I assure you, only terribly grieved by the news of your parents' deaths and your injuries. And you should know that Mr. Granville is not with her at present."

Her eyes darted back to his. "Oh? Really? But why is that?"

"Well, Miss Hollingsworth, I am afraid there is much to tell."

"Please do tell, Dr. Braxton. How did you come to be acquainted with my sister? I have felt so helpless to communicate with her. The letters I sent to the missionary church in Jamaica went unanswered. I cannot tell you how concerned I have been for her since she left us, and especially after the fire."

"Yes, of course I will tell you everything I can, though I must warn you, Miss Hollingsworth, that some of the tale will be distressing to hear."

She held his gaze for a moment as Braxton's heart pounded in his chest. "Please, Doctor," she said urgently, "tell me everything. I promise I will be all right."

"Very well, I will tell you all of it, but before I do, there is one pressing question that I am almost certain you would be able to help me find the answer to. Do you mind?"

"Oh, of course not, Doctor. Please ask freely."

A shaft of evening light lit the side of her porcelain face, lighting her eyes like pale-blue gems. He could just see the scarring on the top of her forehead and more on her right cheek, but her bonnet still covered most of her injuries. Her delicate, small hands were gloved now, and he was relieved to see that her fingers still functioned quite well. In spite of her scars, he found her the most enchanting woman he had ever seen.

"Well, you might think it an extremely unusual question, considering the circumstances, but"—he paused and felt himself redden in the face—"have you ever seen your sister climbing trees?"

"What?!" Josephine's hand flew to her mouth in surprise,

and then, to his amazement and delight, she laughed. Her laughter was sparkling and sweet, like water rippling over stones in a brook, and Braxton saw the hint of dimples accenting her perfect smile.

"Why, yes, Dr. Braxton, many times. Has she never spoken to you about the year we spent with mother and father in India? Our parents went to relieve a missionary couple there for a year when I was ten and Sam was thirteen. Father would take us with him to visit the local people living in the jungle around the mission, and he would let Sam and I run around with the natives as if we were boys!"

Braxton blinked in bewilderment. "Really? And what else did you do with the natives in India?" He chuckled, imagining the picture and could hardly contain his excitement.

"Oh, so many things! We learned how to fish with a spear and light a fire with a bit of flint and a knife, and we made little huts under the trees with whatever we could find lying around. We wove baskets and picked fruit. Oh! But Sam was by far the best at climbing trees. I cannot believe she has never mentioned it. Perhaps she is too embarrassed to admit that she ever did such boyish things."

Braxton sat back and marveled. Yes, it all made sense now. God had known she would need these skills to survive her abandonment on the island years after she ran with the natives in the jungles of India. Again, he stared at Josephine and shook his head in wonder.

"Thank you, Miss Hollingsworth. You have just put the final puzzle piece into place."

❋

THEIR RIDE from north London to Hatfield took the rest of the day but was still barely enough time for Braxton to fill

Josephine in on the details of the adventure that had begun only a couple of months before on a deserted island in the West Indies. He had just finished telling her about their dinner at Lord and Lady Melville's house, when the carriage came to a stop on the gravel drive of the old vicarage.

He helped her down and collected their bags, leading her toward the front door just as the sun began to set. The crickets called to each other around the house, and the distinct scent of autumn wafted through the cool evening air.

Braxton set down the bags by the door and turned to Josephine, who was clasping her hands, her eyes sparkling in the last of the day's light. "Are you ready?"

"Very!" she whispered.

He grasped the handle and, finding it unlocked, flung the door open and motioned Josephine inside.

Standing at the bottom of the stairs, where it met the hallways to the rest of the house, Braxton flashed a mischievous smile down on his companion, then cupped his hands around his mouth and shouted at the top of his lungs, "Samantha! John! Penny and Henry! Come quickly! I have found her!"

# EPILOGUE

The bells of the Carillon in the tower of St. Etheldreda's church rang out in echoing joy over the town of Hatfield. Standing at the transept in the nave of the sanctuary, Reverend Henry Keate had just pronounced the happy couple before him to be husband and wife. The groom bent and kissed his beautiful bride under her elaborately decorated white wedding bonnet, while the best man, the groom's best friend, stood applauding beside him, and the matron of honor, the bride's sister, with her rounded belly conspicuously visible in her light-blue gown, wiped her joyful tears. The lord of nearby Hatfield House stood beside his lady and the rector's wife, all beaming with delight, as well as Mr. and Mrs. Green and two tall and amiable black sailors.

Dr. and Mrs. Braxton followed the small company across the churchyard to the old vicarage, there to enjoy their wedding breakfast in the freshness of a fine spring morning.

# ACKNOWLEDGMENTS

**Editors:** Heidi Kraakevik and Dori Harrell
**Cover design:** Roseanna M. White
**UK Consultant:** Malcolm Caie, Hatfield, Hertfordshire, UK
**Beta Readers:** Geraldine Grey, Karen Laage,
Lorraine Green, Niki Ligouras, Nicolas Hostetler,
Amparo Bellon-Champ
**Nautical Consultant:** Nicolas Hostetler

**Agent:** Rachel McMillan

## About the Author

Sydney F. Grey is a Christian historical fiction author whose work blends
Regency romance, gothic suspense, and
themes of faith. A native of Colorado, she

www.sydsartsongs.com

grew up among the pine forests of the
Rocky Mountains, where her love for stories first took root.
Always captivated by British history, especially the eighteenth
through nineteenth centuries, Sydney draws on her passion for
the era to create richly detailed, faith-driven narratives.

Her debut novel, *Those Who Trespass*, was recognized as a
finalist in the prestigious Crown Awards. Beyond writing, she
is also a fine artist, singer, and vocal coach.

To read Author's Notes, visit the website, www.sydsart
songs.com, or scan QR Code.

www.ingramcontent.com/pod-product-compliance
Lightning Source LLC
Chambersburg PA
CBHW021956130726
47903CB00014B/1482